AMERIKA
STRIKES BACK!

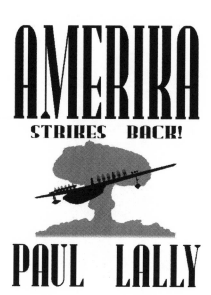

PAUL LALLY

This is a work of alternate history.
And while some persons, organizations, places,
events, and incidents may have existed in the real
world, they're purely fictional in the author's
imaginary world where anything can happen—
and does.

Book cover design: Aaron Ijams
Copyright 2018 Paul Lally
All rights reserved
ISBN-13: 978-1723598197
ISBN-10:1723598194

For Jim Lewis;
Creative artist, gifted engineer, trusted friend.

I am a soldier. I fight where I'm told,
and I win where I fight.
General George S. Patton

Ice belongs in a glass of Kentucky bourbon—not the wings and air intakes of a piece-of-shit Consolidated C-87A *Liberator Express*, transporting General Patton to a "must attend" meeting in Alamogordo, New Mexico.

Such was my predicament on a wintry February night in 1943, as pilot-in-command of a four-engine VIP aircraft that flew like a drunken whale.

And if I didn't solve the icing problem fast, instead of delivering the commanding general of the Western Defense Command safe and sound to his destination, we'd end up scattered in a thousand pieces of shredded aluminum on the scrub-filled empty desert, ten thousand-feet below.

Crew included.

If only we'd been flying Consolidated Aircraft's B-24 *Liberator* bomber, instead of her underpowered, cousin! If so, I'd have been sitting pretty in the left seat, chatting it up with my wife and co-pilot First Lieutenant Ava James about where to have dinner that night.

But no such luck!

The C-87A was the cargo version of the deadly B-24 currently blasting the hell out of Nazi-occupied Netherlands. By contrast, the C-87A's crappy superchargers and unreliable center-of-gravity kept us rocking and rolling like a bad dream on the verge of becoming a nightmare.

"Carb heat?" I hollered like an idiot. But sometimes shouting helps.

"Full on, sir," Ava said.

"Forget the sir."

"No, sir. I'm in the army now and a full bird colonel outranks a first lieutenant, SIR, and we're still losing power, by the way."

"Doesn't make sense," I said.

"Doesn't make sense, SIR." A deep-throated voice behind me echoed, "Number three's about to give up the ghost."

"Jesus, Orlando, when we're alone like this, it's Sam, okay? 'Sam Carter,' your soon-to-become *late* business partner unless we figure out what the hell's happening."

Major Orlando Diaz and I had grown up together as kids in Key West in the late 1920s. Me, a skinny white kid he, a refrigerator-size black kid, we'd fallen in love with aviation each in our own way; me with flying, Orlando with fixing. As young men, we'd made our mark with Juan Trippe's fledgling *Pan American Airways* in the 1930s and risen through the ranks until I became a full-fledged "Master of Ocean Flying Boats" and Orlando Chief Mechanic of *Pan Am's* South American route.

After the Nazis A-bombed New York and Washington D.C. on December 7, 1941, America became a neutral, cringing nation afraid to breathe lest we get nuked again. As for me, the bomb in D.C. killed my wife and infant son. I'd been down in Brazil on a four-day trip when it happened.

Instead of dealing with the loss like a man, I turned into a falling-down, guilt-ridden drunk who belonged in the gutter, not behind the controls of an airplane filled with paying passengers.

But thanks to Orlando, all that changed. And thanks to Ava James and her so-called "Dutch Uncle," George Patton, I climbed out of the gutter and got back to doing what I loved to do with the people I cared about, including fighting like hell for America's freedom from the tyranny of Hitler in the East and the suicidal ambitions of General Tojo in the West.

Another voice blasted like a jackhammer, "What the hell's happening, colonel?"

General Patton blew into the cramped cockpit like the hot air currently colliding with the cold air outside causing the ice to form on this staggering cow of an airplane. I dreaded both forces of nature.

"Touch of ice, general. Heading down to get below it."

"Anything I can do?"

"No, sir. We'll be out of it soon."

"You lying to me colonel to calm me down?"

"Absolutely, sir."

"Nice try. Now, damn it, you've…"

A series of machine-gun like BANGS on the port side interrupted him as the propeller on number two engine flung ice chunks against our thin-skinned fuselage.

"What the hell?" Patton shouted. "We taking fire?"

Ava said, "Mother Nature, Uncle George."

"God DAMN it, lieutenant, you're in the army now."

"Yes, sir, thanks to you, sir. Sorry, General Patton, sir."

The Woman's Army Air Corps, or WAACS had been officially formed six months ago, by President Frances Perkins's executive order and Patton's table-thumping support. Up until that point, the Women's Air Force Service Pilots (WASPS) a non-combative organization had ferried military aircraft around the world. But with Perkins' signature barely dry on the paper, the women happily disbanded, quickly raised their right hands to protect and defend the Constitution of the United States of America and pinned on their second lieutenants' bars. Women had officially entered the war effort.

Ava being a Hollywood movie star, not to mention an experienced multi-rated pilot from her ferrying days, became the pinup girl for the program. Her dazzling smile at War Bond rallies, like the one we'd just finished at the Todd Shipyard in Galveston, Texas, prompted money to fly out of the pockets of the workers and wistful dreams to take hold in the minds of the female workers to join the ranks of the WACS, because "if Ava can do it, so can I!"

More BANGS on the fuselage, this time on the right.

Orlando said, "Number four's giving up the ghost. RPM's dropping fast."

I shoved the control column forward. The plane slowly nosed over like a reluctant mule. "Got to be a bottom to this."

"And if there isn't?" Ava said.

"At ease, lieutenant, and keep an eye on the manifold pressure."

Orlando growled, "Let me worry about that." His meaty paw reached up and enfolded the four engine throttles like he would a baby's face. "This fat girl needs some loving."

"Won't get it from me," I snapped.

Patton turned to go. "I'll be in my office. Let me know if we're going to crash into the side of a mountain so that I can make peace with my Divine Creator."

Ava said, "We won't, Uncle—I mean, General Patton. I promise."

"That's what I like to hear. Confidence!"

Ten seconds later, engine number four died with a spinning gasp.

"This is nuts," I said. "We're doing everything right."

Ten seconds later, RPM began slowly dropping on number three. If we lost that engine, we'd lose hydraulic power too, and this dog of an ice-covered plane would turn into an unflyable monster.

Ava rapped the gauge with her knuckle, but the needle kept falling.

Orlando said, "Maybe it's time we did something wrong, instead."

"What do you mean?"

He didn't bother answering. Instead, he pivoted his massive bulk like a ballerina despite his middle linebacker size. Seconds later, he crouched over Ava's shoulder and aimed a flashlight onto the dead engine.

"Mags off on number four."

"Off? What do you mean, 'off?'"

Instead of answering he reached across and flipped off the magneto switch. "Booster pumps on. Do it NOW!"

After years of flying, there comes a time when you don't question your flight engineer. You simply do *exactly* what he says without hesitation.

"Take over," I snapped.

Ava wiggled the massive control wheel slightly, "I have the aircraft."

Orlando said, "Keep the ignition off until I say so. Mother Nature's gonna' crank the hell out of that engine."

I wanted to shout, "That's ass backwards" but bit my tongue instead.

Orlando said, "Unfeather number four, throttle to auto rich—pardon me, lieutenant, here we go."

He reached across to the engine control panel near Ava and flipped up the spring-loaded toggle switch marked PRIME and held it fast.

While 100 octane fuel gushed into the twin barreled carburetors, I risked a glance outside to witness the motionless propeller blades on the dead engine slowly start rotating in the slipstream and quickly transformed themselves into a spinning blur.

Unignited fuel pouring into a hot engine.

Sparkplugs without power because the ignition switch was off.

A recipe for disaster in the making but I bit my tongue harder.

"Lord GOD in heaven," Orlando boomed in his best preacher voice (during peacetime, back in Key West, besides being my business partner, he was an unordained, self-proclaimed minister.) "Deliver your humble servants to the throne of retribution so that we may wreak havoc upon the enemy. In thy name, we beseech thee. Amen and amen!"

"AMEN!" Ava shouted.

He flipped the ignition switch ON.

In less than a millisecond, the P-1 generator assigned to engine number four shot twenty-four volts of electricity to the waiting sparkplugs of the Pratt & Whitney "Twin Wasp" 1200 horsepower engine. Seconds before, an inert but brilliant piece of engineering, it came to coughing, explosive life in a way I'd never seen. Four explosive BANGS, each one louder than the previous, as unburnt fuel in the fourteen cylinders exploded in massive backfires.

The last series of volcanic explosions blasted from the twin air intake scoops on either side of the nacelle. The force shattered chunks of ice that had formed around the openings, thus starving the engine of much needed air, and why this dog of a plane had been acting like a dying swan.

"Halleluiah!" Ava crowed.

Within seconds the engine stabilized and sang like the beauty she was.

My intercom crackled.

"What the hell's going on, colonel?"

"Cleaning house, sir." I went on to explain, and ended with, "Going to get noisy for a while. Plug your ears."

We repeated the process on the other three engines, and within a few minutes and a cacophony of backfires and shattering ice, all four air intakes were free and clear.

We sat in silence for a long while, listening to the smooth drone of engines, while the adrenaline slowly left our bodies.

"Who would have thought?" I finally said.

"Orlando did," Ava said. "You're our hero, sir."

"No big deal. Fact of life. Can't breathe without air."

"Agreed... but...." I patted the four throttles. "We could have blown those engines. Then where would we have been?"

Orlando's smile lit up the cockpit. "With the choir of angels, Colonel Carter. But it's not our time, yet. We are His fiery sword."

"Literally!"

A sharp series of staccato explosions aft. Three heads swiveled as one. I keyed the intercom. "Pilot to gunner, what the hell's going on back there?"

A tinny voice in my headset instantly replied, "Gunner to pilot. Sir, the general wanted to fire my weapon. Uh... hang on a sec, sir."

Patton's strident voice replaced the gunner's and it cut through the static. "Can't afford to have ice on these babies either, know what I mean, Carter?"

"Yes, sir. You clean your house, I'll clean mine."

"Affirmative. How we doing in that department?"

"We found the bottom to the warm front. The ice is already easing up."

"Excellent. Carry on."

Another short blast from the twin fifties, then silence.

About those machine guns....

While our C-87 was technically a VIP transport, when you wear four stars on your shoulders, you can trick it out any way you damn well please. In Patton's case, he didn't give a hoot about the office quarters they'd rigged up where the bomb bay was in the bomber version. Or the fully-equipped galley where a sergeant/cook prepared great meals for his distinguished visitors.

Nice, but who cares?

Patton packed a pair of pearl-handled, Colt .45s. But he added to his armament by "requesting" Consolidated Aircraft to retrofit .50 caliber waist guns, like their B-24 bomber version, gunners included. When not protecting America's most colorful commanding officer, our tech sergeants pitched in as orderlies, assistant cooks, and whatever other job it took to keep the good general's airplane in good condition and getting to its next destination.

Same was true for Ava, Orlando, and me. Because of our past experiences working for Patton, and then saving General MacArthur's bacon from Tokyo's *samurai* swords, we'd been "temporarily" assigned to "provide aerial crew support to the commanding general when and where determined by commander."

Taxi drivers in the middle of a war? Yes.

Happy about it? Hell no.

But I'd learned the hard way that when there's a war on all bets are off. And was there *ever* a war on. After almost a year and a half of massive rearmament, America was finally done flexing her muscles and about to start swinging for real. When and where the invasions would take place remained a closely guarded secret. But this unexpected order to divert to Alamogordo after our war bond rally meant something was in the wind and I'm not talking ice.

Patton got on the intercom again. "Patton to pilot."

"Yes, sir."

"What's our ETA?"

"Less than an hour to landing."

Another ripple of fifty caliber machine gun fire. "Hope it's good news."

"Me too, sir."

The mysterious news came first.

"Army three-seven-zero divert to alternate airfield, approximately seventy miles northwest your position, heading three-four-five. Contact tower on one-one-niner point one."

"Uh, Alamogordo Approach, my orders are to land your airfield. Top priority passenger. On whose authority for the change, over."

A nice, hefty pause. Then, "Army three-seven-zero, be advised that's classified. Weather at alternate airfield reporting wind two-one-five at ten, gusting to twenty."

Not great news, but I'd landed in worse wind conditions.

"Alamogordo Approach, is this alternate landing site a controlled airfield?"

Another pause. "Roger. Single runway. Macadam."

And so, we passed over a perfectly good Army airfield in favor of some unknown strip of asphalt, most likely covered with snow. Over the years I'd landed on my share of crappy runways – gravel, dirt, grass, but blowing snow made it especially crappy.

I got on the intercom with General Patton and explained what was happening. Instead of the expected explosion, he seemed to take it all in stride. "Classified, huh?"

"Yes, sir."

I could hear his breathing. Then a chuckle.

"Goddamn Mac. Why walk across the room when you can have a parade instead!"

"Sir?"

"Never mind, colonel. You'll find out soon enough."

I let the mystery fade into the background as the complex calculations of navigating to a new airfield took over: Fuel estimates, landing weight, and weather conditions scrambled into the cockpit like a swarm of cats that Ava and I had to herd into a straight line.

Less than twenty minutes later, we were cruising at just over two hundred miles-an-hour with the wind off our port wing and heading for our new destination. I dialed up the mystery tower frequency. It took a few tries, but finally, a voice crackled, "Wind two-one-five at fifteen, gusting to twenty-five, runway three-four, cleared to land."

"Roger, three-four, and is confirm three-four's your only runway?"

"Affirmative."

Not good. The wind was about as close to crosswind as you could get.

"Advise runway length?"

"Nineteen hundred twenty feet."

The voice in the control tower was matter-of-fact, a bit bored, but I could hear the tiniest edge of excitement too. Not every day did a humble enlisted man grant permission to a four-star general to return to earth. Let alone one nicknamed "Blood and Guts." Unfortunately, the earth we were returning to wasn't very hospitable at the moment. But at least the airstrip was long enough for some gymnastics on my part if needed.

Dry and forever dusty Alamogordo, New Mexico gets an average of six inches of snow a year. It seemed like a full years' worth was falling tonight. Gusting too, thanks to a winter storm swooping down from the forever-wet Pacific Northwest and slamming headfirst into the dry desert air.

Ironic.

Only hours ago, we had taken off from warm and sunny Galveston, Texas, seven hundred miles southeast. Not a flake of snow in sight. The War Bond rally at the shipyard had a stupendous turnout. Not because of General Patton, despite his thinking so. The real reason was Ava James on stage, wearing her neatly tailored army lieutenant's uniform with aviator wings, but every inch a Hollywood star, joking and laughing with the massive crowd as if they'd just stopped by for cocktails at her place and she had all the time in the world for them. Not just the men, either. Women too, their faces uplifted, smiling—some even beaming—at a happy woman doing what she wanted and loving every minute of it.

Then Tommy Dorsey's band played.

And Ava sang.

You could almost hear the dollar bills squirming around in peoples' wallets and purses, wanting to jump out and buy war bonds. Ava had that effect on people—including me. But in my case, the gods had smiled down upon us and decided that marriage was perfectly okay with them if we wanted to go through with it.

We most certainly did.

I knew it was the right—and the only—thing to do for me, as a man. But as a father, I worried that my ten-year-old daughter Abby might not agree. My late wife Estelle and baby Eddie had been her world. They were gone forever and here came Hollywood knocking—not just for tea but for good. Would Abby slam the door?

In the end, though, Ava won her over, not me. And not with words but with serene silence, endless patience, and steady love.

I wiggled my control wheel. "Care to dance?"

Ava placed her hands on the controls and wiggled back.

"Only with you, my colonel."

The physical strain of flying a 56,000-pound whale through the air was manageable most of the time. But with blowing snow and wind gusts slamming into us, I needed some extra muscle.

I managed a grin as best I could. "The family that flies together…"

"Don't rhyme that!" Ava snapped.

"Orlando, lend a hand… gear down."

His hand snaked forward and snapped down the lever. The massive main gear dropped by gravity, while a small electric motor nudged the nose gear into the slipstream.

Ava and I horsed the plane into a descending turn to final approach. I called for half-flaps and Orlando moved the control lever back, while watching the deployment needle swing to the mark.

"Turbos off."

"Off."

"Flaps full."

"Going to full."

The slab-like flaps extended downward to forty degrees, while Ava and I fought the corresponding up pressure on the control yokes. Double-controlling an aircraft is a fine art, but after flying a variety of aircraft together, from Pan Am's massive Boeing 314 *Dixie Clipper* to the Martin M-130 *China Clipper*, the two of us had mastered the process as best we could. Not perfect, mind you; sometimes Ava would anticipate my action and throw off my timing.

True, I was pilot-in-command tonight, but a tired one too. After a long day of hauling around General Patton his olive drab, four-engine flying taxi, the last thing I wanted was a dicey landing in snow squalls by hogging the controls all to myself.

I called out "High RPM," but Orlando was already ahead of me as he adjusted the propeller pitch to give us full power. For a man who hated to fly he knew more about my job than I did. He had a sixth sense, not only about what it took to fly a plane, but also how to land it.

"Numbers in sight!" Ava called out.

Our landing lights bathed the end of the snow-swept runway. The wind was doing its part to make things a little easier by whipping the snow around in billows. That's the good news. The bad news was that the crosswind wanted to lift our left wing and cartwheel us into the desert.

After a lifetime in the air, I've come to an understanding with Mother Nature: the minute I'm off the ground and in the air, I'm a guest in her house and behave accordingly. She's the boss, not me. I never act, I *react*.

Which is why tonight I didn't curse her twisted sense of humor, but instead cranked the plane into a forward slip to get us closer to earth before our low-drag wings lost their lift. Wings. Gotta have them to stay in the air. But the Davis wing, designed by aeronautical engineer genius David R. Davis provides great lift at low speed but it ain't no friend when snow and ice come knocking.

Tonight, we had both.

Ava read my mind, shoving full-right rudder to stay on our heading. I joined her by adding my muscle to hers. Out of the corner of my eye I could see Orlando's right hand checking the position of the landing gear lever to make sure it had a full charge, while his left held the throttles like horse reins, ready to chop speed on my call.

"Drinks on me after we land," I said.

"Make mine a double," Ava said.

"Amen," Orlando said.

A plane this big carries a hell of a lot of inertia. Control inputs must be done far in advance of response. In other words, a P-38 *Lightning* it ain't. But it can absorb fifty times the damage that little twin-engine fighter can handle.

Which is why, as the runway numbers flashed beneath our nose and I cranked the elevator trim nose high even more, I thanked God for this rolling whale of a VIP transport that muscled her way through the crosswind like a drunk at a party trying to reach the bar. With this kind of crosswind, a *Lightning* would have flipped over and cartwheeled by now.

"Give me more," I said, and felt Ava help me pull on the heavy yoke.

The nosewheel on this baby was notoriously weak. No matter how many modifications Consolidated had done, it still would collapse on you if you THUMPED down too hard on landing. Even though we had tricycle gear, we always settled on the runway like a taildragger, and then let the nose settle down when it – and Mother Nature – decided enough was enough.

"Power off."

But once again, Orlando was a beat ahead of me. How he could judge the right moment remained a happy mystery. Happy, because he and I had been partners in a small air service currently on hold back in Key West, Florida. But when the war ended, as all wars must and providing America came out on top—no guarantee there, of course—but if so, then *Carter Air* would once again take to the skies.

For now, our only asset, a twin-engine Sikorsky S-38 amphibian, slept in a locked hangar. But thanks to a reconciled friendship with my former boss, *Pan Am* president Juan Trippe, my post-war dreams just might come true—provided I lived through this landing.

A wind gust struck the left wing and we started to roll. Despite full aileron deflection, the right wingtip dipped closer and closer to the macadam. Our self-sealing fuel tanks in the wings were safe from bullets, but not Mother Nature's wrath.

Hell breaking loose always happens like this—at least for me. A millisecond of hesitation. Shock. Disbelief. Anger. Then ACTION. Might be right, might be wrong, but action, not inaction as my mind expanded into the C-87's wings, fuselage, rudder, and elevators until I became part of it, feeling her tipping faster and faster to the right. No more aileron to apply, no rudder to shove. Full deflection on both. What to do? How to do it?

And with questions came answers.

"Right brake!" I shouted and stabbed the right brake pedal as hard as I could.

"With you!" Ava said.

The brakes took hold, the right wheel stuttered and shuddered, and the nose abruptly pivoted further to the right as 45,000 pounds of aluminum, rubber, steel, and flesh-and-blood skidded sideways long enough for the Davis wing to dump its lift.

Before I could call for full power on engines one and two, the RPM indicator needles were already climbing, because Orlando had anticipated my sideways dance and brought all available horses to the party.

"Release brake!"

As the plane's nose swung back to the centerline, we continued our high-speed rollout. Despite a few last-gasp attempts from wind gusts, the left aileron firmly deflected the slipstream and kept the wing planted where it belonged,

When we slowed enough to taxi, I swung the beast off the runway. As always, I whispered a prayer of thanksgiving for arriving in one piece.

The intercom crackled in my headsets. "Patton to pilot."

"Sir."

"Ride 'em cowboy."

"Yes, sir."

Five minutes later, with our plane parked on a narrow apron, engines off, controls locked, mission accomplished, a new one began when the VIP passenger compartment hatch BANGED open and the already-helmeted General George S. Patton jabbed a freshly-lit cigar in our direction.

"Transport's waiting," he barked. "BOQ quarters for you and me, Major Diaz. Our lovebirds, here, get the bridal suite."

"Thanks, sir," Ava said. "But Colonel Carter and I have been married for almost six months now."

"Don't talk back to your superior officer, lieutenant."

Ava grinned and saluted.

We tumbled out of the aircraft and onto a bus-like personnel van. Orlando gave some last-minute instructions to the ground crew, then hopped on board as well, bringing with him a wintry blast of wind.

"Hell of a night," he said.

Patton blew out a stream of cigar smoke. "Clear as a bell by dawn. Mark my words. Not even a breath of wind."

"Want to bet, sir?" Ava said.

"Not a betting man."

Her response disappeared in the roar of the bus engine as we pulled away from the hardstand and headed for a line of single-story, structures huddled together for protection from the blustery weather. Warm light glowed from all the windows, inviting us to rest a while. A fine idea to me. I'd been up for nearly twenty hours and wasn't a young man anymore. Well, thirty-four, is hardly what you'd call old, but after horsing around a four-engine cow with wings through an ice storm, and then landing in below-minimum conditions, my muscles and mind felt twice as old.

As if reading my mind (and I swear she could), Ava's hand sneaked beneath my flight jacket found my weary neck muscles that needed massaging. The darkness of the bouncing van hid her actions, including leaning close to me and whispering, "Carter Air, you are cleared to land on runway Ava."

The van pulled up to the enlisted barracks and our tech sergeant gunners, cook, and radio man tumbled out.

The cook turned. "Orders, sir?"

I looked at Patton, who instead of answering, studiously studied his cigar like a four-star sphinx. Something was in the wind, but damned if I could figure out what.

I shrugged. "Rest up. Report back to the flight line for a briefing at oh-eight-hundred hours."

Patton said, "Make that ten-hundred hours."

He and I exchanged a long look that ended with a wink—not from me, that's for sure. Got to give it to that man. Some people can wink and actually say something with that subtle gesture that says so much without saying anything. Others, like me, just blink.

Patton *winked*.

"Make it ten, sergeant. Do you read?"

"Yes, sir!"

The snow on the ground gave enough light scatter that I could make out a cluster of low-roofed structures, a water tower, and a line of construction cranes with their booms lowered against the storm. Military Police jeeps using four-wheel drive to navigate the snow, roamed the narrow streets like cops on the prowl. Huddled figures hurried back and forth, some carrying crates and boxes, others rolling barrels.

This could be any army forward operation base in the world. But it was here, sixty miles northwest of Alamogordo Army Airfield, in nowhere-land, New Mexico.

The van stopped again. Patton stood and re-seated his Colt .45s like the local sheriff off to capture a rustler. "Major Diaz, this is our stop. You two are just down that row of buildings to the right."

Ava said, "You've been here before?"

He smiled, said nothing, slid open the door and followed Orlando out. "See you two soon," he said over his shoulder, then disappeared into the swirling snow.

We sat there as the van pulled away.

I finally said, "Your uncle's nuts. This storm is here to stay."

"Not if he wants it to go."

Ava was right, of course.

But I didn't know that when the hammering on the flimsy door to the Officers' Quarters started at three in the morning—yes, 0300 hours. We'd been asleep for a total of four hours.

"Colonel Carter, sir?" A muffled, high-pitched voice.

"Yes?"

"Sir, you and Lieutenant James are to report outside on the double."

I wrapped a blanket around my shivering body, cracked open the door and encountered the bright blue, bugged-out eyes, and wildly freckled face of a young, white-helmeted, MP corporal.

"What's going on, son?"

A beaming smile. "We got the 'go' order."

"What's that mean?"

His eyes narrowed ever so slightly in suspicion at my innocent question.

"It's okay, son. I'm with General Patton, you can tell me."

"Oh, yes SIR, I know that and uh… he's waiting for you right now."

"Outside."

"Yes, sir."

"In the snow."

The smile almost broke his face. "What snow, sir? It's long gone, and we've got the green light.'"

Ten hurried minutes later, half-awake and barely dressed, Ava and I scrambled outside into the crisp cold morning. Still pitch-dark, but familiar constellations high above greeted me like old friends. So much better than the gray nothingness of last night's blowing snow.

"Uncle George was right," I said.

"Always is. Even when he's wrong."

We piled into the waiting personnel van. Hard to see much in the darkness except Patton sitting there, penlight in hand, peering at a sheaf of papers and puffing away on a fresh cigar.

"Morning, colonel… lieutenant."

"Sir."

"Sleep well?"

"Like a log, sir," Ava said.

"Find yourselves seats. Should be some left."

He spun around and gestured to the barely distinguishable dark silhouettes of other people packed inside the van. "Gentlemen, allow me to present the two folks who saved Doug MacArthur's bacon."

A slight ripple of laughter and deep chuckles. While it's true that our desperate gamble of hijacking a Japanese, high-performance seaplane and escaping to America had saved General Douglas MacArthur's life, Ava and I had been instruments of wartime need, that's all.

By contrast, military geniuses like Patton and Mac were giants striding the earth like twin Colossuses – Mac leading the fight to the Nazis in Europe and Patton to the Empire of Japan.

Patton turned back to us. "Say hello to various members of congress and assorted VIPs who are about to witness the dawn of a new age, at least for America. Or so *Herr Professor Doktor* Gunter Friedman and Professor J. Robert Oppenheimer have assured me."

He snapped off the penlight.

"Hope to hell they're right."

A half hour later, after a twisting, turning drive across a monotonous landscape of sand, rocks, and scrubby vegetation covered with a mantle of snow that would be long gone after the sun came up, we came to a stop.

I could smell it in the air – the change in weather, I mean – and while I welcomed the lack of crappy weather to screw up our flight plans, I wondered if this diversion of Patton's was going to throw a monkey wrench into the premiere festivities for Paramount Pictures' *Mission to Manila*.

Not that Ava could give a damn. Acting was a job to her, and she was good at it. Good at flying airplanes too. And golfing, and ping pong, and singing. She did many things well—no, I was more concerned that Abby and my mother Rosie wouldn't get a chance to enjoy the bright lights and newspaper photographers' flashbulbs as they climbed out of the limo and made their grand entrance into Oakland's Paramount theater to enjoy *Mission to Manila*, the silver screen version of our rescue mission to save General MacArthur.

So... whatever we were supposed to see this morning had better damn well be worth it. I said as much to Ava—whispered is more like it.

She shrugged. "No worries. We'll make it. Twentieth Century Fox will have Uncle Georgie's hide if he screws up their premiere."

"How can they hurt a four star?"

"You don't want to know."

She patted my arm, which meant she was done with the topic and moving on. Women have a way of doing that without missing a beat.

Men hem and haw as they drag the topic through the dust to a new place, prop it up, and start in all over again.

Ava sailed serenely onward instead. "Abby's dress is divine. She looks so grown up. Your mother looks ten years younger in hers."

"Rosie hasn't worn an evening gown in a long time."

"She'll get her chance tomorrow night."

"You *really* think we'll get there in time?"

"Shush." She patted my arm again. "I wonder what the fuss is all about. A 'new dawn?' What's that supposed to mean?"

"You sound excited."

"I am. When it comes to cloak-and-dagger, America's the best."

A phalanx of security men, both civilian and military, scrutinized our identities as we lined up in front of a wood and sand-covered, bunker-like structure, nestled half in, half out of the New Mexico desert. The dawn sky held only a faint yellow promise but enough light for me to recognize familiar members of congress from our nation's capital back in Philadelphia. Their overcoats and heavy boots hid their shapes, but not their faces.

Their names patiently checked off on a list, they entered the bunker one by one.

Our names weren't on the list. But when you're with General George S. Patton those details become moot.

"They're with me, sergeant," Patton growled around his cigar.

"Yes, sir, but…"

"What's the 'but' for, son? I said they're with me."

The hapless MP darted an anxious glance at the civilian security agent nearby. "Sir, it's General Patton, and…"

The man glided over; trench coat, fedora hat, leather gloves – the epitome of an "I'll take it from here" kind of guy.

Patton said, "You look cold, Agent Andrea."

"Good morning, sir."

"I take it our boss has arrived?"

A slight nod.

"Mind if my friends and I warm up our freezing butts and say hello?"

His eyes narrowed, both in exasperation and defeat. Wordless, he gestured with his close-fitting leather glove, much as a *maître d* would indicate a table.

Patton grinned. "Wife and kids okay?"

"Doing fine, sir."

"Becky lose that tooth yet?"

"Quite a while ago, sir."

"You're a lucky man, Agent Andrea. Don't you ever forget it."

Once inside, it felt like a cocktail party, but with everybody wearing overcoats to keep out the chill as they stood around chatting. The only thing missing in the low-ceiling, timber-raftered space were cocktails and *canapes*.

Patton sailed through the VIP crowd, with Ava and me in his wake. The others parted like the Red Sea before Moses. Not because he did anything, mind you. Some folks exude a kind of unquestionable power that causes the rest of us to sit up, take notice, and stand aside. Patton was that kind of guy.

Against the far wall stood a bank of mysterious-looking instruments. Technicians crowded around them like expectant fathers. A large countdown clock lorded it over the scene, steadily ticking away, showing minus twenty minutes.

"Madam President," Patton called out.

The smokescreen of politicians and hangers-on fell back to reveal Frances Perkins, thirty-third President of the United States, who smiled at the sight of us.

"So glad you could make it, General! Colonel Carter, Lieutenant James, how *are* you?"

Despite the wintry weather, her handshake was warm and strong. She'd come a long way in less than two years. On the night of December 8, 1941, she'd been Secretary of Labor in FDR's cabinet. The next day, president of our nation. She'd been in Philadelphia the night the Nazi's A-Bomb took out Washington, D.C. including the capitol and everybody in it.

Frances Perkins had been the sole survivor of Roosevelt's cabinet. By Constitutional right-of-succession, she took over our broken country. Like most women everywhere, she saved her grieving for later, while getting down to the business of picking up America's broken pieces and trying to put them back together again.

"Lieutenant," she said. "I heard the Galveston bond rally was a great success."

"Yes, ma'am, those Texans know how to build ships and how to buy war bonds."

"I know you need to be at the big event tomorrow night, and I promise we'll get you there in time."

Ava shrugged. "Duty first, Hollywood second."

"But *Mission to Manila's* such a wonderful recounting of your adventure. I saw an advance screening a few days ago."

"That's wonderful, Madam President. How did that happen?"

She pointed to a group across the room. A familiar figure wearing a trench coat and smoking a corncob pipe was holding court with a cluster of junior officers.

"General MacArthur not only knows *what* strings to pull, he knows *how* to pull them—just like you do, George. Am I right?"

Patton mumbled something, while Ava frowned. "But I wanted the movie to be a surprise for General MacArthur."

"Trust me, he'll enjoy being there with you for the premiere. He enjoys crowds."

"So did Caesar," Patton grumped.

Moments later, a swarm of enlisted men herded us to a row of bleacher seats set up at the back of the bunker. Since we were with President Perkins, we got front row seats and a good view of the soldiers and civilians gathered at the consoles in front of us. Some were making notes, others talking on microphones, while others simply sat there staring at the blank wooden wall, lost in thoughts of which I had no conception.

One of the figures detached himself from the crowd and made his way toward a small podium. His beer belly proceeded him and his two stars on his collar did the rest. He cleared his throat loudly, and the sound shushed us to silence.

"Madam President, distinguished guests, I'm General Leslie Groves. On behalf of the dedicated scientists and hardworking soldiers here at

Trinity Test site, I want to thank you for putting up with a snowstorm and very little sleep to make it out here at this godawful hour."

A slight rustle of approval by members of Congress and other VIPs. Groves knew how to work a political crowd, not to mention the President of the United States.

"But in less than five minutes, I promise you it will be worth it. Thanks to the concerted efforts of a nation at war and the teamwork of Doctor Oppenheimer and Professor Friedman, we are about to conduct a test of America's first atomic bomb."

"T-minus four minutes," a voice called out over the loudspeaker.

As if on cue, the wooden wall in front of us shuddered slightly, and then rumbled upward like a roll top desk. A collective intake of breath as we stared out at the vast panorama of the pre-dawn desert. The *Sierra Blanca* Mountain range to the east was an indistinct silhouette, the snow on its peaks still hidden from view. The cloudless winter sky glowed bright yellow from the promise of the rising sun soon to come.

Groves continued, "We have suspended the bomb from a steel girder tower ten miles from our bunker. When it detonates…."

Patton whispered, "*If* it detonates."

President Perkins nudged him. "Shhhh."

"…we have every confidence of your safety at this distance."

Patton muttered. "Famous last words…"

Another nudge.

"Three minutes. All systems optimized. Automatic triggering system engaged."

A voice somewhere behind me called out, "Do we need protective glasses?"

"No, senator, not at this distance. You are free to observe the explosion with the naked eye. That said, we anticipate a bright flash at first, so be prepared."

Patton let out with a slight grunt as Perkins's elbow poke to his ribs intercepted any further wise guy comments.

"Sixty seconds…."

The team behind General Groves tensed up. He joined them and stood beside an emaciated-looking specter of a man.

Patton saw me staring. "That's Oppenheimer. Looks like hell. If he weighs a hundred twenty pounds, it's a goddam miracle. Jesus."

"He's part of the project?" I said.

"The boss."

"What about Professor Friedman?"

"He's Tonto to the Lone Ranger."

"Sounds like a good team to me."

"We're about to find out."

"Thirty seconds."

Patton lit up a cigar, much to the consternation of the president. But it wasn't bravado this time, just plain and simple nerves. We all felt it. So much so, that the entire crowd in the bunker leaned forward, eyes alternating between the red numerals on the countdown clock above the panorama window and the distant darkness.

"Ten… nine… eight…

The voice droned ever onward but I stopped listening and started looking at how everybody rose slightly and leaned forward even more, as if peering over an abyss.

In a way we were: fifty-eight people crowded into an earth-berm bunker in the middle of the New Mexico desert at 5:08 in the morning of February 10, 1943, waiting for history to be made… or not.

"Two… one… DETONATE."

Another second of nothingness. Amazing where the mind can go in one second.

Then pure light.

Everywhere.

Like a flash bulb that won't go out, the entire *Sierra Blanca* range lit up like noontime; its snow-covered peaks white as the light illuminating them. But not from the light of the sun. That would come later when it rose.

Death was in charge for now.

I'd seen this same sky-filling flash almost two years ago. Ava gripped my hand and whispered the exact word I was thinking, "Hanford."

We'd both witnessed Professor Friedman's proof-of-concept Nazi bomb exploding over the Hanford Nuclear Enrichment Facility in Washington State. Our last-ditch mission in the ill-fated *Dixie Clipper* had managed to deny the Nazis their precious plutonium and allowed America to cast off her neutrality declaration and join the war against fascism.

But this far-brighter light in the New Mexico desert was so much more than the small nuclear device we'd dropped in desperation.

By now, the white light had subsided to reveal a reddish-orange, hemispheric-shaped, boiling fireball swelling higher and higher. Then the shockwave struck us from ten miles away like a bouncer at a bar slamming you against the wall just once, but hard enough to warn you not to mess around with muscle.

Our Hanford bomb had one quick punch. *This* bomb had sustained muscle, and plenty of it.

The fading fireball revealed a cyclonic vertical column of sand, rock, and vegetation capped by a mushroom-shaped top that billowed higher and higher with every passing second.

"Son-of-a-BITCH!" Patton hissed. "We just won the war."

Perkins said, "God help us all."

Patton hollered, "Hey, Les, how many we got of these things?"

General Groves shook his head, still mesmerized by the continuing display of what happens when you split the binding force of atoms and don't bother containing the explosive force. All I could think of was what the priest said when he pronounced Ava and me, husband and wife; "What God hath joined together, let no man put asunder."

Yet here we were, slamming neutrons into Uranium-235 and causing it to split so fast that a chain reaction released the binding energy of what God had joined together. President Perkins was right. We'd officially entered the "asunder" game and were now about to reap the whirlwind.

The sound reached us at long last, its ten-mile journey creating a deep-throated, low-frequency rumble that seemed to enter—not just our ears—but permeated our entire bodies.

The column kept climbing until its top flattened out at what I estimated to be at least 30,000 feet. But by now, the politicians and VIPs had turned their attention away from the massive explosion and started their own explosive conversations about what they'd just witnessed.

I had nothing to say. Neither did Ava. We moved trancelike through the crowd until we came upon the coffee urn tucked against the side of the bunker and helped ourselves to the jolt of caffeine. We stood there, munching dry donuts, and listening to the blur of conversation, until President Perkins's voice said, "Colonel Carter?"

I turned to see her standing beside General MacArthur, his hand outstretched.

"Been a while, colonel," he said as we shook hands. "Why didn't you seek me out earlier?"

"You looked busy, sir."

"Not for you two." He bowed slightly to Ava, ever the noble Roman Consul. "Your uniform becomes you, lieutenant. As do your aviator wings."

"Thank you, sir. Women pilots are finally in the fight the way we want to be."

President Perkins added, "Not to mention women presidents."

That got a frosty smile from Mac that quickly turned to a scowl when General Patton swept in from behind, thwacked him on the back, and said, "Jesus H. Christ, Mac, that's one hell of a bomb."

"One day it shall be."

"Can't wait to drop it on the Emperor's palace in Tokyo. The professor here says we just saw twenty-thousand tons of TNT go up. Am I right, Gunter?"

Only then did I notice the diminutive *Herr Professor Doktor* Friedman who had been standing behind Patton all this time. He took a step to one side and said, "*Jawohl*, we estimate the yield to be twenty kilotons."

Patton's grin was maniacal. "Hell of a lot bigger than that firecracker you tossed at Hanford, right, colonel?"

"It did the job, sir."

Patton didn't even hear me. Too lost in his own visions of glory. "Tojo, your days are numbered you son-of-a—"

"—We need to talk, George," President Perkins said quickly.

"With me?"

Her hazel eyes locked with mine. "With all of you."

Patton took in the crowded room filled with politicians and VIPs. The viewing window was still open. Clouds from their wintry breath bloomed over them like a cumulus cloud.

"Bit crowded, don't you think?" Patton said

The president said, "I didn't mean here. We'll talk back at Trinity Base." She checked a small watch pinned to her businesslike dress. "Professor, can you join us?"

Friedman regarded the enthusiastic crowd gathered around Doctor Oppenheimer and General Groves and smiled. "They won't miss me."

"Gentlemen? Lieutenant James? Shall we leave the party early?"

Guided by her secret service detachment, we cleared out. I doubt anybody noticed our leaving. The memory of what we had just witnessed still boggled their mind. They were frantically trying to put it into some kind of perspective by talking about it. But they would fail. Not for lack of trying, though. When you see something for the very first time you have no reference point, and they had none.

By contrast, Ava, Friedman, and I had already witnessed a small mushroom cloud rising over Hanford, thanks to the professor's "proof-of-concept" bomb, no bigger than a steamer trunk. The weapon had effectively destroyed America's plutonium supplies that Hitler wanted to make *his* bombs. We had denied him that pleasure.

Now we had one of ours.

Time for us to "put asunder."

I still remember Patton's face – like a child accidentally dropping his ice cream cone while crossing the street and a truck runs over it. That's how he looked an hour later, when we gathered in the small deserted mess hall at Trinity Base guarded by Secret Service agents.

President Perkins finished her announcement by saying, "I'm sorry, George."

"With all due respect, ma'am, I think you're making a big mistake. Last time Mac and his Joint Chiefs met they said I had the go-ahead for the Hawaii campaign."

Perkins nodded to General MacArthur, who took up the baton. "Hitler's *blitzkrieg* into Spain has altered the situation. We are pushing *Operation Torch* forward without delay."

"North Africa' nothing but sand and scrub, Mac. Like this godforsaken place. Sicily's even worse."

"But is also our first foothold in Europe."

"Providing Rommel doesn't boot your ass out."

MacArthur took this in stride. Julius Caesar was accustomed to doubting generals. "You'll wear that grass skirt yet, George. The Joint Chiefs and I are simply asking you to be patient."

Patton slapped his riding crop on his open palm. "NOT one of my strong points."

The president soothed, "Four to six months, George, that's all we're talking about here. We land in North Africa, establish a firm beachead in Sicily, and then you push east to Hawaii."

The small room fell silent. The ticking of a clock somewhere. Reminded me of a ticking bomb.

Patton tapped the table with his riding crop. "Mac gets the bomb and I get the bum's rush."

"Not quite," Perkins said.

She looked meaningfully at Professor Friedman, who cleared his throat and pushed his glasses up on his nose. A small man, slightly hunched, balding, the epitome of "absent-minded professor. But a brilliant nuclear physicist who'd been brave enough not only to sabotage Hitler's atomic bomb program, but crazy enough to steal a proof-of-concept device and help America buy time to get into the fight. This modest little man proved the adage that appearances can not only be deceiving but also deadly.

Friedman cleared his throat again and said softly, "What you saw this morning was *not* a deployable weapon."

A long pause.

Perkins said, "Did you bring them?"

"Jawohl. Wenn ditcht darf…"

He placed his leather briefcase on the table, opened it and pulled out a manila folder. He dealt out a stack of eight-by-ten glossies like a winning hand in poker as he briefly described the Trinity "device" they'd just seen explode;

1. Bomb assembly building
2. Plutonium sphere
3. Wiring harness
4. Assembled device
5. Tower
6. Installation.

After a cursory glance at the photos, I zeroed in on the "assembled device." It no more looked like a weapon of war than a gigantic weather balloon covered with a spaghetti tangle of wires. It needed tailfin assemblies and streamlined casings to fall through the atmosphere as a stabilized, aerodynamic object. This thing could never leave the ground.

Patton said, "How long before we get the real thing?"

Friedman looked at the president, who said, "It's okay, professor. You can tell them."

"Six months. Maybe a year."

"Why the hell so long?"

Friedman cleared his throat again. "It is always easier to beat a sword into a plowshare than the other way around."

SLAP went Patton's riding crop. "Then Jesus H. Christ, Mac, what's the hurry? Why not let me take a crack at Hawaii, while you wait to get this thing in working order? Then *after* you wipe out Palermo with one of these atomic babies you can take over Sicily like a sleeping baby. Sounds like a plan to me. What do you think?"

Mac considered this for a ponderous moment, but you could tell Patton's protests were so much rain on a tin roof. "We fear Spain will fall long before we have the bomb. That closes the Mediterranean and locks us out of Europe."

"You think that's why they killed Franco?"

"I *know* that's why."

Patton leaned forward on his elbows, a football lineman about to lunge.

"I said this before and I'll say it again. Tokyo's got its eyes on two prizes: the Aleutians and the Panama Canal. If they manage to lock those two doors, America can kiss the Pacific goodbye." He slapped the table. "We've GOT to take back Hawaii before it's too late!"

Another long pause. President Perkins finally said, "Thank you, general, we're more than aware of that strategic threat. But I must repeat, General MacArthur has my go-ahead for *Project Torch*. In the meantime, continue your troop buildup for our drive west across the Pacific. It will commence as soon as we have operational nuclear weapons. Are we in agreement, gentlemen?"

A long moment of silence. While Patton and Mac locked eyes, Professor Friedman cleared his throat. "If I may add one more disturbing item?"

Perkins nodded.

"*Danke.*"

The good professor pulled out another photograph and added it to the pile.

A Japanese man wearing a white linen suit, a white shirt, tightly-knotted tie, a furled umbrella, and a straw hat perfectly aligned on his head. He stood at attention beneath some kind of flowering tree.

"This is a former colleague of mine, Professor Saburo Yamasaki. We did research together in Berlin. We became friends." He sighed. "Seems like an eternity ago."

He paused. Mac puffed on his pipe. "Your point, professor?"

Friedman slid out another photograph. Mac leaned over and examined it. A Japanese man decked out in a costume of sorts; a sleeveless jacket with exaggerated shoulders, puffy pants, and two swords tucked into a cloth belt around his waist. The top of his head was shaved smooth, while the sides remained long.

"Who's he?" Mac said.

"Same man."

Ava slid the photo closer, so she could see it. "He's a *samurai* warrior?"

"You know about such things?"

"MGM has a film in the works. Sent me the script is all. One of the costume sketches looks a lot like this guy, minus a gigantic helmet."

"That is the movies, Miss James. Yamasaki is the real thing. His family is descended from a warrior clan."

"Your point, professor?" Perkins's voice was edged with impatience.

"Yamasaki is a brilliant physicist. As adept in splitting atoms as he is with splitting heads with his sword."

Patton smiled. "My kind of man."

Friedman gathered up the photos. "I have a confession to make." His voice dropped to a whisper, as if somebody was eavesdropping. "Despite this world war between nations, the scientific community is a global family. I have maintained friendships with many of my colleagues in conquered nations – Italy, France, England, and yes, even Germany and Japan. Science recognizes no borders."

"So… what's this *samurai* buddy of yours up to?" Patton said.

"Saburo always believed that it would be possible to create fission without force. That is to say, with the right kind of conditions, the atomic structure would surrender its grip on its electrons and release the binding energy. But not with brute force like we did this morning to explode our atomic bomb. And…" He trailed off, reluctant to continue.

Perkins checked her watch like a frustrated railroad conductor. "I need to be back in Philadelphia, professor. Let's wrap this up, if you don't mind."

"My colleagues and I have come to the conclusion that thanks to Professor Yamasaki, Japan may well have leapfrogged ahead of both Germany and the United States in developing thermonuclear weaponry."

That got everybody's attention.

Perkins, especially, who frowned and said, "You're telling me this *now?*"

Mac straightened up like a shot. "Verified or professorial gossip?"

"Both, I'm afraid."

"Which is which?"

"That's the problem. Fermi thinks Yamasaki's devised a way to fission a trigger explosion that could in turn trigger a fusion one. Szilard and Einstein disagree."

"What about you?"

He closed his eyes for a moment. "*Samurai* warriors were military nobility, fiercely devoted to protecting their *daimyo*, or lords. Knowing Saburo as I do, if he has indeed achieved this breakthrough, then Japan will have—or perhaps already has—thermonuclear weapons to protect her Emperor, much in the same way as Yamasaki's ancestors' swords did so in ages past."

A long silence while his words sank in. Patton's cigar burnt down a full inch from his rapid puffing. He was the first to speak, right in Mac's face. "And *you* want to go after the wops and Nazis in Sicily?" He swung around to Perkins. "Madam President, we've got to cry havoc and slip loose the dogs of war with Tokyo, and we've got to do it *now!*"

Mac said, "Based on scientific gossip? I disagree. Stay the course we've laid out. Besides, it's too late to turn back now."

Perkins' eyebrows lowered ominously. "It's never too late, general. But based on what I've just heard we need to explore this in greater detail."

"Good luck with that," Patton said, "Japan's a closed shop."

"We cracked their code, remember?"

"Yes, ma'am, but that's all we'll ever get."

Perkins stood. "Thank you for being here. The original invasion plans remain in place, but in the meantime, I will direct our intelligence agencies to find out the truth about Professor Friedman's claims."

Friedman said, "I would prefer you consider them as serious warnings, instead, Madam President."

Patton said. "Where the hell is this guy, anyhow? Any way we could get hold of him and make him talk?"

"In Hokkaido for a long while. Then Manila. Szilard told me yesterday that Professor Yamasaki is now somewhere in the Hawaiian Islands."

You could have slapped Patton full in the face and not got a bigger reaction.

"You hear *that*, Madam President? That son-of-a-bitch *samurai* hotshot is brewing up trouble right where *we* need to be."

Perkins nodded but kept moving toward the door. It opened as if by magic and her Secret Service agents stepped in to flank her like bookends. She turned to face us, her face serene.

"You'll find your way back, General MacArthur?"

"Yes, ma'am."

"Lots to do."

"For all of us."

"Enjoy the movie premiere, everyone. Wish I could be there. Such a wonderful film. Everyone did a fine job. Especially you, Miss James."

"Thank you, Madam President. Personally, I thought Bogie stole the show."

"He wasn't nearly as convincing as the real thing." She pointed to me. "Colonel Carter's much taller—braver too, I might add."

I could only nod like an idiot.

"Ava, if you see Mr. Zukor, thank him again for me. So thoughtful of him to provide the White House with a private screening."

"Yes, ma'am."

"Including popcorn."

"Zukie doesn't miss a trick."

She nodded thoughtfully. "Back to work."

And saying that, the thirty-third President of the United States sailed away, leaving the five of us to stare at each other in silence until Patton stubbed out his cigar and growled. "You heard the lady."

The lousy weather that had iced up our C-87 from Galveston to Albuquerque had long since rolled eastward, kicked in the backside by a high-pressure system that drove everything before it like a mule driver. It also packed some powerful headwinds, which cut into our fuel consumption.

That said, we had topped off our tanks with almost three thousand gallons of one-hundred octane AVGAS before leaving the airfield at Trinity. More than enough for the nine hundred-mile flight northwest to San Francisco.

And home.

We were flying at eleven thousand-feet – low enough not to need oxygen, which made life easier on the nostrils and lungs. Plenty of masks on board if needed, though, but Patton hated to use the stuff unless absolutely necessary.

No doubt he and Mac were telling each other lies back in his VIP quarters, while sizing up each other too. Two four-star generals – each with a story to tell and a bone to pick, but the other one not interested in either.

Our flying whale had a reliable automatic pilot (Sperry doesn't make junk) and could easily assume the physical strain of horsing around a twenty-ton bucket of aluminum junk.

That said, Ava was hand-flying at the moment, and I stole a couple glances at her hands gripping the oval-shaped control wheel. The diamond in her wedding ring kept catching the sunlight slanting through the cockpit window and tossing rainbow rays all over the place.

Me. Married to a movie star!

Still hard to believe. But Ava would have laughed at me for characterizing her like that. Being a gifted actress was just one of her many skills. She took as much pride in handling a multi-ton, four-engine airplane as she did performing a dramatic scene with Humphrey Bogart.

"Are you humming?" I said.

"Maybe."

"You look like it, but there's too much noise up here for me to know for sure."

"I'm humming because I'm happy to be going home."

"To a tiny bungalow the size of a closet with no privacy."

"That day will come, darling."

"Can't come too soon."

After the successful Hanford mission. I shuttered *Carter Aviation* in Key West for the duration and accepted a Presidential commission as a lieutenant colonel in the Army Air Corps. General Patton had found quarters for me and what was left of my family near the Presidio in San Francisco, his HQ for Western Command. Not much. A two-bedroom bungalow. My mother Rosie slept in one bedroom, my daughter Abby the other. I had the couch.

Then, Ava and I fell in love and got married. Rosie insisted Abby sleep with her, and we took over my eleven-year-old daughter's room. But ever since we evicted her from her private kingdom, life had been tense at home.

Fortunately, war bond tours and General Patton's long-distance travel took Ava and me away from home a lot, which gave Abby breathing room to haul her cot back into her old bedroom and dream of days gone by.

The plane JOLTED through a touch of turbulence, but Ava's lightning-fast aileron and elevator correction transformed what might have been a momentary nose dive into a tiny pothole.

"Nice catch," I said.

"Just another day at the office, Colonel Carter, sir."

I heard my name and rank repeated in my earpiece in a deep male voice.

"Yes, general?"

"Got a minute?"

"Yes sir."

"Head on back here."

Ava and I exchanged a silent look. She wiggled the yoke. "I have the aircraft sir."

"Share it with General Sperry." (our nickname for the autopilot).

She frowned. "But I—"

"That's an order, lieutenant."

Both Patton and MacArthur were tall men. The former at six-two and the latter, six-feet. I'm in between at six-three. Like a stand of redwoods we gathered in the confines of the C-87's flying office, located aft of the cockpit, where the bomb bay is in the B-24 bomber version. A map of the Hawaiian Islands was mounted on the side wall of the fuselage.

Patton launched right in without preamble. "Sam, when you were with *Pan Am* you used to fly to Oahu, right?"

"Yes, sir. A long haul but worth it when you landed."

He grinned. "Hula-hula girls and coconut cocktails, right?"

"Bed was more like it, sir, after a nineteen-hour flight."

He tapped the island of Oahu with his riding crop. "I'm trying to convince General MacArthur, here, that we need to reconnoiter what the hell's going on out there with that *samurai* professor."

Mac frowned. "The president said she would authorize intelligence-gathering, and that—"

"—when hell freezes over, she might get some answers." Patton's dark brown, almost black, eyes swiveled to me like twin machine guns tracking a target. "Colonel Carter, how well do you know the islands?"

My head buzzed with sudden excitement. No more taxi-cab driving around the country and twiddling my thumbs while Patton beat the war drums and Ava rallied the crowds and sang for the troops. A mission!

"I know them well, sir." (A bit of a stretch, but when in doubt, fake it until you make it.)

Patton continued. "Can't be Oahu, that's for damn sure. The Japs can't afford something going wrong with the bombs and blowing up their fleet." His riding crop slid east to the northwesternmost island. "What about here?"

"That's Kauai. A bit a bit too far off the beaten path."

His crop slid the opposite direction to the chain of islands to the southeast.

"Forget Molokai… the leper colony's there."

Slid again.

"Maui… maybe…."

MacArthur grumbled. "This isn't a guessing game, George. While I agree we have the resources to send a team in by submarine, should that be the case, we need intelligence on the ground before I commit."

"Agreed. And since we're in regular radio contact with guerilla forces on Oahu and Maui, they can find out the who, what, and where. Then I'll authorize a recon team. A sub can land them."

"A submarine would take forever to transit from the west coast."

"We have four on station less than a hundred miles from Hawaii."

"But your recon team is in California—George this is ridiculous."

Patton tapped my shoulder and grinned wickedly. "Colonel Carter, here, could fly them out and rendezvous with the sub."

"In what?"

Patton stared at me. I took the lead. Didn't want to appear too excited, but I was! "Well, sir, we've got one Boeing Clipper left from when the *Lufthansa* was flying them for the Nazis. She's a hangar queen at the moment, but it wouldn't take long to get her ready."

"To *where*, damn it!" Mac snapped. "George, you come up with the damndest ideas."

I scrutinized the islands; Lanai... Hawaii... no... no...and then I knew. Don't ask me how. Life works like that sometimes, but mostly it doesn't.

My finger stabbed a small scrap of an island southwest of Maui. Hardly an island. More like the tip of the underwater mountain from whence it first arrived, born from volcanic eruptions millions of years ago.

"Kaho'olawe." I said. "If they're up to something, it'll be there."

"Why?" Mac said.

"Because nothing else is."

I explained how the tiny island was perpetually caught in the "rain shadow" of Maui, seven miles away to the northeast. Because of this meteorological curse, little or no vegetation grew on this volcanic scrap of real estate. That, plus the lack of fresh water, made the place relatively uninhabitable. Sure, thousands of years ago Polynesian fishing villages dotted the shoreline, and as late as the early 1900s an idiot Wyoming cattle farmer thought he could raise beef on the scrubby land. All efforts ultimately failed.

"Ever been there, colonel?" Patton said.

"Once, when I had a layover. Just before the war. Took a canoe trip from Maui. When I was there, nobody else was except Mother Nature."

Mac said, "And now?"

I regarded the desolate place. "I think your recon team should put this on their list."

"Whereabouts?" Patton said.

"At the top."

In war, you win or lose, live or die —
the difference is just an eyelash.
General Douglas MacArthur

No matter how many times I looked in the mirror, I still didn't recognize the man looking back at me. For good reason – I was wearing the formal United States Army "mess dress" uniform for the very first time.

The dark-blue tail coat sported gold-braided epaulets on the shoulders, and curlicued "Austrian knots," or trefoils, embroidered on the sleeves. Since my rank was full "bird colonel," now, I rated five knots. But had six, counting the one in my nervous stomach.

Nervous because of what Patton and Mac had discussed with me on our flight from Alamogordo to San Francisco. No more "watching the meter" of Patton's four-engine, airborne taxi like I'd been doing for the past year. Looked like I stood a good chance of getting back into the fight again with a mission to Kaho'olawe.

No doubt about it – the mere thought of getting my hands on an ex-*Pan Am* Boeing 314 Clipper again gave me goosebumps. That beautiful flying boat had a special place in my heart. Considered the ultimate in luxury ocean travel, my lofty-sounding rank of "Master of Flying Boats" had entitled me to sit in the left-hand seat and call the shots.

Back in the fight again!

I tried to hide my nervousness by fussing with my bow tie in the mirror.

"You're awfully quiet," Ava said—or sort of said—as she applied lipstick to the same lips I'd kissed five minutes earlier when she said, "How do I look, darling?"

Imagine a dream come true. Then double it. Then triple it. That's what I thought as I took in the full effect of Ava's evening gown that her waiting fans would crane their necks to see when we arrived at the Paramount theater for the world premiere of *Message to Manila*.

Designed by Edith Head, the emerald-green, off-the-shoulder gown neatly framed her shapely bare shoulders for all the world to see. The watered-silk fabric gleamed in the lights on her dressing table, coming from globe-like fixtures marching around the perimeter of the mirror like the makeup tables you see in motion picture studios. Not much space in our tiny bedroom for that sort of thing, but Ava made it work somehow.

She fluffed her long auburn hair, finally freed from its military "jail." It cascaded onto her shoulders.

"How'd you get so many curls?" I said.

"Trade secret—but you, my dear, aren't you a sight for a young maiden's eyes?"

I ran my finger around the tight-fitting collar. "This thing's killing me."

"I see the problem, colonel." Ava tugged my bowtie loose. "Have you ever worn one of these?"

"No."

"It shows—sit, look in the mirror, I'll show you."

She nudged me onto her dressing room chair, reached around from behind and slowly tied the black bow-tie.

After a few practiced twists, flips and loops she said, "You like?"

"Perfect. Like you."

A quick intake of breath and she turned away.

"You okay?"

A couple more deep breaths. "Butterflies in the stomach, that's all."

"The premiere?"

"No. Just a little queasy."

"I'd like to say you don't have to go to this thing, but you do. So...unless...."

Halfway through her objections, a muffled shout from downstairs.

"WHAT?" Ava shouted.

Thundering footsteps stopped outside our bedroom door.

Ava called out, "It's open, dear."

My daughter Abby burst into the bedroom, eyes wide with astonishment. Not at us – she'd already been in here twice, pestering us while we were dressing. She stood there, staring, motionless.

"Cat got your tongue?" I said.

"Humphrey Bogart is in our *house*," she gasped. "And... and... Lauren Bacall *too*!"

Ava was unfazed. "Did you offer them refreshments?"

"Grandma did..."

"Be a dear and tell them Sam and I will be down in a minute."

AMERIKA *Strikes Back* · 43

She twirled around to leave and Ava said, "By the way…Abby?"

Another twirl. Her face expectant.

"It's *Mister* Bogart and *Miss* Bacall, darling."

"I *know* that." She flushed slightly. "I was just—"

"And may I say, you look perfectly wonderful in that dress."

"Me?"

"Yes, you, silly goose."

My daughter's gangly frame barely filled her dark blue evening gown. Temporarily caught in a growth spurt, nothing seemed to fit. But Ava's words seemed to round out the sharp edges she'd been displaying lately.

"One more thing," Ava said.

Abby sighed, trapped in Ava's gunsight, waiting to endure another criticism. "Yes, ma'am?"

"That shade of blue is *absolutely* your color. Don't let anyone ever tell you otherwise."

"Really?"

"Really. It sets off your eyes perfectly. And by the way, it's 'Ava,' not "ma'am'. Okay?'"

Abby grinned, "Okay." She ducked out and slammed the door.

My wonderful wife fussed with my bowtie in silence.

I finally said, "A truce between you two?"

"Sort of. Having us out of the house with Uncle George so much gives her some privacy. We need to do it more often."

"I'd rather have another bedroom."

"That's a wonderful idea. Abby would love that."

"Not for Abby." I kissed her. "For us."

By the time we got downstairs, Orlando, Bogie, and Abby were playing cards at a rickety table, while Lauren and Rosie were chatting away like long lost friends as they sat on the tiny sofa in the tiny living room of our tiny little bungalow. While I was happy to join the crowd, two more bodies added to the cramped confines made for standing-room-only.

Unlike our current housing situation, Bogey and Lauren were staying at the luxurious *Sir Francis Drake* hotel in downtown San Francisco – *the* Hollywood hideout whenever movie stars were in town. Compared to our wartime "closet" called a house, they were slumming it when they came here.

But you wouldn't know it from the contented looks on both their faces. Something to be said for just living your life *outside* the limelight for a change, even if it means rubbing shoulders whenever you move.

Bogey examined his cards, shook his head, and growled, "Go fish!"

Orlando frowned. "You *sure* you don't have hearts?"

Abby crooned, "Uncle Orlando, you heard *Mister* Bogart. Go fish."

As he did so, Lauren Bacall rose from the couch like Botticelli's *Birth of Venus* and said in her famously-seductive low voice. "I don't want to be a spoilsport, Steve, but if we don't leave soon, we're going to be late."

"In a sec, Slim," Bogie said. "I'm winning."

"Not for long, darling." She glided over, reached down, and examined his hand. "Who are you kidding? Abby wins—or I should say *would* win, but she can't because we have to go." She kissed Bogie's head. "Scoot, scoot—Abby and Orlando, you two as well—Ava you look delicious. How do you keep your figure?"

"Starvation."

My mother Rosie observed their movie star banter with a mixture of wonder, awe, and delight flitting across her face like happy clouds. I confess I felt like she did – it really *was* like having a movie happening in your own house, albeit a tiny bungalow-sized one.

The good news was that the two army staff cars assigned to us were regular limousines by comparison to the normal Jeeps I was accustomed to bouncing around in. The cars' olive drab paint, white stars painted on the side doors, and blackout shields over the headlights couldn't hide the familiar lines of Cadillac *Fleetwoods* – ready for war on the outside, but ready for presidents, generals, and heads-of-state on the inside.

Tonight, thanks to General Patton, they'd carry movie stars and regular folks to the world premiere of *Message to Manila*, the quasi-fictional, mostly true story of our daring rescue of General Douglas MacArthur by hopscotching an ex-*Pan American Airways* M-130 flying boat across the South Pacific to Corregidor, and to many adventures beyond. Bogie played the part of me while Ava appeared as herself.

We moved like a Conga line out of the bungalow down to curbside, where Bacall stopped us like a ringmaster. "We're heading over to the Persian Room after the show to celebrate—my treat!"

"Who's 'we,' darling?" Ava said.

She swept her arm around to take in the world. "Everyone, of course."

"The Persian Room!" Abby said. "Ooooh, can I come, daddy? Puh-leez?"

Typical that Bogey and Bacall would choose the historic hangout at the Drake Hotel for their after-show party. Everyone who's someone always has cocktails at "The Persian," both to see and be seen. Needless to say, being an official nobody, I'd never been there. But I figured Ava had downed many a *mai tai* there over the years. Yes, *mai tais*. Makes a straight bourbon man like me shudder to even write the words that describe that super-sweet, fruity concoction. But anything that brings a smile to my wife's face brings a smile to mine.

But not at the moment.

Bogey spotted the beginnings of my reluctant fatherly frown regarding Abby's request and said, "I hear they make a mean *Shirley Temple*. Abby'll love it."

One doesn't refuse Humphrey Bogart. Not because of his size, mind you. He's not really that tall. But there's something absolutely and unequivocally *certain* about his demeanor. Whatever he says, *goes*.

"What do you say, Sam?" he said. "Give the kid a night on the town, why don't you?"

I agreed, and Abby beamed. Bacall kept the good times going by saying, "Abby, you ride with us, darling. Rosie, you too. C'mon, troops, let's roll!"

Their army driver stood ramrod stiff by the open car door. He automatically saluted Bogey and Bacall, like visiting generals. In a way they were worthy of such acclaim, at least as far as millions of Americans were concerned. Myself included.

Our driver, a whip-thin, Ichabod Crane-like corporal snapped off a sharp salute to Orlando and me as befitting our ranks, but his eyes were riveted on Ava's sinuous entry into our staff car. Couldn't blame the kid. Just because you're on a diet doesn't mean you can't look at the menu.

Unexpectedly warm air for February was busy swirling down from the northwest and meeting the cool waters of San Francisco Bay. The result? Dense clouds of marine-layer fog. Based on the forecasts, destined to hang around for a long time. Not that it mattered much, since I was sitting comfortably in the back of a Cadillac limousine, while somebody else was being the chauffeur for a change.

Ava slipped her hand in mine and took a couple of deep breaths.

"Easy, Miss James," I said. "Your public needs you."

Orlando grinned. "Opening night jitters, huh?"

Ava shook her head but said nothing, which pushed my "Daddy" button. "You should have grabbed something to eat before we left."

"The thought of food makes me even more nauseous."

"Not even popcorn?" Orlando said.

She moaned, "Who writes your material?"

"I do."

"Thought so."

The car sped up, which would be fine under normal circumstances, but the fog made things a bit dicey. I said to the driver as casually as I could, but with enough bite to make it known I was concerned, "Need to get there in one piece, corporal."

"Yes, sir. But I can't lose sight of the other car. We've got orders to arrive at the same time."

He took a corner a bit too fast and we fought for balance. Ava slid closer to me and laughed. "Follow that car, officer!"

"Got him, Miss James!" the driver said, then immediately slowed down. "Sorry sir, but these blackout lights are pretty much useless."

Ava said, "Tonight's fog hides us from General Tojo much better than they do."

"Yes, ma'am."

She brightened and leaned forward. "You coming to the premiere, corporal?"

"I wish."

She fussed around inside the smallest clutch purse on earth. No bigger than my wallet, sparkling like mad, covered with what she said were rhinestones, but I knew for a fact—because Rosie told me—they were diamond chips—a long-ago gift from a studio head who had made a fortune from one of her movies.

"Got a pen, dear?"

I always have a pen.

She jotted something on one of her cards and handed it to him.

"Once everybody's inside, give this to the folks in the box office. They'll sneak you in the back."

"You mean it, ma'am?"

"Enjoy the show—oops, almost forgot." She pulled out a twenty-dollar bill. "Buy yourself lots of popcorn."

General Patton's fingerprints were all over the premiere. The familiar rows of searchlights swooping and sweeping the skies were absent tonight, of course. We were at war and didn't want to make it easier for the Japanese find us. But everything else you'd expect was there in full force – crowds, of course, lining the street, held back by Military Police—a nice touch, instead of cops—holding the barrier ropes, while the happy mob leaned forward for an adoring glimpse of their stars.

Bogey's Cadillac pulled up first, the doors opened, flashbulbs went off like a strafing attack as he and Lauren, and Abby and Rosie made their way up the red carpet toward the entrance to the most remarkable theater I'd ever seen in my life. Even though Ava had described it to me, to see it for real made me get a crick in my neck from looking up.

The exterior façade towered at least two hundred feet in the air. The word, **PARAMOUNT,** marched across the marquee. Directly beneath it in big, bold block letters:

MISSION TO MANILA

Directly beneath that, almost as big:

AVA JAMES * HUMPHREY BOGART

Can you imagine your name up in lights? I can't. But then again, I'm not an actor. The stories they tell on the silver screen are blended together inside movie sets, with musical scores and special effects. The movie theater is where we come to pay homage to their hard work.

And what a theater!

Rising up like a skyscraper, a mosaic of two exotic-looking women holding marionette strings attached to dancing puppets. That's just for starters. The gold, blue, silver, and black mosaic pieces that made up the figures sparkled from the moisture of the drifting fog.

Bisecting the two beautiful puppeteers was a one-hundred-twenty-five foot high slab, emblazoned on both sides with the famous word spelled out vertically:

P
A
R
A
M
O
U
N
T

Then, right before my astonished eyes, the gigantic letters lit up in bright neon red, with neon-gold around the edges, glowing proudly in the night.

The crowd gasped as one, then cheered. To hell with the blackout! Tonight's pea soup fog was the best ally we could have had against Tokyo's prying eyes. Someone must have thought about this possibility early on and planned accordingly.

Ava laughed. "Good old Uncle George. He *knows* how to throw a party."

"Even when it's for Mac?"

She whispered in my ear, "Daddy may be cantankerous and a bully but he's not vindictive."

And yes, for the record, General George S. Patton *was* Ava's biological father. But back then, only three people knew it, counting me. A long story not to be told here, but suffice to say, "Uncle Georgie" wasn't one of those three people, nor would Ava ever tell him.

At least not yet. And probably never.

My wife was the kind of woman who believed more in knowing the truth than the telling of it—if that makes sense. In other words, it was enough that *she* knew that her feisty, headstrong, determined, widowed mother had wanted a baby, but not a husband to go with it, and devised a way to seduce a young, handsome, unsuspecting Army captain to fulfil her wishes in a loving one-night stand that also created Ava James.

Only in the past year or so, had Ava learned the true story of her birth parents. For years, her mother had told her she was adopted—to protect Patton's reputation as a solid, Bible-reading, family man. And if that ever needed protecting, it was now as America charged full speed into a world war.

More flashbulbs and a roar from the crowd as Patton and Macarthur climbed out of their staff car and paused to acknowledge the deafening applause. Nothing like heroes to make you feel heroic.

Ava whispered in my ear. "With all those stars on their shoulders, gonna' be a tough act for me to follow."

"You're the only star these folks steer by."

Ava whispered, "Love you, Sam Carter."

A kiss in my ear and I was in la-la land again. Tonight, the world would get to watch a fabulous forty-foot-high version of Ava James on the silver screen, but I had the real one just kiss my ear.

"Curtain going up!" she said.

The army driver swung open the door with a flourish and saluted. The deliriously happy look on his face was mirrored by the crowd that surged against the ropes.

The whole world wanted Ava James.

Lucky me.

In the distance, Bogey and the gang were almost inside the main entrance. Flashbulbs were still going off like popcorn. Warmed my heart to see Bogey holding Abby's hand, with Bacall and Rosie arm-in-arm, waving at the crowd. Didn't matter that the crowd didn't know who the hell my daughter and mother were. The fact that they were on the red carpet warranted wild applause.

Ava made a quick adjustment to her gown and took a deep breath. "That's our cue. Here we go. Look sharp!"

Orlando and I paused to let her lead the parade. But the instant she saw our tactic, she linked arms with us, making a happy threesome, then shouted to the crowd, "Hello, my darlings! Meet the team!"

Ka-BOOM went their answering cheer. And in that moment, I loved my wife for leapfrogging over the racial barriers that crisscrossed Hollywood, preventing black performers from working with white performers except as secondary citizens like "Stepin Fetchit."

Here she was, arm-in-arm with Orlando Diaz, a man as black as you could ever find—played in the movie by Freddie O'Neal, a somber, dead-serious, negro stage actor, who agreed to change his somewhat reserved persona to more closely match Orlando's boisterous, assertive ways.

The premiere crowd? One look at the *real* Orlando Diaz and knowing what they knew about his heroic actions in the war, they cheered their heads off.

People are funny that way. If by your actions you can rise above the color of your skin and be a man or woman who deserves and demands equality, folks go color-blind real fast. We're wired that way. But it's not easy.

That said, Orlando made it look easy. Especially the way he smiled and waved at the crowd like they were drinking buddies. I just hoped Freddie O'Neal could do justice to my lifelong friend.

The short answer is, he did.

Orlando never looked better on screen that night as the courageous flight engineer firing his fifty-caliber machine guns at the attacking Japanese fighters, when we bombed downtown Tokyo as part of the Doolittle mission.

The audience moaned when they pulled the gravely wounded Orlando from our bullet-riddled B-25 after we landed at the Soviet airfield. And then they cheered in the fourth reel when they found out he'd survived.

Ava was astonishing, as always. You'd think it'd be easy to play yourself, but as she constantly reminded me, acting is portraying "enhanced reality." And because so little "space" existed between the real person and the person she was portraying, her acting was masterful in *Mission to Manila*.

Me? I winced at Bogart's portrayal of myself as a stoic, determined pilot who never gave up, especially when bobbing in a life raft in the South China Sea with Ava and General MacArthur, just as the Japanese super-sub surfaced. Don't get me wrong. All that stuff happened, but it the *real* world, not on the silver screen with music and sound effects.

"You were wonderful," Ava said afterwards as she squeezed my arm.

"That was Bogey, not me."

"You know what I mean."

We stood waiting in Paramount's cavernous grand lobby for the crowd in the street to thin out a bit before we left for the after-party. But so far, it didn't look like anyone had left. Patton and MacArthur and their retinues clustered near the "fountain of light," a sheet of backlit translucent panels and gold-beaded fabric that created the illusion of a waterfall. Flanked by bright red pillars that held up the cathedral-like space, you could fit thousands of people inside. As it was, only a handful of us meandered around like tiny ants in search of a picnic.

Bacall glided up to us, holding Abby's hand. "Such a thrilling movie. Like a fairy tale."

"You did all that stuff, daddy?"

I shrugged, preferring silence.

"And more," Ava said, then turned to Bacall. "Bogey was spot-on. He always makes it look so easy."

"That's my guy."

Bacall's "guy" was politely listening to Rosie telling him something I couldn't hear. But from the way my mother was waving her hands and the look on her face, it had something to do with flying.

The small air service she and I had founded after I left *Pan Am* was a dream come true for her. She'd spent her teenage years rolling cigars in Key West with Orlando's mother (it's how the two of us met). Then she fell in love with my father, who worked for the *Florida East Coast Railway*.

On weekends she and I would ride our bikes over to the small Key West airstrip and "watch the planes take off and land." I eventually "took off" at seventeen and started my life in aviation. Rosie stayed put, but never lost her love for being above the ground and dancing with the clouds.

She finished her story with Bogey and towed him over to us. "Didn't Mister Bogart do grand, Sam?"

I saluted Bogey, and meant it.

He returned the salute while giving me his familiar, lopsided, crooked-tooth grin. "Hope at least I *looked* like I was flying those planes of yours."

"I believed you."

"Tell me something, was that Jap seaplane really that fast?"

"Like the wind."

Bogey meant the Aichi M6A *Seiran*, the Japanese super-sub's sleek, high-performance fighter that Ava, Mac, and I had hijacked to escape from the *I-401*.

Abby-the-aviation-expert made a face. "The Martin M-130 looked like a toy."

"Now Abby…" Rosie said.

"The kid's right," Lauren said. "Isn't she, dear?"

Bogie rubbed his face. "They wanted more time to work on it, but principal photography was done, Zanuck wanted it in theaters by March, soooo…"

"Doesn't matter one bit." Orlando grinned. "When you landed the *Seiran* at the Presidio, the audience bought it hook, line, and sinker. The happily-ever-after is all that ever matters."

You can't argue with that, and nobody did, especially Abby, who stifled a yawn. She caught me watching, shook her head, and grinned. "Not tired, daddy, honest."

"Good, because I don't want you sleeping at the big party."

Her face lit up like one of the news photographer's flashbulbs. "That's right!" She glanced around at the empty space. "When can we leave?"

Bacall took her hand. "Now."

Like a movie in reverse, our exit matched our entrance – cue the mob scene, flashbulbs, cheering, fog swirling everywhere, waving, smiling, army staff cars curbside, drivers by the open doors.

Patton and Mac conferred by the lead vehicle. He waved me over.

"Colonel, can you give the good general a lift over to the hotel? I've got a forest fire going full bore at HQ."

"Literally," Mac added.

"More sub shelling?"

Patton puffed his cigar like a freight train. "Damned Japanese raids will be the death of me. The minute I scramble planes to search for the subs, they button up, dive, and are long gone."

The Japanese Navy's offshore shelling of the California coastline had been going on ever since Pearl Harbor. Not a Japanese battle fleet out there with battleships lobbing eighteen-inch shells on Los Angeles. More like a submarine's deck gun firing five-inch incendiary rounds into the forested hills overlooking Los Angeles, or high-explosives shell pulverizing a hapless truck on Route One along the coast. Not much in terms of material damage, but a powerful psychological weapon used on American citizens to great effect.

Especially Patton.

He hopped in the staff car, then hopped out, like toast from a toaster. "Tell them I'll try to make it to the party, but no guarantees."

"Yes, sir."

He and Mac shook hands. "Colonel Carter will fly you back to Philly first thing in the morning."

"I appreciate that, George."

I groaned inwardly at the thought of another long, dreary flight across the wintry United States, while freezing my butt off in our drafty C-87. At least Ava and Orlando and my flight crew would suffer along with me.

Patton hopped back into the staff car and the driver shut the door. The general leaned out the window, all grins at MacArthur. "Any time you want to change places leading the charge, you let me know, okay?"

MacArthur managed a weary smile. "Your day will come, George. As will mine."

As Patton sped away, Mac and I wove our way through the crowd still gathered around our two staff cars. Bogie and Bacall's Cadillac sounded its horn, ready to go. The crowd pulled back, while I hurried to our car, where a heavyset sergeant held the door open. I thought his arm would snap off from the force of the salute he gave Mac, who returned it and climbed inside.

Ava called out from inside, "General, what a *delight!*"

Puzzled, I said to the sergeant, "What happened to our driver?"

"Called back to the motor pool, sir. Priority."

An army military police captain untangled himself from the crowd of shouting fans. All business, but from the looks of his weathered face, not a kid by any stretch of the imagination. He'd probably seen his share of drunken riots and broken up many a fist fight in his years of wrangling the disruptive behaviors off-duty peacetime soldiers.

He saluted. "We're ready to go, sir."

"Joining the party, captain?"

Too tired to smile at my joke, he said, "Just dropping you off, sir. We got balloons going up back at the Presidio and they need all hands on deck."

"Need any help?"

He gestured to the crowd. "You've already done your part, sir."

I surrendered and climbed into the back, while he and the sergeant hopped in front. Orlando and Mac sat on the jump seats facing Ava and me.

I said, "Got enough room, general?"

Mac's knees were around his ears, so were Orlando's. "I'm perfectly fine. Major? How about you?"

"Couldn't be more comfortable if I tried."

The captain leaned back slightly and said, "We're heading out, sir."

An exchange of horns between Bogie's car and ours, then we nudged our way onto Broadway.

Ava said, "Need to wave, darling—sergeant, toot your horn, please. Thanks!"

While he did so, Ava leaned across me and waved at the crowd who walked along beside us for a while; some holding out autograph books, others 8x10 glossies of Ava, and some just reaching out, beseeching, imploring.

The fog quickly swallowed us up as we moved further away. You could still hear the crowd but no longer see them in the silvery nothingness.

Laughing, Ava flopped back in her seat. "Such dears—every single one of them."

Mac said, "You gave them your money's worth, Lieutenant James. Quite a stirring performance."

"Thank you, sir. And how did you like Laurence Olivier's portrayal of you?"

A long pause while Mac puffed meditatively on his pipe. "That actor was Laurence *Olivier?*"

"Yes, sir. Didn't you see his name in the credits?"

"I was otherwise engaged in conversation with General Patton at that time."

"And?"

"I thought his performance most convincing. Especially the flag-lowering ceremony at Corregidor."

"I wept," she said.

He nodded.

She brightened like a light bulb. "Can't wait to tell Larry you didn't even *recognize* him!"

"By all means do not. I would hate to hurt his feelings."

"Just the opposite, sir, I assure you. Every actor strives for what Olivier does seemingly without effort – he becomes another person so convincingly that his own *persona* disappears without a trace." She chuckled. "He'll be tickled pink!"

Mac pondered some more. Shook his head and muttered, "Laurence *Olivier!*"

I was pondering too, but not about actors. For the past few minutes my internal compass was having fits. We should be heading northwest to the Oakland Bridge, where we'd cross the bay and head up Market Street to the Drake Hotel on Powell.

But we weren't.

Out of habit, I had familiarized myself with our route before we left home. It's a pilot-thing that you may not understand, but after a lifetime of flying, I've learned to read maps like palm readers analyze their customers' hands. I don't stop until I can literally *feel* my internal compass agreeing with what I'm envisioning. And at the moment, the opposite was happening. So much so, that I leaned forward between Orlando and General MacArthur and tapped the driver on the shoulder.

"Lost in the fog, sergeant?"

His shoulders rose slightly. "No, sir, we're heading for the bridge."

"Negative, your last. Can you see the other staff car?"

"Uh… sort of, sir."

"Negative again, sergeant." We're heading due south. Find a cross street you can turn onto and let's get straightened out. Don't want to be late for the party."

A pause. The sergeant said nothing. He looked at the captain, who cleared his throat and said, "There's been a change in plans, Colonel Carter."

The odd tone in his voice made me turn to face him. Even though the light was dim, I had no trouble recognizing the muzzle of a nine-millimeter Luger pistol aimed at me. I *did* have trouble sorting out why an American army officer was holding a *Wehrmacht* officer's pistol, instead a standard-issue Colt .45 automatic.

"It's locked and loaded, sir. Sit back and don't move." He lifted his other hand – holding the familiar Colt automatic. "So's this one."

"Whose side are you fighting on, captain?"

The shot, when it rang out, was an explosive CRACK that made everybody jump. Fortunately, the round went straight through the roof.

"Sit back!" he shouted, and I obeyed.

The acrid smell of gunpowder filled the close confines of the staff car like a fog that echoed the real one outside. Ava, coughing, wound down the window, leaned out and screamed, "Help! Somebody HELP!"

The captain shook his head and smiled. "Colonel, please reel in our damsel in distress or I will be forced to kill her."

All along, I'd been subconsciously noticing the crisp edges to his voice. Earlier I had attributed it to his manner of speaking. But now I knew differently.

Ava sat back and glared.

I said, "You're the bad guys?"

He smiled. "Actually, where I come from, *you're* the bad guys."

"That would be… Berlin?"

"In a roundabout way, yes."

Mac turned around to speak but the Luger's barrel prodded him hard. "Eyes, front, general."

He rattled off some German to the driver, who answered in the same authoritative-sounding tongue and sped up.

I said, "Mind telling us what's going on?"

"This is not the movies, colonel, where the villain provides backstory while the audience eats popcorn."

At the mention of the word, I remembered Ava giving our star-struck corporal a twenty-dollar bill and sending him off to enjoy the movie. "What happened to our driver?"

He shrugged. "That was Jürgen's job, not mine."

"I said—"

The captain sighed in weary frustration and said to the driver, "*Was hast du mit dem Fahrer gemacht?*"

The sergeant shook his head but said nothing.

The captain sighed. "Sorry, but Jürgen has his own ways of doing business and I never pry."

As our staff car continued rolling through the thick fog, my internal compass kept whispering "south." I tried to envision what was there, other than wharfside bars and closed shops. Then I remembered. The ferry connection between Oakland and Alameda. My guess was that we were heading south to eventually head west, but on a *boat*, not the bridge.

"Where are you taking us?" Ava's voice had a surprisingly plaintive, fearful edge to it. (Not for nothing was she a good actress.)

The captain grinned. "Somewhere a lot warmer than San Francisco on a foggy night."

"Mexico?" she said.

"No, but I hear Hawaii is nice this time of year—watch out for your street," he snapped at the driver.

Jürgen snapped right back, "Quiet! You talk, I drive."

Ava said, "You mean Honolulu? Where the—"

"Where our dear allies, the Japanese hold court, yes, at least for now. And thanks to some arm-twisting in Berlin, they enlisted the *Abwehr* in helping them save face—or, as you Americans say—get rid of egg on their face. And a *lot* of it as far as they're concerned."

"What's that got to do with us?" I said. "I'm just a schmuck in the Army Air Corps."

"Yes and no. 'Yes' you are a footnote to Tokyo's main target. But no, you're heading there too, because once upon a time you and your glamorous Hollywood actress rescued General MacArthur, from his appointment with the *samurai* sword at their precious Yasukuni shrine."

"But why—"

"No more twenty questions, colonel. I've given you the storyline, you figure out the plot—ah, here we are, right on time. Hope they are too."

The car slowed. Unseen in the gloom, I slid my foot over and tapped Orlando's shoe twice. He answered back. Mac caught my eye and I nodded once. Guns or no guns, we'd have something to say about what happened next.

The captain got out. As he opened the passenger door on the right, Orlando yanked opened the opposite one on the left and dove headlong onto the street.

Jürgen shouted, *"Verdammt Schwarzer!"* and scrambled out after him. A crackle of gunfire. A shout. From Orlando or the other guy? Impossible to tell.

The captain, distracted, looked up and over the car roof just long enough for me to dive straight at his midsection in what I hoped was a flying tackle. We connected with a common GRUNT and the backward motion flung us onto the sidewalk. Over the years, I've had my share of fist fights and barroom brawls. Lost more than I ever won, but I'd never faced a banshee Nazi masquerading as a U.S. Army captain. His fists were like pistons, alternating between my chest and my head. At this rate he would have me down for the count before I knew what happened.

I had enough weight advantage to finally roll over on top of him, but that only made him punch harder. This was one wild bronco I would have given anything to stop riding.

General MacArthur's right foot brought my reluctant rodeo to a quick end as it connected smartly with the captain's head and it bounced on the sidewalk, knocking him senseless.

I got to my feet, grabbed Mac, and shoved him forward. "Go, go GO!"

As he took off, I spotted Ava, grabbed her arm and we started running. Within seconds the dense fog wrapped around us like a blanket. With streetlights, I could have at least figured out where the hell we were, but the coastal blackout had shuttered them long ago.

A pole materialized. If I was lucky—and I was—it led upward to a street sign proclaiming the intersection of Washington and Water Street.

"What about Orlando?" she said.

"He'll find us. Keep moving."

As ornery kids in Key West, Orlando and I had our share of running from the cops who didn't like our brand of practical jokes. Tonight, I prayed my friend hadn't lost the knack of getting away. Could we as well?

Through the swirling mist... a golden rectangle of light, a burst of laughter, and music. A door opening and closing? Then it came to me in a rush. It had to be *Heinold's First and Last Chance Saloon*, a famous local bar. Nothing else open at this hour. With that Oakland historic landmark planted in my mental map, I knew exactly where we were.

The place had been here since the late 1800s. Back then, prospectors heading north to Alaska and whalers heading out to sea would stop for a cold one and a *bon voyage*. Nowadays, soldiers and sailors on their way to war were doing the same.

"This way," I whispered to Mac.

The three of us hustled down the deserted sidewalk, being careful to hug the sides of the buildings. The dense fog muted familiar noises like the nearby water slapping against the pilings, street traffic and foot traffic.

Mac's kick to the kidnapper's head had been a short-term thing. He'd be in hot pursuit by now. At almost the same instant I had that thought, the squeal of tires and a car engine racing.

"Heinold's to your right!" I shouted. "Head for it!"

"You sure?" Ava said.

"Go, GO!"

She and Mac ran across the small open plaza between us and salvation. Again, the small door on the wooden building opened briefly, the volume of shouting voices and blaring music increased, the light within glowed gold, then darkness fell as it closed and swallowed them up. Once inside and in the company of strangers, we could get help.

I plastered myself against a palm tree in the courtyard and waited until the staff car slowly cruised past. I recognized it from the white star painted on the driver's side door. This time however, the captain was at the wheel, hatless, peering into the fog like a crystal ball.

Where the hell was Jürgen?

No question about it, this *Abwehr* guy was good at his job. I mean, he'd almost kidnapped us. What I didn't know was that he was a mind-reader too, because he suddenly stood on the brakes. The car rocked to a stop and he sounded his horn—not in alarm—but clearly some kind of signal. In response, the pinpoint stab of blackout lights as two more cars materialized from out of the fog.

I didn't bother waiting to see what happened next. I took off running as fast as I could for Heinold's.

I burst inside the bar, where a young Jack London used to hang out and ran smack into a solid wall of soldiers and sailors raising happy hell as they crowded around General MacArthur and Ava, who stood there dazed, like grand prizes in a treasure hunt.

The soldiers and sailors had started the night in this most famous of hangouts, expecting to have a few beers and tell a few lies. Now, they beheld a four-star general and a Hollywood star, who looked back at them, equally astounded.

The light from the gaslight fixtures barely penetrated the fog of tobacco smoke. Ava spotted me as I hollered, "Out the back way! They're coming!"

"Who's coming?" said one of the soldiers.

"You don't want to know—listen up, fellas!" I shouted. "If you want to live to see another day, sit down at your tables and pretend you never saw us."

A long beat of silence. A sea of blank looks.

"That's a direct order from a commissioned officer. Take your SEATS!"

Stunned by the intensity of my voice, the mob of young men fell back. Mac added his two cents. "On the DOUBLE!"

That did the trick. Four stars trump silver eagles every time.

While they rumbled and muttered and sat down to nurse their beers, I threaded my way through the mob, grabbed Mac and Ava and steered them to the door leading to the kitchen.

Once I got them in the back, I stopped, spun around, and said to the crowd. "You never saw what you just saw. Do you read me loud and clear?"

A mixed bag of heads nodding, and "yes, sirs" filled the tiny space.

I ducked back inside and peered through a crack in the swinging double doors. A millisecond later the front door BANGED open and the Nazi captain, still hatless, strode in like he owned the joint. Partly because he was one determined S.O.B., but also because two gangster-type goon civilians beside him carried Thompson submachine guns at the ready.

He nodded to one of them, who blasted a few rounds into the bar's famous ceiling, dotted with hundreds of caps and hats, and thousands of slips of faded United States currency signed by sailors who never returned to claim them when they sailed away long ago.

A rainstorm of ripped and torn five and ten-dollar bills drifted over the stunned crowd. Not a soul moved. But I sure as hell did.

"Hi, Johnny," Ava whispered to Heinold's short order cook, who stood there like a statue, eyes wide, spatula in hand, a hamburger patty balanced on it.

"You didn't see anything, got it?"

He could only nod.

The bar owner, George Heinold, stood by the back door, ready to open it, while Ava and Mac waited for me.

Muffled voices from the bar. Wouldn't be long now.

"Thanks, Heinie," Ava patted his cheek. "You're a lifesaver."

"Wish to hell I knew what was going on," he said.

"So do we," she said.

"Go... NOW!" I whispered.

The back door swung open and we darted into the pitch blackness of the foggy night—straight into the arms of four men the size of boxcars. One of them spun me around like a toy doll and pinned my arms so tight I could hardly breathe.

"Hold it right there, soldier boy," he growled.

Ava cried out to her assailant, "Let me GO, you lug!"

"Not a chance, sweetheart."

Heinold's back door BANGED opened again, and I was not surprised to see our Nazi "captain" stride out like he was taking a Sunday stroll, followed by his goons. The door BANGED shut and foggy gloom surrounded us again.

"Nice try," the captain said. "You almost made it. But 'almost' only counts in horseshoes." He checked his watch. "We're late, boys, let's move it."

"Yes sir."

As his hired goons shoved us along, I said to the captain, "What happened to your driver?"

A beat of silence. "Jürgen is dead, thanks to your friend."

"Orlando?"

"One and the same."

"Is he—"

"On the run. But not for long. The *Abwehr* doesn't like loose ends."

"What the hell are Nazis doing in California?"

His sigh was audible. "Cleaning up after Tokyo's mess."

"What do you mean?"

He didn't answer. Instead, he hurried ahead until the fog swallowed him up, leaving us at the mercy of the phalanx of heavyweight gangsters who hustled us like underworld enemies who had an appointment with cement shoes.

At least that fate wasn't on our dance card. If they'd wanted us dead, we would have been cold corpses floating in the bay by now. No, they wanted us alive and kicking, and I was beginning to suspect why.

The Municipal Dock in Oakland's inner harbor was filled with all sorts of boats tied up for the night. Ranging from sailboats to shrimpers, to deep-water fishing trawlers, nothing was moving in tonight's fog. Neither were people—besides us, that is.

In vain, I'd hoped for a rescue mission from Heinold's to come thundering after us. But apparently a Tommy gun blasting the ceiling was incentive enough for the guys to stay put, instead of saving the head of the Joint Chiefs and his two sidekicks. Couldn't blame them, though. Forty-five caliber bullets make a uniquely convincing argument for not moving a muscle.

Our underworld escort shoved us down a dock ramp leading to a long string of private yachts and motor boats painted battleship grey with "CGR" white lettering on the bows. It stood for "Coast Guard Reserve." Days after declaring war, President Perkins had urged Congress to pass legislation that allowed the Coast Guard to commandeer thousands of private vessels and volunteer crews to join the fight against Fascism.

But no fighting tonight – lights out, shuttered up, sails folded on those that had them, crews home in bed, the flotilla bobbed slightly in the waves kicked up by some fog-shrouded tanker heading to the Bay and points beyond.

Except for CGR 2502, a former fishing trawler that had exchanged its sieve nets for a forty-millimeter Bofors deck gun and what looked like "Hedgehog" depth charges in the stern. Figures moved around in dim silhouette. People who could help?

I took a chance and shouted, "Ahoy on deck, lend a hand!"

The figures stopped moving, and so did we.

But instead of my guard pistol-whipping me, he chuckled and then shouted, *"Ciao, Capitano Angelo. Siamo pronti."*

"Si, si." The answering voice weary. *"Sali a bordo."*

The Nazi captain gestured with his tommy gun to the boarding ramp, "After you, Miss James."

"And if I refuse?"

Instead of answering, he prodded her forward. She took a step, turned, and said, "You're on the wrong side of this war, mister, and don't you forget it."

He smiled and prodded her again. Point made, Ava glided up the ramp with regal bearing like it was Oscar night and she was taking the stage to make her acceptance speech.

General MacArthur followed, his face a mask of neutrality. Here was a man who'd proven himself a courageous fighter in World War One, and up until tonight, a farsighted leader of the nation's military in World War Two. Yes, he was walking up the ramp, but not the plank. He was compliant but not complicit—my kind of fighter.

My turn next. I paused long enough to turn and say to my mafia captor, *"Arrivederci,* asshole."

That brought his pistol to bear, but the *Abwehr* captain shoved it away. "Get the hell out here, Guido, and take your boys with you."

"You sure you donna' need us, boss?"

"Scram, I said."

Guido and his henchman melted into the fog, disappearing quickly. The foggy weather and the drama of what was going on made the moment seem more like a nightmare than reality. But the Tommy gun barrel prodding my lower back reminded me that we were still in deep trouble.

The captain shouted, *"Scartato!"*

One of the sailors jumped across to the dock like a flying monkey, untied the lines wound around the cleats, then just as quickly jumped back on board, while holding a single painter that held us to the dock.

The deck vibrated as the trawler's diesel engine came up to full power.

The armed crewman motioned for Ava, Mac, and me to go below.

I said to our Nazi captain, "How did these bad guys get on a good guys boat?"

He smiled. "All depends on who you're calling 'bad.'"

"But this is a Coast Guard Auxiliary boat."

"You're absolutely right. It really *does* look like one, doesn't it?"

"With an Italian crew."

"Axis allies."

His comment stopped me cold. I continued taking in our predicament the way I'd take in an inflight emergency – stay calm, count to ten, know that even though there's no answer yet, something will turn up. It always did, right? Otherwise I wouldn't be standing here kidnapped, about to head for Tokyo—*again*, I might add, except by way of Hawaii this time around.

We'd been through all this before when we rescued General MacArthur from Corregidor almost a year ago. Back then, America, fresh into the fight, was teetering on the brink of disaster. President Perkins needed Mac back in the states to take up the reins of the military. This fried Patton's ambitions to a crisp because he wanted to lead the fight east to Nazi-land. Instead, she tapped Mac, which meant plucking him from the fortress island of Corregidor before it fell.

All conventional rescue efforts had failed.

That's when Ava and I and a team of actors did what couldn't be done – snatched the general and were on our way home, taking the long way around the world—that is, until an American P-40 mistook our Japanese-marked flying boat for the enemy and sent us into the drink.

Despite the adventures that followed, we still made it back, and Mac was in the fight again. Until tonight turned into *déjà vu* all over again. This time around, we had become three tiny pawns in a deadly game of Axis chess played by Germany, Japan, and Italy.

By the time I got below, the trawler was underway in Oakland's inner harbor. So maddening that nearby military installations paralleled our course, not to mention a U.S. Navy airfield. But thanks to the damned fog and the dogged expertise of our Nazi captor, nobody was aware of what was happening right beneath their noses.

"Over there," he ordered me to take my place in the cramped confines of what passed for a combination galley and crew dining area. Ava and Mac were already sitting at the table, hands folded, like they were waiting to say grace. The trawler's cook was busy in the corner stirring something in a pot on the stove. From here, it looked like tomato sauce. His cheery face and contented smile was in stark contrast to the chiseled-sharp features of our Nazi villain – a real poster boy for what the Third Reich had in store for America and the rest the world if they came out on top.

"Where precisely are we going?" General MacArthur said.

A simple question, but sounded like an order coming from a man like Mac – an enemy combatant who happened to be a high-ranking officer used to getting his way.

"I believe I already told you, sir. You're on your way to the Yasukuni Shrine in Tokyo to deposit your head in a bamboo basket, courtesy of the *samurai* sword of Emperor Hirohito's Royal Executioner."

Mac took in the crowded confines of the boat.

"To Japan in *this?*"

"Merely the first step in a long journey—now if you'll excuse me, I must return to my duties."

With that, he pivoted around and made his way aft to the ladder leading topside. He took a step then stopped.

"I forgot to add, that on the off-chance we should be stopped on our way into the bay, I strongly urge you to keep silent. Massimo, here, will make sure you do so, *e vero, Massimo?*

The smiling cook turned from his stirring. His smile vanished as he reached beneath the apron stretched over the vast expanse of his barrel-shaped belly. A moment later, he brandished a silencer-equipped machine pistol.

Mac's voice was calm and collected. "I believe that is a Mauser semi-automatic?"

"Indeed, sir."

"Silencer-equipped. Didn't know the *Wehrmacht* had that variant."

"The Italians created it—not surprisingly considering their penchant for secrecy."

"Menacing to be sure."

"Indeed. Life is one big opera to them." He grinned at Massimo. *"La vita è un'opera, non e vero?"*

"Si, si, hai ragione, capitano!"

"Max is a good cook, but an even better shot."

Up the ladder he went, leaving us to watch our chef at work, stirring the pasta sauce with his left hand while aiming the pistol at us with his right.

From the way the trawler encountered more active wave action, we were leaving Oakland's inner harbor and heading west. Made sense if Tokyo was going to be our ultimate destination.

If only I could have opened the tightly-dogged porthole – which was impossible – I could have seen Treasure Island to starboard. Not literally, of course, because the fog continued doing its part in aiding and abetting our kidnappers.

But in my mind, I saw with perfect clarity the immense *Pan American Airways* hangars on the island that once housed Martin and Boeing clippers. Many's the time I had marched down the boarding ramp with my fellow *Pan Am* aviators, proudly wearing dark-blue uniforms, white caps, and in my case, gold wings with three stars pinned on my chest that declared Samuel B. Carter a "Master of Ocean Flying Boats." A hell of a title, and a hell of a job.

All those memories passed to starboard as the sluggish trawler continued making ten knots—if she was lucky.

Ava sighed. "At this rate, the war will be over before we even clear the bay."

Mac wasn't listening. Just watching.

I said softly. "You thinking what I'm thinking, general?"

He nodded fractionally.

"And if we manage to get cookie's gun?"

Mac's blue eyes calculated the dimensions of the room the way a surgeon analyzes the operating area before his first slash of the scalpel. His eyes narrowed into a squint. "It would be a steep uphill climb, I'm afraid."

"With an armed crew topside."

He pondered some more, then said, "But they would be distracted if their boat were on fire."

Ava whispered, "Get ready, boys." She cleared her throat and said in pitch-perfect Italian, *"Signor, per favore, che tipo di salsa?"*

The cook looked at her in surprise, so did Mac and me. Where the hell did she learn Italian? Her sidewise glance kept our mouths shut.

The cook stirred his creation while he ticked off the ingredients, *"E pomidori fresca, aglio, olive di oliva, e cippole."*

"Basta?"

"Basta cosi."

"Simplice.'

"Sempre simplice."

Ava rubbed her stomach. *"Ho molto fame."*

He frowned and gestured overhead at the powers-that-be, especially the trawler's captain. *"Non possibile, signora."*

She pinched her fingers together and said pathetically, *"Un piccolo assagio?"*

He looked around furtively, then ladled a tiny bit of sauce into a coffee cup, plunked a spoon into it and waddled over to our table. Mac tapped my foot with his shoe and I got ready to pin the cook's arms, while he would go for the gun. After that, we'd improvise. The stove was coal-fired, which meant plenty of red-hot embers to set a whopping-big fire.

A half-ass plan? You bet. But better to be doing something instead of sitting there like French nobles on our way to the guillotine. Screw that. We were about to leap out of our "tumbrel" and get the hell out of Paris.

The cook placed the cup on the table, his round, red face a mixture of pride in his work and awe of Ava's beauty. Say what you will about movie stars, good or bad, you have to agree that there's "something" about them that the rest of us don't have.

Impossible to describe in words what that 'something' is, but people like Ava, Bogie, and Bacall take up all the space in your brain when they decide to be "on." When that happens, like it was happening now between Ava and the cook, her star power was like standing outside on a sunny day, arms outstretched, eyes lifted heavenward as the sunshine bakes you like a warm dinner roll, fresh from the oven.

Ava smiled her radiant smile and whispered, *"Mille grazie."*

She slowly—almost seductively—lifted the spoon to her perfect mouth, pursed her lips and blew slightly to cool it down. Then she opened those same, oh-so-kissable lips, and took a taste.

The outline of the Mauser machine pistol hidden beneath the cook's apron was plain as day. Its long, rod-like silencer might prove a problem as Mac yanked it out. He and I exchanged a minuscule nod, and both tensed to spring. Now or never....

The *Abwehr* captain's voice rang out behind me, "I said, *guard* the prisoners, not *feed* them!"

The cook sprang back as if touching a live wire. *"Scusa mi, capitano!"*

The Nazi turned to the deckhand standing beside him. "Tell him."

The sailor half-shouted, *"Doveve proteggere i prigionieri, non dar loro da mangiare."*

A flood of invective filled the small galley as the two men went back and forth in machine-gun-fast Italian. Their voices rose higher and higher as each tried to outshout the other. Meanwhile, Ava calmly continued sampling the sauce like it was popcorn at the movies and she was watching a film about dueling Italians.

She finished and plunked down the cup. "Needs salt." She turned to the cook and shouted. *"Signor, sale per la salsa."*

He stopped arguing and turned to her, all business. *"Impossible."*

She shook her head and frowned. *"Sale."*

The Nazi captain shouted, "Enough!" He tossed three pairs of handcuffs on the table. "Should have done this from the start."

Ava stared at them. "You're joking."

"I don't joke." Neither did the Luger he pointed at us, while the sailor quickly cuffed us, then just as quickly unwound a small-linked chain from around his waist, looped it through our bound wrists, then around a steam line directly overhead.

We sat there like three gaffed fish.

To his credit, Mac still managed to look like a four-star as he said with a measure of dignity, "If you would be so kind as to remove my cap and place it beside me? I neglected to do so it when we first arrived."

The Nazi captain did so with precision.

"Thank you," Mac said.

"You are most welcome."

Mac smoothed his tousled comb-over with grave dignity, like making one's bed. Minus his famous officer's cap with its embroidered eagle insignia and "scrambled eggs" laurel leaves, and his signature, long-bodied corncob pipe, he seemed diminished as the leader of America's military. But one look at his firm, uplifted jaw made you think twice.

Mac took in the Nazi *Abwehr* agent and gave him his famous gimlet eye. "You know of course, dress as you are, you will be shot for impersonating an American Army Officer."

"They need to catch me first, general."

"Oh, we shall. Make no mistake, *herr kapitan*, the mills of the gods grind slow but exceeding fine."

That got a laugh from him as he returned topside and left us sitting there with the deckhand training his pistol on us, while the cook returned to his sauce. He occasionally glanced our way. Maybe I was imagining things, but it seemed he looked sympathetic at our plight—or Ava's, more likely than not.

I said to her, "Where the heck did you learn Italian?"

Ava shrugged. "College. Had to learn enough to survive singing *Carmen*."

Mac said, "You spoke it quite fluently."

"Amazing what the mind can do when it's in high-panic mode. I doubt I could ever do it again."

"Never say never."

Ava was right, of course, because as our journey continued ever westward, our two guards would occasionally talk to each other in Italian, but Ava didn't have a clue what they were saying. I guess she was right about finding her "inner Italian" at just the right moment and giving us a fighting chance at getting the cook's gun.

We failed to do so of course, but not for lack of trying. Timing is everything in life. Especially in war. This time, it had worked against us. Had we sixty seconds more, we could have gone on the offensive. But as it turned out, we sat chained together like convicts in a chugging old trawler tricked out like a Coast Guard Reserve vessel. Sea fog notwithstanding, the Italian's boat presented a logical, unquestioned presence to authorities.

By now, we must be heading past the Presidium to port. Had I been on deck and with the help of a little land breeze to lift the lower layers of fog high enough, I could have spotted the dim, blacked-out outlines of the Southern Defense Command headquarters perched high atop the cusp of land anchored to the south end of the Golden Gate suspension bridge.

Ava must have been thinking the same thing because she said, "Wonder if Uncle George has a clue what's happened to us."

"Don't see how."

"Orlando?"

That brought back the memory of the gunshots in the fog during our escape. Where'd the bullets hit? The Nazi said his driver was dead, but what about my friend?

A rattle of chains. The deckhand looked sharply in our direction as Mac gestured to his shirt pocket then said to Ava, "How do you say smoke?"

Without missing a beat she rattled off, *"Fumare una pipa?"*

The guard shrugged like he could care less and casually waved his pistol in Mac's direction. The general fished out his corncob pipe and matches. Despite being handcuffed, he managed to tamp the tobacco, strike a match, and fire up his trusty trademark.

His dexterity impressed everyone, including the sailor who grinned and said, *"Ecco bravo!"*

Funny how such an ordinary thing centered my thinking and calmed me down. Before Mac struck that match, my worries had trapped me in an inverted spin of my own devising and I couldn't pull out.

An inverted spin, by the way, is the worst situation you can encounter in flying – no reference to the ground, everything spinning, including your mind as you try to sort out which way is up and how to get there before you hit the ground.

In this case, images of Rosie and Abby sitting in the Persian Room, wondering why the guests of honor hadn't arrived. Then I spun even faster because by now, everybody must be alarmed at the vanishing act that we pulled off somewhere in the fog between the Paramount theater and the Sir Francis Drake hotel.

That "somewhere" now must be the open sea, because the rising and falling motion of the trawler as it met the waves meant we must have passed the Point Bonita lighthouse, darkened because of wartime blackout restrictions. In peacetime its flashing beacon always helped me line up my Sikorsky S-24 Pan Am clipper for a long, slow approach to landing in the bay near Treasure Island.

Captain Fatt had been my mentor up until his death during a Nazi *Kampfschwimmer* raid on Patton's secret base in the Louisiana swamp back before America declared war. With Fatt gone, I had taken over command of the Boeing 314 *Dixie Clipper* for an epic mission to bomb the plutonium storage facility in Radford, Washington. With Fatt gone, I was in command once again in a crisis that needed resolving—a bit difficult, considering I was handcuffed.

But thoughts of Fatt cleared up my confusion. He'd forgotten more about flying than I'd ever remembered. And the mental image of him sitting in the "left seat" in this particular situation, helped me kick opposite rudder, snap back the stick and my inverted spin surrendered its grip and got me thinking straight again.

I said to Mac, "Submarine, you think?"

He winced slightly at the thought. "If so, I pray it's not the one from which we made our escape."

Ava grinned. "Irony, anyone?"

Mac looked sharply at me. "Let me be perfectly clear, Colonel Carter. I will never kneel to an enemy and await his blade."

"You will if they tie you up and shove your neck on the block."

He puffed his pipe harder but said nothing.

I pondered some more, trying to get into the bad guys' heads. "Forget the submarine. It would take way too long to transit to Pearl. Tokyo wants you *now*."

"They want *us*, you mean," Mac said.

"Yes sir, but the difference between pawns like Ava and me and a king like you is a big one in the game they're playing."

Less than a half-hour later, the steady pounding of the engines slacked off. I still felt like we'd been sailing due west. Time to find out for certain, because seconds later, the hatch BANGED opened and the *Abwehr* agent shouted down, *"Andiamo!"*

"Si, si, capitano!" the sailor answered and quickly unlocked the chain holding us together like circus elephants.

I shook my handcuffed wrists "What about these?"

Ava smiled that smile of hers. *"Liberato, per favore?"*

"Si, si, signorina. momento." He fumbled with the handcuff key and freed us, while the cook covered us with his pistol.

We made our way to the ladder leading topside. Ava called out to the cook. *"Buona fortuna, caro!"*

His red face got redder as he nodded, grinned, then saluted with both his ladle and his Luger.

"Anche lei, anche lei!"

The fog was still with us, but not as dense as back on land. The sound of breakers told me instantly where we were, and it sure as hell wasn't the California coastline. I turned to the *Abwehr* agent to confirm it, while he scanned the sea with his binoculars – a useless activity, if you ask me.

"Farallon islands?" I said.

He nodded without speaking.

Forget the submarine. No way would it take a chance sailing anywhere near this group of small, rocky, forlorn islands about thirty-five miles southwest of San Francisco in the Gulf of Farallon. These desolate islands were fatal to passing ships. A submarine's ballast tanks and steel hull wouldn't last long if they ripped into a hidden sea stack.

To our right was Seal Island, sticking up from the sea floor like a giant's thumb. Come spring, seals would swarm over it like ants as they started their mating season.

Back in the early 1800s the fur trade decimated the Farallon's seal population, leaving only seabirds to lay eggs by the millions, which enterprising San Franciscans gladly carted off to markets up and down the California coastline.

Once both trades died out and the sparse tribes of Kodiak native Indians either got killed or escaped with their lives, Teddy Roosevelt got

Congress to declare this unforgiving, lonely place a National Wildlife Refuge.

For birds, maybe, but for people? No way.

Tonight, nothing remained but an Coast Guard lighthouse up on Tower hill to our right, closed and shuttered for the war. But once upon a happier time it had been a familiar, flashing landmark—just like the Point Bonita lighthouse—as I flew my Pan Am clipper on her last leg that had begun in Hong Kong and would end at Treasure Island.

Back then, the foaming ocean waves crashing against the rocks were a welcome symbol—albeit harsh and unforgiving—of home sweet home waiting for me, my passengers, and my crew at the end of our long journey.

"Rendezvous here?" I said to the Nazi.

"Almost." He lowered his binoculars. "On the other side of the island."

"Fisherman Bay?"

This guy never acted surprised, but even so, I heard a trace of it in his voice when he said, "How do you know that?"

"Flew over this these islands many a time—which must mean—"

He raised his binoculars again. "You ask too many questions, colonel."

But I knew the answer already—well almost. Only time would tell.

And not much of it at that, because five minutes later, after traversing the south side of the island, the wave action calmed down enough for the trawler to swing around to the east side of the island.

Sheltered from the relentless reach of the west wind and waves, the sea action smoothed out almost immediately. The booming roar of the pounding surf diminished just as quickly, replaced by the chug-chug-chugging beat of the trawler's diesel engine as it edged us perilously close to the shoreline.

Out of habit, I calculated the wave action, much as I would if I were attempting to land in its cove. Most folks think seaplanes land in the open ocean. They do not. Unless it's a flat-out emergency. Seaplanes are built to land in sheltered lagoons or harbors with breakwaters that transform ocean-sized waves into peaceful ripples, onto which any pilot worth his salt can kiss the seaplane's hull upon the waters so gently that the passengers don't know when flying ends and sailing begins.

No such gentle place like that tonight, even though they called it "Fisherman's Bay." True, island's mass shielded the waters from the west winds and broke the back of the larger wave action surging and crashing upon the empty shoreline elsewhere. But make no mistake, this was still open ocean, barely sheltered by the mass of the Farallons.

My palms felt a prickle, before I realized what it meant. Even with moderate seas, landing a flying boat here would be a challenge for even the most experienced pilot.

"They're up there somewhere," I said. Not a question but a statement of fact.

"Idiots." The *Abwehr* captain lowered his binoculars, useless in the fog. "Bad enough we've got spaghetti-eaters in the Axis, we have to work with slant-eyes stuck in the fifteenth century. Swords, horses—who knows what else."

"Seaplanes," I said. "Not to mention battleships, aircraft carriers, tanks, submarines…"

He made a face. But his disdain turned to wonder seconds later at the faraway throaty roar of radial engines.

"Speak of the devil," I said.

Muted by the fog, airplane engines without a doubt. Not perfectly synchronized, that's for sure, but the pilot was to be forgiven, considering what he was trying to do as he adjusted pitch and RPM in preparation for landing.

A quick surge of power, then another. I couldn't help wishing good luck and safe landing to whoever was at the controls. Yes, he was an enemy combatant, and yes, I had taken an oath to defend the Constitution of the United States against all aggressors, but hear me out: airplane pilots are a breed apart from folks who walk on the earth.

Yes, we have allegiance to our countries, and yes, we'll fight each other in the air if war crashes its way into our world and jabs us with its pointy stick. But in the end, we're brothers—and sisters—who have seen the world from on high and understand that the only thing separating nation from nation are borders drawn by politicians on maps. We know better. No borders looking down from above. Just the world.

Sermon ended, go in peace.

That's why I secretly wished that Japanese pilot good luck that night. If our positions had been reversed, he would have done the same for me.

That's how aviators are wired. And yes, in case of war, we would then pull out pointy sticks and start jabbing, or in our case, machine guns and open fire.

"He'll never make it," the Nazi said.

"Never say never."

Another blip of the engines as he refined his glide slope. From the wind on my left cheek, I turned to the right and waited for whatever it was to emerge upwind from the fog.

Ava cried out, "Eleven o'clock!"

A second before, only dim grayness, now a four-engine flying boat materialized barely two hundred feet above the waves and descending fast. Maybe too fast.

The art of landing on wave-tossed water is to choose a trough and slide onto the backside.

Problem #1: waves keep moving, so you have to judge far enough in advance.

Problem #2: when the magic moment comes and you're *just* above stalling speed and have to commit to landing, that wave may—or may not—be where it's supposed to be.

Problem #3: if it's where it belongs, then there's no problem, you're home free. But a BIG problem if it's not, because you get slammed sideways and can lose a wing.

When you dance with Mother Nature she always leads.

"Not carrying enough power," I said.

"Affirmative," Ava said.

MacArthur pointed to the flying boat painted flat black, "A *Kawanishi*. No markings."

"Must be an Emily," I said.

We'd seen our share of the broad-shouldered maritime patrol bomber last year when snatching General MacArthur away from the *samurai* chopping block. Up until tonight, our daring rescue operation had been a feather in Ava's and my cap—not to mention medals for our uniforms and a Hollywood movie about how we pulled it off.

But Tokyo had other plans, and so far, they were working to perfection, including this long-nosed, high-winged H8K flying boat searching for the backside of the right wave to set down.

"There he goes," Ava said.

The murky night lit up with a needle-thin streak of foaming-white water beneath the H8K's broad, slab-sided fuselage as she found the sweet spot of the wave pattern and settled her massive bulk safely onto it.

I admired the pilot's skill in not only flying all the way from Hawaii and being able to navigate his way to this fingernail-sized scrap of land, but also descending into a dense fog bank, not certain where it would end—if ever—and manhandling a multi-ton airplane onto an active ocean like it was a glass-calm lagoon.

"Nice landing," I said.

"Nice airplane," Ava added.

A major provider of maritime patrol aircraft to the Japanese Navy, *Kawanishi* made solid seaplanes. No surprise they'd painted her flat black for their kidnapping mission. While Tokyo had America by the throat, she dared not get too close to polish us off. That's why her submarines were regular visitors to the west coast to keep up the pressure, and the occasional long-range bomber, too, of which they had precious few. In the war to date, the Emperor had wisely kept his celestial hands off our sacred shores.

But after tonight, everything had changed. The egg we'd unceremoniously tossed on his face could only be washed away with our blood.

Let the die be cast!
Julius Caesar

The Italian crew transferred us from the trawler to the waiting seaplane with their dinghy. They did so with such deft maneuvering skill, that you would have thought we were still back in Oakland's glass-calm inner harbor, instead of an active sea with wave action beginning to pick up serious chop. If I'd been alone in this predicament, I may have jumped overboard and tried for shore, or maybe grabbed the gun away from our captor.

What I did, instad, was sit and stare at Ava and Mac who stared back at me. Then I regarded the massive *Kawanishi* H8K seaplane, its engines ticking over to keep position as it slowly rose and fell on the waves like a pitch-black Moby Dick. Then, finally, I regarded the Luger in the Nazi's hand, trained unwaveringly on me because he *knew* I was plotting and planning.

So, I stopped triangulating my options like a hawk about to dive on its prey. When you've got a lot of moving parts to a problem, it's best to acknowledge that from the start. Makes for better decisions later when you've *got* to do something or else.

I looked at the woman I fell in love with, who smiled at me like she was on a movie set, not shivering in an emerald-green gown, bobbing up and down in the middle of the ocean.

"Great first act," she said. "Wonder what happens next?"

"How about, we wake up from this nightmare?"

"Pinch me, darling and let's find out."

"Quiet!" the Nazi shouted.

The dinghy slewed to port to avoid the *Kawanishi's* massive wing float the size of a canoe. The seaplane's nearly hundred-foot length and hundred-fifty-foot wingspan made it a kissing cousin to *Pan Am's* Boeing 314. But the resemblance ended there. This bird was packing machine guns in her tail, with dorsal turrets and waist blisters, too—all currently tracking us like enemy targets—not ticket-holding passengers.

The plane's port side boarding hatch aft of the wing was already open and a short ladder attached. The unreality of our current situation sunk in — three short hours ago we were sitting in comfy seats at the Paramount theater eating popcorn. Now, instead of helping my wife unzip her evening gown in our bungalow while we talked about what fun we had at the party in the *Persian Room*, we were getting soaked with sea spray from the ticking-over engines of an enemy flying boat.

I had a fleeting memory of being snatched up by the Japanese super-sub I-401 in the South China Sea a year ago and being held captive.

Mac must have been thinking the same thing because he said, *"Déjà vu, colonel."*

"Yes, sir. Only this one flies instead of sinks."

The Nazi cupped his hands and shouted to be heard over the engines, "Ready to board prisoners?"

A voice called out in accent-free English, "Make fast the line!"

Did they have an American on board? I bristled at the idea of a traitor.

Cast in silhouette by the red-light of the interior, the man stood in the hatchway and expertly snaked a line out to our boat. Once the Italians made it fast, *Kawanishi* crew members pulled us closer, hand-over-hand, while their gun turrets tracked us as targets until ordered otherwise.

The Nazi motioned for General MacArthur to enter first. He clamped his hat and sprung onto the ladder like a teenager, not a sixty-three-year-old. From the set of his shoulders, I got the feeling that, contrary to surrendering to his fate, Mac was heading to the center of the boxing ring spoiling for a fight. I felt the same way.

Ava climbed the ladder next. Long-experienced with being graceful under trying circumstances, she gathered the shimmering green gown around her legs to preserve a modicum of modesty while navigating the six rungs leading upward.

The Italian crew members, ever gallant gentlemen, avoided looking at Ava's ascent, but the Nazi enjoyed every rung of her climb.

I bristled at the nerve of this guy and growled, "Look at the menu all you want, mister, you'll never order from it."

He prodded me with the Luger. *"Raus, schwein."*

I started climbing the ladder and said over my shoulder. "Can't wait to kick your ass when we get to Honolulu."

He shook his head. "Once that plane takes off, you belong to the Yellow Peril. I am returning to Germany to win the war."

"Then I'll see you and Hitler in hell."

"A distinct possibility. *Raus, raus!*"

A jumble of confusion when we first entered the cavernous interior of the *Kawanishi*. Crew members shouted back and forth as they retreated to resume their combat stations. If I hadn't been around the enemy during our captivity on the *I-401* last year, I would have thought they were angry with each other.

But after weeks under the ocean watching the sailors in action, I'd learned that when it comes to giving and taking orders, the Japanese have a broken volume switch – always stuck on LOUD.

With the shouting finished and crew dispersed, Ava and Mac sat on a long bench that ran the length the interior like disobedient students waiting to see the principal. Two armed crew members sat directly across from them, *Nambu* pistols held at the ready, their eyes locked on target.

The primitive benches seemed to go on forever. This *Kawanishi* must be their troop transport variant. Could carry almost a hundred soldiers a hell of a long way. Felt like being inside a barn, with every wire and rib exposed, no insulation, purely utilitarian.

By contrast, every inch of *Pan Am's* flying boats were padded, upholstered, painted, trimmed, and polished for the wealthy passengers who could afford to buy a trans-Pacific ticket that cost two months wages for your average working man.

"Over THERE!" the man who could speak English shouted at me. "Seatbelts. Fasten. We're taking off."

"Okay, okay."

But I already knew that from the engine sounds and hull vibration. Lack of insulation made the flying boat act like a gigantic tuning fork as her engines advanced to take-off power. Despite our grim circumstances, my pilot's brain had enough room for jealousy of engines that could crank out almost nineteen-hundred horsepower each. The *Kawanishi* had four *Mitsubishi Kasai* radials to shove her massive bulk around the sky. If we'd had those on the Boeing 314s, we could have flown rings around our competition.

I took my seat beside Ava and fumbled with the tangled straps the Japanese called seatbelts. More like cheap suspenders – clips everywhere, but nothing to clip them onto.

"Here, let me," she said.

"Thanks, mom."

The engines sang at full power. The plane nosed down slightly as she encountered a side-swell, then surged forward like a whale set free from a net.

Ava said, "I can't believe this is happening."

"Me either."

I didn't envy the pilot his task of lifting off in an active sea. The number one rule in getting an airplane into the air is to face the wind. That way, Mother Nature helps you get to flying speed faster. But in an open ocean, the wind's *creating* waves and if you face the wind, you'll face the waves too. That's like slamming into Mother Nature the wrong way. And she always wins…always.

Instead, you go about it diagonally, finding a forgiving trough that follows the crests. Then you start a rock-skipping game that drives you faster and faster along the narrow passageway, ever mindful that another wave is bearing down on you, so you've got to time it just right. What you lose in relative airspeed you gain by knowing you're *cooperating* with Mother Nature, not defying her.

The *Kawanishi* accelerated faster and faster, then leaned ponderously to starboard to "chase" a promising trough. Within seconds she quickly gained "the step," a point about midway along the hull where her longitudinal lines "step up" vertically, and by doing so, break the surface tension of the water. So far in the takeoff, it seemed her pilot was doing exactly what I would do under the circumstances. I admired his skill.

"This guy knows his business," I said.

"Wish he'd peddle it somewhere else," Ava snapped.

I looked at Mac, expecting him to chime in with some orotund observation (four-star generals tend to be that way). But he sat in stony silence, chin out, eyes narrowed, lips firm, presenting a profile that belonged on Mount Rushmore not a flying boat on its way to Tokyo.

I *felt* it before I my mind thought it—up until now, just the drumming, booming, hissing sound of the hull and roar of the engines slugging it out with the water—then suddenly, we were *flying*.

You've probably *felt* it too – that precise moment when your body's sensory apparatus registers a change in horizontal/vertical orientation. Sometimes it's a slight touch of negative-G if you hit a crosswind pocket and balloon up a bit. But no matter how you rise up into the air, your body knows it before your mind does. Not by much, though, because it's damned important information that your brain receives like an all-points bulletin. "HEY, were flying!!!"

The moment we got above the waves, the *Kawanishi* weathervaned into the prevailing wind to avoid a wing-down situation that could easily rip off one of her floats.

We spent the next few minutes in relative silence—meaning no talk—because instead of climbing above the fog and crappy weather, we stayed—by my guess—about two hundred feet above the waves.

"Radar," I shouted to Mac, who nodded.

America's less-than-stellar radar was still in its infancy. The odds of it spotting a flying boat this close to the water were minuscule. That said, radar *was* radar, so the pilot was playing it safe.

Fortunately for us, just before Germany occupied England, we managed to rescue Henry Tizard and his brilliant group of scientists who'd forgotten more about radar than we'd ever learned. With their brain trust going full bore in America, we would soon have new and improved systems for our inventory, both for use at sea and in the air.

But not tonight.

While Rosie and Abby, and Patton and the others wondered what the hell had happened to us, our flying boat flew "under the radar" like a homing pigeon... in search of Pearl Harbor.

About a half-hour into what would be at least a nineteen-hour, bone-weary flight (I used to fly this for *Pan Am*, remember*)* our translator rattled of a long string of Japanese to our guards. Grins split their faces, then guffaws. How nice that these bastards were having a grand old time while we shivered in the chilly warehouse of a flying boat.

I gave our captor the quick once-over. Taller than most Japanese; narrow shoulders, bean-pole thin, full head of hair, straggly beard, slightly stooped. Something *about* him... what was it???

Just as I opened my mouth to say something, he turned to me and put his finger to his lips. Then he stepped closer and pretended to check my seatbelt.

"They don't speak a word of English, Colonel Carter, but the walls have ears." He grinned. "Or in this case, the fuselage."

Ava whispered wonderingly, "Takeo, is that you?"

"One and the same. Did my beard fool you?"

He brushed its sparse shape, then raised his finger to quell any response. He turned and scowled at the guards, pulled out his *Nambu* pistol, waved it menacingly at us, and rattled off something in Japanese over his shoulder. They grinned at his exaggerated pantomime and scuttled away into the darkness.

Once they were gone he said, "They've been wanting their damned tea ever since we took off. Give me coffee any time – strong, black, and hot."

General MacArthur cut to the chase, "What *are* you doing here, young man? We left you swimming in the South China Sea."

"They fished me out and gave me a medal."

Mac scowled, but I felt relieved. Somehow this was going to work out all right. It *had* to. Or at least I hoped so, because the man standing before us had helped us escape from the I-401 super-sub.

We had first met Takeo when they dragged us on board from our raft, adrift in ocean, after a friendly P-40 *Warhawk* logically mistook our Japanese Navy-painted Martin M-130 for the enemy and shot us down.

The Japanese submarine captain quickly saw through Ava's and my ruse of claiming to be Methodist missionaries and Mac being a civilian contractor, partly because his crew fished out the general's damned hat from the ocean (he'd ditched it when the sub first surfaced). But when you think about it, back then, General Douglas MacArthur's face was as familiar to Americans FDR's, or Errol Flynn, or Chiang Kai-shek.

The submarine captain had landed a "fish of all fishes" into his net.

Because of Takeo's impeccable English accent and smooth knowledge of slang and idiomatic phrases, we had thought for sure he was one of the hundreds of Japanese-American *Nisei* that the enemy had lured back to Japan before the war with lies and deceit, but then forced them to become translators and, in Takeo's case, do radio propaganda broadcasts.

To listen to this guy, he could have hailed from Milwaukee or Minneapolis, or anywhere in the United States. He was a *Nisei* if there ever was one. But as we came to learn, he was a *native* Japanese, who'd gone to college in America, then ran his family's silk business in their New York City branch until the bottom fell out of the market in the late 1930s, when embargoes cut off Japan at the knees. Home he went to convert his family's production from silk stockings to silk parachutes.

When the war broke out, the Japanese Navy snatched him away from his radio duties and used him as a civilian translator. Because of his impeccable accent, they assigned him to be part of their ultra-secret mission to attack California with highly radioactive, cesium-filled "dirty bombs" dropped by high-performance *Seiran* seaplanes tucked away in the two super-subs' deck hangars.

Takeo's job on the radio was to have posed as a lost U.S. Navy pilot, and by doing so, decoy any interception attempt by American fighter planes on coastal patrol. But after our capture, he became our translator as well.

"So, they didn't hang you, after all?" I said.

"Hell no. After you slugged me, and I hit the water, I rescued the pilot *you* slugged. For my bravery I ended up high in their pecking order. When I got wind about how they were still after General MacArthur, I weaseled my way into the mission as the ideal translator."

"Damned clever," Mac said.

Ava touched his arm. "We've got to get out of here."

Takeo shook his head. "Not this time, I'm afraid. You've got to admit the Nazis had your kidnapping figured out to the nth degree—thanks to the admiral who dreamed it up in the first place—three guesses who."

"Don't bother," I said. "Just spill the beans."

"Vice-Admiral Seizō Hidaka."

Mac sat up straight. "The base commander at Pearl?"

"The very same guy that Sam and Ava made a fool of when they landed in Oahu in that Nazi-plane—"

"No," I said. "It was a Pan Am clipper *painted* in Nazi colors. A Martin M-130."

"I stand corrected." He turned to Mac. "Anyhow, general, these two here pulled the wool over Hidaka's eyes with their bogus story of carrying a top-secret Nazi weapon to Tokyo. But after they refueled, they headed to Corregidor to rescue you instead."

Mac fingered his famous hat. "I was most reluctant to leave those brave men and women."

"Officers give orders, sir," I said. "And they take them. Especially when they come from the commander-in-chief herself."

He pursed his lips as if tasting something bitter. "President Perkins is a complex woman."

Takeo grinned. "This is so amazing. We bow down to an emperor who honestly believes he is a direct descendant from the sun god, while you Americans obey the commands of a woman."

"What's wrong with that?" Ava snapped.

Takeo backpedaled. "I was only suggesting that there's a deep divide between our two cultures."

"The Grand Canyon if you ask me," she said.

I added, "So, how do we escape your damned culture—*with* our necks still attached to our bodies?"

"An excellent question. The answer to which I don't have—at least not yet."

"What's that supposed to mean?"

"It means I'm not just here to be your friendly translator—although that's what Hidaka thinks—and I say, let him think so, until…"

"Until…"

Takeo looked around as if someone was eavesdropping. "The fuselage has ears."

Mac said, "You're telling me that Admiral Hidaka is responsible for…" He swept his arm out to take in the plane. "For this outrageous kidnapping?"

"Yes, sir, but not at first. He lost so much face, that he reached for his *Seppuku* knife to rip open his belly—and it's *some* belly—like a sumo wrestler, except it's fat, not muscle. But then…."

"Then?"

"His wife reminded him of a famous Japanese Proverb; 'A man who chases two hares catches neither.'"

Ava laughed. "His *wife*, ladies and gentlemen of the jury, the brains behind the brawn."

Takeo bowed slightly, absorbing the blow. "So... Admiral Hidaka, with the help of some of his *Kempeitai* secret police friends, concentrated on catching just one hare instead; General Douglas MacArthur. And with the help of Nazi *Abwehr* agents in the United States, they snared you, sir, but good."

Mac bristled but said nothing.

I said, "Three for the price of one."

Takeo grinned. "I'm sure Hidaka's dancing for joy. Not only is he the man-of-the-hour back in Tokyo, he'll get to rub yours and Ava's noses in it when we land at Pearl."

"I'd like to sock his," Ava said.

"I don't advise that."

"What *do* you advise?"

Takeo's turn to fall silent.

I could tell Ava was sorting out something, because she got that look in her eyes and tilted her head just a fraction off center, "Say, hot-shot, how'd you know it was Hidaka's *wife* that got him on the kidnapping trail?"

He grinned. "Been giving her English lessons."

"For the great day when Japan rules the world?"

"Yeah, something like that."

"So, you two talk a lot."

"You bet."

"Not just *talk*, though, right?"

A long pause.

Ava lowered her head like a prosecuting attorney. "Am I right?"

Takeo's pleasant smile lit up like a searchlight in the darkened interior.

Ava added, "What's she been teaching *you*?"

His smile grew even wider saying everything by saying nothing.

While he gloated, I recalled that when I flew for *Pan Am* just before the war broke out, it took our fuel-heavy, passenger-packed Boeing 314 *Clipper* on average, nineteen hours to slug along at a stately, hundred-fifty miles-an-hour to reach the Promised Land of palm trees, sandy beaches, and *Hula* girls.

But from what I'd learned about the H8K from our military intelligence folks, she could hit 400 mph max, and easily topped 200 mph cruising. My guess was the pilot was "damning the torpedoes and full speed ahead-ing" way faster than cruise to get us to Pearl as quickly as possible.

From there, some version of *Pan Am's* island-skipping plan would fall into place that would end us up in Tokyo. I knew our San Francisco-Hong Kong six-stop route by heart – first, Pearl Harbor for overnight refueling and maintenance, then an early morning takeoff for Midway Atoll 1200 miles northwest. Ditto there for gas and another overnight, then an 1100-mile hop southwest to Wake Island, then onto Manila, and finally, Hong Kong.

But the *Kawanishi* was a marine patrol plane, which meant, essentially, a flying gas tank. She could cruise four thousand miles without blinking an eye. That's a *lot* of miles. But a lot of strain on her twenty-man crew and sometimes-cantankerous radial engines.

My educated guess is that they would do it in "legs," but as few as possible. We'd layover at Pearl Harbor, then a quick stop at Midway to "top off the tanks," then the final leap to our appointment with the *samurai* sword in Tokyo.

From somewhere in the vast darkness of the interior, Takeo found rough woolen blankets for us to bundle up in for our long trip into the unknown. As we snuggled down, by reflex I rubbed my neck.

Ava spotted it and began rubbing my shoulders. "We'll think of something, darling. We always do."

Our guards returned from their tea party to take up their positions like stalwart library lions. Their rock-steady pistols aimed directly at us discouraged any further attempts at conversation. But then, what more was there to say? The Japanese had us dead to rights. All that was missing was the "dead" part.

The drone of the engines hour after hour hypnotized everyone. No longer in danger of radar detection, we'd climbed to cruising altitude. My guess was ten thousand feet or so, since the plane wasn't pressurized, and oxygen wasn't available.

Pointedly ignoring us, the aerial gunners crouched at their various turret positions at the waist, top, and the tail. But their posture was anything but vigilant. Who could blame them? The *Kawanishi's* twenty-man crew had little to do except maybe to daydream—or in their case, nightdream of home-sweet-home as the plane flew through uncontested skies towards our destination.

I purposely avoided any thoughts of home, because the moment I let my mind drift back to the long-departed California coastline, I would picture Rosie and Abby being stupefied as to our complete and utter disappearance. As for General MacArthur being among the missing, every conceivable alarm had to have been sounded for sure, with Patton's voice the only one heard over the racket.

I watched as Takeo made his way back from the small toilet and stop next to me.

"If you want to use the *benjo*, it's up there. The can, I mean."

"Thanks, I'm okay for now."

He smiled. "No, you're not. You need to use it right *now*. Look behind the flush valve—that's a long handle you pump to empty the bowl. A little something for you, compliments of the management."

As I unwound myself from the blanket and stood, Takeo changed his tune and barked at me in Japanese, then waved his *Nambu* threateningly. That got the guards attention.

Takeo said something else, and while I don't understand Japanese words, his tone matched the singsong, taunting rhythms that children use worldwide to make fun of someone. The guards laughed appreciatively as Takeo shoved me slightly to get me moving.

Ava stirred from her sleep. "What's going on?"

"Bathroom break," I said.

Mac sat up. "I need to do the same."

Takeo spun around. "Wait for Sam to return."

"But…"

"I said, wait!"

The prisoner/guard tableau stayed frozen in time as I shuffled forward to the tiny crew toilet located on the bulkhead separating the passenger section from the cockpit.

The red-light inside—to preserve night-vision—made it hard to see much of anything in the cramped and foul-smelling space. But after some fumbling and groping I located the rod-shaped flush handle Takeo had described.

And something else.

Slipped over the rod through its finger-guard was a compact *Nambu* Type 94 pistol. Much smaller than its parent, the Luger-sized *Nambu* 14, this 8mm pistol was the darling of aircrews. Its six-round clip was fully loaded.

I stood there for a long time.

It's one thing to have a gun. But where, when, and how to use it remained a complete mystery.

At least I could tackle the "how" part. Despite the dim reddish light, I was able to familiarize myself with the gun's safety, its cocking mechanism, the cross bolt, the clip release—the kinds of basic things that, when completed, I no longer held an unfamiliar pistol but a lethal weapon.

Where to hide it was the next challenge. Only one choice: Tucked inside my belt in the small of my back, the cold metal reminded me of both of its foreignness...and my fear.

Flying in the opposite direction of the earth's rotation has its small rewards – we arrived over the Hawaiian Islands in late afternoon of the preceding day, after seventeen hours of engine-droning flight. Sleep had come and gone sporadically during the long night.

Our inflight breakfast—if you could call it that—was cold rice, fermented soy beans, and *daikon* radish pickles. Ava has a stomach of cast iron born of terrible meals served on movie sets for years, so she dug right in. Mac was just as eager to eat, but that came from long experience of living in countries other than the United States. For him, it was "when in Rome..." He grabbed his crude bamboo chopsticks and dug right in.

Me? I yearned for two eggs over-easy, home fries, toast, and endless cups of strong, black coffee. I got tea instead, and heartburn from the pickles.

But thoughts of stomach trouble faded away when I caught sight of the familiar shape of Oahu, third island in the Hawaiian chain. From our slowly-descending altitude of what was now about five thousand feet, the historic Makapu'u Point lighthouse on the southeastern most tip of the island rose up like a tiny, red lantern-roofed friend to remind me of its nighttime flashing that warned ships to avoid the island's unforgiving rocky, volcanic coastline.

In years gone by, during layovers before catching my return trip to San Francisco, I'd hike up the trail and stare in wonder at the Coast Guard-maintained lighthouse. I'd always time my journey to get there just at dusk, so I could witness its massive, twelve-foot-high, conical-shaped Fresnel light come alive and start slowly rotating its brilliant-white signal to captains—both at sea and in the air—as far out as twenty miles on a clear night.

No such beacon today for our late afternoon arrival, but by tonight it would once again be doing what it had done for over thirty years. One day, I prayed, Coast Guard personnel would be operating it once again instead of Japanese soldiers.

"Victory" was a hard thing to imagine while being prisoners I admit, but I imagined it anyhow, and did so until I felt the *feeling* of standing at the base of the lighthouse and waving at a Coast Guardsman standing on the balcony and shouting, "Nice day, isn't it?"

And he shouts back, "You bet, mister."

"Mind if I come up and take a gander?"

"Sure thing." He points down. "Door's open!"

And when I could actually *feel* my hand on the doorknob, I smiled and thought to myself, "So glad we won the war."

And then I "woke up to my present."

It's a trick my father taught me as a young boy and I've done it all my life – imagining a different reality than the one I'm currently in. And I keep doing it creatively until I can *feel* what it would be like to have my wish come true. That way, I make my wish no longer a possibility but an *inevitability*.

Here's another way to think of it: imagine if you will, plotting a course to an island in the middle of the ocean – drawing a line, making an "X" on the map, calculating the distance, and picturing your arrival. Don't leave out any details. Palm trees, beaches, cocoanuts, bananas, fancy drinks with tiny umbrellas in them… imaginative details are the secret.

Does it always work? Hell, no. But do I always try? Hell, yes. Like I was doing right now, by picturing that young Coastguardsman smiling down at me from the Makapu'u lighthouse.

I'd watched my father use the same technique to rise from being a grease-covered, coal-grimy hostler "dropping fires" from *Florida East Coast* steam locomotives, to become the chief engineer on a crack Miami/Key West passenger run over the Key West Extension that whisked high-rolling customers down to the tip of the island. From there, they'd pile onto a steamer and cruise down to Cuba to lose their trust-fund money on Havana's crap tables.

Thinking and feeling in this imaginative, positive way, got my father his dream job. And in a way, it got me mine. His was steam locomotives, mine was high-flying airplanes. That said, it didn't keep him from losing his life in the Hurricane of 1938, and it didn't keep me from losing my wife and baby boy when the Nazis wiped out Washington D.C. in 1941.

Still, you try. I owed my father that.

I reached out and held Ava's hand.

She looked at me wonderingly, and I just smiled.

"You're doing that thing again, right?" she said.

"You bet."

This time I imagined a different version: I'm walking along the trail that runs along a ridge six hundred feet above the ocean to reach the cliff where the Makapuʻu lighthouse stands. Ava's beside me, and Abby's running far ahead, like a rabbit let loose from her cage. She's laughing at something and Ava squeezes my hand. I *feel* it—not only in my mind but also in reality because Ava's in both places at the same time.

She leaned close and whispered. "Got a plan yet, colonel?"

"Sort of. Rub my back. Down low."

"Sore again?"

"You'll see."

Slowly, ever so slowly, her hand snaked behind me… then froze when she reached the *Nambu*.

She whispered, "Is that a gun, or are you just glad to see me?"

"Both."

As our *Kawanishi* began its final approach for landing on the sheltered waters of Pearl Harbor's Middle Loch, I leaned into the descending turn as though I were the pilot instead of a prisoner.

I pressed my right foot on the deck as if applying right rudder to coordinate the turn and not disturb my high-paying *Pan Am* passengers. I caught myself doing this and smiled.

But one glimpse out the side window and my smile faded.

No doubt in my mind who Pearl Harbor belonged to now – the Japanese battleships and heavy cruisers moored on Ford Island along what we used to call "Battleship Row" made that all too clear. Black clouds of smoke from their funnels rose into the air and drifted south. Lots of vessels getting underway. Something was brewing, that's for sure.

The pilot in me instinctively noted the southward drift of the smoke, and I approved of our pilot's decision to land into the wind—just like I would have done had my hands been on the controls instead of folded helplessly in my lap.

Then they clenched into fists at what I saw next.

A behemoth-sized flying boat was moored alongside the sunken hulk of the USS *Enterprise* aircraft carrier on the north side of Ford Island. Sunk during the attack on Pearl Harbor, she had settled straight onto the mud. Because her flight deck and hangar deck remained above water, instead of raising her, the Japanese had sliced off her island and funnel and were using her for storage and for servicing a *twelve*-engine monster flying boat three times the size of any aircraft I'd ever seen. How the hell could that thing fly?

Decked out in Japanese Navy colors of dark sea green, and sporting twenty-foot diameter, blood-red roundels, the flying boat's slab-like wings and boxy fuselage dwarfed the two H5K *Bettys* moored forward and aft, nose-to-tail, like sparrows guarding a Condor.

I bet you could have stacked five, Boeing 314 Clippers on top of it. Yes, I said five, because this beast was at least four hundred feet long. Yes, I said four *hundred*. Longer than a football field!

"What the hell *is* that?" I said to Takeo, who had joined me. Our guards had departed for their landing stations, so we could speak freely.

"Isn't she something else? They call her the *Tokyo Express*. Makes three trips a week out and back."

"Nonstop?"

"Absolutely." He grinned. "She's got enough fuel to fly twelve thousand miles."

"Must use a hell of a lot of it."

I counted her powerplants. Mounted on pylons in regimented rows along the top of each wing, six to a side, four of the twelve engines were ticking over, emitting a blue haze of exhaust that rippled the waters behind them. Flanking the propeller engines on either side were cylindrical objects also mounted on pylons. My stomach dropped—those *had* to be operational turbojets.

I knew from General Patton that Frank Whittle and the Brits had been furiously working to get a functional jet fighter into the war. But the Nazis' invasion of England had sent them hustling to American shores, where they were still at it but not making much progress in the airframe department—or if they were, I didn't know about it.

I turned to Mac who was now glued to the window as well.

"Looks like Tokyo's got operational jet engines."

"Blazes and damnation."

"That thing's as big as a ship, for God's sake."

"Bigger," Mac muttered. "Lay odds it could carry eight hundred troops."

"A thousand, they say," Takeo said. "We're a short race, remember?"

Further south, a Japanese fleet aircraft carrier was underway in Ford Island Channel. A fussing and fuming escort of destroyers flanked her, determined to protect her from dangers both seen and unseen.

"Damned busy down there," I said.

"They're always busy," Takeo said.

Mac said, "Doing what?"

"Sorry, general, they don't share their secret plans."

I said, "What's the scuttlebutt then?"

"The what?"

"The rumors, the hearsay, the gossip."

Takeo grinned. "'Scuttlebutt,' *that's* a great word, Gotta' remember it."

Mac lowered his famous eyebrows in warning, "Answer the question, young man."

"All I know so far, is that they've issued cold weather gear to the ships' crews."

Mac and I glanced at each other. Then he nodded permission for me to proceed, so I said, "Any talk about Alaska or the Aleutians?"

"Of course. Why else would they be getting ready to bundle up? The average temperature here is close to twenty-five—what's that in Fahrenheit, general?"

"Near eighty," Mac's shoulders slumped slightly. But only for an unguarded moment before straightening into a board-hard, West Point brace. "It would seem obvious that they've begun their move to cut off America from the Pacific and all points further west."

Takeo said, "Makes sense to me, but then, I'm just a translator. You're the professional soldier."

Mac's smile was razor-thin. "Lately I've spent more time being kidnapped than commanding."

No welcoming parades this time, no thumping drums, no pulling the wool over the glittering black eyes of Vice-Admiral Seizō Hidaka, who the last time we met, was bowing in obeisance to a fake Nazi SS General played by a Hollywood actor. Me? I was tricked out as the *Lufthansa* pilot of our *Luftwaffe*-painted Martin M-130, while Ava was the glamorous "assistant" to the "general."

Our creative ruse to get enough fuel to reach our destination had worked its magic. Hidaka and his fellow-idiot Japanese bought the whole nine yards of being on a secret Axis mission and feted us, while their ground crews topped off our tanks. We soon took off to hop, skip, and island-jump our way—not to Tokyo—but to rescue General MacArthur just before the fall of Corregidor.

But that was then. This was now.

In the late afternoon sunshine of a February day, we stood on the boarding dock – three forlorn, wrinkled-clothing prisoners facing Admiral Hidaka who regarded us the way you do butterflies pinned to wax in a museum display case.

I figured, what the hell, and bowed slightly. "Long time no see, admiral."

He stiffened slightly.

Takeo started to translate but Hidaka raised his slab-like hand. "I heard."

"It's an idiomatic phrase, sir, and I thought—"

"I *said* I heard," he shouted.

At that, Hidaka's retinue of officers and guards flanking him on both sides reared back slightly, as if an artillery shell had landed in their midst. And it had, metaphorically, for if you think hell hath no fury like a woman scorned, try scorning a Japanese man. Their idea of "face" is not a Westerner's idea. For us, it's where our eyes, ears, nose, and mouth belong. To them, it's where their soul belongs.

Don't forget, almost a year earlier, Ava and I, and our team of Hollywood impersonators on a hairbrained mission—if there ever was one—tiptoed inside Japan's house uninvited and slapped Tokyo's face as hard as we could; then we grabbed the "silverware" (General MacArthur) and got away clean.

Hidaka's polished boots flashing in the sun, as he CLOMPED his way over to Mac and stood before him. To my surprise, he bowed. And even more surprise, Mac bowed back.

"We meet at last," Hidaka said.

Mac took his measure of the man. In stature, the admiral was a foot-and-a-half shorter, but much broader in the beam. A bowling ball to Mac's ten pin.

Mac finally said, "I have no sword to offer in surrender."

Hidaka grinned. "You *yourself* are the sword, general."

Mac said nothing.

A quick burst of Japanese between Hidaka and Takeo, while the rest of us took turns staring at each other.

I've learned many things from being with the Japanese, both as a prisoner and years later after the war as an honored guest. One of the most impressive things is that while they may *seem* to be somewhat aloof to the goings on in the world around them—marching to a different drum, so to speak—they don't miss a damn trick.

As proof, while the various officers and enlisted in Hidaka's entourage stood at rigid attention and *seemed* to be staring forward into space like polite, brainless statues, their mental gears were turning at the speed of light.

So were mine, except I wasn't getting much traction at the moment.

Where were our handcuffs? Where were the ropes tied around us, dragging us to our doom? Instead, Hidaka was calmly talking with Mac, while alternating between Takeo's translating for him and speaking

English. I couldn't hear what they were saying because they had moved off to the edge of the boarding ramp.

A nod from Mac, an answering half-bow from Hidaka. Takeo glanced over his shoulder and shot me a look that said, "Stay tuned."

While waiting for the outcome, I risked a look around the familiar buildings that once housed *Pan American Airways'* passengers and crews. The terminal, the service hangar, and the fuel depot remained, but no longer painted bright-white with sea-blue lettering proclaiming Juan Trippe's globe-spanning airline. Now they were painted a soul-killing, drab gray, as if to match Japan's stern resolve to rule the Pacific no matter the cost.

Across the waters at Ford Island, the *Tokyo Express* monster-sized flying boat towered like a surfaced whale over the sunken remains of the *USS Enterprise*. But her "nose" wasn't thick-headed and blunt like a sperm whale. More like a streamlined Blue Whale with a smoothly contoured pointed snout. I counted *five* separate machine-gun turrets topside and four along her boxy fuselage. The crew must be thirty-plus.

Had to be a *Kawanishi* creation. No other Japanese aircraft company had the expertise—or the daring—to have not only dreamed up this titan of the skies, but to have actually built and entered her into fleet service. The good news was that I'd soon see the aircraft close up. The bad news was that we'd be heading to Tokyo inside it.

While I examined the massive airplane and pondered my fate, a pair of *Nakajima* A6M *Rufes*—the seaplane version of the Mitsubishi *Zero*—flashed overhead at two hundred feet, then zoom-climbed to begin their combat approach to landing in the waters adjacent to the Ford Island airport. Elegantly-streamlined, rearward-slanting pylons held their single floats in place. They not only looked fast, they *were* fast.

Everyone on the boarding ramp followed their progress, including Hidaka and Mac. Something about the snarl of high-performance radial engines always stills conversation into mute observation. And in the case of the *Rufes*, beautiful planes to behold doing what they do best.

According to Allied intelligence, the seaplane cruised out at nearly two-hundred-seventy miles-an-hour. That, plus machine guns and bomb racks, made her an ocean-born yellow jacket – the bane of existence to our PT boat fleets in the early days of the war by dropping flares and turning night into bloody day. Some of our fast-moving "Mosquito

Boats" were still hiding out in secret bases – striking fast and getting away even faster. But like phantoms in the night, no one knew where.

Ford Island airport was a busy place. The bomb craters and burning hulks of American fighters and bombers were long-gone memories of the devastating Pearl Harbor attack almost two years ago. In their place, neat rows of Japanese Navy fighters and patrol bombers lined the revetments. But they were hardly needed because Japan ruled the Pacific…at least for now.

When Mac returned from his *téte-à-té* with Hidaka he said, "The admiral informed me that we are to be his honored guests at the Royal Hawaiian Hotel until such time that we become his prisoners once again tomorrow morning."

Takeo said, "Including dinner at the admiral's quarters. Eight o'clock sharp. Laundry services provided to make you presentable."

"Nothing I'd like better." Ava fingered her wrinkled gown that had stopped the show when she and I walked the red carpet at the Paramount premiere. Now it could stop clocks.

"You're familiar with the Royal Hawaiian?" Takeo said.

Was I ever.

Back in the late thirties, I spent many a stopover night there as a *Pan Am* crew member. We'd land at Pearl in the late afternoon, surrender our flying boat to the maintenance crew who'd swarm over it like a flock of worried hens and have it ready for our early morning departure.

As for our ten-person flight crew, including the stewards, we'd check in to the famous, eye-catching, coral-pink-painted hotel, put on swim trunks, then race to Waikiki beach to see who would be first to dive into the waves. When you came up for air, the view of Diamond Head would always take your breath away. At least, it did for me every time.

That's because I was a kid from flat and featureless Key West, where the two highest landmarks in town were a three-story, wooden hotel of dubious repute and the First Methodist Church – each attracting its own discerning clientele.

But here on an island created by the volcanic upheaval of forces trapped thousands of feet below in the earth's crust, what you saw was what happened eons ago when volcanoes rose up from the depths of the sea, blew their tops and spewed the insides of the earth to the outsides.

In Oahu's case, these lava-spewing monsters created the Punchbowl Crater, Hanauma Bay, Koko Head, and Mañana Island, not to mention majestic Diamond Head.

It's called that because back in the nineteenth century, British sailors thought the calcite crystals they found on the nearby beach were precious gems. The native Hawaiians call it *Lēʻahi*, because its ridgeline looks like a tuna's dorsal fin (it really does). But everyone agrees that it's one hell of a volcanic cone with a massive crater two thousand feet across. Must have been one hell of a blast when it first happened.

For me, the volcano was constant reminder that whatever power human beings *think* they have is laughable compared to the almost limitless power that created the Hawaiian Island chain.

That opinion was shaken two years ago, however, when we exploded the Nazis' miniature atomic bomb over the Radford Plant in Washington State. For a split second that felt like forever, I witnessed firsthand what happens when you crack open the atomic force that binds matter. Instead of Mother Nature doing only what she can do, mankind stepped in and did it too.

That small, rising mushroom cloud from the Hanford detonation delayed America's race to get its own atomic bomb, but by doing so, it also had kept the Nazis from getting their mitts on our plutonium to build more bombs for themselves. But the nuclear Pandora was long gone out of the box and the race continued, with just a few laps lost. Still, it bought America enough time to draw even with Berlin.

(Which seemed unimportant at the moment, because Tokyo was on *our* dance card, with far different consequences).

What a shock to see a Japanese manager overseeing the front desk at the Royal Hawaiian, along with all his staff. In the past, the workforce was a dazzling mix of Caucasians, Hawaiians, Japanese, Chinese, and various blends in between. For as ritzy a place as the hotel had been before the war, nowadays, the Japanese wanted it as racially pure as possible for their exclusively Japanese clientele and occasional visiting Axis member. Show anybody a beach like Waikiki, whether they be Nazi or Fascist, odds are they'd race down the beach and dive into the waves like a ten-year-old.

Takeo did his share of translating with the staff, because, contrary to days gone by, English was no longer a familiar tongue to the current occupiers.

"These folks from around here?" I finally said, but already suspected the answer.

He shook his head. "Imports from the Land of the Rising Sun."

"So… not just food and supplies arrive on the *Tokyo Express?*"

He rolled his eyes to shut me up. So, I did.

But I kept thinking—mostly about the *Nisei* Japanese who still remained on Oahu. Word was that most had escaped to other islands like Maui and Kauai where the Japanese military maintained only token garrisons, more for show than enforcement, and by and large left them alone. Like the Nazis who currently were keeping order in England, Denmark, France, and other conquered European nations with garrison troops, the occupied always outnumbers the occupier. But fear of reprisal keeps order in check. Same must be true here.

The female desk clerk DINGED a small bell and I laughed. "Why bother? No baggage."

Takeo said, "The bellhop will show you to your rooms."

I'm not kidding… the floor literally shook as a native Hawaiian the size of a Mack truck, decked out in the Royal Hawaiian bellhop uniform thundered across the hotel lobby. The tiny pill-box shaped cap perched on top of his melon-sized head looked like a bottle cap. But you didn't notice much more because his enormous grin and brilliant white teeth made it feel like a sunrise was happening right before your eyes.

He put on the brakes and came to a halt. His smile—impossibly— grew wider. His deep bass voice boomed in perfect English, "Welcome to the Royal Hawaiian!"

The desk clerk, decidedly unimpressed with the arrival of this mountain of a man, snapped off a string of Japanese.

The behemoth bellhop pondered her words, his heavy brow lowered in concentration, then he bowed and said meekly, *"Yukkuri hanasu, kudasai?"*

She started up again, her voice even more shrill, but Takeo intervened with a raised hand was all smiles as he turned to the bellhop and translated. "Our guests have rooms on the third floor. Three-oh-seven and nine."

The bellhop bowed his thanks to Takeo, to the desk clerk, to us, and to anyone else he could see in the lobby. The Japanese must have the healthiest backs in the world because of their constant exercise. At the rate this hefty Hawaiian was bowing, he soon would too.

We could barely fit inside the elevator because our bellhop insisted on coming with us. Still, we managed. My view was limited to the vast expanse of purple uniform cloth it took to cover his broad back. Ava's eyes were understandably wide from being this close to this much of a man.

General MacArthur suffered in silence. But I knew his mind was on some astral plane, sorting out God knows what. Me? I listened to the giant hum a tune, his chest vibrating like a bass drum.

Takeo prodded him. "Enough with the music, Hek."

A deep chuckle. "You recognize it, my friend?"

"No, but you're going to tell me, aren't you?"

"It's the Hawaiian national anthem. We used to sing it before the Americans rammed theirs down our throats. No offense, General MacArthur."

Mac shrugged but remained silent.

The elevator doors opened, the bell dinged, and we pried ourselves out like anchovies from a tin.

"This way, please," Hek said.

I said to Takeo, "How do you know this guy?"

Hek laughed, "Takeo knows everyone, right, Braddah?"

"Keep a lid on it, wise guy."

A chuckle, but Hek said no more.

A few minutes later, after having shown Ava and me our room—a suite, really, if you can believe it—Hek did the same for Mac. Then came a timid knock on the door. Hek back again, this time holding Mac's uniform in a tight bundle.

"Your clothes, please. We'll make them tiptop for the dinner."

"What do we wear in the meantime?" I said.

"Kimonos in the closet."

"I checked my watch. "You've got less than two hours before this dinner thing."

"Back in one, colonel."

"Hek's right," Takeo stepped out from behind the giant, where he'd been hiding all along. "Great support staff here."

"Hawaiian is why," Hek said, then frowned. "Clothes please."

Five minutes later, Ava and I wore bath towels as we stared at the Japanese clothing hanging neatly in the cedar-lined closet.

Ava said, "It's like they knew we were coming."

"They did."

She shook out her hair. "I need a bath first."

"I need to watch."

She leaned against me. "Scrub my back?"

"Promise."

"Promise to tell me your escape plan too?"

"Not quite formulated yet."

Ava sighed, turned, and nestled close. Don't get me wrong, I dearly loved my first wife Estelle. Always will. A fine woman, a great wife, and loving mother too. But Ava fit my body and soul like a second skin – so damned close that half the time I didn't know where I ended, and she began.

While Ava ran the bath water, I went out onto the balcony and stood there for a moment, taking in the view of Waikiki beach, still dotted with a few umbrellas of last-stand Japanese who wanted to squeeze every second out of this paradisiacal setting of beach and ocean. Who could blame them? Contrary to their close-quartered, asshole-to-elbow living conditions in Tokyo, Kyoto, Hokkaido, and cities like that, where you took turns breathing, here, waving palm trees, comfy lounge chairs, and attentive beach stewards delivered amazing drinks with tiny umbrellas in them, and plates of salty snacks.

Problem was, of course, no matter where you go, there you are.

A heavy-drinking friend of my father once told him the reason he finally stopped the booze was that it got so bad one day he hopped a *Florida East Coast* passenger train, and kept traveling north until he got to a small town in Georgia he'd never heard of, and got off, figuring "Hey, things have *got* to be better here, right?"

They call that useless strategy, "change of venue" because it never works. I wondered how many Japanese down on the beach beneath their umbrellas were staring at their drinks or munching their snacks and thinking, "Uh oh, I'm still me."

I certainly was still me, wearing only a bath towel and being held on house arrest at a five-star hotel. Make no mistake, we were guests but prisoners too. From where I stood, I could spot the guards standing outside the main entrance three stories down below. Funny thing is, last time I checked, Oahu was an island in the middle of the vast Pacific Ocean. The empty horizon stretched out before me in a knife-sharp, dark blue line. Why bother guarding us? Where the hell could we run?

Above me, towering tens of thousands of feet high, cumulonimbus clouds had begun picking up the delicate coral tinge of the sun as it moved lower in the sky. Hard to sort out the direction of the storm brewing inside that monster. Most likely moving to the east, because of west-to-east prevailing winds. But wind can be as unpredictable as human beings. The minute you think you've got somebody figured out, they pull a fast one on you.

Wind's even worse.

How many hundreds of hours had I stared at horizons like this, while flying *Pan Am* clippers across open ocean? How many times had my mouth gone dry at the thought of having to fly through a sixty thousand-foot-high, lightning-flashing, rain-pummeling cumulonimbus thunderstorm because we couldn't climb over it?

I sighed.

"Not enough times," I whispered.

"My back, darling," Ava called out. "Needs your attention."

I wouldn't exactly call a formal dinner at the base commanding officer's residence a "last meal," but in truth it was, because tomorrow morning at 6:45am, the *Tokyo Express's* massive wings would lift us off the waters of Pearl and whisk us nonstop northwest to Tokyo.

Takeo's compact, *Nambu* Type 94 pistol tucked in my belt didn't assuage my fears. Its six-bullet magazine of eight-millimeter shells were no match for the Japanese battleships, aircraft carriers, cruisers, and destroyers operating from what was—once upon a time—America's foothold in the Pacific. Not to mention tens of thousands of Japanese troops spread out over Oahu to keep a tight rein on its terrified populace.

A handful of locals had miraculously escaped to "the mainland" (America) during the past year and described in grisly detail the various reprisals they'd witnessed, ranging from on-the-street executions by bayonetting and hanging, to outright gunning down of guerilla members unlucky enough fall into the *Kempeitai* secret police snares.

No such interrogation chambers tonight, though. We were dining with the victor who enjoyed the spoils of war; Vice-Admiral Seizō Hidaka.

His two-story, stucco house had once belonged to Admiral Kimmel, the U.S. Navy commandant of Pearl Harbor, who firmly believed the Japanese would attack Midway Island not Pearl—until the bombs started falling and the battlewagons started sinking. Kimmel died in the front yard, gunned down by a strafing Japanese *Zero* while courageously firing his useless shotgun at it.

The outside of Hidaka's house was the only part left that suggested Western culture. The interior had been completely gutted and converted into a Japanese-style home, complete with a step-up entryway, where we removed our shoes before stepping down onto *tatami* mats spread throughout the house. None of the wood was painted, of course, just stained. And wood was everywhere you looked – beams, sliding doors, low tables.

How odd to spot Admiral Hidaka's *tokonoma*, a small alcove, set into the wall, when we first entered. Graced with a simple flower arrangement and a scroll, I imagined Admiral Kimmel's shotgun shells there instead, and that thought helped quell my anger for the Japanese culinary immersion experience I was soon to experience.

I stared at my bowl of soup, served by a *kimono*-clad side boy who was most likely enlisted, and smiled at the thought of waving my *Nambu* at Hidaka and saying, "This is a stickup. Give us our freedom."

"Our *miso* soup amuses you, colonel?" Admiral Hidaka said.

"No, sir, it's quite good. Strong flavor."

Hidaka's wife, Michiko, sat at the opposite end of the low table. She smiled and said in halting English, "Red *miso*, we use." She turned in mild confusion to Takeo who sat beside me. "I say correct?"

Takeo nodded. "Almost. Next time put the verb at the beginning. 'We *use* red miso.'"

She frowned slightly, but it only made her porcelain-doll face look even more charming. If she was half Admiral Hidaka's age it would be a miracle. The size of him versus the size of her, and visions of a bull in a china shop suddenly turned loose in bed almost got me smiling again. No wonder she enchanted Takeo. Still waters run deep. Still women even deeper.

Michiko bowed slightly, "Your movies, Miss James, I watch. Before war. Very good."

Ava bowed and glanced at Takeo. "Thank you is '*arigatō*,' right?"

He nodded, and Ava thanked her. More nodding.

Bored, Hidaka observed their exchange of praise like he would two birds grooming each other.

Ava turned to Takeo. "Ask her about the lovely appetizer we had. Such a striking flavor and texture."

He did so in rapid Japanese. A beaming Michiko answered promptly, and he translated. "The Japanese call appetizers, *sakizuke*. In this case, it was a *Parmigiano Reggiano pannacotta*."

"But that's Italian!" Ava said.

Admiral Hidaka butted in smoothly. "In honor of our Roman allies. My wife is clever in many ways."

Michiko and Ava exchanged slight bows and even slighter smiles. I thought about Takeo's English lessons, and how she was teaching him too. And how.

Our *miso* soup was followed by *ahi tuna sashimi*, then a dish of simmered vegetables, then grilled salmon, followed by the inevitable pickle platter, and finally—getting close to the finish line—a tiny bowl of steaming-hot white rice.

By contrast, the multi-course dinner we enjoyed had been a far cry from the down-and-dirty meals we three had endured while prisoners on board the I-401 Japanese super sub cruising beneath the waves – its steel bulkheads dripped water as we downed cold rice and gobbled half-cooked vegetables.

Here in this tropical Hawaiian paradise were silk tablecloths, candles, attentive servants, and a charming host and hostess, who tomorrow morning I pictured them still in bed, momentarily awakened by the roar of turboprops and turbojets as the *Tokyo Express* took off. Then they'd roll over and go back to sleep, while we watched Oahu shrink to a small thumbprint in the Pacific from our flying jail.

Just before tea was served to end the meal, Mac cleared his throat. His general's stars gleamed in the candlelight, as did his polished brass buttons. The Royal Hawaiian staff had restored our clothes to spotless condition. Ava looked ready to walk the red carpet again in her gown, and I looked like I'd just taken the oath to uphold the Constitution. Mac, being Mac, looked the best of all.

We turned to him the way flowers turn to the sun. Generals with stars on their shoulders clearing their throats cause that kind of reaction. So do admirals.

Mac bowed ever so slightly. "Thank you, Admiral Hidaka, and the lovely Mrs. Hidaka, for an enjoyable evening."

They both bowed slightly but said nothing.

"Admiral, you could make it more enjoyable by treating us as proper prisoners of war, according to the Geneva Convention. The three of us are, in fact, commissioned officers in the United States Army."

"I am well aware of that. As are you are equally aware that Japan is not a signatory to the Geneva Convention, and accordingly need not follow its accords."

"But your allies, Germany and Italy, follow them."

Hidaka shrugged slightly and you could almost hear his chest of medals jingle on his dress uniform.

I figured these two were at an impasse, so I said, "What's with all your ships setting sail? Hirohito planning on invading Hollywood?"

Before Hidaka could respond to my wise-guy approach, Ava chimed in. "If so, I've got to warn some friends of mine, like Louie Mayer over at Metro. He's such a dear."

Hidaka said, "I do not know what you are talking about."

"Sure you do," I leaned forward. What the hell, turn the screws. What did I have to lose? "When we landed today, it looked like everything that could float was getting up steam and heading out to sea."

He sipped his tea. Clearly a dodge to buy time. Finally, he said, "The Japanese Navy regularly conducts training maneuvers to maintain its readiness. That is what you observed."

Mac and I exchanged a quick look that said, "case closed."

Mac smoothly uncrossed his legs and stood. When the pops and creaks stopped coming from his knees and hips after two hours of sitting at the low table, he towered over all of us as we scrambled to follow suit.

Mac intoned, "You know, of course, as American military officers, we are obliged to make every effort to escape captivity."

Hidaka pursed his fat lips, as if tasting something sweet. "May I remind you, general, this is not a submarine, nor is there a convenient seaplane in sight, like before. You three are on an island two thousand miles from America, and here you will stay as my guests, until tomorrow's flight to Tokyo."

I said, "Coming along for the three-ring circus, admiral?"

"What do you mean?"

"To Tokyo. To watch our heads roll into the basket, like the good old days when *Samurai* warriors roamed the land."

"Since you ask, yes." His chest swelled slightly. "I am to be honored for my service to the Emperor. Admiral Tojo himself wishes me to deliver my final report in person."

"An honor," I said. And an empty side of the bed for Michiko's English teacher, I thought.

Mac said, "Before or after our execution?"

A weighty pause as captive and captor stared each other down across the bright-red lacquered dinner table. Hidaka broke first and bowed slightly.

"That has not yet been decided."

"A minor detail," Mac said.

More silence. I filled it.

"All because you dreamed this whole thing up, right? The *Abwehr* grab-guys… The Italians on the trawler… You did all that because we made a fool of you the last time we were here?" I turned to Ava. "Right, *Fraulein*?"

"Jawohl, kapitan."

Hidaka came to a rolling boil. "Westerners do not understand the Japanese concept of 'face.'"

"We sure as hell don't, but you lost plenty of it, right?"

His face got redder but said nothing.

"So, you dreamed up one hell of an amazing kidnapping plan. Admiral, let me be the first to say…" I gave him a knife-sharp salute and held it. "We who are about to die, salute you."

Puzzled, he hesitated, then returned my gesture, more from reaction than comprehension, while Mac intoned in perfect Latin, "*'Ave, Imperator, morituri te salutant.'*

I explained, "That's what gladiators used to say to the Emperor in Rome's Coliseum."

Hidaka pondered this for a moment and a cynical smile brushed his fat, complacent lips. "American gladiators."

Ava added her salute. "Who know how to fight."

If ever there was a great "curtain line" to end Act One of our Hawaiian adventure, it was Ava's snappy comeback to Hidaka. What followed next, were the ordinary rituals of ending a Japanese evening – saying farewells, more bowing than I'd done in a lifetime, and soon we found ourselves in a (confiscated) Chrysler limousine that once had ferried American admirals on their daily rounds of being mini-potentates on an island that America begged, borrowed, and finally stole from the Hawaiians back in the late 1800s. The Japanese had it now and were holding on like a bull terrier.

A moonless night. Cloud cover low. The towering cumulonimbus I'd seen earlier had moved closer, not further, away. Now and then, a faraway, purplish-white flash of lightning flickered deep inside the murky clouds. Always a foreboding sight when flying, especially when you know you can't climb over it or go around—a lot like the current predicament we found ourselves in.

Days before England fell to the Nazis, Winston Churchill said, "If you're going through hell, keep going."

After his capture, he was placed under house arrest at the *Reichstag* in Berlin. The photos the Nazis released to gain propaganda featured Great Britain's aging leader, slack-jawed, sitting in a chair in an empty room, staring into space. Not a cigar in sight. His hell was far from over.

Ours too.

From my vantage point next to the limo's window, I couldn't help but notice Honolulu's bright streetlights blazing away. So different from the blackout-darkened streets of San Francisco. Not a strip of tape in sight either, crisscrossed over store windows to absorb shock waves from bomb blasts. By all observable measures, Pearl Harbor was wide open for business—Japanese business, that is.

It took me a while to get my bearings during our brief, seven-mile drive to the Royal Hawaiian. Mostly because Japanese *Kanji* and *Katekana* lettering had replaced all the English store signs along the main drag. The neon light industry was making a killing for sure, as red, green, yellow, orange, blue, and violet Japanese words flashed, flickered, and glowed over theaters, restaurants, even fish markets and *sushi* bars.

Takeo heard me mutter my disapproval and said, "Welcome to the Greater Asian Prosperity Sphere."

"I only wish America had half your industry and drive."

"We shall one day," Mac chuffed, "Our nation's strength grows with every second of every minute of every hour of every day."

Ava said, "Meanwhile, we sit inside a captured American Army staff car driven by a Japanese soldier."

"Don't forget the armed guard," I added, motioning to the other young soldier sitting beside the driver, staring stolidly forward.

Takeo chuckled.

"What's so funny?" Ava said.

"Hidaka's *tatami* mats…"

"What about them?"

"Japanese floor mats are edged with simple black cloth. Very traditional. Everybody does it. Except his were embroidered."

"That amuses you?"

"I like to watch people on high pedestals… they fall farther."

Ava said, "What about four-star generals?"

Mac stirred but stayed silent. That man could say more by saying nothing than anyone I know.

Takeo grinned, "If things turn out right, he just might bounce."

Before I could ask him what he meant by that, Ava said, "Hidaka's really coming with us to Tokyo?"

"You bet. Hail the conquering hero and all that. If I know how my country works—and I do—he'll probably get the *Order of the Rising Sun*—do you know that one, general?"

Of course, Mac did. He knew everything, it seemed.

He intoned, "Awarded for meritorious service in the performance of military duties. Admiral Hidaka captured the commanding general of the combined armed forces of the United States. I should think Emperor Hirohito himself will pin the glorious medal on that fat man's despicable chest."

Ava slid her foot over to tap Takeo's toe. "And while the cat's away?"

He smiled. "Michiko's something else, isn't she?"

"She is indeed. But the last time I checked, she's also the admiral's wife."

"You know what I mean."

"Word of advice, my friend – tread carefully with those action verbs. Hidaka's paper walls have mighty big ears—attached to their servants."

"Thanks for the warning."

Takeo turned away and pondered the gaudy store signs streaming past. Japanese sailors and soldiers, intent on having a good time with what little time they had left, packed the narrow sidewalks,. Not a smile in sight, though, just fierce determination of going somewhere and getting there.

Takeo turned back. "I hope you realize exactly who and what you're dealing with when you come up against the Japanese. We're not like the Nazi goose-steppers or Mussolini's pasta-eaters."

Mac said, "I believe we are more than aware of your ruthless determination to win."

"Not win, general, *die*. When it comes to diving into a fight, it's not about winning a battle, it's about winning an honorable death."

Ava said, "That makes no sense."

"It does if your Japanese. We have one foot in the grave and the other on a banana peel."

I said, "Fact or opinion?"

He grinned. "You'll find out soon enough."

The staff car turned off Kamehameha highway and headed for the beachfront road leading to the hotel. Less traffic here, but still surprising to see cars approaching from the opposite direction with headlights blazing away.

Back in San Francisco, automobiles skulked around at night with blackout shields on their headlights for fear of attracting attention from marauding Japanese submarines. They had a nasty habit of popping up, lobbing a few rounds into the city, then ducking down again. Despite what
scientists claimed was the latest version of sonar, the Navy could never find those elusive sons-of-bitches.

And with that thought, the floodgates of memory broke open again, and swept away Hidaka's embroidered tatami mats and neon lights to reveal my daughter Abby, and Rosie two thousand miles away in San Francisco, and along with them, the memory of another life, with other plans that had nothing to do with Pearl Harbor and being captives in an Army staff car that reeked of tobacco. The enemy had stolen Admiral Kimmel's cigars too, I guess.

Takeo rattled off some Japanese to the driver and guard. They laughed good-naturedly. Then he added something else and they roared. The driver pounded the steering wheel it was so damned funny. Takeo leaned forward between them and pointed at something on the dashboard.

Seconds later, the radio blared out a tidal wave of Japanese music that spilled into our ears. After the rather conventional dance band introduction, a woman started singing, and to my western ears her high-pitched, squealing voice could have peeled paint. But the way our guard and driver swayed back and forth in deep appreciation, it was right down their alley.

Takeo got into it, too, as he tapped his finger on his knee in time to the music. "It's called *Cute Girl Standing at the Prow*." The guys are crazy about it."

Ava shook her head. "To each his own, I guess."

Takeo, facing us on the limo's jump seat, leaned forward and motioned us to lean closer. "So, here's the escape plan, kids."

Mac shot a stern look at the driver and guard, but Takeo waved him away. "They wouldn't know a word of English if it bit them on the nose.

Besides, it's all about music for them at the moment, so listen up good. I'll only say this once, because we'll be at the hotel any minute."

The wise warrior avoids the battle.
Sun Tzu, The Art of War

When we entered the Royal Hawaiian hotel, I expected a military escort to goose-step us down the long hallway, up the elevator, and then lock us inside our rooms. Instead, an "army" of Hawaiian bellboys stood at attention along an "avenue" of plant-filled, porcelain urns. As we passed, they bowed like we were visiting royalty.

Once inside the spacious main lobby, the Japanese night clerk at the front desk almost broke her nose bowing so low to the counter top, while a beaming Hek thumped across the polished marble floor and came to a halt in front of us, his face a radiant, South Pacific sunrise.

"*Aloha ahiahi*, my friends."

He quickly followed up the classic Hawaiian greeting with a proper Japanese bow, to which the desk clerk repeated, as did the two bell boys standing at attention on either side of the registration desk.

By contrast, the few Japanese guests gathered here and there in the lobby made a point of pretending we were invisible. But make no mistake, like an ocean wave that ripples through the water and eventually crashes on the beach, they damn well knew that the VIP *gaijin* prisoner-of-war General Douglas MacArthur, had arrived.

Takeo smiled broadly but spoke so softly that only we could hear. "You're in good hands with Hek, aren't they, braddah?"

"All-time good."

"Do what he says, and all will be well."

Takeo bowed, turned to leave, then pivoted around. "Colonel Carter?"

"Yes?"

"When you see my uncle, tell him that everything's going to turn out right in the end."

"I promise."

"And that my mother prays for him every day."

While it's true that Takeo was Japanese, born and bred, when Ava and Mac and I were trapped on board the I-401, we learned that his uncle had emigrated to America years earlier to live and work in Oakland, California, the unlucky bullseye for Tokyo's dirty-bomb attack. It had proven to be a turning point in our relationship. From then on, Takeo was on our side. And he still was, thank God.

Ava said, "Watch out for those active verbs with your lovely student, Romeo."

Takeo smiled, winked, and then hurried away.

Off the elevator, we followed Hek down the deserted third floor hallway like tailgating a Mack truck – hard to miss, plus the distinct feeling of being in the shadow of a giant.

"Wiki wiki," he said over his shoulder.

"What's that mean?" Ava said.

He walked even faster. "Hurry, hurry."

We stopped at our room. He fished out his master key and unlocked the door. His voice dropped to a whisper. "Look under your bed. Put them on. Back at two o'clock." He turned to General MacArthur. "You, too, sir, got that?"

"Affirmative."

Hek's voice rose to normal pitch, which for him was like a klaxon. *"Hiamoe maika'i,* sleep well."

While he and Mac went next door, Ava and I ducked inside.

True to his word, while we were gone, someone had hidden a large, flat cardboard box underneath the bed. The Japanese might own the Royal Hawaiian, but folks like Hek and others were obviously running the show.

Proof in point – two pairs of indigo blue, *samue* work clothes. Normally worn by Japanese Buddhist monks to perform their daily chores, the kimono-style top and bottom trousers were also worn by your average Japanese—and your average American prisoners, Ava and me.

We stripped down and tried them on. After wearing a dress uniform for days, my *samue* were loose-fitting and extremely comfortable. So were Ava's.

The thong sandals fit perfectly. How did they know our shoe size? Not a clue. As for the conical-shaped straw hats – at first, I thought they had only included one, but then realized the weave was so tight that two were nestled together. I pried one free, handed it to Ava and whispered (the walls having ears).

"Try this on for size."

"In a second." She finished folding the Edith Head-designed gown she'd been wearing for two days straight and slipped it into the cardboard box. "Sayonara, my beautiful movie star dress. May some tall Japanese woman wear you in good health one day."

I regarded my folded-up, dress uniform. The gold-braided trefoils on the sleeves and gold epaulets gleamed in the dim light. "They'll burn my uniform in effigy."

"I hope to hell these people know what they're doing."

On the drive back, Takeo had told us that a group of Hawaiian resistance fighters planned to rescue us from the Japanese. All we had to was do keep doing what we were doing and hope they were on the way.

Ava didn't answer. Too busy folding and re-folding the front of her *samue* top. "Did I do this right?"

"You're asking me?"

"Yours looks perfect, that's why."

"Undo the side ties again."

She fussed a bit with the front tie until it fell free, then twisted around to reach the other one. "How can something so simple be so complicated."

"Allow me."

Seconds later, the jacket-type front fell free and revealed Ava's beautiful naked bosom. My mind came to a halt, but not my hands.

"For God's sake, Sam!" she whispered. "We need to be ready when they get here."

I reluctantly drew back. "I'm a lucky guy."

"Roger that. Now please tie me up."

I grabbed her wrists, "My pleasure."

"I MEANT the *samue*, silly man."

I managed to get a brief thank-you kiss after doing so.

"Another kiss, please?" I said.

This one was much more promising, as we knelt there on the floor like two teenagers in a steamy car. All that was missing was the car—and the United States of America to go along with it.

"What's the time?" Ava said.

"Little after one."

She sighed but said nothing. We stood and then sat at the end of one of the double beds, holding hands, waiting for the bus....

"Won't even get a chance to sleep on these nice, soft beds." She flopped back onto the soft mattress and pulled me to her.

"Ouch." I said.

"What's wrong?"

"My pistol." I wriggled it around and tucked in into the front folds of the jacket.

"Don't go to sleep," she said.

"Don't worry."

"They'll knock, right?"

"Right."

"Just a second." She hopped up, grabbed the box with her evening dress and my uniform and placed it on the small table in the entryway, then lay down beside me again. A couple deep breaths.

"You okay?" I said.

"Probably something I ate."

"Everything you ate. What a hell of a meal."

"Michiko's a pretty thing. Way too young for Admiral Sleazebag."

"Takeo will ease the pain."

"What a guy."

A long silence. Just the two of us, holding hands in a darkened hotel room, stuck on an island in the middle of the Pacific, with nothing but a cheap-ass *Nambu* pistol between us and perdition.

I whispered, "Did I ever tell you I loved you?"

"A zillion times."

"I love you. A zillion and one."

A soft knock, Ava shot up like a lightning bolt and hissed. "They're early!"

I pulled out my gun. Another knock. But not from the front door.

I scrambled over to the one adjoining Mac's room and tapped on it.

A tap back.

I unlocked it and opened it a crack.

Mac whispered, "Are you presentable?"

I opened it all the way to behold the Chairman of the Joint Chiefs of Staff of the United States Army, Navy, Marines, and Coast Guard dressed like a Japanese peasant.

"What do you think of the hat?" he whispered.

"You look ridiculous, sir. But keep it on."

He sighed and yanked it off. "Thing's too small." He stooped and picked up a cardboard box. "A pity to surrender my uniform. It's been through a lot of history."

"Still more to make, sir." I took it from him. "Come on in."

"The last place I thought I would ever end up.".

"Roger that, sir. But not for long."

He strode into our room like a general, even though wearing *samue*, which proves you can take the general out of the man but not vice versa. He sailed past us and out onto the narrow veranda that overlooked Waikiki Beach. There he stood, silently gazing at the vast ocean beyond. No moonlight to paint the wave tops silver tonight. Far from looking romantic and South Sea Island-y, the wind had shifted to the east, bringing with it the earlier storm I saw gathering before our dinner at Hidaka's. The rain was falling faster, as if tapping us on the shoulders to say, "Get ready, my friends."

Mac turned back to face us. "I fear we are in the hands of amateurs."

I said, "Don't know about that, sir. Seems this Hek character is running the show pretty well, so far."

"Not *very* far as yet—your sidearm's secured?"

I patted its now-familiar shape beneath my kimono top. "Yes, sir."

Ava said, "Better come inside, general. They might spot you out there."

"At this hour? Honolulu's sleeping the sleep of the conquered."

A gust of wind and a splattering of raindrops did what Ava couldn't. Mac retreated into the darkness of our room.

She patted the bed. "Take a load off, sir. Long night ahead."

The three of us sat like statues for what seemed forever, but could only have been a few minutes, when a a soft knock came on the door.

Ava kissed my cheek and said, "We're wanted on the set."

"You come, you come!" whispered the short, dumpy hotel maid standing beside a laundry hamper on wheels. Her broad, gentle face, a blend of native Hawaiian and Chinese, was so serious that I almost laughed.

She lifted the wooden lid to reveal its empty interior and pointed to Mac. "Number One … you inside, inside… les' go."

Without a moment's hesitation, Mac piled in and folded his gangly arms and legs like a praying mantis. I boosted Ava in next then followed. Our noses nearly touched, so close were the quarters in this damp canvas hideout that smelled of laundry soap.

The maid hissed, "Mo bettah you bend down now."

She draped a loose tangle of wrinkled sheets over the three of us. The light turned silvery. I could just make out Ava's face. Then everything went dark when the lid flipped closed.

"Ho brah, this some night. We go!"

By my calculations of our combined body weight, the laundry cart tipped the scales at nearly five hundred pounds. But after a mighty HEAVE, the woman rolled us along like triplets in a baby carriage out for a Sunday stroll on the streets of Honolulu.

Hidden in the pitch-black darkness, I registered nothing but continuous back-and-forth motion and the noise the cart's wheels made. First, they hissed over the hallway carpeting, then halted.

An elevator "ding" and then we rolled inside what must have been a service elevator.

A blur of conversation in Hawaiian between the maid and elevator operator that I didn't understand. But from the hushed intensity of their back-and-forth conversation, he must have been in on the escape plan, too.

We began our descent. Ava grabbed my hand and squeezed. I squeezed back, and then patted my *Nambu* to make sure it hadn't slipped.

The elevator stopped. The doors CLASHED open.

The operator thumped the top of our laundry cart and whispered, *"Hele me ke akua."*

The maid whispered, *"A'o'oe."*

Wheel noise skittering over concrete.

A male voice called out something in Japanese. Had to be a guard of some sort.

Scraps of conversation.

The maid's voice turned whining and meek, *"Sumimasen, sumimasen."*

Male grunts, then our laundry cart sped up as we descended what must have been a ramp, BANGED through two sets of doors, and then slowed to a crawl as the maid shoved us up an incline, grunting like an ox. Five hundred pounds. How the hell was she doing this?

Another male voice, *"Teishi maru!"*

The laundry cart rocked to a halt and I lost my balance.

"Sumimasen," the maid's voice begged.

More Japanese – curt, demanding. The woman had no choice but to repeat her single world. The guard snarled something. Then the darkness disappeared as he flipped open the wooden lid. The sheets over us glowed white. Faraway shadows shifting.

I reached for my pistol.

Gone.

Fallen out.

Where?

As I scrabbled around to find it, the sheets vanished, and we stared at the wide-eyed face of a Japanese soldier. He took one look at our Caucasian faces and shouted, *"Gaijin!"*

I tried to bat away his bayonet-tipped rifle, but he pulled it back in time. As he counter-thrust, the muffled CRACK of the *Nambu*.

The eight-millimeter bullet slammed into his chest at point-blank range, spun him around, and toppled him, half-in, half out of the cart. As he did so, his rifle tipped over and followed suit.

I caught it just before the bayonet stabbed Ava, who crouched with her back against the side of the cart, hand shaking beneath the jumbled white sheet. Upon it, a smoking, gunpowder-smudged hole. She slowly pulled out her shaking hand, still holding my *Nambu*.

"My God, is he dead?" she said.

The maid's smile was grim. "Dat *moke* be gone. Les' go, les' GO!"

She started to manhandle the body free from the cart, when it seemed rise into the air on its own as if by magic, but in fact, was lifted by Hek, our ever-smiling bellboy. He tucked the soldier's dead body beneath his arm like an immense loaf of bread.

"Out of the cart, folks, and pile into that truck, *wicki, wicki.*"

Only then did I realize we were outside on the Royal Hawaiian's loading dock. A step-van was parked there, its rear doors open. Bright red Chinese lettering emblazoned the truck's sides. Beneath it, English words translated; "Honolulu Hop-Sing Laundry. Tel. HN 2556." A man who must have been the driver quickly shoved a laundry hamper identical to ours into the back of the van, then frantically waved for Hek to hurry.

Mac clambered out of the cart first, then helped Ava while I lent our mysterious, heavyweight boxer bellboy a hand in flopping the dead soldier into the hamper and covering him up with the bunched-up sheets.

The maid slammed the wooden lid shut. *"You pau hanna, moke."*

Hek grinned and embraced her. She squirmed like a happy toddler at the attention, and then turned to us, her liquid brown eyes brimming with tears as she gravely whispered, *"Aloha...Mai hoʻopoina iā mākou."*

"She says not to forget us," Hek said.

Mac straightened ramrod stiff and stuck out his hand. "We dare not!"

She shyly shook his hand, curtsied, turned, and waddled off. The shadows swallowed her whole.

By the dim overhead light I noticed for the first time that Hek's Royal Hawaiian bellboy uniform was long gone. In its place, he wore a camouflaged tunic and cargo pants, a webbing harness, a sidearm— looked to be a Colt U.S. Army-issue automatic—and a sock cap snugged down tight.

We hurried over to the truck. Hek rolled the laundry cart behind us, and Mac said over his shoulder, "Young man, by any chance are you—?"

"Later, sir... in you go!"

The driver, to my stunned surprise, was a full-bearded Caucasian. As he guided Ava and Mac on board he said in perfect English, "Watch your step, watch your step," Then he grinned as he shoved me inside, *"Pan American Airways* welcomes you aboard, Captain Carter. Enjoy your flight."

His voice was familiar, but before I could say anything, he slammed the door shut. Seconds later, the step van roared away from the loading dock and onto the rain swept, darkened streets of Honolulu, with three escapees, a dead soldier, a mystery American driver, and a happy

Hawaiian muscle man who was no more a hotel bellboy than Mac was a burlesque stripper.

My limited knowledge of Honolulu made the drive more mysterious than meaningful. We were heading somewhere specific for sure, as the driver turned down one street, then over two blocks, then a sharp left, followed by an equally sharp right.

Then the twisting and turning stopped, and we accelerated onto what looked like a coastline road. Hard to be sure exactly where, because the only time I could get my bearings was by looking out the rear-door windows when the lightning flashed—fortunately it did so a lot. This storm was turning out to be a whopper—another flash—the countryside lit up blue-white and the ocean waves crashing along the shore to my right.

"Heading north," I said.

And just as I said that, the small panel separating us from Hek and the driver slid open.

Hek boomed, "How we doing back there, my friends?"

"Where we heading?"

"You're going to love it."

"Where?"

"The perfect hideout."

Thanks to lightning flashes, I managed to chart our escape route as we raced north, away from Pearl Harbor. About ten minutes later, we swung northwest along a road that hugged the coastline. At this early hour—which by my watch—was almost 3AM—the two-lane highway was deserted.

Ava, Mac, and I sat on makeshift boxes in the cargo area, dimly lit by an overhead light that cast its cold beams on two laundry hampers – one filled with dirty linen, the other, a dead soldier.

I said to Ava, "Thank God you found my gun. Where the hell was it?"

She shook her head but said nothing.

"Can't believe it came loose. No idea how."

More silence. The step van roared along, tires singing on the open highway. Mac cleared his throat, the way generals do, when about to make a pronouncement. But then he said nothing, so I put in my two-cents.

"Look, it was either him or us."

"Darling." Ava touched my arm. "I don't regret shooting that son-of-a-bitch. I just feel awful killing him."

Mac cleared his throat again. "Lieutenant James, you swore an oath to defend the Constitution against all enemies. You did so, admirably."

"Tell that to his wife and kids, sir."

"Would you have preferred the War Department inform Rosie and Abby of yours and Colonel Carter's demise instead?"

"You don't make this easy, sir."

"War is not easy. When it begins, soldiers must do their duty until it ends with surrender, victory, or—in the case of that young man—death."

"Duty," she said.

"Yes. He died honorably, serving his emperor. His family will be proud."

"How will they ever know?"

"I'll make certain they dispose of the body in a way that guarantees its discovery."

Something in Mac's tone of voice convinced me they would.

After a further half-hour of twisting and turning along the coastline road, the van slowed, swerved to the right and left the smooth macadam. Its wheels rumbled over gravel as it climbed a shallow incline and finally came to a stop. Rain drummed on the metal roof; didn't seem as torrential as before, but still rain.

"Home sweet home," Hek said.

We scrambled out the back and onto the ground. Too dark to see more than a few feet in front of your eyes. But what I did see was sparse grass rippling in the wind, a distant tree doing the same, and the crashing sound of breaking surf, not thirty yards down to my right.

But instead of heading for the water, Hek motioned us to follow him single file up a narrow, climbing path, starting with Mac, Ava, me, then the driver, who laughed and patted me on the back. "Well, you kept your word, skipper, you came back for me, after all."

I kept moving but twisted around and said, "Who the hell—holy cow, is that *you*, Tony?"

"One and the same." He rubbed his beard. "Like the whiskers?"

Tony Esposito's dense black beard hid most of my former *Pan Am* head mechanic's face, but not his dancing eyes and New York City accent. The last we saw each other had been last year, when Ava and the actors and I landed at Pearl Harbor to refuel, before heading to Corregidor to evacuate General MacArthur.

After occupying Oahu, the Japanese had forced the *Pan Am* maintenance crews into servicing their Navy flying boats. They interned families, like Tony's, at a dismal work camp east of Honolulu, where the wives and children served as hostages to prevent sabotage from Tony and his crews.

"You put on some weight," I said. "Last time we met you were at death's door."

"All that great food the Japs eat, sir. Especially the raw octopus—kidding."

"Amy and the kids?"

He grinned. "Long gone from that dump in the Punch Bowl. Escaped to Kauai about six months ago, along with three other families. We got a regular underground railway working, except it's on water."

I wanted to know more, but by now, we'd reached a level stretch of ground about fifty feet above the highway and set back around the same distance. Too dark to see much more than a sheer volcanic wall against the rain-streaked, pre-dawn sky. At the base of the wall, torch light glistened off the water-dripping walls of an oval-shaped cave opening about twenty feet high by fifty feet across.

"Move it, move it!" Hek shouted.

Tony and I arrived just in time to witness Ava and Mac disappear down a long tunnel leading deep inside. Their elongated shadows swayed on the cave ceiling.

"Follow them," Hek said. *"Wicki wicki."*

"What *is* this place?"

"Kaneana Cave." Hek's voice echoed off the walls, "Where the world began."

While Tony and I made our way down the twisting and turning tunnel, Hek explained we were inside the remains of an ancient lava tube. One hundred fifty thousand years ago, white-hot, molten lava surged up from deep beneath the earth's crust and spewed molten basalt into the sea. As its outer edge cooled and the volcanic flow stopped, it formed a passageway leading deep into the earth from whence it came.

Hek's torchlight revealed the corrugated, curved surface cause by cooling lava and underfoot, a series of wooden planks that made walking easier.

"People come here?" I said.

"Never! Kaneana cave is big time *kapu*—taboo. You get anywhere near here and the shapeshifter, *Nanaue*, turns into a shark, swims through the air, bites your head, drags you into the cave and eats you up."

"Nice bedtime story," Tony said.

Hek chuckled. "It works with the locals, and even more so with the Japanese—watch your head."

We crouched lower and lower, until I was doubled over. A sharp turn right, then left, then a pause, while Hek spoke Hawaiian to a figure in shadows holding a submachine gun across his chest. When I passed, he nodded to me and smiled, his white teeth like a beacon in the gloomy darkness.

After five more minutes of steady crouched-over walking, and just when I thought I'd have to go down on my knees, the tunnel widened...then widened more as we entered a cathedral-like space with a ceiling at least a hundred feet high. Torches along the curving walls did their best to light up the place.

I didn't look up for long, though, considering the crowd of people gathered around a woman seated on a chair placed on a small dais in the center of the cavern. The others—maybe ten or fifteen men and women—sat cross-legged, facing her, their clothing a hodgepodge of cargo pants, fatigues, ammo belts, and boots. The common denominator was that they all carried weapons of some sort – mostly rifles, but some submachine guns, too.

The stately figure arose from her chair. Hard to see her face at first, encircled as it was by a tall stack of colorful *leis* encircling her neck. But more and more of her round, placid, smiling face became visible as she took them off, one by one, and proceeded to drape them around Ava's neck, then Mac's, and then she turned to me.

"*Aloha*, my friend. The great *Kane* welcomes you." The way she pronounced the word, "KAH-nay," was more a prayer than a word.

"Your hat, you take off, please."

I removed my straw field hand hat and felt the cool brush of flower petals as she draped a pale-yellow *lei* around my neck.

The woman was impressive, both in size and in gravity of manner. And while her dark blue and white, floral-print *muumuu* must have used ten yards of fabric to cover her immense girth, something told me that, like Hek, her clothing wasn't hiding fat, but muscle.

Her voice was like a church organ sounding a deep bass chord, "I am Kalola Kahkili. We have come to set you free."

A long pause. Hek must have seen my puzzlement and said, "Kalola is a *Kahuna kilokilo*. A sorceress who can predict the future, right, my friend?"

She bowed slightly, "Yes, my king."

Hek laughed, and the others smiled, but Kalola grew stern. "Mark my words. One day you shall rule the islands as your ancestors once did. The Hawaiian people will call you 'king.' I have seen it come to pass. Here…" She touched her temple. "Where the world lives beyond sight but not beyond mind."

Hek hefted his submachine gun. "We've got other business to attend to first. Right, my friends?"

The group stirred and smiled, clearly charmed by this bellhop who wasn't a bellhop.

Kalola wasn't buying any of it. "One day you will be *Ali'i nui*. This I know, for it is ordained by the gods and by the spirit of the great Kamehameha himself."

Hek smiled. "May I ask a question, oh, mighty *kahuna*?"

"For you, I always have answers."

"How much *okolehao* you drink tonight?"

"Enough to see the future. Enough to know one day you will wear the cape."

From a place behind her chair she lifted a vibrantly-colored, red and yellow feathered cape and brandished it like a bullfighter. At the sight of it, the other guerilla fighters sucked in their breath. So did I, at the beauty of the handiwork. Each of the thousands of delicately-plumed feathers had been painstakingly attached.

Hek, not nearly as impressed as the rest of us, grinned. "Don't forget my hat."

Undeterred by his nonchalance, Kalola reached inside the folds of the cape and pulled out a helmet-shaped headpiece with a curved crown. Tiny feathers covered it like felt. She held out both to him, *'O ka hekeli Kolani*, lead your people!"

A long pause. The guerillas were silent. So were we.

Finally, Hek shook his head. "I'm just a bellboy with a gun. You want a leader?" He pointed to MacArthur. "That cape belongs on him, not me."

Kalola shook her head. "His cape not feathers. It is stars."

Mac nodded in agreement, then turned to Hek. "She called you *O ka hekili Kolani*. That is your given name?"

"Hek for short."

Kalola added, "*Hekili* mean thunder."

He grinned. "She's one of my biggest fans."

"What she said about your lineage…you are in fact related to the great King Kamehameha who once ruled these islands?"

"That was a hundred years ago. A lot has happened since. Including America ruling us, and now the Japanese."

"Indeed."

Hek frowned. "But not forever."

"You didn't answer my question. Are you of royal blood?"

"Does it matter? All blood is red. Besides, Kalola can see into the future. She's the *kahuna*, not me."

"I am a *kilokilo*," Kalola added proudly. She clutched the feather cape and cap to her massive bosom like a baby to the breast. "One day you will wear this crown, and all of Hawaii will be yours, my prince."

"I'll settle for a nice cabana by the sea."

The others laughed, but Kalola silenced them with a glare.

Hek continued. "First things first. Let's get our American friends on their way home." He turned to Tony. "You set with what you need to do next?"

He nodded. "On my way, brah."

MacArthur stepped forward and raised his hand. "You're not to dispose of that enemy soldier's body in a way unbecoming of the sacrifice he made to his emperor."

"Are you kidding me?" Tony snapped. "He's a damned Jap. And as soon as I reach the next bend in the road, he joins his ancestors in the sea."

I said, "Do as the general says."

"How? Drive back to the hotel and say, 'Hey, everybody, look at what I found.'"

"You're more creative than that."

Tony looked back and forth between Hek and me.

Hek added, "You heard the man. Use that thick head of yours. And be sure you get Hop-Sing's truck back to his laundry before dawn. I promised him we would. Then meet us back here."

Tony pondered his options while scratching at his beard like it was the enemy. "I think I know a place where I can dump—I mean put—the guy's body. They'll find him within a day or so."

Mac said, "You will honor his sacrifice by doing so."

"You're the boss, sir."

"I am indeed."

I put out my hand. "Thanks for saving the day, my friend."

He took it and grinned. "You're welcome, skipper, but it ain't over yet."

He turned and was gone.

We stood there in silence. Ava and Mac joined me – three convicts on the lam – with a sorceress and prince-in-waiting as our guides.

Ava said to Hek, "So… this is your gang's hideout?"

"One of many."

"You're their leader I gather."

He nodded.

"When you're not carrying bags to guests' rooms."

He laughed. "I took the day off."

Mac said, "How did you know of our capture by the German agents? We are thousands of miles away from San Francisco and yet…"

"Simple, really, sir. Got a flash radio signal yesterday morning. Relayed by one of the picket subs that patrol out here."

I spoke up. "That means Orlando must have made it out alive!"

Ava added, "And told General Patton who—"

"—set the ball rolling," Mac said. "What happens next?"

Hek stretched like a lion after a big meal. "We sleep, we eat, we hide...until tomorrow at midnight."

I said, "And then?"

"*Aloha*, Oahu."

Sleep came, but not for long. Seems like I'd barely drifted off before someone was shaking my shoulder and hissing in my ear.

"Skipper, wake up," Tony said. "You've gotta' see this."

By my watch, a little after six o'clock in the morning. I'd managed a few hours after all.

"Back already?" I mumbled.

"Friends in high places. C'mon!"

My joints ached as I rolled over and tossed off the thin blanket I'd used to ward off the rheumatism-inducing dampness of Kaneana cave. While the subterranean hideout offered protection from enemies without, its humid, spore-laden air clogged my throat and lungs. I coughed repeatedly as I stumbled after Tony.

Ava and Mac stayed curled up like caterpillar cocoons, lost to the world. Off to my left, two Hawaiian guerilla fighters looked up from the cooking fire they were tending. They grinned and waved, then went back to work, stirring a pot big enough to roast a missionary.

"Coming any second now," Tony said over his shoulder. "You won't believe this bird."

His torch got help from the dim daylight as we finished our long ascent from the bowels of the cave and neared the opening. He snuffed the torch by stuffing it into a small pipe conveniently fixed into the volcanic rock. Beside it, hung a smaller can with matches. When it came to unconventional warfare, these guerillas knew how to dot their 'i's and cross their "t's."

"C'mon outside, skipper." Tony shouted. "Coast is clear,"

I heard the ocean long before I saw it. Last night's storm was a passing memory. The faraway bank of clouds hugging the western horizon would most likely dissipate during the day. Waves crashed on the rough-hewn beach about five hundred yards down the hill and directly across the highway from us. The repetitive sound was oddly soothing.

Tony swung up his binoculars and scanned the sky to the south.

"What time you got, skipper?"

"Little after six."

"Good. She's not taken off yet. We would have heard her by now. It's like all hell breaks out."

"Clue me in, Tony."

"It's the *Kawanishi*."

"You got me out here for—"

"Not the dinky one you guys came in on. I'm talking the *Tokyo Express*. Biggest damn bird you've ever seen."

The memory of the king-sized flying boat I spotted when we landed came back to me. While Tony scanned the distant horizon, he babbled on and on about its being a *Kawanishi* (no surprise there. They were the masters of flying boats), and having twelve turboprop engines and four turbojets, and armed like a small destroyer.

"Shhhh…" he put his finger to his lips. Then he cocked his head to one side. "It's the damndest sound."

All I could hear was the ocean.

Then something else.

Music—sort of. The kind bagpipes make—not the flute part—but those tall, stick-shaped drones attached to the bag that sound the constant chords.

Tony thrust his binoculars into my hands. "Look just beyond Kephui Point. She'll be at about two hundred feet AGL."

The "bagpipe" sound grew louder, and the chord grew higher, this time joined by the roaring noise a river makes when you're shooting the rapids. But still no sight of the flying boat, the details of which I could barely remember, other than its astonishing size.

Morning mist clung to the rising mountain above Kephui Point. In the brief time we'd been here, the dawn sky had already shifted from pearlescent gray to pastel blue.

Tony kept up a running commentary, like we were at a football game. "Straight shot, non-stop, three times a week, Pearl Harbor to Tokyo Bay. Three thousand, seven hundred eight-eight miles as the crow flies. Can you believe it? A hell of plane. Hell of a range. Word is, the bird can fly twelve *thousand* miles not-stop. Swear to God, you could fit three of our clippers inside her and still have room for a Fokker. How the *hell* could they make a plane like that and we never knew about it?"

On and on he rambled...

A dot at first... then it slowly grew wings... and a tail... and got larger and larger as she swung clear of the shore line and lifted her starboard wing in an oh-so-gradual, ten-degree bank to port and continued a slow climb to a westward heading.

"Looks like she's flying in syrup don't it?" Tony said.

The optical illusion was convincing. Anything that big *appears* to be moving slowly, but the plane was easily flying well over one hundred knots and constantly accelerating. It's just that a flying boat four *hundred* feet long takes a long time to pass in review.

"Turbojets," Tony said. "Can you believe it? Thought they were joking when she first started landing here."

"You worked on her?"

"Only for a couple of months. After I got the wife and kids to Kauai, I made a career change and headed for the hills to fight with Hek's guerillas."

I lowered my binoculars. By now, the *Kawanishi* filled the lenses and the only way to see all of her was with the naked eye.

No matter how big or small a plane, they all fly the same, including seaplanes – evidenced by her slow climbing turn to port. Now that the pilot had plenty of flying speed he no longer needed ground effect to buoy up his massive aircraft.

From our vantage point just inside the opening of the cave, we were hidden from view. Was Admiral Hidaka onboard the *Tokyo Express?* No way. Not after his prized prisoners had escaped, leaving him with double the humiliation as when we first pulled the wool over his scheming eyes a year ago. Bet your bottom dollar, he'd loosed his hounds to snatch us back.

Tony shouted, "*Sayonara*, you big-ass beautiful bird."

We laughed at that. Me, a tall, gangly ex-*Pan Am* pilot wearing ratty *samue*, and Tony Esposito, a bearded wild-eyed looking ex-*Pan Am* chief mechanic wearing tattered fatigues. We made quite the pair.

As I turned to leave, Tony grabbed my arm. "Listen! This is great!"

All I could hear was the fading snarl of the *Kawanishi's* turboprops and the roar of its jet engines.

"That her again?"

He shook his head. "Listen harder."

I cocked my head and cupped my ear. A different sound this time. Much higher-pitched, almost a buzzing sound. Up came my binoculars and suddenly I was staring at flying *barrels*.

Tony echoed my thinking out loud. "Funny looking damn things, ain't they?"

Three of the odd-shaped Japanese aircraft flew echelon-right, easily twice as fast as the flying boat and catching up fast. Instead of the fuselages sporting wings like airplanes do, they protruded from cylindrical tubes like pencils stuck in a doughnut.

"Never seen anything like it," I said.

"Me neither, until a squadron of them arrived a couple months ago."

"No wings... how do they..."

"Fly? Something called a ducted-fan—a big-ass propeller back in the tail. The airfoil-shaped barrel sucks air from the front and spits it out the back. They call it a 'ring wing.' I barely know how it works, but it damn well does. Look at them go! *Mitsubishi's* got a winner on its hands with those birds."

We crouched down as the single-seat fighters flashed past, going at least two hundred knots and accelerating fast. But instead of following the flying boat, they began zoom-climbing like skyrockets, almost straight up.

"Holy hell," I said.

"Twenty-millimeter cannon in the nose and fifty calibers in the wing sponsons for good luck. You do NOT want to mess with these bad boys."

Another snarl. Getting louder. This sounded more familiar.

"She's turning back?"

We hurried back outside and crouched down. The monster *Kawanishi* was an ever-dwindling black silhouette in the pale blue sky to the west.

Tendrils of exhaust from her props and jets drifted lazily down to the sea. The escort fighters were nowhere to be seen.

"I'll be damned." Tony pressed the binoculars to his eyes. "Party ain't over yet, skipper, check out Kephui Point again!"

All I could see was the blunt shape of the stubby mountain poking up from the sea, but Tony saw something more.

"Tojo had twins, baby!"

Kawanishi monster flying boat number *two* cleared the point. Like her sister before her, her massive wingspan swept the skies like a vulture in search of a meal. Flying lower than the previous one, she came on steadily, gaining altitude with every second.

"They've got *two* Tokyo Expresses?" I said.

"No way. This one landed a couple hours ago. Saw her when I took the truck back. But now she's taking off again? Thought she was here for backup. But go figure the Japs."

By the time the flying boat was abreast of us, she had reached four hundred feet—about as high as she was long—and like her predecessor, she began a slow climbing turn—but to the *east*, this time, not west.

"Tokyo's that way, doll," Tony said.

But nobody heard him inside that flying boat as big as a small ocean liner. Based on its size, it must have a crew of at least thirty, counting gunners and cargo loaders. On this one, I got a closer look at the cockpit area. Not stepped down in front, like conventional transport aircraft, the slender, teardrop-shaped enclosure sat on top of the fuselage—fighter plane-style—just aft of her sharply-pointed nose.

Being a pilot, I couldn't resist imagining the pilot-in-command at work inside that plane – his hands on the yoke, eyes sweeping the sky, and then each of his many instruments – all the while monitoring the incoming status reports from his co-pilot, flight engineer and navigator. Oh, to be a Master of Ocean Flying Boats again, happy in my element, climbing for the distant clouds with a load of happy passengers, instead of crouched down in a cave opening, yearning for the sky, scratching fleas.

We watched as both monster planes disappeared from view, each to her own destination. But we didn't leave until the last humming resonance of their well-synchronized engines faded, replaced by the sounds of the surf.

Tony pointed to the cloudless morning sky, now a blushing pink, and sighed. "Gonna' be a nice day."

"Indeed."

"Too bad we ain't gonna' see any of it. Back to the depths——after you, skipper."

Sleep helped. No surprise there. I'd been going flat out for what seemed forever and my body needed a break. But the nightmares didn't help – wild imaginings of Nazi agents, chopping blocks in Tokyo, Ava screaming and my being unable to reach her——those kinds of things, where you can't do anything but watch helplessly.

Every time I woke up, I'd forget where I was. The cave, perpetually dark, had only a small central fire during the day for general illumination. Everywhere else was shadows.

Sometime after my hundredth nightmare, to get my bearings I reached out and gently stroked Ava's huddled shape. Sound asleep on a small cot, all wrapped up in a Royal Hawaiian Hotel blanket, she moaned her happy moan, but kept on dreaming. I envied her whatever it was that made her smile.

I rolled over and saw that General MacArthur was sitting up, wide awake, puffing on his ever-present corncob pipe. Seeing me, he checked his watch. "Two hours until our rendezvous."

"Yes, sir."

"Can't understand why Hek didn't give us more detail about the rescue mission."

"Need to know, I suppose. He's got to protect his people."

"I loathe being out of touch with operational plans."

"Understandable, sir. Before all this happened, you were about to invade Europe."

"North Africa to be precise, and yes, everything was moving smoothly toward that fateful day when our ships would set sail." He knocked the ashes out of his pipe. "And then *this!*"

"At least we're not on that plane for Tokyo."

"There is that consolation."

He got his pipe going until it was puffing like a steam engine. "And these ridiculous clothes. Not being in uniform, we could be shot for spies. Why did I agree to such a monstrous thing?"

"It was either that or your neck."

More puffing of tobacco. He was working up a major head of steam. Fortunately, Hek came THUMPING out of the shadows, his ever-present smile like a beacon of cheer in the midst of dark peril.

He stopped, hunkered down and whispered so as to not wake up Ava, "Got a little something for you, general."

Mac turned listlessly to Hek, but then his face lit up like a Christmas tree—only for a moment, mind you—at the sight of his battered uniform cap with the famous embroidered "scrambled eggs" on the brim and around the sides. Like Mac, this hat had been through a lot.

He accepted his "cover" like Caesar would his laurel leaf crown. But he didn't put it on. "You're suggesting I substitute this for my infernal straw hat?"

Hek grinned. "No, sir. Just thought you'd like a memento of your stay at the Royal Hawaiian."

Mac's eyes dimmed slightly as he fingered his beloved hat. Nobody in the Army had a hat quite like his. It was as though he was heading up his own personal army.

Hek continued, "When you get back stateside, you can add the rest of your uniform, and then drive the Nazis off the face of the earth."

Mac pondered this for a moment. "What about the Japanese?"

"Me and my fighters will take care of them, won't we colonel?"

"Agreed. Nothing worse than a Japanese losing face. Admiral Hidaka has precious little left after what you and your team pulled off."

"We skunked him good, didn't we, general?"

"So far," Mac said. "But we still remain hiding out in a damp cave on a small island in the middle of the Pacific Ocean, thousands of miles from the United States. What happens next?"

"We get you a little closer." He checked his wrist watch. "I've got five of nine."

Mac checked his, "I have twenty-fifty-five hours."

"Same church, different pew, sir." Hek stood and gazed into the darkness. "Chow line at nine, then away you go."

"You coming with us?" I said.

"Wouldn't miss it for the world."

"What about your hotel job?"

He patted the Thompson submachine gun slung over his shoulder. "Career change."

Hek's promised "Chow line" was more like "Feast Line." *Kalua* pork, chicken long rice, *poi* (of course), and deep-fried, sugar-coated pastries called *malasadas*—all you can eat.

Twenty or so guerilla fighters gathered in a loose circle around the fire, legs crossed, relaxed, chatting and smiling like they were at a happy *luau*. For me it felt like the Last Supper, albeit a mighty tasty one. Ava chatted with the sorceress Kalola, while Mac listened in on their conversation with grave attention. Hek sat beside me, hunched over, as he plowed through the food with fierce intensity.

"When's the last time you ate?" I said.

"Couple hours ago."

"You're packing it in."

"Growing boy—pass the pork."

I passed over the platter. As he took it, the seams on his fatigue shirt sleeves strained at the bulging force of his biceps.

I pulled off a chunk of the tender meat. Rubbed with salt, wrapped with *Ti* leaves, then baked underground for hours, it tasted fantastic.

"Where'd all this stuff come from?" I said. "You couldn't have cooked it here."

"Friends."

"Guerilla fighters, you mean?"

He nodded. "Japanese *think* they control the islands. But they're learning to keep their distance, if they want to stay alive—had any soup yet?"

"No."

"Time you did."

A female fighter was ladling out a steaming-hot bowlful of chicken soup. When she finished, she handed me the ladle.

"Does it taste good?" I said.

Huge grin, perfect teeth. "Broke da mout, brah."

As I slurped down the delicious concoction, Hek revealed the secret to its unique taste was chicken broth spiked with ginger and soy sauce. The slippery soybean noodles swimming with the meat chunks went down practically without chewing.

"Can't believe all this great food," I said between mouthfuls.

"Americans know how to work. Hawaiians know how to live."

"And how to eat."

I regarded the hunkered-down collection of guerilla fighters, mostly male, but some female, all age ranges.

"Seems to me they know how to fight, too."

"For the right cause, you bet." Hek slammed his massive fist onto the cave floor. "Never again!"

"Meaning?"

He brooded a while before answering. Me? I just kept slurping soup.

Across the way, Kalola laughed, and Ava joined in. At what, I had no idea but even Mac managed a tight grin.

Then somewhere in the shadows, ukulele music; soft, sweet, comforting—and surreal, considering we were fugitives from Admiral Hidaka. His soldiers must be combing every inch of the island, but not the taboo Kaneana cave—at least so far.

Hek smiled at the ukulele chords. "Used to be Hawaiians would much rather play music than fight."

"From the looks of things, they've changed their minds."

"All it took was everybody wanting our paradise. Last ones we listened to, were you guys."

"Americans?"

"Big time mistake. Know what we call you?"

"Not a clue."

"*Ha'a'ole.* Means without breath."

He explained that a traditional native Hawaiian greeting involved two people touching foreheads and exchanging the "breath of life." But when white people first came to Hawaii, they just shook hands and took over.

He sat back, cocked his head, and listened to the music. But his face was far from peaceful. "When this war is over, we're taking it back."

"Thought you said all you wanted was a cabana by the sea."

"That comes after."

"But 'King Hek' first?"

His mouth smiled, but not his eyes. "Something like that... maybe."

An hour later, with my *luau* feast barely digested, a whispered cry came from the shadows and the banquet atmosphere shifted from peace to war. The guerilla fighters rose as one. They gathered in a tight-knit group, their faces turned to their leader. Hek spoke Hawaiian in hushed tones. In response, one by one the fighters peeled off and disappeared, each with his or her own assignment.

Ours was simple – follow Hek.

After a swift, single-file, twisting, turning journey out of the depths of Kaneana cave, we emerged at its broad oval opening. Below, all was in darkness. No moon tonight. That was in our favor. To the north, tiny dots of yellowish light here and there from the occasional native huts and small dwellings, but mostly dark, brooding, vegetation covered hillsides that drop straight to the sea. Same to the south. Hek and his fighters had picked a good hideout for us, that's for sure.

Yesterday's storm was long gone. In its place, an infinity of stars filled the heavens and disappeared behind the razor-sharp edge of the horizon. From long habit, I quickly found old navigation friends, like Capella, Castor, and Pollux, high overhead. And even though I'd seen the stars a thousand times and used their unfailing positions to guide my airplane safely home, they still took my breath away. Especially when they appeared without the moon to diminish their distant brilliance.

But before I could continue my reunion with the heavens, Hek motioned us to follow him down the same trail we had climbed the night before.

The ever-present night wind plucked at my *samue*, and my sandals skittered and slithered on the volcanic gravel. I offered my arm to Ava, but she wisely declined, preferring to keep her own balance. Only hard work with my straw hat kept it in one place. Always easier to climb than descend. True in climbing. Flying too.

The guerillas acting as rear guard chatted softly among themselves, their voices hushed and excited, almost like school kids instead of killers. But make no mistake, freedom fighters fight for something far more than a flag, or a constitution – they fight for a cause.

And if I could trust Hek, their cause was to be free from Japanese occupation. America had the same cause – with her treasured Pearl

Harbor and the clout it once gave to her Pacific plans now in Japanese hands, she wanted it to be free again, too.

But all that was out the window until Patton got his game going in the South Pacific. And *that* wouldn't happen until this ramrod-straight, *samue*-wearing, four-star general marching along the path like a steam train, got safely home.

We finally arrived at the bottom of the steep incline that led back to Kaneana cave. Hek stopped the group and sent out scouts along the narrow, two-lane highway. They scuttled off like high-speed land crabs, visible only for an instant, then swallowed up by the night. A minute later—or more—hard to estimate when adrenaline's going full-speed through your bloodstream, a tiny pinprick of blue light flashed twice.

"All clear," Hek whispered.

We darted across the road and then down the shallow embankment. The slippery volcanic rubble was a challenge, but we managed without tripping and breaking an arm or leg. Hek's fighters, by contrast, moved like Swiss Alp mountain goats when, with a series of sharp whistles and hand signals, he fanned them out to protect our flanks and provide a rear-guard.

By now, my eyes had adjusted enough to the darkness to see foaming white surf breaking on a crude beach of black, basaltic rocks about thirty yards ahead.

Ava gingerly stepped over the sharp-edged, crumbly volcanic stone. "Where's the sand of Waikiki when we need it?"

"Tokyo's got it," I said.

"Very funny—your hand!"

I caught her from falling. Together this time, we danced from rock to rock, until Hek motioned us to crouch down behind a small pile of boulders. He took out a flashlight fitted with a blue lens and sent a series of dots and dashes.

My years as a *Pan Am* radio operator had long accustomed my ear to the rhythmic pulses of Morse code, whether they were "DIT-DAH-DITs" in my headsets or bright dots and dashes of light, like Hek was doing.

"You sent 'OK.'" I said.

Hek nodded without looking at me and pointed at the velvet-black surface of a moonless sea. The starlight barely made a dent in its depths. Then, in the midst of nothingness, about two points to port, a blue light appeared long enough to flash a long series of dots and dashes,

Took me a second to read it all, then I whispered to Hek, "Did just he say, *"Party* time?"

Hek laughed. "Jack's boys like to have fun."

Moments later, a dark shape materialized out of the gloom and drew closer, until it halted about fifty yards off shore and held its position. A motorized boat of some kind, it engines a deep-throated rumble, with the sound mostly masked by the crashing surf.

To our right, a slender outrigger canoe glided out of the same darkness, crosswise to the approaching waves. Two paddlers, bow and stern, dug in their tulip-shaped oars and quickly swung the bow ninety degrees until it headed straight for our beach.

Hek whistled, and four of his fighters darted into the surf to wait for the outrigger to make its approach precisely in between wave intervals. When the moment arrived, the paddlers increased their speed, and so did Hek as he stood and said, "Follow me!"

Ava, Mac, and I trailed him across the boulders to a gravely beach no deeper than a few feet. But that's all the outrigger needed as its needle-sharp prow, safeguarded by the guerillas, gritted into the volcanic sand. The paddlers wore nothing but loincloths and head bands.

I turned to Hek. "Where we heading?"

"A short ride to a beautiful island." He gripped my shoulder and leaned closer to be heard over the noise of the waves. "Just wait until you see *that* hideout."

He gave a series of crisp orders in his native tongue. The fighters nodded, grinned, and rattled off a string of Hawaiian words. The only one I recognized was *"Aloha."*

Ava and Mac and I returned their timeless greeting. Then, guided by Hek and assisted by the guerillas and Tony, we climbed aboard the narrow canoe, knelt onto soft, woven fiber knee pads and waited for Hek, who landed like a thunderclap, grabbed a paddle and banged it on the gunwale.

"Wait for me, fellas!" Tony flipped into the dugout like a gaffed fish. "Full speed ahead, King Hek!"

The guerillas shoved us into the surf and spun us around until we faced bow-first. Then the rear paddler thumped a series of beats on the hull. Hek and the bow paddler answered.

They counted... sixth wave... seventh wave... then came a brief interval while the next set of waves approached...and in that brief grace period, they fiercely paddled to meet the incoming wave as its master not its victim.

A sharp climb to the peak, a spray of watery sea foam arched overhead... then a slippery slide down the backside and we were finally in open water, heading parallel to the trough of the approaching waves, steering straight for the waiting boat.

Mac said, "By God, that's a PT boat! George told me they still had a few out here, but I didn't believe him."

Before the war, I'd seen my share of newsreel footage of pristine squadrons of the sleek, dark green, eighty foot-long Elco motor torpedo boats slashing through the waters, dropping torpedoes and haul-assing in rooster-tail turns away from their targets.

Capable of hitting fifty-miles-an-hour, these wooden-hulled hotrods were the dashing, adventurous, cutting edge of an otherwise plodding navy of battleships and cruisers. Yes, we had aircraft carriers and were building more every day, and yes, we had flyboys as our dashing heroes. But those were *pilots*, not sailors – a big difference to a Navy man more at home with the sea than the air.

As we approached the PT boat, two figures knelt aft of a deck-mounted cylindrical torpedo tube, waiting for us. One of them threw a line. I caught it and made it fast, while Hek and his paddlers skillfully maneuvered the canoe alongside. Willing hands hoisted Ava up, and then guided Mac, Tony, and me onto the deck.

Hek shouted, "Gangway, fellas."

He planted his broad legs on the canoe gunwales, crouched, then vaulted high enough to grab a deck stanchion, then pulled himself onboard. The outrigger canoe veered off, mission accomplished, and glided back into the darkness. The muffled sounds of the PT's engines vibrated the plywood deck beneath my feet.

Despite no moon, there was enough starlight to see the face of the grinning sailor who led us across the gently heaving deck past a twin fifty-caliber machine gun tub mount. The sailor who gripped both gun triggers didn't even look at us, so intent was he upon potential danger elsewhere. His blotchy-patterned shirt looked out of place – not your standard Navy denim blue.

But I didn't pay much attention beyond that, considering that everything else during the past seventy-two hours of my life had been straight out of a screenplay for an adventure film that I'd would have been more than happy to watch, eating popcorn with Abby, not living it for real. If I were sitting in a theater, I could pretty much count on a happy ending. Not here, that's for sure. Not a clue what would happen next.

"Watch your step," the sailor said over his shoulder.

We wound our away around cleats, toe-rails, stanchions, and odd-shaped gear mounted on the deck as we followed him forward, then climbed up to the tiny flying bridge. As the boat's speed slowly increased, the wind kept trying to steal my straw hat. I gave up and slung it around my neck. Damned thing. Ava did the same, while Mac, in a fit of frustration flung his out to sea.

A high tenor voice called out, "Welcome aboard!"

A skinny young man stood inside a chest-high cupula about the size of a telephone booth that passed for the helm. His hands gripped a small wooden-spoked wheel. The reddish-glow from the engine instruments and the binnacle compass light lit up his incandescent smile.

Behind him, just outside the cupula, another young man stood, knees flexed, easily handling the choppy water. His scraggly, sandy beard barely covered his youthful face.

The man at the helm said, "Lenny, take ov-ah the helm, okay?"

"Aye, aye, sir."

"Course zero-three-eight until we clee-ah the point. You know the way from they-ah."

His crisp New England accent was like a fresh breeze on a hot night.

"Affirmative, skipper."

The two men changed places like trapeze artists – four hands momentarily grasping the wheel, then two. The former helmsman who greeted us was shirtless in the warm, tropical night, his crunched-down officers' cap lent authority to his boyish face.

Casual uniform notwithstanding, he delivered a razor-sharp salute and held it until General MacArthur returned it.

"Lieutenant Kennedy, United States Navy, sir. We've come to take you home."

Mac regarded the wooden "Mosquito Boat," now going at such a fast clip that I had to hold on to the lip of the bulkhead to keep my balance.

"I doubt this craft has the range, young man."

"Let me rephrase that, sir. We've come to *start* you on your way home."

Mac pondered this, then finally said. "How is it you have managed to stay alive out here in the midst of enemy forces?"

"Well, sir, we—"

"And furthermore, how many of you remain—the boats, I mean?"

"Just two operational PTs left in the squadron, sir. The 109 and the 124. The 146 got shot up pretty badly a couple months ago, so now we cannibalizing her for spare parts. And in answer to your first question, sir, we have *him* to thank."

Kennedy pointed to Hek, who stood looking out to sea, seemingly more concerned with the waves than our conversation. "Right, Hek? You and those guerilla fighters of yours?"

Hek swung around and smiled. "Affirmative, lieutenant. Just because you *Haoles* stole our country, doesn't mean we can't still be friends."

Kennedy laughed. "And friends help other friends, right? We *huli-huli* the bad guys all time, don't we?"

"All time give dirty-lickings, braddah."

They both laughed at their pidgin exchange.

"How am I doing with your lingo?" Kennedy said.

"Better and better. We'll get you a grass skirt pretty soon. But you need to put on some belly fat before that happens, brah." He slapped his stomach and it sounded like thumping a concrete wall.

Kennedy turned and introduced the young officer at the helm as Ensign Leonard Thom, his exec. Smiles and salutes exchanged, but a bit odd, considering Thom wore a brightly-patterned Hawaiian shirt, with one sleeve missing, and half its buttons. But he, like Kennedy, kept his hat on as a mark of rank.

Mac took all this in. "Gentlemen, if I were not sporting these infernal pajamas, I would have questioned your uniform choices. But all things considered...." He fingered his frayed blue collar. "There *is* a war on, and we must make the best with what we have."

"About the clothes and beards, sir..." Kennedy said. "It's been a long time since these boys have seen home. Some of them..." he hesitated at the catch in his voice. "Well, not all of them who came out here in forty-one will ever see home again. That's why I try to boost morale wherever I can."

An awkward silence fell over the group. But Mac knew how to handle things like this. "How long is our journey, son?"

"Molokai's a little under a hundred miles from here. At our rate of speed, we'll be there around oh-four-hundred hours—all things considered."

"Meaning?"

"The Japs have night patrols out of Kawela Bay. But they're lazy as hell. Once we get past them, we'll pour on the coal."

"I'll say you will!" Tony bounded up onto the small platform like a kid let out of school early. "Pappy was showing me your setup down below. Never got a chance to see it before. Almost five thousand horses! Burning AVGAS. Fantastic."

"We do know how to move," Kennedy said.

"I'll say."

Kennedy indicated a small hatch to his right. "If you folks don't mind, I think it's best if you head below until we get in the clear. I'll call down when I think it's safe to come topside."

We managed to worm our way below into the cramped wheelhouse of the PT boat. The waves were getting a bit choppy, which meant the ride would be getting bumpy. Better to have something to hold on to.

Not an inch of wasted space in these boats, and most spaces had a dual purpose. A hook with a helmet hanging from it, could become one end of a laundry line when needed.

The small radio compartment on the starboard side included a radioman. He was so busy smoking cigarette and jotting down a Morse signal at the same time that he regarded our motley group like we were the most natural thing in the world.

Hek gave him a playful pat on his head. "Staying out of trouble, Johnny?"

The radio operator grinned at Hek's familiarity but kept on writing. Duty called.

"You know all these guys?" I said.

"Most of them, yeah."

Tony said, "This was the PT-boat that took Amy and the kids to Kauai. Should have seen it. Thirty-plus folks crowding the decks, and Lieutenant Kennedy and the boys cruising over to Kauai like it was a holiday instead of the great escape. To this day, I don't think the Japs know we pulled it off."

Hek said, "Oh, they know it all right, but they also know if they try going after them, they'll never see Mount Fuji again."

"Many enemy troops on Kauai?" I said.

"No way. Oahu is Tokyo's only prime real estate. The rest of the islands have skeleton-crews of garrison troops. I mean, c'mon, we're in the middle of the South Pacific. Where are folks going to run?"

I said, "You've got guerilla forces on *all* the islands?"

"Affirmative"

"How the hell do you coordinate things?"

"Brah, we Hawaiians been conquering islands long before Christopher Columbus tripped over the New World. We got *much* better ways than Johnny's radio here."

Johnny blew a smoke ring. "Yeah, but without this baby you're a bunch of canoe paddlers." He patted the well-worn device dotted with a profusion of glowing dials and meters.

Hek said, "I will admit that technology has helped in this particular situation."

"Impossible without it. Admit it, oh mighty prince."

He grinned and saluted. "I surrender."

We continued making our way aft until we reached the day room, where a narrow table and benches were tucked against the sides of the sloping hull. We crowded onto the benches like spectators at a football game and proceeded to stare at each other.

Being just forward of the engine room, the vibration made the deck buzz beneath our feet. While mufflers masked the noise outside, the

3000-plus horsepower aviation engines made a major dent in our peace and quiet. For everyone that is, except Tony who sat there, happily drumming his fingers to the beat.

"Pappy's got those babies purring like kittens. *Pan Am* should have snatched him up long ago."

A long moment of silence—sort of—providing you discounted the sound of waves slamming against the bow and the creaks and groans of wood and metal shifting and flexing from the multiple play of forces at work required to drive a patrol torpedo boat through the water at almost fifty-miles-an-hour.

"Did I hear the lieutenant say 'Molokai'," Ava said. "Isn't that where..."

"The leper colony is?" Hek said. "You bet."

He was fussing with the coffee pot at the small mess sink. He opened a small compartment and grabbed the coffee grounds. "But Molokai's a big island and there's lots more going on over there than that. The leper colony is isolated on the Kalaupapa peninsula on the north side of the island, pretty much cut off from the rest of Molokai."

"I didn't realize."

"That's why they picked it way back when."

"Poor things."

"We picked it too, for our purposes."

"The guerillas?"

"Times change."

"What do you mean?"

"You'll see."

"You live with *lepers?*"

"We live with friends—how you take your coffee?"

A short while later, nature called, and I left the group in search of the head. After a couple of wrong turns inside the incredibly cramped and crowded boat, including the exec officer's quarters, I located the postage stamp-sized compartment.

Even here, I could feel the vibration from the powerful Packard twelve-cylinder engines driving us to Molokai. All I knew was that the island lay southeast of Oahu. That was about it. How much more I would discover remained to be seen, because if all went well, we'd be landing there in less than two hours.

The combined smells of AVGAS and engine oil were overpowering. To escape the fumes, I went topside to clear my head and met Tony Esposito coming my way.

"The head's below, if you need it," I said.

"Negative your last, skipper." He hefted a small green thermos. "Fresh coffee out of the pot. Gonna' visit Pappy. Wanna' come along with me and check out his toys?"

There's something to be said about groups of men standing around powerful engines. Whether they're working or not, a male camaraderie inevitably springs up—especially when they're not. In that case, everyone will immediately have an opinion as to how to get them working again. But in our case, thanks to Pappy's expert touch, PT-109's three Packards were furiously firing away.

This "standing-around" male phenomenon's been going on a long time. Five hundred years ago, Pappy, Tony, and I could have been standing around a British warhorse watching it stamp its hooves and strain at the bit to ride into the Battle of Agincourt, while carrying one of the knights of King Henry the Fifth. While a horse isn't technically an engine, back then those monster-sized, four-legged brutes were war machines in their own right.

A few centuries later, steam replaced horses, driving locomotives over steel rails and spinning dynamos to bring electric lights to a city. Later on, gasoline and diesel engines took up the task of being magnets for men to scratch their armpits, smoke tobacco, and opine upon the art of power.

A little hard to do that as we stood in the engine room in the midst of thirty-six cylinders beating living hell out of their crankshafts. Despite the noise, Pappy managed to shout his description of the four-stroke, sixty-degree, V-12, supercharged Packard engines with aluminum blocks and aircraft carburetors vaporizing AVGAS at a dizzying rate of speed.

For space reasons, the two outboard engines faced backward, their power transmitted through V-Drive boxes to the prop shafts. The center engine faced forward, the way God intended, with its output delivered directly to the center propeller.

Tony shouted, "How much juice onboard?"

"We left Maui with three thousand gallons."

That stumped me. "Where the hell are you finding one-hundred octane?"

"Subs. Every thirty days, if we're lucky. Sometimes we ain't, though, so the skipper takes it easy or we make do with crappier-octane bug juice."

Pappy had been smoking a cigarette the whole time. He chain-lit a fresh one. I couldn't help myself from hollering as politely as I could, "Chief, you worried about fire down here with all this fuel?"

"Least of my worries, sir."

He pinched the cigarette butt with his bare fingers and dropped it on the deck, then stubbed it out with a grease-stained shoe.

Tony said, "Nice shirt."

"Thanks." Pappy fingered his slightly-worse-for-wear Hawaiian shirt, a bit faded, but its bright red hibiscus and green leaves still had plenty of oomph.

"Where do you boys get them?"

"Some Jap who runs a souvenir shop on Maui."

"A local?"

He snorted. "You ought to know better than that. Nah, he showed up when the garrison forces landed. Tokyo's got a whole civil service racket going on. Police, doctors, teachers, street cleaners, merchants, they're planning on staying a long time."

"Not if we can help it, right, skipper—I mean, colonel?"

"We're coming back, make no mistake," I said.

Pappy patted the center engine with a grimy hand. "None too soon, sir."

In most ships, the captain observes while someone else mans the helm. But the small size of the PT boat's crew—and Lieutenant Kennedy's obvious joy in "driving" his pride and joy—were the perfect excuses for him to guide us closer and closer to our destination on the northern side of Molokai.

The reddish light from the instrument panel cast his gaunt face in shadows, and I said, "You could stand a few more pounds on that frame of yours, lieutenant."

"Aye, aye, sir. Don't want to get *too* fat, though. Wouldn't fit behind the wheel—ahoy, your one o'clock."

I swung around and caught sight of Molokai looming on the distant horizon. It seemed to have materialized out of nowhere. One minute, open sea and nothing but stars, the next, low lying land and looming mountains.

What an island!

I'd seen it from the air many times. It's the fifth largest of the eight-island chain that makes up Hawaii. As for its shape, imagine a fish laying on its side, its head facing San Francisco. Now, imagine a dorsal fin on top, about halfway down its spine. That's the Kalaupapa peninsula, home to the leper colony, completely isolated from the rest of the "fish" by mountains, ridges, and near-vertical "sea cliffs" running almost the full length of the island. Born from two shield volcanoes, the northern one collapsed a million years ago, leaving an open plain that runs east to west, and whose height captures passing rain clouds and blesses the land with green.

As for the Kalaupapa peninsula, the Hawaiian government knew what it was doing when it rounded up the lepers and dumped them onto this forsaken spot to eke out their miserable lives until they died. And died they did by the thousands. Even though the word "leper" is no longer accurate nowadays ("Hansen's Disease" is the clinical term), back then, most of the world still feared what was on Kalaupapa.

So did I.

I turned to Kennedy. "You come here often?"

"Like a bus, sir."

"Do you... What I mean is..."

"It's not what you think, sir. Otherwise, I wouldn't endanger my crew. Joanie will explain everything soon enough."

"And 'Joanie' is..."

"Lieutenant Joan Robinson, Navy nurse. Escaped to Molokai with the guerillas after they bombed Pearl. She works in the colony along with an American civilian doc who got trapped on Molokai about the same time. He's with some big drug company, name I forgot—wait, Parke-Davis, that's it. My dad has stock in them. I do too—I think. Anyhow, they're turning leprosy upside down with a new sulfa drug. We get periodic supplies from the subs. When we do, we haul them over there."

"What do you mean by 'upside down?'"

"Easier for Joanie to explain than me, sir."

We cruised along in comfortable silence for a few minutes. Kennedy guided his craft with the kind of confidence that only comes with a lot of experience.

"Enjoy being on the water?" I said.

"Yes, sir. But I'm done with the South Seas. Give me Martha's Vineyard over Molokai any day."

"That day will come, lieutenant."

"Yes sir."

"And when it does, what'll you do—for a living, I mean?"

He patted the wheel. "Sail around the world, maybe."

"And then? To stay alive?"

He fell silent.

Then, "A good question, sir."

The approaching dawn light washed the sky a faint blue.

"Fair weather ahead." I said.

"Nothing bet-ah."

Minutes later, at a terse command from Kennedy, a group of sailors wormed their way out of a hatch near the bow. Three of them started limbering up an impressive-looking deck gun. A series of cables and turnbuckles held it in place, as well as U-bolts riveted into the wood deck. An oddly-shaped magazine encircled the breech. For sure, a "field modification" of some sort that nobody knew about but the perpetrators.

"What are you packing forward?" I said.

"Thirty-seven-millimeter cannon. Came off a busted-up P-39 *Airacobra*. Pilot survived, plane didn't."

"Not standard-issue, that's for sure."

Kennedy grinned. "Too bad you won't get to meet the madman who rigged it – Marine Gunnery Sergeant Jeremiah James Lewis. A regular one-man armory. But he's out on a recon mission to Kaho'olawe. Something big's brewing on that little piece of hell. The word is, somebody's ready to make like a turncoat. Gunny intends to find out what he's got to say."

The island's name rang a distant bell. President Perkins and Professor Friedman had mentioned Hawaii during the briefing at Alamogordo. Something about a Japanese scientist being there. I had immediately thought of Kaho'olawe too.

"What do you know about the place?"

"Exactly zero, sir. Just scuttlebutt. The Japanese are masters at shadow puppets, if you know what I mean. You think one thing, but it's completely the other."

Another group of sailors limbered up the smaller deck gun.

"What's that one over there?"

"Your basic twenty-millimeter. Getting low on ammo, though. Hek's guys raided an army munition dump on Maui last month, but we're starting to run low again. "

"Expecting trouble on Molokai?"

"No, sir, just the way we do business."

"Many enemy troops there?"

"Japs have less than a battalion, almost all of them on the other side of the island. Half of them are down most of the time with malaria, while Hek's guerillas keep the healthy ones busy. As for Kalaupapa, nobody wants anything to do with the lepers."

"I feel the same way."

He laughed. "That's okay, sir, I did too until I met Joanie—oh, before I forget, more scuttlebutt – General Patton's invasion fleet coming to take back Pearl. That for real? They tell me you've got his ear."

"Used to, until I started wearing pajamas."

"So... do I tell the boys that General Tojo still owns these islands or don't I?"

"Let's just say if things go as planned we're about to foreclose on his sorry ass."

Big grin. "Any idea when?"

"That I can't say."

"Because you can't?"

"Because I haven't a clue."

He swung the boat a few points to starboard and Maui drifted to port. "Speaking of scuttlebutt, sir. Can you keep this to yourself?"

"Depends."

"If things go right—and they occasionally do out here—you should be seeing the Golden Gate sooner than you think."

"Keep talking."

"We've got a picket line of submarines strung out between here and Mare Island, California. Slow-moving once they get in range of Oahu patrols and have to go under, but otherwise they can move fairly fast on the surface. Word is, one's inbound already. Should arrive within a few days to get you and General MacArthur back in the fight. Lieutenant James, too."

The idea of such a thing overwhelmed me at first. To wake up from this nightmare in a couple of days seemed impossible.

I finally said, "How much of this is scuttlebutt and how much the truth?"

"About half, I'd say. Sparks is mighty good at reading the tea leaves of radio chatter. Plus, our code books are pretty much up to date. But most of all, he's got great instincts. A man you never want to play poker with."

"Sounds like you have."

"Too many times."

"Hek know about this?"

Kennedy nodded. "He'll spill the beans to the general when he thinks the time is right."

"Why'd you spill them now to me?"

He shrugged. "You've got family back home worried about you. Be nice to see them again."

"So do you."

"Sir, I'm an unmarried, naval lieutenant. About as expendable a commodity as they come. But my men have families. And if it's all the same to you, I'll tell them what you said about General Patton foreclosing on Tokyo's mortgage. It'll give them hope."

"Do so. And I'll keep your good news about the submarine under this stupid straw hat."

"Perfect place, sir."

A half-hour later, Kalaupapa's landing dock slowly materialized out of the darkness. The ever-lightening sky promised another day soon to come. But Molokai's precipitous, thousand-foot-high cliffs to the east would block the sun's warming rays until later in the morning.

The shadows the cliffs would soon cast upon this small settlement were minor compared to the shadows of rejection and fear that had plagued this tiny, disease-riddled settlement ever since the Hawaiian government isolated folks from the rest of the population.

The disease itself has been with us long before the Bible times, when people first started writing about it. The word comes from "leprous," meaning "covered with scales," and it pretty much describes the condition of the skin when a mycobacterium called—not surprisingly—*leprae* attacks the unsuspecting victim.

There are slower deaths, I suppose, but death by leprosy is an especially slow and cruel one. The body literally crumbles away bit by bit; starved of nerve endings, the nose, fingers, toes fall away first. Then the respiratory system goes, then cardiac, and finally the patient stops breathing and joins the legions of sufferers that populate the heavens.

Whether or not their bodies are restored to their original pristine beauty is something for theologians to sort out. What I do know, is that their endless suffering on earth is finally over.

But none of the above did I know when PT-109 tied up to the dock to disembark her passengers. After a swift exchange of "thank-yous" to Lieutenant Kennedy and his crew, and a rather long-winded pronouncement from Mac about the "courage of men to go in harm's way," Hek bounded down the narrow boarding ramp, turned and held out his hand for Ava to follow suit. She did so, followed by General

MacArthur, who, even when wearing *samue*, looked like a full-fledged, bona-fide general. Then Tony, and finally me.

A neatly-stacked pile of fifty-gallon fuel drums flanked the back of the dock. Oddly-shaped wooden crates too. Here and there, small heads poked up to spy on us, their eyes bright with childlike curiosity. Just enough dawn light for me to glimpse a cluster low-roofed shacks spread out in fairly neat rows, a few small buildings that looked like they might be stores or meeting halls, and in the distance a white church steeple.

Her lines quickly cast off, engines burbling in reverse, PT-109 backed into the surf, wheeled around, and took off like a jackrabbit in search of shelter before enemy patrols showed up.

When I finally turned back from witnessing the departure of our rescuers, a small delegation stood waiting patiently before me. They had appeared out of nowhere it seemed—or perhaps had been hiding behind the barrels all along.

In any event, their impact was impressive: an older man wore a light green cape on his shoulders, a thick grass skirt, and around his swollen ankles, shark teeth bracelets. Beside him, two young girls, also wearing grass skirts, but of simpler construction, their arms filled with *leis*.

Towering over them all stood an American woman, wearing a slightly-tattered but neatly-laundered khaki uniform dress with the twin silver bars of a U.S. Navy lieutenant on her collar. Her eyes locked onto General Douglas MacArthur like sighting the Great White Whale. Up came her hand in a precise salute.

"Sir, Lieutenant Joan Robinson, United States Navy Nurse's Corps. Welcome to the leper colony of Molokai."

Mac returned the salute. Then Ava saluted Robinson a touch later, as the nurse outranked her.

Robinson turned to the man standing beside her and said, "E *'olu'olu.*"

The man smiled, took a deep breath, and the fact that he didn't have a nose seemed unimportant at that moment. Nor did it seem out of the ordinary that his right hand was more stump than fingers. What mattered was the tone of his voice; strong, confident, proud, as he rattled off a long commentary in his native tongue—a tongue blunted by the disease.

But Hek had no trouble translating the man's welcoming message. As the tribal elder, he thanked us for coming across the wide ocean to find safety in their humble home. What was theirs was ours. Whatever we wanted, we could have. The sky was the limit—in his glowing words at least, even though this tiny, forlorn settlement seemed to have barely enough to survive upon.

When he finished, he waved impatiently at the two girls who shyly stepped forward and held up their *lei*-filled arms to Robinson. She said, "Please allow me to complete the traditional welcome,"

She took a *lei* of orchids woven with *maile* leaves. "General MacArthur? *Aloha* to Molokai."

He hesitated a fraction and Robinson whispered with the speed of a machine gun. "Sir, you have nothing to fear. No contagion, perfectly safe, I'll explain the medical situation later, but for now, please bend down, you're awfully tall."

He did so, like a king accepting his crown. Ava next, then finally me. Hek and Tony stood to one side enjoying the action; clearly, they were more than just visitors here.

During the welcoming ceremony, I kept having the feeling of being watched. That tingly sensation on your scalp…. Must be an ancient reflex we've carried in our genes since the days of the caveman.

We were *not* alone.

But every time I looked out onto the village, nothing but motionless palms trees, smoke curling from a chimney, and here and there, stray dogs skulking about, looking for just the right spot to relieve themselves.

The morning light continued slowly building in strength. Still gloomy, though, because the high sea cliffs hid the sunrise. Somewhere up there curious eyes looked down on us. And not necessarily friendly.

Hek must have felt the same way. "Let's saddle up and ride, folks."

I looked around for horses, because they're the easiest way of getting around on the remote parts of the Hawaiian Islands. And Kalaupapa was remote with a capital "R."

But instead of whinnying horses, the surprising bark of an unmuffled truck engine broke the peaceful quiet. Not much of a ride, mind you, but the battered vehicle had enough room for Ava, Mac, Tony, and me to crouch knee-to-knee in the back beneath a raggedy canvas cover, while Hek rode up front with the driver.

The man behind the wheel steered with his left hand because that's the one with the most fingers. All that was left of his right hand was a thumb and a stump, but he shifted gears with practiced ease and chatted nonstop in Hawaiian as the truck bumped and thumped along the rough streets—more like pathways.

Tony sat back and smiled like he was flying on a *Pan Am* clipper. "Wait 'til you see our hideout, skipper. Puts Jesse James to shame."

"Whereabouts is it?"

"Keep your eye peeled for the only thing that rises above the plain."

We drove inland along the open land for about two miles. Nothing to see but those ever-present cliffs brooding over us in the distance. Cliffs that millions of years ago had led straight down to the sea, but now overlooked a small peninsula that housed a leper colony and guerilla fighters.

Kalaupapa was a volcanic "afterthought" to the original cataclysmic birth of the island. After the double eruptions of its east and west volcanos millions of years ago, things slowed down to a steady upwelling of molten lava that cooled and formed fertile land.

Only much later, did a smaller side vent burst up from the depths, and with it, bring enough lava to create this flat plain above the water. In time, vegetation found its way here, too, with low grass and scrub, as did migratory birds rest long enough to breed and then fly ever onward. Eventually Polynesian people found their way here, too.

The natives who first settled on Kalaupapa named the eruption crater *Kauhakō*. But once the leper colony came, the natives who had lived here hurriedly relocated "topside" of Molokai by wending their way up a torturous, three-mile switchback trail that climbs over sixteen hundred feet before reaching the top. From there, they fled the dread disease that has afflicted so many poor souls over the years.

We soon neared the gentle rise in the land that signaled the beginning swell of the *Kauhakō* crater. More vegetation too. An occasional orchard with regimented rows of fruit trees here and there – signs of ongoing civilization and practical examples of the leper village's industrious inhabitants. Plus, a sound I'd been hearing but not paying attention because I thought it was the unending surf.

Ava spotted it for what it actually was. She leaned out of the truck and shouted. "Waterfalls!

Clefts in the tall ridges of the sea cliffs spouted jets of water—not white, but reddish from the mineral-rich volcanic mud gathered in the gullies above and dislodged by the overnight rains. These temporary mini-rivers cascaded down the *pali* face and kicked up a vaporous spray that the rising sun behind the cliffs transformed into rainbows.

This breathtaking Garden of Eden splendor was old hat to Tony, who complained, "Should be running white by now."

As if on cue, one of the multiple water streams slowly shifted to pale pink, then brilliant white.

"There you go. That's more like it."

When we finally stopped at the crater's edge, Tony hopped out of the back of the truck and made a sweeping bow. "Home sweet home, folks. Follow me."

Hek was already scrambling down a trail that disappeared into thick underbrush. Soon there was nothing left but his booming voice rising up from the mysterious depths – "You heard the man. Breakfast is waiting."

The crater was almost four hundred feet above sea level, but our climb to it along the dusty road was so gentle that I didn't realize our height until I looked back along the plain where the distant leper colony's tiny huts and structures made their settlement appear even more forlorn and isolated.

The sound of hoofbeats.

A rising pall of red dust, and minutes later, Nurse Robinson appeared on horseback, galloping over a rise, her dark blue cape flying horizontal like Superman, while she sat firmly upon the saddle as if in a steeplechase.

She reined in, stopped, and dismounted in one graceful, fluid motion. Her face was flushed—not with fear—but more from the exhilaration of the ride.

"Forgot the sulfa," she said. "They ran out of it up here yesterday."

She looped the reins over a nearby scrub bush and breezed past us. "I'll show you the way—Tony, grab that package for me, will you?"

"Aye, aye, lieutenant."

"Don't drop it."

"No, ma'am."

"Like you did last time."

"Yes, ma'am."

Ava and I joined her as she peered over the edge of the crater. Four hundred feet below, the pink clouds of dawn reflected off the water of a small lake at the bottom, about two hundred feet in diameter.

Robinson explained, "Tribal legend says that the goddesses Pele and Hi'iaka dug this crater in search of fire. But when they found water, they flew away to the Big Island instead."

Ava said, "Like you flew here from Oahu."

Her face tightened slightly. "After what happened to the nurses and doctors, at Pearl, I was lucky to get out in time."

"Where are they now?"

She shrugged. "Hard to say. The Japs loaded them onto freighters and sailed away. Prison camps I figure, but some say labor camps, working in their factories."

"Like the Nazis."

"Or worse."

We stared in silence for a moment, then I thought of how thirsty I was.

"That fresh water down there?"

"Brackish. But all the rain we've been getting floats on the top layer and all sorts of little critters show up."

Ava, being who she is, cut to the chase of another script running in her head. "What's the sulfa do?"

"I'll explain as I go down. We're sticking out like sore thumbs up here. C'mon."

Saying no more, she wrapped her nurse's cape around her shoulders and set off down the switchback trail leading to the bottom of the crater. Along the way, she explained that the main reason it was safe for us to be here with the lepers on Kalaupapa was that ninety-five percent of human beings have a natural immunity to the crippling disease. You couldn't get it if you tried.

And thanks to recent advances in sulfonamide "miracle" drugs, the unfortunate five percent were now able to see their symptoms reduced, and in many cases actually reversed, if treatment was started early enough.

Did it bring back missing fingers? No. But for the first time in history, a "miracle medicine" was able to ease the pain, bring hope to those who had none, and provide a measure of prevention to those who were not naturally immune from being infected with the tuberculosis-like bacillus.

The shadows from the overhanging vegetation provided a perfect cover for our progress. Every fifty yards or so, Robinson would stop and whisper something in Hawaiian. What seconds before had been underbrush and scrub trees, suddenly blossomed with smiling and nodding guerilla fighters, both men and women, emerging from caves carved into the lava rock hillside.

She turned to Tony. "Make like Santa Claus, mister."

He dug into the parcel and hauled out handfuls of small cardboard boxes. The fighters grabbed at them like Crackerjacks. They broke out their canteens and gulped down the "prize" of sulfa drugs, manufactured thousands of miles away by swing-shift workers in the Parke-Davis plant in Detroit, Michigan.

Robinson sighed. "If Father Damien had had this medicine, the nightmare would have been long gone."

Ava said, "He must have prayed for this all the time."

"And wrapped bandages around rotting flesh while he did it—don't forget yours, Tony—then do the honors for our guests."

I gulped mine down. "What are those odds again?"

"Ninety-five percent will never contract the disease."

General MacArthur held the tiny orange tablet between his fingers, as if examining a pearl beyond price. "Here's to that five percent of which I may be a part—please pass the canteen."

By the time our caravan reached the small lake at the bottom, Hek was already holding court with a small band of guerillas outside one of the larger caves.

One man towered over the group like a scarecrow over a crop of summer corn. The grizzled, middle-aged man wore an odd combination of military issue gear, including a "steel pot" with the distinctive U.S. Marine Corps camouflage cover.

But he also sported shorts with cargo pockets and straw sandals that laced up and around his skinny calves. He looked like a malnourished Roman Centurion.

The man's early-warning "officer detection," system, born from years in the military, caused him to turn in our direction the moment we cleared the underbrush.

"Atten-HUT!" he bellowed, his voice a cross between a frog and a giant Komodo dragon—if such a creature could speak.

The other guerilla fighters instantly came to parade-ground-perfect attention, including Hek.

The centurion barked, "General MacArthur, SIR, Gunnery Sergeant Jeremiah James Lewis reports all present and accounted for, SIR!"

The guerillas stood like perfect tenpins, backs straight, salutes held, until Mac saluted back and said, "Stand at ease."

I noticed a man standing off to one side. Early 40s, medium height, skinny arms crossed over an equally skinny chest. Wearing only a swimsuit and wrapped in a raggedy blanket, he looked like something the cat dragged in—from the beach.

Even though the morning air was warm, he seemed to shiver as he stared at us with a kind of fierce attention, as if physically trying to restrain himself from talking.

Hek turned to Mac. "Sergeant Lewis was just briefing me on their mission."

MacArthur said to the Marine, "You're back early, aren't you?"

"Sir, when you hit the jackpot, it's best to cash in your chips and head home with the loot."

"Explain your colorful analogy, sergeant."

"Sir, I'd rather the professor, here, do that himself."

He nodded to the man the cat dragged in, who looked questioningly from Hek to Gunny.

Hek said, "Go ahead, doc, tell him what you told us."

The man frowned, shook his head, then said, "But who is this man? Can he be trusted?" He spoke English with a pronounced Italian accent.

Gunny laughed out loud. "Are you kidding me? This here's the commanding general of the United States of America's Army, Navy, and Marines."

Ava quipped, "Don't forget the Air Corps."

"Aye, aye, ma'am."

Mac drew himself up and smoothed the fabric of his *samue*. "Despite my appearance, I am indeed the person with whom you need to speak. I can assure you I can be trusted with whatever information you have to share with us—I assume you are *not* a medical doctor?"

"*Mai, mai.* Nuclear physics."

"Ah, yes." Mac didn't bat an eyelash. "I presumed as such, considering our adjacency to—" He turned to me. "What's the name of that infernal island, Colonel Carter?"

It took me a second, but then I remembered. "Kaho'olawe."

The professor lit up. "Unbelievable what is happening over there. And to think I was a willing part of it." He shook his head violently, as if trying to shake the memory loose. "No longer. *Mai piu!*"

Between Doctor-Professor Franco Rasetti (we finally learned his name) and "Gunny" Lewis, they unfolded the story of what was happening on the tiny, desolate island directly across from Maui that once held the promise of ranching and farming, but because of overgrazing and lumber cutting, combined with persistent drought conditions, had become a no-man's land.

Except for the Japanese, of course, who, according to Rasetti's operatic-like descriptions, were developing a nuclear weapon unlike anyone had ever seen before. One that would consign the current kiloton designs that America and Nazi Germany were working on to the wastebasket in favor of *megaton* yields.

He gripped his hands together to demonstrate. "Atomic bombs…they split atoms to *release* their binding energy. That kind of explosion goes like-a dis –

He yanked open his hands to demonstrate. "Boom."

"It is called atomic fission. But hydrogen *fusion* bombs work the opposite. Saburo Yamasaki—my *former* friend and colleague—developed a tritium trigger that does this instead."

He slowly brought his hands together and squeezed and squeezed. "The fission trigger pushes *in* on the fissile core with such force that it finally implodes, and… BOOM!"

He yanked his hands apart and swept his arms open as wide as he could. The blanket fell from his shoulders. "A thousand times more powerful. Ten thousand times. There is no limit."

How in hell did an Italian nuclear physicist end up on an island in the middle of the Pacific Ocean? Who *was* this guy? More importantly, how did he escape from Kaho'olawe? Mac's persistent questions about this and much more gained us a tidal wave of information not only from Rasetti, but also Gunny, and even Hek.

First of all, Professor Franco Rasetti was a *bona-fide* Italian university-trained nuclear scientist, whose peaceful pursuit of atomic physics got caught up in the fever of war and swept him along like a piece of flotsam on the sea. He bounced from Italian to German research facilities, until he finally found refuge with a Japanese nuclear physicist whose peaceful philosophy matched his.

Peaceful.

Got that?

At first, that is.

And seemingly for all times.

But the fortunes of war had their way, and Rasetti found himself teaming up with Yamasaki on a deserted Hawaiian island, his—formerly--pacifist fellow scientist, now in charge of overseeing the final touches on a thermonuclear weapon developed independently from any German influence.

According to Rasetti, the design was light-years in advance what the rest of the scientific community had conceived to date.

How the man managed to get off the island to tell us this fantastic tale was more a tribute to Hek's masterful use of guerilla tactics than by a mighty show of force.

The Japanese used conscripted locals to do the dirty work of maintaining their base of operation, from cooking, to laundry, to cleaning latrines. Fortunately, half the Hawaiians were Hek's guerilla fighters with their ears to the ground and noses poking everywhere, finding out as best they could the mysterious goings-on on that lonely island. They learned a lot and shared a lot, but Rasetti was the key. And how he managed to get off the island without raising suspicion was a simple one.

"They think I drowned," he said.

The Italian went swimming every evening before turning in. Did so, month after month, like clockwork. Routine, same old thing… in the water, then to bed. But last night, he hit the waves, while Gunny Lewis and his team of irregulars in a twin-hulled dugout canoe waited off shore, just north of the point where the bay begins.

According to the plan, Rasetti had left his belongings on the beach like he always did. But instead of striking straight out past the breakers, he swam north to the point, and there, just before midnight, deserted the land of the enemy and joined the other side.

Mac said, "They have this bomb now?"

"*Sì*, and soon they will have *two* of them. The second one, she arrived today from Tokyo."

A long pause.

Rasetti continued. "But not the kind of bomb you see drop from an airplane. Much too unfinished for that. But it is big enough to explode. And they are going to explode *both* of them very soon."

"Where?" Mac said.

He shrugged his shoulders. "It changes every day. California, Alaska, the Panama Canal. The navy admirals are like children with a new toy— except it is deadly."

At the mention of the possible targets, Mac and I exchanged a look that spoke volumes. This Rasetti guy was connecting the dots in a way we didn't want them connected. Especially when the dots could be targets for super-bombs.

Mac said, "What do they say about Panama?"

"The admirals, they want to destroy the locks at both ends. The blast and radiation would close the canal for years. Everything sent by boat would have to come around Cape Horn."

I said, "Ever heard of Professor Ernst Friedman?"

He smiled for the first time and looked years younger. "He and Enrico are—or I should say—were my colleagues, before... before all this."

I knew of Fermi from my connections with Professor Friedman. The Italian nuclear physicist was the famous nuclear pioneer who, after a disastrous attempt to get a controlled reaction with his "Chicago Pile One" in Chicago, finally managed to do so in Berkeley. and became—in the eyes of the American scientific community—the Leonardo da Vinci of nuclear physics.

The connection between Rasetti and Fermi was that they were fellow Italians and professional colleagues—at least at the beginning of Fermi's research into splitting the atom. According to Rasetti, Enrico Fermi was wholly committed to doing that and *only* that. What happened after it split was not his concern, morally, ethically, or politically. Rasetti was just the opposite.

He viewed the work essential, but treated it like "Pandora's Box." So, while Enrico went his apolitical, amoral way, Franco went his and cozied up to Saburo Yamasaki, who not only claimed to be sympathetic with the Italian's troubled conscience, but also had made top-secret progress in nuclear research that eclipsed both German and American research.

The Nazis, being deeply racist, had never treated the Japanese as their equals, politically, diplomatically, or socially. And because of this, they had no idea that the "Slant-Eyed Devils" had leapfrogged light-years ahead of them in nuclear weapons research and development. But Friedman had, and if Rasetti was to be believed, those suspicions were now inescapable facts.

Rasetti looked at us like we were a pack of doubting Thomas's. "Enrico wanted to break the chains, but Saburo and I...we wanted to make a new sun to power the world forever." He slapped his hands together. "And we *did* it."

Mac said, "So, why are you here instead of on that island?"

A long pause and his face grew somber. "Because the sun that Saburo and I created, the others now want to rain down its fire upon innocent people." He looked away, then back at us. "And so does Saburo."

A moment of silence as Rasetti's words took hold.

I finally said, "Why'd he change his mind?"

Rasetti shook his head. "*Chissà?* All I know is that his ancestors were *Samurai* warriors. Maybe the air he breathed on Kaho'olawe was so filled with war that his *Bushido* spirit came alive again. Whatever the reason, he is not the man I once knew."

Hek said, "We knew the Japs were working on some kind of super-weapon. But not this."

Mac said, "They must be stopped."

"Of course—except..."

Mac's frown deepened. "Except?"

"We're a guerilla force, sir, not a standing army. We strike when we can and disappear before they can strike back. This is a job for a special assault team. An army Ranger battalion, for instance."

Gunny growled, "Nothing wrong with good old United States marines."

"I agree with you both, gentlemen," Mac said. "But such forces are thousands of miles away and the clock is ticking. That being the inescapable case…" He swept his eyes over the ragtag group of fighters standing by the still-smoking fire. "I think this group of warriors will do splendidly in their stead."

Then he smiled. Which is about as rare as a solar eclipse. And the effect was just as remarkable. How an ordinary man wearing ratty, water-soaked *samue* could exert a nearly hypnotic force over a group of men and women was a mystery. But I confess, I found myself being just as smitten.

"We'll do this together!" Mac said.

Leaders are born, not made. MacArthur and Patton, Eisenhower and Bradley, Halsey and King, are men that history delivered at the just the right time and place—and in our case, at the bottom of an extinct volcanic crater on Kalaupapa—and set General Douglas MacArthur turning the gears of war in the direction of victory.

A distinct stirring of energy seemed to sweep through the group of guerillas. For a few minutes, the conversations multiplied into various groups speaking a wild mixture of Hawaiian, pidgin, and English. But one thing was in common; the eager look on their faces and the determined set of their shoulders. Here stood men and women with their minds clear with purpose and their hearts filled with the kind of joy that comes with commitment—not turning back—no matter what.

And all this without the slightest notion of a plan, mind you. Mac's confidence in them was the trigger that started a chain reaction similar to the one Professor Rasetti had just described, where the energy kept growing exponentially as more and more atoms kept splitting. In the case of Tokyo's devastating bombs, the chain reaction was intentionally designed to be uncontained and result in a cataclysmic explosion. But our chain reaction would be rigorously contained to achieve maximum effect with the minimum of loss.

The seeds of General MacArthur's plan for a guerilla assault on Kaho'olawe sprouted during a hastily gathered briefing. It took place in one of the deeper caves carved out of the volcanic rock. Oil lamps illuminated the walls and cast their yellowish light onto the incongruous sight of a blackboard attached to the wall.

We could have been in a schoolroom, providing you didn't look beyond the detailed chalk drawing of the enemy's base of operations on Kaho'olawe, not ten miles due west from the island of Maui. If you had, though, you'd have seen the crudely-hacked out space that long ago had sheltered leper colonists from a world that had cast them to the winds of fate with barely a backward glance except to shiver in revulsion. And you would think—as did I—"There but for the grace of God…"

The flow of information began with Gunny Lewis. Professor Rasetti chimed in when needed with particulars. Between the two of them, they described the basic layout of the enemy's research and testing base located on the eastern side of the island on the shores of in Kanaupu Bay.

Established within months of the Japanese possession of the Hawaiian Island chain, the base combined research with aggressive testing. According to Rasetti, Professor Yamasaki had quickly upgraded his unique tritium trigger to a proof-of-concept device that—tested underwater for secrecy reasons—performed flawlessly, delivering over three hundred kilotons of explosive energy while consuming the barest fraction of their available precious fissile-trigger material.

Rasetti continued. "I should have known by then that Saburo had deceived me all along, but the pursuit of science can blind you with its light."

Ava said, "Glad you saw the light of reason instead."

"*Si, signora.* Better late than never, because if his calculations are correct—and God forgive me, I corroborated them to be so—these two weapons are supposed to yield fifty *megatons* of TNT."

I said, "That's fifty *million* tons?"

"*Si, e veramente.* If one of them exploded by accident, it would destroy Kaho'olawe, Maui, and a good part of the Big Island in one blast."

The whole time we were talking, Mac was pondering the map. "How large is the device and where are they keeping it?"

"The one we just completed on the island weighs close to seven tons."

"*Tons?*" I said.

"*Si.* The other device from Tokyo weighs more because it has a heavier containment shell."

"That's over twenty-four thousand pounds. What's their delivery system, an ocean liner?"

Rasetti didn't smile, let alone laugh. "I said before that no ordinary plane could lift such a primitive device. But never underestimate the Japanese, for they have *un gigante* flying boat they say can lift both of them and do so with ease."

Tony and I exchanged a quick look, then said in unison, "*The Tokyo Express!*"

"I do not understand that expression."

Mac added "Nor do I."

It didn't take long for us to describe the two gargantuan-sized *Kawanishi* flying boats we saw fly past us that morning off the coast of Oahu – one bound for the Tokyo, but the other one, apparently carrying the second H-bomb to pair up with its twin on Kaho'olawe.

When we finished, Mac turned to Tony, "What kind of range does this aircraft has?"

"I'm only guessing, sir, but something that big has got to be at least ten thousand miles—maybe more."

"Dear God."

"Yes, sir, it can pretty damn well fly anywhere it pleases."

"And detonate weapons unlike the world has ever seen—at least according to what Professor Rasetti suggests."

The Italian frowned. "I do not, as you say, 'suggest.' I myself saw the underwater test explosion. The sea turned itself inside out."

We pondered that image in silence.

Ava finally said softly. "No plane, no bomb."

Mac smiled slightly. "My thinking precisely, lieutenant." He swung around to me. "What was your flying rank—in *Pan Am*, I mean?"

"Master of Ocean-Flying Boats, sir."

"How would you keep this one from doing just that?"

I didn't need to think too long. "Well, sir, Tony's right about the fuel it can carry. Plenty of it. I figure half in the wings and half in the fuselage—along the keel, most likely. Seems to me, if we could place explosives alongside the hull in the right place, we could send it up in flames."

"Sounds simple."

"Except…flying boats have bulkheads that guarantee buoyancy. We'd have to find out exactly where the fuel tanks are located, otherwise we'd just be poking holes that they could fix."

Mac leaned closer to the map and tapped the Kanaupu Bay area. Then he said to Hek, "What kind of explosive devices do you have on hand?"

"Not much, sir. Mostly hand grenades some mortar rounds."

"Not nearly enough blast force for what we need."

Gunny Lewis cleared his throat. "Begging the general's pardon, sir, but I know how we could blow up that big-ass bird—begging the lieutenant's pardon for my language, ma'am."

"No worries, Gunny, Hollywood could teach you jarheads a thing or two about swearing."

Relieved, Gunny sailed onward. "We could chain-gang a bunch of hand grenades onto a steel plate, then rig it to the gunwale of a dugout. We could float that beside the plane and set it off. When it blows, those steel plates would RAM the blast forward instead of going in all directions. It'd poke a mighty big hole in its side, not to mention sending up that fuel in a hell of a fireball too. Mission accomplished."

Mac mused, half to himself, "The Misznay-Shardin Effect. Out of the mouths of babes—Marines in this case."

"Sir?"

"A blast occurring upon a perpendicular surface multiplies itself exponentially."

"Sir?"

"Named after a Hungarian scientist who first devised it—unfortunately, he did it for the Nazis, not us. But the principle remains. Remarkable that you intuited this on your own, independent of outside influence."

Gunny grinned. "Ma always said I was handy with my hands."

"She was right in this case—those steel plates you described. You can find something like that?"

Gunny shrugged. "I can find any damn thing you want, sir. Plus, I've got an acetylene torch topside."

"Excellent."

A long beat of silence. Lots of bland stares. And puzzled frowns from the rest of us who weren't following their exchange. Gunny finally said, "Permission to draw what I'm thinking, sir?"

Mac nodded. "Share your plan."

In less than a minute, accompanied by enthusiastic descriptions, Gunny sketched a half-inch steel plate, eighteen-inches square, onto which were wired a cluster of ten Mark II fragmentation grenades. He even went to the trouble of drawing the small "pineapple" segments that would shatter into steel shards upon detonation.

Your average fragmentary grenade holds about two ounces of TNT, which delivers a considerable BANG to be sure if it goes off in a crowd of soldiers or in a machine gun nest. But against a plane as big as the Kawanishi? Like throwing BBs.

But Gunny's "reflective" design was ingenious. And who cared if it duplicated the "Misznay-Shardin Effect"? What were the Nazis going to do? Sue him from Budapest for patent infringement? Besides, the way he figured "chain-ganging" the grenades with a common loop of wire threaded through a series of eyelets and yanked at a safe distance was Marines field expediency all the way.

Tony Esposito watched with intense concentration the whole time Gunny worked at the blackboard. I could almost hear his engineer wheels turning. Gunny finished up with a drawing of an overhead view of a small dugout canoe tied up alongside, about midway down the Kawanishi.

"Great idea," Tony said. "But unless you set it off near the fuel tanks, you'll slow them down but never stop them cold."

Gunny frowned. "I ain't a mind reader."

"But the skipper is." Tony pointed to me. "What do you think? She ain't got sponsons like the Boeins. So, she's got to be carrying most of the juice in those big-ass box-girder wings of hers. Too high up to get at. But I figure the fuselage, too. Whereabouts you think?"

"I'd have to get close enough to see. The tanks will have fuel-filler ports. Once we spot them, we'll know for sure."

Gunny grinned. "Did somebody say 'recon mission?'"

Mac looked at me questioningly.

I shrugged and said, "Request permission to sort this out on-site, sir?"

Mac turned to Hek. "What's security like at their base?"

"Sir, when you rule half the Pacific and two thirds of Asia, you tend to get complacent."

"Even with our recent escape?"

"That's Oahu's problem, not Kaho'olawe's. These islands are separate nations, like the good old days before your missionaries came. Each one has its 'king commandant'—Kauai, Oahu, Molokai, Maui, the Big Island—Sergeant Lewis, you agree?"

"Affirmative. I've scouted Kaho'olawe with my team three times so far, and never once met any kind of guard perimeter that meant business. Sure, they've got the weapons and know how to use them. The Japs ain't stupid. But their commandant is more egghead than kickass, and his troopers have been stuck on that tiny, treeless island so long that they're going native—no offense, Hek."

"None taken. But the world would be a better place if we all went that way."

"I ain't saying there ain't no danger," Gunny continued, unfazed. "But let's just say Colonel Carter, here, and Tony will be able to get their recon job done in no time flat and return to base."

Ava looped her arm in mine, "Without getting his head blown off."

"Yes, ma'am—or anyone else's for that matter."

"Good, because I like having this fella' around, even though he outranks me."

"Yes, ma'am, he's one lucky man."

Mac stood up. His knees cracked like faraway popcorn. "I'm getting too old for hiding out in caves."

Everyone smiled but wisely said nothing. He shook hands with Professor Rasetti.

"Thank you for risking your life to bring us this critical information. The free world salutes you, as do I."

Up went Mac's hand in a somber salute.

Rasetti bowed slightly. "Pandora's Box. You know the story, general?"

"Indeed. When she opened it, untold evil escaped to rule the world."

"*Si, e vero.* But did you also know that one item remained at the bottom of that box?"

Rasetti waited in silence for an answer that nobody had—except him.

"Hope."

The guerilla hideout was a complex system of interconnecting caves dug into the sloping sides of the Kauhakō crater. Ava and I took possession of one of the smaller ones a bit higher on the slope, while Mac chose one closer to the action near the lake below.

From our vantage point looking down on them, I could smell the cooking fires going, while Nurse Robinson wove in and out of the overhanging foliage making her rounds with the sulfa drugs.

I said to Ava, "That woman's a regular Florence Nightingale."

"A tough cookie if there ever was one."

"She can't weigh more than a hundred pounds dripping wet."

"It's not the muscle that makes her mighty—hold still, darling, this stuff goes on like frozen butter."

Ava brandished a thick camouflage stick and proceeded to rub it diagonally across my face. She was right, it took a lot of elbow grease to get the sticky stuff on my cheeks and forehead. Time was of the essence. Gunny's recon mission was that very night. But unless I got a couple hours sleep, I'd fall over from exhaustion. I was running on fumes. Ava couldn't have been far behind. Even so, she worked with diligence.

"Stop yawning," she said.

"Sorry—didn't know you could do this camo thing."

"They taught us in O.C.S—a place you never went to, flyboy."

"Got a direct commission, baby."

"Hold STILL, colonel. I still have the brown to go."

When Ava finished her green, black, and brown camouflage handiwork on my face and hands she frowned. "Wally Westmore, I'm not, but I think you'll blend in with the others—promise to be careful."

"Don't you worry about—"

She gripped my wrist. Gone was her wise guy look. In its place, wifely concern. "Why the hell can't I come with you?"

"Not enough room in the PT boat."

"That thing can carry fifty!"

"I meant Gunny's dugout later. Ten folks, including me. That's what we're using for the final leg of the mission."

"Not fair."

"Nothing is in war."

She made a face and stood up. "Did you write that line? It's awful."

I held her by the shoulders. "Listen up, I'll talk to Mac. When the time comes to for us to blow up that plane, I'll make sure you lend a hand."

"Promise?"

"Scouts honor."

"I'm not a woman who knits by the fire and waits for the man of the house to come home."

"No kidding."

"Not that there's anything wrong with that. I mean—"

Sometimes the best way to have a difficult discussion with Ava is to kiss her. So I did. And she's right, I'm a lousy screenwriter. Better action than words, every time.

Dinner was the ever-present *poi*. Ours was "two fingers" meaning that's how many you needed to scoop it up, twirl it once or twice until it took hold, then slurped it down.

Plus, we had raw fish salad called *Poke*. Sort of like *seviche*, but packing a bigger wallop with spices added to chunks of tuna and octopus. To go along with it, we had *limu kohu*, shredded seaweed sprinkled with crushed and roasted *kukui* nuts mixed with sea salt.

Not exactly steak and baked potato, but tasty nonetheless.

As I sat there eating, I continued to be amazed at how calm and relaxed the guerillas seemed to be. I expected them to be like the ones I'd seen in the "war movies" that Hollywood was cranking out at a furious rate; desperados clenching knives in their teeth and leaping into raging battles.

But those were stuntmen in backlots who went home at night to their families and friends. These freedom fighters before me were the real deal – cast adrift from their everyday lives and committed to warfare against an unforgiving enemy. But forget knives in their teeth, they lounged around the campfire as relaxed as the rich American tourists I used to see sprawled out on Waikiki Beach, baking in the sun.

We even had ukulele music that came from somewhere in the shadows. Good ukulele music. So good that groups of fighters would sway in time to the tune now and then. Some would hum, while others sang softly in melodic, vowel-drenched, Hawaiian.

I was still learning how to make that little hiccup of a pause when I said "Kaho'olawe." Not easy. Modern English is packed to the brim with brick-hard consonants, whereas Hawaiian is more like Swiss cheese, full of unexpected "ahs" and "ees" and "ohs."

A big "OH" escaped my mouth when two Japanese soldiers marched into the crowd. One carried a Type 99 *Arisaka* short rifle and the other some kind of ammo case.

I scrambled to my feet, ready for anything. But their grim faces broke into broad grins as the crowd of twenty or so men and women guerillas laughed and applauded.

Hek, all smiles, said. "The bad guys bring dessert."

One of the Japanese soldiers popped open the ammo case, reached inside and pulled out a red cellophane ball about the size of a large walnut. He tipped back his helmet, smiled and whispered, *"Daifuku!*

The crowd "oohed" and "ahh'd."

He marched over to Ava, bowed, and held it out to her. "You eat, please.'

Ava has always been the braver of the two of us when it comes to food. Without hesitation she took the treat, bowed in return, then unwrapped it to reveal a small, pillow-soft ball of dough dusted with confectioners' sugar. One bite, and her face lit up like Christmas morning.

She showed me what was inside. "A strawberry!"

Thank-you bows, big smiles, and gales of laughter as the Japanese soldier scurried from guerilla to guerilla, dispensing the sweet treats like the ice cream man, including me and Hek, who did all the explaining, while I devoured the chewy, gooey, Japanese dessert treat called *mochi*. In this case, a fresh strawberry covered in a sweet, red bean paste, then wrapped in dough made from cooked and mashed-together rice.

Hek pointed out the two soldiers and said between mouthfuls, "Those are the Kagusaki brothers. They used to run a bakery in Oahu before the war. Had to close up shop when Tojo came to town. Lucky for us, they're *Nisei* to the core. Took to the hills and joined the fight."

"Where'd they get the Jap uniforms?"

Hek gave me a meaningful look. "Where do you *think*?"

One of the brothers was on the chubby side, the other slender and austere. Looked to be in their mid-thirties. Hard to tell. Soldiers dressed for war tend to hide the man inside.

Hek continued, "They've got all kinds of outfits – officers, NCOs, enlisted—whatever we need, they supply. Tonight, they're wearing what they wore for the recon mission over on Kaho'olawe."

"They've been over there before?"

"Plenty of times."

"But—"

"These two guys are masters of deception. They're like these…." He held up a *Daifuku*. "What you see on the outside…." He bit into it to reveal the lush red shape of the strawberry. "Is not what's on the inside."

"They have families?"

He nodded. "Everyone does. They're scattered over the islands like migratory birds. Kauai, Maui, the Big Island… one of these days they'll all come home again."

"And you'll be their king—like that *kahuna* lady said?"

He smiled. "Kalola gets some wild ideas."

"True?"

Hek said nothing as he unwrapped another *Daifuku* and popped it into his mouth. Whole.

Hours later, we rode our canoe out through the waves to meet our PT "taxi" that would take us to Maui, sixty miles away. From there we'd continue on to Kaho'olawe.

Our slender craft was a more modern design than the traditional dugouts carved from *koa* trees. Its hull was made from thin planks lapstraked like clapboard on a house. The design was a carryover from the missionary days in the nineteenth century, when the saintly New England missionaries brought the white man's Jesus to the Hawaiian shores.

And while they were busy converting the natives with one hand, they used the other to spread communicative diseases like smallpox that decimated the population. Add to that, whaling ships that brought new boat-building ideas, but also stir-crazy, drunken sailors who rambled the streets while on leave.

Progress always comes at a price. In the case of Hek and his ancestors, the white man's pineapple plantations and cane sugar farms buried their Polynesian cultural heritage for good.

Ten of those natives, along with Gunny and me, sat like peas in a pod, hunched over, lost in our thoughts, while four rowers easily cleared the last of the waves breaking on the graveled beach of Kalaupapa.

Sixty miles away on Maui, a twin-hulled outrigger canoe waited for us in the PT boats' secret hideout. Because time was of the essence, and travel by day was fatal, Kaho'olawe was only seven short miles from Maui—an easy paddle to accomplish a not-so-easy task.

Our "Maui taxi" the familiar, low-slung menacing shape of PT-109 soon cleared the point and hove into view. Its "speedboat" shape deceived the eye at first. Your average Chris Craft runabout is sixteen or seventeen feet long. These menacing Elco beauties were eighty-footers. And the closer she got, the bigger she became, until she towered over us, a grey-green, triple-screw, high-horsepower engine of war.

Whereas the original Elco boats had relatively clean foredecks, PT-109's "field modification" gun placements of twenty and thirty-millimeter bow-mounted cannons trebled her firepower.

The menacing noses of her four torpedoes protruded about three feet from their launch tubes like Moray Eels ready to dart from their lairs. I remembered Lieutenant Kennedy telling me that the warheads carried almost five hundred pounds of TNT.

I tapped Gunny on the shoulder. "Be nice to put one of those babies into that plane's belly."

Before he could answer, the boarding scramble began. In less than thirty seconds, our recon team was safely on board and clustered around the bridge.

The Kalaupapa launch swung away, Kennedy signaled Lieutenant Thom, his XO, who opened the throttles wide. Pappy's pampered engines, until now a burbling mumble, cleared their throats and delivered almost five thousand horses to the three bronze propellers that would drive us to Maui in a little over an hour.

But less than a half-hour later, our on-again, off-again S-Band radar picked up a surface target. By now, Kennedy had the helm, while Thom pressed his eyes to the rubber eyepiece of the radar screen. Because I stood next to him, he leaned back and grinned.

"It's the milkman again, sir. Take a look."

I gazed at the yellowish-green screen with a vertical line that swept back and forth in an arc like a windshield wiper. How did any of this make sense?

"Check out your two o'clock, sir."

A faint, greenish dot glowed, then died, then glowed again when brushed by the 4GHz microwave as it pulsed out from the radar unit enclosed in a dome perched on top of a sturdy tripod mast directly behind Kennedy.

Thom described the target "dot" as a tubby Japanese Navy Auxiliary Patrol Boat chugging along with all the confidence of a milkman making his morning deliveries. Once upon a time, these beat-up boats had been fishing trawlers. But with a coat of grey paint, a navy crew, some deck guns and depth charges, they had become "auxiliary craft" not unlike the boats America was using to take up the slack during war shortages.

The deck of PT-109 leaned slightly to starboard as Kennedy angled us away from the enemy.

"He knows you're here?"

"Yes, sir, and vice-versa. But as long as nobody starts a shooting match, we leave well enough alone. They protect their own and we protect ours."

"You're kidding me."

"Scouts honor—but it took them losing three boats before they realized that we'd blow them out of the water if they messed with us. Now it's a Mexican standoff."

"Between Americans and Japanese."

Thom laughed. But just as he did so, his face lit up from a distant burst of gunfire off the port bow.

"What the hell's he doing?" Kennedy said.

Glowing orange blobs of enemy twenty-millimeter tracers missed us by a scant few feet.

Kennedy said, "Somebody didn't get the memo. Hang on!"

I lost my balance as he spun the helm *toward* the enemy. The PT's triple rudders shoved us into a slewing, sliding turn.

"Commence firing!" Kennedy bellowed.

Lots of shouting going on, but his voice cut through like a scalpel. Pappy's engines screamed full throttle as Kennedy drove the boat straight down the throat of the enemy, while jinking and juking at random intervals to throw off their fire, which seemed to be increasing.

Thom shouted to me, "Lend me a hand with the ammo!"

He dashed up and out of the small compartment and I followed. By now, both deck guns were returning fire. The ex-P-39's thirty-seven millimeter cannon made a SLAMMING sound as its rounds pumped out across the water. The twenty-millimeter, by contrast, made a CHATTERING sound as it imitated its larger brother.

Thom joined the "water brigade" of sailors handing over magazines for both guns. I could barely lift the *Airacobra's* barrel-shaped one, but the beefy sailor who took it from me grabbed it like it was empty.

The gunfire noise was deafening but didn't last long.

Whatever had caused the calm and collected, dreary old "milkman" decide to go full "*BANZAI*" on us remained a mystery—maybe a new skipper who was out for blood, or a drunken one out for dreams of glory. What *wasn't* a mystery was the way our heavier firepower soon found the trawler's ammo magazine and depth charges, and up they went in a deafening explosion of streaming tracers, cooking off and arcing chunks of burning metal.

Within seconds, our quiet night on the Pacific Ocean became a macabre Fourth of July that you couldn't help but watch in dazzled amazement. The trawler's keel broke cleanly in two from the force of the exploding depth charges. The last I saw of the spluttering, burning hulk before we swung away and resumed our course for Maui were her sailors leaping into the water that, fortunately for them, was not filled with burning fuel.

Lieutenant Thom and I joined the crew in gathering up the rolling, tumbling, empty brass cartridges before they went over the side. Many were still warm from firing.

"Waste not, want not," Thom said. "We'll reload them back at the base."

"You can do that?"

"When you're on your own, sir, you can damn well do anything."

I surrendered my canvas sack jampacked with thirty-seven-millimeter casings to a waiting sailor, who grabbed the load of heavy brass like it was cotton candy.

Thom whistled a tune as he scooped up shell after shell.

"Why do you figure he did it?" I said. "Come after us, I mean. After what you said..."

"Every once in a while, you get a *Bushido* warrior-type who finds himself stuck in a dead-end job. He follows orders like a good *samurai* for a while, but sooner or later he goes native."

"You figure that's what happened tonight?"

"Seen it plenty of times. Odds are if he didn't go down with the ship, he'll make sure of it by ripping open his belly, *seppuku*-style. Stupid bastards."

He spat, then laughed and wiped his face. "Just broke rule one while on a United States Navy vessel. 'Don't ever spit into the wind."

I've never had motion sickness a day in my life, but when I went below to grab some water, I lost my horizon reference and fell victim for about ten queasy minutes. I think the reason was because of the boat's rising and falling motion when we encountered the cross currents of Lahaina Roads, the southern passage between Molokai and Maui.

Fortunately, when I returned topside, Hek spotted my dilemma and found a mysteriously magical spot on my palm at base of my middle finger and pressed down like he was drilling for oil.

"That help?" he said.

"Hurts like hell."

"Still feel like puking?"

"Feel like punching you to make you stop."

"Give me five more seconds."

I gave him ten, and when he relaxed his grip on my hand, I felt a chill run through my body.

"Got the shakes?" he said.

"Affirmative."

"Means it's working."

The man was right. My nausea beat a fast retreat.

Hek rose to a crouch and leaned forward, staring intently at the ocean.

"Something wrong?" I said.

Gunny, who had witnessed "Doctor Hek" at work on my hand, laughed. "Hek's sniffing the trail, is all."

The Hawaiian said over his shoulder, "I am looking for the *'ale kuloko*, which will tell me we are nearing Maui."

"You don't trust the Navy charts?"

"I trust my ancestors more."

"Show me."

"You must not puke."

"Promise."

"Come with me."

We left Gunny and crouched down at the bow of the boat. Other than a few scudding clouds, the moonless sky held an explosion of stars.

I said, "You navigate by the stars, don't you? Just like us."

"By water too—look to your right, see those approaching waves?"

"Affirmative."

"Watch the swells just ahead of them. Bigger or the same?"

"Look the same to me."

"Exactly. Now notice the ones behind."

"Identical. So?"

"So, when they begin to *kupu*, or grow, as they approach, it means the waters are hitting Maui and reflecting back the *'ale kuloko* swells."

"You can tell this going almost fifty-miles-an-hour?"

"When I navigate the waters of *moana*, I look with my eyes and feel with my heart."

"Makes no sense."

"... said the missionary to the savage."

Hek left to check on his men. Shortly thereafter, Gunny joined me on the foredeck where the gun crews remained at battle stations. The darkness muted the bright colors of their outlandish Hawaiian shirts and cutoff shorts. One of the sailors wore a stained and crumpled white cowboy hat. "Because we're the good guys," he had told me earlier.

I regarded the ragtag but deadly-efficient young men. "I feel like I'm on a pirate ship."

Gunny chuckled. "Aye, aye, sir."

"These guys as good as jarheads?"

"Better—but don't tell them I said that."

"I promise."

"Wait until you see their hideout. It's something else."

"That where we're picking up the war canoe?"

"Affirmative. They've rigged up a twin-hull job that'll get us over there and back in no time. And wait until you see what they've rigged up amidships for you, and me, and Tony."

"What about the others?"

"My guys, you mean?"

"Yes."

"They'll be in our escort canoes, in case something goes haywire."

"Never happen."

Gunny grinned. "Oo-rah."

I bet you every postcard you've ever seen of an idyllic white sand beach with palm trees, flowers, happy hula girls, and "Wish you were here!" sentiments was taken on Maui. None of the above was visible tonight, of course, as we slipped down its western coastline past Maalaea, Kihei, and Wailea-Makena toward Makena Cove, the PT squadron's secret base of operations.

The cove itself wasn't a bit out of the ordinary – a small promontory protected its inner waters from heavy wave action, which made our final approach smooth sailing——a far cry from the earlier heaving up and down in the open ocean when we passed through Lahaina Roads.

What followed next, came as a total surprise. We didn't turn into the cove like I thought we would. Instead, we continued an additional hundred yards or so, and then swung into a much smaller cove lined with overhanging trees. Tiny by comparison with the larger cove and utterly unremarkable, we drew closer and closer to shore. I thought for sure we were going to run aground at any second.

A sailor crouched on the bow, Aldis light in hand, blue lens in place. He flashed a complex series of dots and dashes.

Two answering dashes from the shore.

Seconds later, the leaves on a tall stand of trees shivered. Odd, because the wind was practically zero. Then, a slender strip of darkness appeared between two of the trees and began to widen as the tree trunks seemed to *move*.

As they did, it became clear that they had no upper branches. They were fake trunks. Seconds ago, they had blended into the grove without notice. Now they had become gateways to the darkness beyond, into which we sailed past the trees, and then deeper into a lava tube cave similar to the one on Oahu. Only this one had been formed at water level.

Once inside, the burbling exhaust of our PT boat echoed and re-echoed off the curved, volcanic rock-ribbed ceiling. My eyes quickly adjusted to the flickering, wall-mounted torches that delivered yellowish, smoky light. The cave had wooden walkways on both sides, upon which stood sailors here and there, dressed like they were on their way to a *luau*. They waved their 'hello's'' and shouted back and forth with our pirate-like, freewheeling crew.

As we swung to starboard, the cave widened dramatically. Another PT boat was tied up directly ahead of us. Its crew was busy refueling by hand-pumping fifty-gallon barrels of gasoline through hoses. They barely paused to look up and wave.

Just another day at war in the South Pacific.

Lieutenant Kennedy stood beside Hek and me on the flying bridge while Thom smoothly guided the boat to its landing dock. Although the young commanding officer chatted with me in a relaxed manner, not for an instant did he take his eyes off the proceedings. His ship might be only eighty-feet long, but by God, every foot was *his*.

I know the feeling.

After years of climbing the long ladder to full command, I'd captained many a *Pan Am* plane and felt exactly the same way. When you're the boss, there's nobody to turn to but yourself. Sure, others work with you and for you, and the success of your command depends on your skill in building a team that depends on implicit trust of each other. But in the end, *you're* the boss. And sink or swim, fly or crash, life goes on...or ends because of your decisions.

Hek's guerilla team tumbled off the boat, chattering and joking like they were on a school outing. Gunny herded them along the dock like an impatient schoolmarm. Further down, the cannibalized remains of another PT boat from the original squadron. Kennedy explained they used it for parts.

Then he pointed to the roof of volcanic rock that towered over us, lost in shadows. "The men call this place, 'Skull Island.'"

"As in *King Kong?*"

"Yes sir, minus the big monkey, of course."

Hek stopped my laughter by adding, "Back in the olden times they did human sacrifices here. That's what the *kahunas* say."

Kennedy grinned. "I'd like to start that up again with the Japs."

"How'd you ever find this place?" I said.

I learned that the local underground had offered them the sheltered cave as a refuge when the Japanese first occupied the islands. Was it a great secret? Kennedy doubted it. But then he gave a good reason why Tokyo steered clear of Skull Island.

"These islands are full of active volcanoes," he said. "Rule one is that if you get too close to the hot stuff, you'll suffer the consequences. The guerillas and us are equally red-hot. The Japanese lost a lot of soldiers that way in the beginning—Hek and Gunny's guys in the mountains, our PT boats peppering them with torpedoes at sea. Now they know better. Not for nothing are we called 'Mosquito Boats.' By and large they leave us alone. But if they come after these mosquitoes they turn into yellow jackets."

"But what about that picket boat we blasted to kingdom come? Won't they come after you for that?"

He hesitated because lines were being tossed onto shore to tie up the boat. He gave a few sharp orders to coordinate things. Once they started snugging up properly, he continued.

"That joker we sunk was nowhere near his picket line. The Jap Navy doesn't like lone wolves any more than we do. Mr. *Samurai* paid the price and Tokyo knows it—or they soon will when his boat's reported missing."

"Hell of a way to run a war."

"Welcome to the South Pacific, sir." He pulled out a leather case. "Cigars, gentlemen?"

Hek and I both accepted one. Smelled like they cost a lot.

Kennedy caught smile of appreciation. "My dad gets these from Cuba."

"How do *you* get them?"

"By sub." He turned and shouted, "Now hear this; the smoking lamp is lit!"

The ritual of getting tobacco up and running took a bit of time, but that's part of the pleasure offered by cigars. Compared to that, cigarettes are a waste of time and lung power.

Once we were puffing like a trio of steam engines, Kennedy continued monitoring the orderly progression of his crew rigging the boat for shore, while simultaneously replenishing the depleted ammunition and food stores.

Pappy flustered and fussed around the engine room hatch. Then he dove below, only to pop up now and then like a prairie dog and shout for a certain tool or a specific kind of wrench.

I said, "Nothing like a man and his machine."

"Pappy's got triplets," Kennedy said.

By now, my eyes had adjusted enough to the torch-lit gloom to notice another lava tube tunnel to my right that branched off from the main tunnel. Dimly lit from deep inside, elongated human shadows flickered eerily upon the walls of the chamber. Creepy.

I tried to be clever. "Preparing for a human sacrifice over there?"

Hek puffed a bit on his stogie. "Hell no, sir, that's our ride."

Valor grows by daring, fear by holding back
Publius Sirus, Roman Senator

W e followed Hek off the PT boat, single file, onto the rickety wooden dock, then over to the side lava tube. The closer we got, the larger the shadows loomed inside that mysterious opening. Tens of thousands of years ago, molten lava had gushed up from the earth's belly. Something else was about to do the same.

Just as we arrived at the cave, a twin-hulled Hawaiian war canoe slowly emerged, guided by a team of native workers. Painted flat black, its elegantly curved bows swept upward. By the time it fully revealed itself, I estimated it to be at least forty-feet long, with a single mainmast and a slender, thatch-roofed platform spanning the space between the two hulls. No fanciful decorations to appease the gods, no colorful paintings, just a flat- black killer canoe, top to bottom, specifically designed for the life-or-death business of war.

Hek smiled as he pointed to the tightly-furled sail. "Black sail to match. *Kahuna* Anakoni loves theater."

"Who's he?"

"Great-grandson of one of Oahu's finest canoe builders, way back when."

From deep inside the tunnel, a man's high-pitched voice shouted something in Hawaiian.

"The only thing Anakoni hates more than a badly-built canoe are the Japanese who ruined his business and killed his brother. Speaking of the *kahuna*, here the master himself."

I expected a tyrannical old man to come hobbling out wearing a grass skirt and a shell necklace. Instead, a man in his mid-thirties emerged wearing a spotless-white Panama suit, white shirt, and red silk bowtie. His polished, two-toned wingtip shoes and gold-rimmed, round eyeglasses gleamed in the torchlight as he came to a halt.

Hek said, "Looking sharp, brah."

Anakoni ignored him at first, fully occupied with making sure his workers properly tied up the canoe to the dock. Everybody seemed to know exactly what to do, but their *kahuna* made sure of it with sharp, precise commands. His high tenor voice cut like a scalpel through the humid air of the cave.

Just as his workers finished mooring the sleek double canoe, more action came from inside the cave as four smaller, single hull outriggers glided out under their own power, each paddled by a man sitting in the back. Painted flat black as well, the sight of them elicited appreciative whistles and cheers from the Gunny's guerillas gathered on the dock.

Anakoni waved to the waiting fighters and hollered, *"E'e!"*

Like a single organism, the guerillas reached for broad bladed, tulip-petal shaped, wooden paddles from a neatly-stacked pile. Then, with Gunny acting as the traffic cop, he hustled the fighters into their assigned places in the small canoes, five to a boat, four to paddle, one as paddler/steersman.

Hek nudged me. "Anakoni's navy."

"Seems a bit much for just a recon mission."

"Not if we get jumped. That's what the smaller canoes are for – sort of like destroyers to our battleship."

Hek explained that he, Tony, Gunny and I would ride in the double war canoe, while the guerillas acted as an armed escort for the brief, ten-mile journey across the straights from Maui to Kaho'olawe.

Hek called out, "Gunny, got a second?"

Gunnery Sergeant Lewis detached himself from his guerilla gang and strode over. On his way, he passed Anakoni and saluted him smartly. The meticulously-dressed young man merely nodded in return.

Hek turned to Anakoni, "Okay if we have a briefing, braddah? Colonel Carter here, he needs to *hele on.*"

Anakoni ignored him and gave a final set of brisk orders to his men, then turned and faced me expectantly.

Hek introduced me to him. His grip was as hard as his stare, but with a twinkle in it to confuse things. He gave me the once-over, then smiled and said, "That's interesting face camouflage you're wearing, colonel."

"My wife got carried away."

"Hear she's an army officer? That true?"

"Affirmative."

"But you outrank her."

"Want to bet?"

Gunny butted in. "Hey, the colonel's makeup ain't no more than mine."

Hek smiled and shook his head. "You *Haoles*. White skin like cocoanut meat. Not like me and my good brah, here. We're brown like the husk."

He nudged Anakoni good naturedly. "Did you know that two years ago, my friend, here, was canoe-surfing with Bing Crosby and Bob Hope on Waikiki. Right, brah?"

Anakoni shook his head. "'Beachboy Hale' worked the *On the Road* movie gig, not me."

"But you handled the ladies. Dorothy Lamour? Ginger Rogers…"

"Among others—colonel, the wind's picking up. How are you in rough seas?"

"How rough?"

"Hard to say. My guess is not too bad, but smooth as glass it is not."

"You coming with us?"

A slight smile. "I have other plans. But Sergeant Lewis knows the way like the back of his hand, right, Gunny?"

"My home away from home."

Anakoni stepped lightly onto the hull of the war canoe. "Check out what's waiting for you." He balanced himself and then reached out and patted the thatched palms covering a long narrow compartment mounted between the hulls.

"In the old days, a Hawaiian chief would travel in this, his *hale lanana*. Sheltered from the sun, wind, and rain, his paddlers would take him from place to place while he reclined in comfort and regarded his kingdom."

"Those were the days, bra," Hek said.

"You four men will sit here during the crossing. But not on a throne."

He heaved upward, and the roof flipped open like a Zippo lighter on a clever set of hinges to reveal the sleek outline of a slender canoe about fifteen feet in length nestled inside.

He turned and smiled. "Your needle in a haystack."

Hek whistled. "She's a beauty. What's her freeboard?"

"Barely." Anakoni ran his hand along the smoothly-polished surface. "But if you sit right, nobody will see anything but four heads."

"Five, counting mine," Tony said as he joined us, all smiles, like a kid with a new bike. "That's not a Hawaiian rig, brah. Where the hell did you find it?"

"Friend of mine on the Big Island loaned it to me. It's a Tahitian racing canoe."

"You do get around, my friend."

He shrugged.

Tony added, "He know you painted it black?"

"Not yet."

We climbed on board to examine the sleek-looking, needle-sharp, pencil-thin canoe in more detail. Anakoni pointed out our narrow seats. The paddles were narrower than the broad-bladed Hawaiian ones. Designed for calm waters, we wouldn't disembark in this fragile-looking craft until Anakoni's much larger war canoe gained the leeward shelter of Kanapou Bay.

I admired how they'd cleverly stowed the *Ama*, the outrigger float, alongside the racing hull, next to the two *Iakus*, outrigger poles, that would hold the float in place and provide counterbalance to prevent our capsizing. Anakoni explained they would rig them onto the canoe just before we disembarked.

Tony said, "Ever paddle a canoe, skipper?"

"Sure," I lied. "But it's been a while."

"That's okay, I'll dust off the cobwebs on the way over."

The whole time we were talking, the noise level in the tunnel kept rising – a combination of men's voices, CLANGING of steel on steel, the occasional whistle, a laugh here, a shout there, all of it blending into a kind of rising tide of expectancy.

I could feel it in my chest as my breathing grew shallower and my rate-of-respiration increased. Knowing this was happening was the easy part. Trying to calm down wasn't.

How many times had I faced a "jump-off" point in my life? Turning base to final and lining up on an ice-choked runway with snow pounding my windscreen. Or scrambling into that Japanese seaplane with Ava and Mac to escape from the *I-401* Super Sub.

A compass has three hundred-sixty degrees of possible headings. Life's the same way – it encircles you from all angles and presents situations that demand that, sooner or later, sink or swim, now or never, you have to "jump off" and let life take you where you want to go. Me? I wanted to go to Kaho'olawe and feast my eyes on that big mother of a flying boat and figure out how to send her to the bottom, mission *un*-accomplished.

Anakoni checked his watch and frowned. "Jap picket boat's due in half an hour. I suggest that you—"

Hek said, "May I do the honors?"

"Be my guest."

He straightened up, cupped his hands and bellowed, *"E, e"*

I counted eighteen paddlers running toward us before the echo died out. Wearing only loincloths and carrying their one-piece paddles, our muscular motive power hopped into the twin canoes and took their places like powerful peas in a pod. Approaching at a much slower pace came the helmsman – an older man sporting a hat woven from palm fronds and dotted with small flowers.

Anakoni caught me staring and said, "My uncle's cousin's brother."

"Glad he's on our side."

"Me too."

The man touched his straw hat in salute, and then took his place in the stern of the starboard hull. He THUMPED the side of the canoe. The others THUMPED in answer.

"Lele mākou i ka moana?"

They shouted back, *"MAKOU!"*

Anakoni said, "He says, 'Do we fly over the ocean?' They answer, 'yes'"

"Time to go, I guess," I said.

Anakoni touched my arm. "Hek says you are a famous pilot?"

"Not famous. But I do know thing or two about airplanes. Especially flying boats."

"You saw this plane they have?"

I nodded.

"We must stop it."

"That's why we're here." I stuck out my hand. He observed it for a moment, then took it. Cool, dry, just like the man.

I said, "Hek told me about your brother. I'm sorry."

"Me too. He took five of them with him before he died."

"He fought with the guerillas?"

"From the very first. Captured during a raid, betrayed by a coward."

I looked around at the cave filled with PT boats and war canoes. "You're a guerilla too."

"Of course I am. " He touched his bowtie. "Better dressed, is all."

A shrill whistle. The helmsman shouted at me.

Anakoni said, *"Maika'i maika'i"*

"Which means?"

"Good hunting."

The PT boat crews barely looked up as "Anakoni's Navy" departed the secret base. For good reason. They had their hands full trying to keep their two boats shipshape, while being stranded thousands of miles from home. That said, Lieutenant Kennedy, his arms filled with a stack of twenty-millimeter ammo magazines, grinned and shouted Anakoni's "good hunting" wish to us as we passed them on the way out. Pappy stuck his head out of the engine room hatch and whistled.

We waved back.

Brave men come in all shapes and sizes. So do cowards. You never know which one you are until danger shows up.

You can *think* all you want, *plan* all you want, *train* all you want about how to act when the shit hits the fan. But when it *really* does—like that picket boat lobbing live ammunition at us—the world as you once knew it vanishes, adrenaline takes over, and you'll do one of three things: take decisive action, freeze like a deer in the headlights, or run like a jackrabbit. I'd seen all three happen with people, not only when the Nazis forced America to be neutral but also now when she was finally at war.

The guerilla fighters dug their paddles into the still waters, Ahead of us, the smaller, one-hulled outrigger escorts glided past the two "trees" that formed the gateway to the PT boats' secret base. We were next.

Once cleared, they magically slid back to hide the sailors and canoe-builders from prying enemy eyes. Would be interesting as hell to see how they rigged up the mechanism to pull off this theatrical effect. Necessity is the mother of invention, but in Hawaii, it's the queen.

Felt odd to be sitting inside a canoe that was on top of *another* canoe. But that was the plan, and in lieu of a better one, I shifted my weight on the narrow seat. Not exactly an easy chair, that's for sure. I turned to Hek who sat behind me. He'd be the steersman when we took to the water.

"Where are the paddles for this thing?" I said.

"Reach down by the keel."

I pulled up a slender, blade-shaped paddle. Not at all like the heavier, tulip-shaped ones the guerillas were using to drive us toward the approaching waves.

"Not much to them," I said.

"Used for racing, not sailing—hold on here we go."

Tony, Gunny, and I white-knuckled the gunwales as the twin-hulled canoe SLAMMED into the first set of waves breaking along this stretch of Maui's rocky volcanic shoreline.

The smaller, single-hulled "escort" canoes slid up and over the waves like an elegant afterthought. Not us, though. We pounded *through* them, our steersman shouting at the paddlers like a harried housewife. The paddlers, in turn, dug deeper and deeper to raise the twin bows up and over the curling combers.

The broad, spatulate-shaped, wooden-carved *Manu* on the bows were designed to part the waves like parting your hair. True to form, they neatly split the thrusting force of the water into two separate, less powerful parts and sent it back to the sea instead of inside the boat.

Then suddenly, we were past the problem and into more peaceful waters. Maui and her towering mountains merged into a velvet-black mass against the star-studded, but moonless sky. Seeing all my familiar constellations beaming down upon me comforted my soul. Their steadfast position in the sky kept me from getting seasick.

Hek said, "Here we go. Watch this."

"*E holo nei,*" the helmsman called out.

Four paddlers leapt up from their seats and freed the lines holding the mainsail wrapped tightly around a boom snugged up against the mast.

"Watch your heads, gents," Hek cautioned. "This thing's got a pretty long foot."

Two of the guerillas, each holding a line, scampered like monkeys to a point near the stern and took up position on either side of the helmsman. At a word from him, they yanked hard. The boom swung down from the mast like a jackknife blade and unfurled a pitch-black, triangular shaped sail, its point facing downward. Its graceful shape scooped up the wind, and the canoe yawed immediately. No surprise there, considering we didn't have a keel.

The helmsman quickly counteracted this by digging his paddle deep into the water to serve as a rudder. He shouted to the paddlers to shift their stroke to a different rhythm. One of them began chanting and the others joined in. Almost a song, but not quite, as they plunged their heavy *Koa* wood paddles into the waters over and over again. Not only were they adding speed to our canoe as we sailed to windward, but their combined force reduced our lee drift by at least forty-five degrees. Not bad for a round-bottom twin hull canoe without a keel!

I said as much to Hek whose smile lit up the night like the missing moon. "We know *moana* and the stars like you know your fancy maps and sextants."

"Even better, I'll bet."

He raised his eyebrows and dialed up his smile.

The desolate island of Kaho'olawe lay ten miles to the southwest. Our specific destination was Kanapou Bay, located at the island's fishhook-shaped southernmost tip. Tucked into the curve of that hook was the research and assembly station, where Professor Rasetti back on Molokai had described the enemy's furious activities to ready their "*bomba horribile*," as he described it.

Make that two of the damned *bombas*.

Plus a plane to carry them five thousand miles across the Pacific and drop them on opposite ends of the Panama Canal, then mosey on back to Tokyo and be smothered in a cherry blossom parade. All on *one* tank of gas. A ten thousand-mile round trip! I couldn't conceive of such a feat.

But my failure of imagination didn't stop the Japanese from not only dreaming up such a behemoth flying boat, but building one too—or three or four—or God knows how many. My mouth went dry at the thought.

While I pondered such grave matters, Gunny stretched out in our racing canoe, arms behind his back, staring up at the stars, the very picture of relaxation.

I leaned forward. "You know this plane is a beast, right?"

"Yes, sir. But you and Tony know where its Achilles Heel is, right?"

"We will after tonight."

He reached around and pulled out his Marine-issue Ka-Bar knife and brushed his thumb across its razor-sharp edge. "The way I figure it, colonel. The bigger they are the harder they fall."

Tony joined in the chorus. "Skipper, with all those turboprop and turbojet engines, the cross-feed piping inside that bird must look like a plate of spaghetti."

Gunny stabbed at an imaginary enemy in the sky. "You find out where plate is, and my bombs will blow it to kingdom come."

"How do you set them off?" Tony said. "You don't look like the *kamikaze* type."

"Got me a fifty-yard reel of Army phone wire. We'll rig it, so the pineapple pins are already pulled, and the release levers held down with a secondary wire. One good yank and five seconds later, *Aloha 'oe.*"

I said, "You ever test this?"

"Once is all we could afford."

"And?"

A long pause. Gunny and Hek exchanged a quick look.

"It pretty much worked," Gunny said.

"What's 'pretty much' mean?"

Hek interrupted my inquisition by shouting, "Here we go!"

The helmsman THUMPED the hull three times in quick succession, paused, then two more times. On the final thump, the paddlers slowed their stroking rhythm.

"Heads up," Hek said.

The sail boom swung over us and the canoe heeled to port as we took up a different course. While Hek and the helmsman spoke in Hawaiian, the older man held his right hand to the sky and opened his thumb. Hek did the same. More Hawaiian back and forth.

Then Hek said something.

The helmsman laughed, then made a fist and shook it. More thumping on the hull and the stroke rhythm changed again. The water hissing along the hull grew louder. I figured we were going at least ten knots, if not more so. At this rate we'd be there within the hour; 0200 by my watch.

I said to Hek, "What was that all about?"

"Comparing notes about where we are," Hek said. "He was right, I was wrong—as usual."

"Hawaiians can navigate without instruments, but damned if I know how."

"Piece of cake, colonel. Open your hand. Palm facing out, fingers together, thumb straight out—like you're going to shake hands."

"Like so?"

"Perfect. Now place the tip of your thumb on the horizon and your index finger beside the north star. Got it?"

"Got it."

"What's the height in angle-degrees, horizon to the star? Figure the width of your little finger is ten degrees. Count it out."

I did my best to hold my hand steady against the rise and fall of the boat, but it wasn't easy. "How the hell do you do this?"

"Practice."

I managed a quick degree count. "Twenty degrees?"

"Close. Hawaii's twenty-one degrees latitude."

"I'd need to check my Weems tables."

He looked blank.

"Name of a guy who wrote *the* book on navigation. Pilots use it all the time. But if memory serves, twenty-one degrees is about right."

"I guarantee you it's right, just like it was right three thousand years ago when my ancestors took the high road for Hawaii—minus your fancy Mister Weems."

I looked at my palm. "With just this?"

Hek smiled tapped his head. "And plenty of this."

A little more than an hour later, within a mile of our destination, our 'escort" fleet of canoes peeled off. Comforting thought to know that the guerilla fighters were heavily armed and would come to our aid if the Japs discovered us.

But, according to Gunny, the base had an almost non-existent guard setup. No surprise there, considering the island was thousands of miles away from the states. As far as Tokyo was concerned, America was still taking baby steps toward waging war – building planes, tanks, and ships but not fully engaged just yet.

Admiral Yamamoto had cautioned his fellow war lords that bombing Pearl Harbor would "awaken the sleeping giant." And that had happened, for sure. Any wonder the Japanese wanted to act like *Jack and the Beanstalk* – steal the gold from the giant, race down the vine, and then blow it up with an H-bomb before the big guy ground their bones to make his bread.

I didn't feel much like a giant at the moment, though, as Hek and I carefully slid the featherlight racing canoe free from its mounting brackets and lowered it into the water. Three of the war canoe paddlers lashed the fore and aft outrigger poles, to the canoe's gunnels, while Hek and another paddler attached the outrigger float. Tony and Gunny climbed in first, with Gunny taking up position in the bow. I followed, then Hek, who would act as the paddler/steersman.

By comparison, the war canoe loomed beside our wisp of an outrigger canoe like a battleship – sail furled to minimize detection. When we were fully rigged, the elderly helmsmen gently tapped the hull – the signal for the paddlers to back full-astern, rotate their canoe away from the beach, and retreat to a rendezvous spot to await our return.

Hek said, "This is as far as he can go. Lots of shoals from here on out."

"But the plane's tied up there."

Gunny said, "They dynamited a channel for it—ready Hek?"

"Full speed ahead," he whispered.

Both men dug their streamlined paddles into the wave-less water. A good thing we had set off in the more wind-sheltered area of the bay, because our freeboard was just a few inches above the water. Our javelin-like Tahitian racing canoe wouldn't last thirty seconds in the open ocean.

"What can Tony and I do?" I said.

Hek said, "Grab those gourds and start bailing."

He was right, because seconds later an errant wave broke over the gunwale. Tony and I began the tedious, repetitious, but essential work of getting rid of an ocean that was determined to join us inside the canoe.

While we bailed and Hek and Gunny paddled, the Hawaiian prince-to-be said between strokes, "Protect us *Hine-ke-ka*... guide us true... keep your sacred waters... close to you."

Gunny said, "Goddess or god?"

"Goddess."

"Of what?"

"Canoe bailers."

"Love your Hawaiian ladies. Think maybe I'll settle down here after the war."

"Need to win it first."

"Affirmative your last, oh mighty prince."

"Button your lip, Gunny, and dig in."

We seemed to fly over the calm waters. If anyone was watching from shore, we'd be nearly invisible, so close were we to the water. Without a moon—thank God—our black hull and face camouflage melted us into the mystery of the ocean at night.

I risked an occasional glimpse at the shoreline but could only see a dark, featureless mass that blocked out the otherwise dazzling display of stars that filled the sky all the way down to the knife-sharp horizon. Because the seas were remarkably calm (some Hawaiian god in charge of reconnaissance missions was at work, maybe) the waters reflected the stars in a mirror-like display, thus doubling their visual effect.

If the baling hadn't fully occupied me, I could have stared forever at the immensity of the universe giving a hint of its incalculable size to four desperately-focused men in a slender canoe, racing across the sea toward the unknown.

I paused my bailing for a moment, held up my palm and spread out my thumb the way Hek had taught me. Within seconds I found Arcturus, the brightest star in the Boötes constellation.

"Which one you find" Hek said.

I told him, and he chuckled. "What's Mister Weems say about that one?"

"Not much. Just lists it as a quadrant referent."

"After the war, maybe I'll translate his book into Hawaiian. What you think about that, brah?"

"Need to win it first."

He laughed. So did Gunny. But not too loud. We were getting close.

The immense black shape of the *Kawanishi* HX-3 flying boat merged effortlessly with Kaho'olawe's equally black sea cliffs towering behind it. Instead of moored to a pier, they'd anchored the massive aircraft to a buoy about forty yards from shore. Not surprising, considering its tremendous wingspan that overhung the beach itself. What little illumination there was came from a string of lights strung along a wooden loading ramp stretching from the beach all the way out to the plane.

I tried to picture the drawing of the research and assembly base that Gunny and the Italian scientist had shown us back on Molokai. Nestled deep at the bottom of *Kaukamaka* gulch, the facility was protected from attack on all sides except the sea. Conversely, its remote location also protected its supply base on the south side of the island from any "accidents" that might happen during bomb assembly. This particular "fireworks factory" meant business.

A sprinkling of lights further up in the gulch. Two rows of small structures—probably barracks—and three long, narrow warehouses that fanned out from a common center like spokes on a wheel—minus the wheel. At this hour, not much going on inside any of them. But from what Rasetti said, they were flat-out hustling to get the bombs ready, so caution was in order, regardless.

Not a sign of life from the *Kawanishi*. It floated motionless upon the water like Moby Dick, its multi-ton mass far greater than the small wavelets passing beneath its keel.

"Which side?" Hek said.

"Starboard," Tony said. "Away from the beach."

"Makes sense."

Hek and Gunny expertly paddled without making a sound. For an old-time jarhead, Gunny was pulling his weight as good as any native Hawaiian.

I whispered to Hek, "Where's our escort fleet?"

He waved vaguely to his right, "Closer to shore than we are. If anything happens, they'll cover our escape."

His words gave me courage. It's great to fly solo. We all have to do it to get started in life. But after that, it's best to be part of a team if things get risky. In our case, we had Hawaiian guerilla fighters who'd rather slit your throat than shake your hand—providing you were the enemy.

Tony turned on his Army-issue flashlight and played its faint dot of light over the fuselage of the approaching plane. Our search for the fuel intakes began.

I don't know if you've ever walked the length of an entire football field, and then walked another hundred feet, and then ten more for good measure. That's how long the Kawanishi's fuselage was. Tonight, we didn't have to traverse its entire four hundred-foot-plus length, but the mere idea that something this huge could take to the air was astonishing.

Yet here she was – like some dark green, gigantic-winged, prehistoric beast that had begun its life as a curving pencil line on a piece of paper by a Japanese aircraft design engineer who said, "Why not?" A line that later added twelve pylon-mounted turboprop engines stacked along the top of the wing—six to a side—to keep the air intakes clear of water spray. Same with her turbojet engines too.

We drew closer still. The flying boat's slab-sided fuselage rose up like an aluminum wall as we slowly traversed the area directly beneath the wing root. The fuel inlets had to be here somewhere. There's no way they could gas up this behemoth by scampering along the top of her wings and pumping it into her tanks.

"Back, back, BINGO!" Tony hissed.

The light circled round and round a constellation of circular filler caps that could only be our target. But the constellation was spread out over a twenty-foot span.

"She's one thirsty girl," Tony said.

I pictured Gunny's measly-sized, multiple hand grenade "bomb." No way in hell was that thing going to have any major effect on this ocean-liner of an airplane. Not a dozen of them for that matter. Like poking her with an icepick.

I tapped Gunny on the shoulder and whispered, "You thinking what I'm thinking?"

"Yes, sir, but maybe we could double or triple them up."

"Negative. You'd mess up some of the piping, but that's about it. Their flight engineers would re-route it in no time—right Tony?"

"Affirmative, skipper. They'll have backup plans for their backup plans. Time for us to make some lemonade out of these lemons."

Gunny slumped slightly. "Hell and damnation. Never thought it'd be this big."

"Welcome to the future," I said. "Got a plan B?"

"Not yet, sir."

"*Yameru!*"

The hoarse shout came from behind us. A boarding hatch was open about mid-way down the fuselage. Yellowish light from within reflected upon the water. A helmeted silhouette stood there holding a rifle. Its bayonet gleamed in the light.

Message clear.

"Hands up, fellas," Hek said.

We did so.

The soldier motioned us to paddle closer. He emphasized his command by aiming his rifle at us. A bayonet-tipped weapon is a great aid in overcoming language barriers. One with a chambered round in its breech is even better.

Hek and Gunny paddled the dugout closer to the hatch that, as we got closer, turned out to be some kind of king-size cargo hatch. No surprise there. Everything about this aircraft was on a scale I'd never seen before.

The dim outline of a second soldier standing in the shadows behind our captor, his rifle pointed at us, too. Things were not looking up.

Like I said before, the Japanese language is an odd bird. When a native speaker gets steamed-up, whether it be anger, joy, rage, or ecstasy, his vocabulary fails miserably to keep up with the passion at hand. In lieu of English, which has a treasure trove of possible words to convey feeling, the Japanese just shout.

A lot.

And from the way this enemy soldier was bellowing at us, we had no trouble understanding that he wanted us to get the hell out of our racing canoe, climb into the flying boat, and surrender as his prisoners so that he could deal with as he so desired.

And in the process, likely gain a promotion for his courageous action of stopping the *gaijin* "Round Eyes" from whatever nefarious activity they were up to. No longer would he be a lowly corporal. Maybe sergeant. Maybe even an officer!

With all of this racing through his one-track mind and words to that effect roaring out of his mouth, the poor guy had no time to consider the possibility of a bullet passing through his chest, fired from behind by his fellow soldier.

The report was sharp and distinct. As was the way our captor looked at us, then looked into eternity before dropping to his knees and collapsing on the deck.

The other soldier stepped forward into the light.

"Brah!" Hek said.

The short, chubby Kagusaki bakery brother bowed slightly, then straightened up. His face a round moon of pleasure. "Happy to be of service, gentlemen."

Gunny said, "Jesus, how the hell did you get over here so fast?"

"Caught a shore leave boat from Kihei, back on Maui."

Hek said, "Where's your brother?"

"Day duty. As far as they know, he's a regimental spy from Oahu. Got them eating out of his hand—what do you think? About this plane. Can you guys do it?"

A long pause. Finally, Gunny said, "This thing's got me whipped."

The Kagusaki brother looked around the cavernous interior. "They say it can carry nine hundred troops."

"Or two bombs," I said.

His eyes lit up. "Got a minute?"

Hek pondered. "Be quick."

"Tie up your boat and follow me—wait, do me a favor first. Dump that bastard's body, will you? Use this."

He dragged a sandbag toward us. "I found a pile of these in the back."

I found some line and handed it to Kagusaki. He took a few turns around the dead soldier's ankles. Satisfied with the knots, he sat back on his heels and patted the soldier's leg. "Wrong time, wrong place, pal."

I could hear MacArthur's voice in my head. I fumbled inside the young man's uniform jacket until I found his identity tag – an oval brass disc, and yanked it free. My own dog tags were stamped with my name, service number, blood type and religious preference. The *kanji* lettering stamped onto tags his proclaimed this man to be who he was by name and by number, too. We both were numbers in somebody's game.

I said, "Drop his tags someplace, where they'll find them."

Kagusaki gave me a "look."

"That's an order."

"You're not my superior officer, and besides that guy's the enemy."

"Do it for his family. So they'll know."

I held them out again. His frown softened, but not by much. Even so, he took them.

"I'll figure out something."

Nothing worse than the weight of a dead body. I swear, when people die something heavier replaces their elusive spirit. Whatever the hell that is, it's heavier than that indefinable "something" that flies away to the stars.

Tony and I dragged the soldier's body to the edge of the deck, while Hek hefted the heavy sandbag like a briefcase and followed.

Hek peered into the darkness. "Water's too shallow and too clear. We'll have to take him along with us."

Gunny said, "Are you kidding? He'll swamp the canoe."

"Not that far, just clear of the shoreline. Get in and we'll hand him down."

Gunny grumbled but hopped into the canoe.

We manhandled him the corpse. He wrestled it, arms flopping, legs askew, athwart the gunnels and lashed it secure.

Kagusaki said, "Step on it, fellas. Guard change in less than an hour."

"What about the dead guy?" I said.

"I'll just shrug my shoulders and say, 'I think he's probably sleeping somewhere.' By the time they finish searching this huge thing top to bottom, they'll be exhausted."

"How the hell do you and your brother get away with all this?"

His innocent face grew sly. For a nanosecond the jovial, chubby persona vanished. His voice hardened. "Not every Japanese soldier and scientist you see on this island is an enemy."

"You mean—"

"I mean, colonel, you need to stop asking questions and follow me. This thing's unbelievable."

He marched into the darkness. We followed him aft along the lower deck of what had two be a two-decker flying boat, minimum, probably three. No lights save for dim, overhead illumination that must be drawing juice from D.C. power run out from the shore to the mooring buoy. That's how *Pan Am* did it in Manila when we couldn't tie up at the docks.

I played the bright beam of Tony's flashlight over the fuselage interior. Unlike the cushioned and padded insides of *Pan Am's* luxurious Clippers, every stringer, bulkhead, wiring bundle and rivet of the *Kawanishi* was clearly visible—and accessible to the crew if something went wrong. A lot like the innards of the *I-401* super-sub that Mac, Ava and I were held captives on a year ago. That immense tube of steel could submerge, this aluminum skyscraper could fly.

For an instant, all thoughts of war vanished. All concerns about what we were doing here, of facing high peril and imminent disaster if the enemy found us, faded into the background of a higher passion that swept over me like a sunrise at 10.000 feet – all I wanted to do was walk the other way and climb however many flights of stairs, ladders or whatever it took, and feast my eyes on what must be a flight deck of epic proportions.

And in particular, the *left* seat. Because, to a pilot, no matter the function, no matter the mission, the ultimate objective of being in an airplane is putting your hands on the controls and lifting it up in the air and you along with it.

Instead, we kept walking… and walking… and walking… the opposite direction toward whatever it was Kagusaki was so eager to show us.

We passed a fully-equipped galley with stoves, refrigerators, cabinets and work tables arranged so that you could move past them without interfering with the culinary labors taking place. Considering the astonishing range of this aircraft, they had relief crews that ate around the clock.

"The size of this girl," Tony said, "I feel like that guy Jonah in the whale."

Hek laughed. "You *Haole* missionaries are all alike."

"I'm an atheist, brother and don't you forget it."

I said to Kagusaki, "Where is everybody?"

"Sacked out in the barracks on shore. The *sake* flowed in abundance to celebrate their arrival with the atomic twin."

"Twin?"

"Right this way, gentlemen."

Two more compartments, a set of stairs, and finally to a hatch that he undogged and swung open to gain entry into the tail section of the flying boat.

I expected a narrow, confined space where all the component parts of the airplane begin converging into the bracing structures that support the vertical and horizontal stabilizers. Instead, it felt like we were entering a basketball arena-sized space. Yes, you could see the interlacing girders high overhead that cross-braced the supports needed to stabilize the plane's towering twin tail in flight, but that's not what captured your attention.

What was sitting on the deck did the trick.

At first glance, it resembled a gigantic, ten-foot high steel egg smothered with silver spaghetti. But upon closer observation the "spaghetti" turned out to be a combination of electrical wiring, hydraulic lines, and frost-covered piping leading from a bewildering array of outlet ports that connected to inlet ports that led, in turn, to rectangular-shaped junction boxes. And on and on, leaving only about thirty percent of the dark-green ball visible.

I reached out and touched it, almost thinking the damn thing should be warm, considering all the wiring and piping involved. But cold as ice. Even colder.

Tony whispered, "Boom, you're dead."

Kagusaki laughed. "You're half right. The other one will go back here."

He pointed to an open area about ten yards beyond where we stood. By my guess on how far we'd come, we were approximately aligned with the "step" of the hull – that notched part of a seaplane's fuselage that allows the hull to break the surface tension of the water during takeoff run and rise into the air.

I confirmed this by playing my flashlight onto massive hinges that lined both sides of the fuselage. Must be some sort of rear cargo door that swiveled up, clamshell like, to facilitate rapid loading, and unloading of men and material.

And hydrogen bombs.

But how could that wire-covered blob be considered a weapon of war? Like Frankenstein's brain without the body. What more did they have to do with it to make it go "Boom" like Tony said? A lot, by my estimate. But then again, what the hell did I know about something like this?

Kagusaki said, "Word is, they're forty-eight hours from loading the other one."

"Scuttlebutt or true?" Gunny said.

His moon-round face widened in a grin. "The top brass is acting like everything's right on schedule, but that's officers for you. Ask the troops and they roll their eyes. The scientists don't even do that. They just look like this…" His features took on a frantic stare. "They were in here until midnight working on this one. I thought for sure they'd never leave."

"Times up," Hek said. "We've got to rendezvous with the canoe. Got everything you need here, colonel? Tony, you all set?"

Tony and I exchanged a meaningful stare. Then I said, "I say no dice with Plan A."

"Affirmative, skipper, you'll need to punch a hole in this thing as big as a bus—make that a steam locomotive to have any effect. Got any of those back at the base, Gunny?"

The old Marine spat. "How the hell did I know this thing was so big?"

"You didn't," Tony said. "That's why God invented recons."

"Plan B, where are you?" I said.

Gunny didn't say anything, but I knew his gears were turning. So were Tony's. Mine kept stripping.

We made our way back to the loading hatch where we first climbed in. So much had happened in so little time. Instead of finalizing a way to send this plane to kingdom come, we were back at the starting point.

As we got ready to leave, I blurted, "Give me two minutes, will you? Just two. Want to see the cockpit layout."

Hek laughed. "Planning on flying us back to Molokai, colonel?"

"Not a chance. Just want a quick look at what makes her tick."

With the clock ticking too, I took off like a sprinter along the lower deck. Enough overhead lighting for me to navigate around neatly-stacked barrels and crates of God knows what they'd brought in from Tokyo along with the bomb. And who knows what else was on the upper deck? No time to find out, that's for sure.

I stopped at a ladder and aimed my flashlight upward to see how high it went. As I did, pounding footsteps behind me – Tony, huffing and puffing.

"C'mon, skipper, let's check out this big-ass girl together."

Before I could answer, he scrambled up the ladder ahead of me. "All roads lead to Rome!"

I followed suit. And just before I reached the open hatchway through which Tony had disappeared, I regarded the *Kawanishi's* vast interior. Like standing inside a cathedral, complete with flying buttress-like side girders that held the mega-flying boat together.

How in God's name could they have built such a thing? Correction— you can build anything you want if you've got the materials. But for something this huge to take to the air and efficiently lift thousands of tons of cargo, not to mention equally heavy amounts of fuel and fly for thousands of miles nonstop, you needed two things; genius aeronautical designers and engineers who weren't afraid to dream, and had enough engine power to defy gravity and lift their creation above the clouds.

"Getting closer!" Tony's faraway voice called out.

I followed him down an ever-narrowing passageway, which meant we were nearing the business end of this giantess. One more ladder, shorter this time. I could feel my excitement growing.

Yes, excitement.

Yes, I know we were at war, and yes, violent death waited for us at every turn, and yes, the sooner we got off this ocean liner the sooner we would improve our chances of surviving.

But…

What I beheld as I finally entered the cockpit defied anything I'd ever seen in all my years of flying. And no surprise, because there'd never been anything like this before in the history of aviation. *Pan Am's* Boeing 314 had been the biggest flying boat anyone had ever seen. But it's hundred fifty-foot wingspan and hundred fifty-two-foot length? Peanuts. Three of them could fit inside the *Kawanishi.*

And the cockpit!

Tony said, "*Madonna mia!*"

He wasn't kidding. The Boeing 314s were the darlings of newsreel cameramen who loved filming the vast expanse of the first-class real estate we had inside that aircraft, plus plenty of room for the pilot, co-pilot, navigator, engineer, and radio operator, with room to walk around and stretch out legs

But the Boeing was an outhouse, a shanty, a pup tent, compared to the *Kawanishi's* flight deck, where you could put together a quick game of soccer for all the room you had. I'm exaggerating but you get my drift.

Tony and I glanced at the engineering station that had positions for *three* crewmembers.

"Three!" Tony echoed. "Are you kidding me?"

"Look at all the bells and whistles, my friend."

Twelve conventional, red-knobbed throttles and four yellow and black, zebra-striped knobs, motionless in their respective quadrants.

"I'm guessing the striped ones are for the turbojets," Tony said. "And these are the prop jobs… one…two… three… and just LOOK at the fuel-flow dials. I was right, skipper, this thing is cross-fed like nobody's business. Those input lines down at the waterline are like a zillion train tracks at Grand Central Station."

His right hand brushed over the throttles while left hand "tagged" the controls like a conductor would before giving the orchestra the downbeat. He had that glazed look in his eye – the kind that comes when you get lost inside an idea. I had to nudge him. Hard.

"Clock's ticking let's get a move on."

"Yeah, yeah."

The pilot station was elevated on a raised platform above the engineering, navigation, and radio operating stations. A quick scramble up the access ladder brought me in direct contact with my original objective – the pilot's control yoke.

There was the familiar, half-wheel shape, mounted on a column, rotated slightly to the left and lashed to a restraint buckle to prevent aileron and elevator movement. Something I'd done thousands of times on hundreds of planes.

Mysterious, indecipherable Japanese *kanji* lettering filled the instrument panel placards. But the instruments themselves were like old friends with easily recognizable functions – turn-and-bank indicator, artificial horizon, airspeed indicator, rate-of-climb indicator…not that many engine performance instruments, however, like manifold pressure, oil pressure, and tachometers. But no surprise there. They were located down at the flight engineer's station, where Tony stood hypnotized, his hands caressing the toggles and controls like a blind person figuring out Braille.

I couldn't help but do the same by familiarizing myself with the buttons, switches, levers, and dials, as if I were going to fly it. I wasn't, of course, but that's what pilots do. They can't help themselves.

The man captaining an airplane of this size was more than a guy shoving a stick back and forth. He was more like an orchestra conductor, his control wheel the baton, with key players to make beautiful music – the flight engineers, radio operators, navigator, relief pilots, and aerial gunners to follow his lead.

The co-pilot's seat was to my right, and two jump seats behind us, plus a short walkway aft to what looked like a gun turret on the rear portion of the highly unconventional canopy. This plane bristled with defensive firepower – dorsal, ventral, and tail cannons, and maybe in the belly somehow, too. Although I couldn't imagine such a thing and still maintaining watertight integrity. But hey, some mighty talented aeronautical engineers created this whale of a flying boat. Anything was possible because they hadn't stuck to convention.

For example, instead of the expected stepped-window canopy design used on multi-engine aircraft—both bombers and transports alike—the *Kawanishi* had a tear drop-shaped canopy that stretched at least twenty-five feet along the *top* of the fuselage. Sort of like fighter planes with their bubble-like canopies, only this multi-paned version—like everything else on the plane—was big as a greenhouse.

For sure, the aviators had a much better view of the engines from up here, but her faraway nose kept on going for an additional fifty feet, thus blocking a lot of the world immediately in front of your line-of-sight. Aviation design is one compromise after another. In this case, a great top view in exchange for lousy forward view that could hamper your depth perception when judging your height-above-water before flaring for landing.

Tony, standing below, said, "I count five dorsal turrets including the one breathing down your neck. *Five!*"

"She's lot of plane."

"And a lot of folks to fly her—what's your guess on the crew?"

"Thirty, depending on relief and gunners."

"Madonna mia!"

Time was up. We had to abandon our enemy candy store and hustle back to Hek. I barely had a chance to register anything more about the plane except it felt like running through a warehouse instead of an airplane. I finally stopped thinking about it because my mind couldn't comprehend the immensity of the experience.

Hek's angry face helped me focus on our present, perilous situation. He was already in the racing canoe. The sight of the soldier's dead body draped over the gunwales honed my focus razor-sharp.

"Jesus Christ, where the hell have you *been?*" Hek said.

Tony, still out of breath from our running, said, "Climbing Mount Everest."

I described what we'd seen as we hopped down into the canoe. But Hek only half-heard, so intent was he on freeing the line that held us fast to the plane.

Kagusaki knelt by the hatch, calmly observing our activity. "Guard changes soon, fellas."

Hek snapped, "If you don't stop your nagging, I'm never going into your bakery again."

"And if you don't blow up this plane, they're won't *be* a bakery."

I said to Kagusaki, "Promise you'll do the right thing with this guy's dog tags?"

He half-saluted. "Scout's honor, colonel—here, don't forget these." He handed down the dead soldier's rifle and helmet. "Drop those about ten meters from here. They'll think he drowned and the tide pulled his body out. Dump him beyond the shoals. The sharks will make short work of him. They love *sushi.*"

False dawn brought a glow to the otherwise pitch-black sky as we shoved off. The added weight of the soldier's dead body slowed our progress. But after we committed him to the deep—and to the hungry sharks—we seemed to fly through the water toward the war canoe waiting for us at the northern end of Kanapou Bay. About halfway there, our guerilla outrigger convoy joined up to make a small flotilla of determined fighters returning from a mission.

Had we been successful? Not in Gunny's mind. His ingenious idea of ganging up grenades into a focused blast would never accomplish what we needed; to sink that fabulous aeronautical creation into the bay and the bombs along with it and put a kink so hard in the Japanese plans to take out the Panama Canal that it would remain a dream—maybe forever—or at least long enough for America to get the hell over here and take back Hawaii.

Hek exchanged a flurry of Hawaiian with the tillerman of the canoe closest to us. When done, he veered off and sped ahead, leaving Gunny and Hek to dig into the increasingly active sea. Because the Tahitian racing canoe's freeboard was so close to the water, we dared not venture too far into open water.

Not having a paddle, or knowing the first thing about racing canoes, all I could do was admire how our slender craft slashed through the water like a barracuda, minus its deadly-sharp teeth that snags prey and gobbles it up.

It was the shortest step in the world from imagining a barracuda to imagining a torpedo, and I took it.

"Gunny, what if we torpedoed her?"

"Who's 'her?'"

"The plane."

"Oh." He paddled a few more strokes but said nothing.

Tony said, all innocent-like, "I never thought of that. Did you, Gunny?"

He kept paddling.

Tony continued. "If you blew up a tin fish at the right spot you'd break her back. Great idea, skipper. Wish I'd thought of it. Right, Gunny?"

Gunny kept paddling.

Hek said, "Might work."

Gunny finally said, "How would you even fire the damn thing?"

"Couldn't we float it over somehow, and then set it off."

"That's not how they work, colonel."

"Sorry, but this is not my line of work."

"No kidding," Tony chirped, "The colonel's an idea guy, right, Gunny?"

In between strokes the old marine said, "Would… you… mind… shutting… the… fuck… UP?"

Tony chuckled. "Yes, sir, Gunnery Sergeant Lewis, sir."

Before I could calm the stormy waters between them, Gunny said, "There it is."

The twin war canoe seemed to emerge from the darkness like a dream, its sail furled, making it difficult to see. That space between the hulls… I suddenly imagined a torpedo slung there, ready to fire.

"Gunny, what if we hung the torpedo between the hulls?"

"Of what, sir?"

"The war canoe."

He kept paddling, but his sigh of frustration was audible, despite the rushing sounds of water all around us.

Tony said, "I agree with the good sergeant, sir. That's a boneheaded idea."

"Why? It's the perfect place to put one."

"You tell him, Gunny. He won't listen to a *Pan Am* mechanic."

""Look, sir, by the time you drop the thing in the water and the engine kicks in, that canoe would be so close to the shore that the Japs would blow it to kingdom come—and the crew along with it."

Tony added, "And who's to say they wouldn't spot it even earlier and sink both the canoe and the tin fish. Right, Gunny?"

"You know something Esposito? You're—"

"—like a penicillin shot – a pain in your ass but good for you."

That got a laugh from all of us—Gunny the loudest.

By now, the immense war canoe was fast upon us. While our guerilla outrigger fleet fanned out to take up a protective perimeter, willing hands snatched us onto the larger craft, followed by the racing canoe. Two of the paddlers helped make fast the canoe and covered it with the thatched roof, while the rest of the paddlers took up the steady, tireless rhythm of dipping their heavy, broad-billed paddles into the water, while the tillerman oversaw their efforts.

He made course-and speed-corrections with a coded set of THUMPS on the hull with his wooden blade, that, when otherwise not engaged, he pressed hard against the hull to act as a rudder.

After we'd travelled about a mile northeast toward the secret base on Maui, he gave the command to set sail. With the westerlies now at our back, we fairly flew across the water.

The PT boats' lava tube tunnel on the Maui coastline was in full swing when we arrived. Sailors swarmed over both vessels like ants at a picnic. A caterpillar-tracked crane hovered over PT-124. Dangling from its hook was a twelve-cylinder Packard engine.

According to Tony, it weighed almost three thousand pounds. But the crane and the sweating sailors made quick work of lowering it into the aft engine access hatch. A lot of whistling, laughing, and hollering going on. You would have thought it was a frat party instead of a war party.

From the forlorn looks of the bedraggled, cut-up PT moored in the back of the cave, the cannibalization was going strong. An engine here, a fuel tank here – bit by bit, these young men were determined to take the fight to the Japanese. Some talented sailor had painted "nose art" on the front of the derelict boat's ill-fated, bullet-riddled wheelhouse – a Hollywood pinup girl, reclining, arms stretched out, smiling away, with the words, "Lucky Lady" proclaiming her invincibility.

Not lucky anymore.

As we glided past PT-109. Lieutenant Kennedy flashed me a bright grin in response to my "thumbs-up" gesture.

"Pay dirt, sir?" he shouted to be heard over the noise of the hammering.

"Depends. We need to talk."

"Who's 'we?'"

Gunny, Hek, and Tony raised their hands. I added mine.

Where they found coffee I'll never know. The rating, who brought a tray of thick, ceramic Navy cups filled with steaming-hot Java into the tiny dayroom aft of the wheelhouse just smiled when I asked him.

Kennedy added, "Seaman Diengott still has many friends back at Pearl. Right, Andy?"

Still not a word, just a secretive smile and nod.

Hek said, "I hear those friends of yours who took to the hills to join my guys have officially gone native."

"Yes, sir," Diengott said.

"Not your thing?"

Diengott plunked down the cups. "I like raising hell here, with the lieutenant and the guys."

Hek slugged his coffee with condensed milk and sugar. Tony did the same. Gunny, Kennedy, and I drank it black.

Gunny savored the brew, slammed down his cup, smacked his lips, and leaned forward. "Sir, these guys torpedoed my plan."

I piled on for good measure. "We need one of yours instead. One should do it, providing it hits the target just right."

Kennedy gave us a good long look. His smile might be contagious, but his eyes were hard as flint. "Do me a favor, colonel. Find your reverse gear, back up and start over."

When we finished recounting what we'd discovered during our recon mission, and how we needed a better way to take out that monster plane, Kennedy's flint-like gaze took on a gentler aspect. And when Gunny put it in tactical terms of PT-109 dashing in at full speed, firing a torpedo, and racing away, his eyes sharpened like a hunter spotting game.

"Exciting stuff," he said.

"Plenty dangerous, too." I said. "Lots of shoals."

"Could rip out my boat's belly in no time."

"Agreed, but they've blasted out a good-sized channel for the flying boat to get in and out. Stick to that and you should be in good shape."

"'Should' be..." Kennedy leaned back and finished off his coffee. "What you're saying is that one of my Mark Eights would act like a fuse that lights up the whole shebang."

"Exactly. Am I right, Tony?"

The ex-*Pan Am* maintenance expert showed off his knowledge of what makes airplanes tick by describing the sophisticated fuel cross-feed we had both seen. A well-placed torpedo hit at the heart of the *Kawanishi* could break her back, and with it, shatter Tokyo's plans to turn the Panama Canal into high-and-dry real estate.

When Tony finished, Kennedy said, "I agree completely."

A long beat. Hek finally said, "You're on board with this, Lieutenant?"

"One hundred percent—with one small exception."

We waited.

He stood. "Watch your heads. And follow me."

We gathered topside by the forward torpedo tube on the port side. The grey-painted bulbous nose of the Mark 8 peeked out the tube like a car that didn't quite fit in the garage. In this case the "garage" was a heavily-greased steel cylinder that housed the torpedo.

Kennedy said, "We kick these babies out using this thing back here."

He flipped open a small hatch at the back of the launch tube and pulled out a brass cartridge. Filled with black powder, it had the same explosive punch as a five-inch shell. When the "Fire torpedo" command came, the launch officer pressed a button on a firing panel on the flying bridge that, in turn, sent an electrical charge to the explosive cartridge, that punched the torpedo out and into the water.

Tony said, "How much punch you got packed in the warhead?"

Before Kennedy could answer, Gunny said, "Four hundred sixty-six pounds. Not enough to sink a ship, but—"

"—in the right place on that *Kawanishi*, that's another story," I said.

"Providing the damn thing explodes," Kennedy said slowly.

The look of disgust on his face made me say, "I gather *that's* your 'small problem?'"

Kennedy slapped the launch tube. "We've got a sixty-percent failure rate on these pieces of crap. Sometimes, they'll stick in the launch tube, sometimes set fire to the lube, sometimes run in circles, or even jump out of the water like a porpoise for everybody and their brother to see."

"But sometimes they work," I said.

"Right, but you never know."

"Aye, aye." Gunny spat over the side, "I served on tin cans in World War One. They used these same damned Mark Eights."

Hek said, "But you won that war, as I recall."

"No thanks to these, right, lieutenant?"

Kennedy nodded as we stared at the torpedo like it was an axe murderer.

I finally said, "Gentlemen, let's decide that we who fight on the side of democracy do so on the side of this torpedo's forty-percent *success* rate."

Kennedy managed a tight smile. "I can't argue with your way of thinking, sir. Just a bit on the high-hatted side."

"I'm with the colonel," Tony said, then turned to Hek. "But let's up the ante a bit. You got any gods you can call on?"

He gave this some thought. "*Kūka'ilimoku* comes to mind. *Kū*, for short."

"He or she?"

"He."

"Big time?"

"The biggest. And for this mission, we shall call upon his war name of *Kū-nui-akea.*"

Tony tried saying it but got tongue tied with all the syllables. He patted the launch tube. "Between your god and Jesus H. Christ, this damn thing might work."

"Did Jesus accept human sacrifice like *Kū-nui-akea?*"

"Nope. Just his own. On a cross."

Hek shook his head. "No way to run a religion."

"Don't know about that. It worked pretty good on you guys."

"You're talking missionaries?"

"Amen, brother."

Hek's spat over the side.

I turned to Kennedy and stuck out my hand. "Green light, lieutenant?"

He took it.

PT-109's crew continued clattering, chattering, hammering, and laughing as they raced to replenish and refuel their boat for our return to the guerilla's operating base at the leper colony at Kalaupapa. There we would report back on our recon mission and present the revised "Plan A." The sooner we left the better I'd feel.

While the others shoved off to find some chow, I made my way over to the side tunnel where I found *Kahuna* Anakoni. His spotless, white linen suitcoat hanging on a hook, his shirtsleeves rolled up, and his tie tucked into his shirt, the master canoe builder was carrying an armful of heavy wooden paddles off the twin-hulled war canoe and onto the dock.

"Need a hand?" I said.

"Put these over there."

He indicated two men sitting cross-legged against the volcanic rock wall, busily sanding and smoothing a stack of hand-carved paddles with rounded, softball-sized chunks of pumice. I handed over the paddles. They grunted their thanks without looking up.

A third man knelt by a wooden bowl of what looked like oil, and from it pulled a rag, wrung it out, and proceeded to rub the paddle's freshly-sanded surface. As he did so, the dusty, tan-colored wood magically transformed itself into a glowing golden-brown.

When I returned to the war canoe, Anakoni was on board retying the lines that held the black sail furled against the boom. His face was oddly placid, as if in a dream. I hesitated to say anything to disturb his silence but wanted to thank him for the fine performance of his canoe during our reconnaissance mission. So I did so.

He nodded his appreciation. "A canoe is only as good as its paddles and its paddlers."

"And its maker."

He nodded again, accepting my compliment with a sort of noble grace befitting a *kahuna*. He gazed at me, his brown eyes a bit magnified by the gold-rimmed glasses. "I hear you have come up with a plan?"

"How did you know?"

He shrugged but said nothing.

"Well, you're right, but not the ones we thought would work."

"Which was?"

I explained Gunny's failed idea, and my equally flawed one of firing the torpedo from a war canoe. When I finally mentioned PT-109's role as the aggressor, Anakoni gestured toward the shadowy tunnel, where a long line of smaller, single-hull outriggers were tethered bow-to-bow like a herd of sheep.

"You will be needing these of course. I'll make certain they're in good shape."

His statement caught me off guard. My brain had barely finished processing Lieutenant Kennedy's smile of agreement, let alone any details of how we might mount the mission. So I did what *Pan Am's*

Captain Fatt used to do when he was stumped but didn't want to appear to appear like an idiot.

"Uh, what did you have in mind?" I said.

"It may not look like it, but I am an excellent wrestler."

"And?"

"Hek and I attended the same high school at the same time."

I had no idea where this was going so I just nodded.

"I went to McKinley high, he went to Roosevelt."

"As in FDR?"

"Teddy."

"And?"

"Both schools had wrestling teams. Hek and I were both on them. My weight class was nowhere near his, so we never competed—officially that is." His features softened into a smile.

"But unofficially?"

"I pinned him every time." He paused, eyes closed at the memory. Then, "Want to know my secret?"

"Yes, and I bet Hek would too."

Anakoni laughed. "Oh, he knows alright—now that is. But not back then. To win a match against him all I had to do was divert his attention. I'd make my distracting move, he'd react, and after that, it was all about leverage. Never failed. And he never figured it out. Want to know how wrestling figures into your mission?"

"You bet I do."

"Could I trouble you for my coat, please, Colonel Carter?"

He carefully rolled down his sleeves while I retrieved it for him. Once attired, he snugged his tie against his tightly-buttoned collar, thus becoming the best-dressed man in a lava tube cave, otherwise filled with sailors wearing faded Hawaiian shirts and ratty Panama hats and guerilla troops wearing whatever they could scrounge up.

Anakoni's high-pitched voice softened to a near whisper. "Right about now, Hek's organizing a diversionary force on the ground that will pull the enemy troops away from your main attack on the plane. Which is the right decision, of course. You need as many diversions as possible. In his mind, he's already on Kaho'olawe, scheming about how he'll deploy his men to attack the main supply base—which is located on the southwest side, by the way."

"You've been there, I presume?"

He grinned. "Many times—before the war. It has a tiny beach, the perfect place to take a pretty girl." His face darkened. "But now, the Japanese guard garrison is stationed there instead. Hek will need to fix them in place so they don't come running."

I noticed his use of the verb "to fix," an oft-heard military expression. "You serve with Hek's guerillas?"

His eyes narrowed, and his lips tightened. "Every Hawaiian does, man, woman and child, whether they carry a rifle or not. We fight for our freedom. We—" He stopped and laughed. "Listen to me, I sound like I'm in one of your war movies. Maybe your wife could get me a job in Hollywood when all this is over?"

"I'll see what I can do—but tell me, what does wrestling have to do with all this?"

"Easy. While Hek's sorting out his next move, I'm already moving to get these outriggers ready. I'm a step ahead of him all the time, like old times"

"That's how you beat him back then?"

"Exactly. And it's how we'll beat the Japanese now."

"But we still need to get approval, from General MacArthur."

"Chain of command, and all that?"

"Big time."

This time, we had the rising moon to contend with on our way back to Kalaupapa. After experiencing either full cloud cover or moonless skies, it felt mighty exposed to be on the open ocean, bathed in its silvery light, racing through the night with the distinct possibility of enemy detection.

Hek and I sat on a torpedo launch tube. But from the way he propped his feet up, he could have been on a pleasant nighttime cruise, unlike myself, who kept wondering when a Japanese picket might stumble upon us and open fire.

"Their radar is for shit," Hek said, when I mentioned this to him. He pointed toward the bulbous device mounted on a tripod just aft of PT 109's wheelhouse. "Ours is not much better, but it gets the job done."

"'Ours?' I thought you and your guerillas were a separate army."

"We are. But that's how allies talk. England, Canada, Mexico—"

"Those are nations. Hawaii's a U.S. territory. We're on the same side."

"For the time being."

"Meaning?"

Hek didn't respond. Instead, he stared out at the open ocean. The wind was nearly calm, making for a glassy surface of rolling swells instead of sharp-edged whitecaps. Now and then, he'd raise his palm to the sky to measure the degree-arc of Arcturus. I couldn't help but join him.

"Amazing how this actually works," I said.

"Lots of amazing things about Hawaiians you don't know about."

"I'm learning."

"Good for you, sir. Keep it up. Who knows? When Hawaii becomes an independent nation again, we just might grant you dual citizenship."

"Independent nation? I'll have whatever your drinking."

Instead of laughing, Hek reached inside his fatigue jacket and pulled out a pint flask. "Have a slug, sir."

"You're kidding me."

"Find out."

I took the flask, opened it and sniffed. "Pineapple juice?"

"Partly. Down the hatch, sir."

I took a wary sip. Sweetness first, then the alcohol hit like a blowtorch. "What...kind...of..."

"Grain alcohol. Hundred-eighty proof. Torpedo engines run on it. They've got a fifty-gallon barrel of it back at the Maui base. Two parts ethyl alcohol, three parts good old Hawaiian pineapple juice—my turn."

He took a swig and smacked his lips.

"Not straight out of the can, though. The alcohol arrives from the states with red dye and methanol mixed in to keep guys from drinking it like we are. Poisonous stuff. So they distill it until it turns into torpedo juice."

"Who's 'they?'"

"Rather not say—what do you think?"

"I'll tell you what I think—after another slug."

Not wise to be hitting the booze while in enemy waters, so we backed off on party time and got down to the business at hand; how to put Japan out of the bomb-building business.

When Hek began spelling out his diversionary plan that would take place during PT-109's torpedo run, I mentioned my earlier conversation with *Kahuna* Anakoni and his uncanny foreknowledge of Hek's scheme.

Hek stiffened. "That guy is a royal pain in my royal ass…sir."

"Makes sense what he says, though. We can't go racing up to that flying boat and firing torpedoes without drawing off enemy fire. Otherwise—""

"Oh, I didn't mean that. Anakoni's right, his outrigger navy has to land a large enough force of my guys on the supply base to make the Japs scream bloody murder and call back the cavalry from your side of the island."

"You sound like John Wayne talking. Watch a lot of American movies?"

Hek grinned, "Know thine enemy…"

"You mean America?"

"In a manner of speaking… yes. If only your missionaries hadn't shown up, then we—"

"Baloney. If not us, then Japan would have shown up, or the Dutch, or some other damn nation. Pineapples do more than spruce up torpedo juice. And don't forget sugar. You can't expect that kind of gold to stay on islands, and it didn't. In fact—"

Hek waved me into silence. "Sir, we're starting to sound like two drunks arguing in a bar."

The image made me laugh. "You're right. Hand me that flask, will you?"

"But I thought—"

"One for the road—or the ocean in this case."

God takes care of drunks and babies.

I think that's how the saying goes. In any event, it proved right—our arriving safely, that is, back at the guerilla base. Truth be told, Hek and I were far from drunk—not even tipsy—when Kennedy's crew tossed out lines to the lepers waiting for us on Kalaupapa's rickety loading dock. The way the waves broke upon the rugged shoreline reminded me of Kennedy's concern about getting close enough to fire his torpedoes without ripping out her keel on the volcanic rock.

The way he nervously watched his crew tie up at the leper colony reminded me of a father watching his kids cross a busy highway. That's why I kept my mouth shut as I stood beside him. Not until the mooring lines were made fast and the boat drifted closer to the pier did I risk saying anything.

"We'll lay out the plan to the general," I said.

Kennedy looked surprised. "What's he got to do with it?"

I laughed. "Lieutenant, I'm barely qualified to be a commissioned officer, but even I understand 'chain-of-command.' General MacArthur's got to approve this crazy idea of mine."

"Of *our* crazy idea, sir. Don't forget, no boat, no 'boom.'"

"Mac can't help but approve the mission. The alternative is unthinkable."

Kennedy looked skeptical. "You never know about top brass, sir. That's something you need to learn."

"After two years of working for General Patton, I already know what you mean."

He checked his watch. "Can we seal the deal in less than an hour, you think? Need to get my mahogany princess back to her castle before dawn."

"Here comes our taxi."

A canvas-covered truck arrived on the dock in a cloud of exhaust. Its overworked engine needed a ring job, but that was a dream. Hek, Gunny, Tony, and Kennedy piled into the back. Being the ranking officer, I smiled as I hopped in front.

The driver lunged at me with open arms and kissed me full on the lips. When I caught my breath I said, "I'd know those lips anywhere."

"Yours, darling, forever—how was your day?"

"Busy, busy."

"How busy?"

You'll find out when we meet with the boss."

She slammed the truck into gear. The clutch stuttered a bit as the truck lurched forward. "Better make it quick."

"Got to. That PT boat's a sitting duck when the sun comes up. "

Ava adroitly steered the truck through the settlement's narrow streets, lined with small houses in various states of repair. Inside, the lepers still slept. Dawn would come as it always had, and with it, the return of their affliction. But for now, they dreamed of a time when their bodies had been whole and their hopes alive.

We began the slow climb toward Kauhakō crater. Hard to pick out the features of the scrub-covered landscape because a cloud layer had moved in during the past hour. Dawn would come as it had for eons, just not as soon and not as bright.

Ava reached over and squeezed my shoulder. "Promise to act surprised?"

"For what?"

"For the good news that Mac's going to tell you, but I'm telling you first because I can't stand keeping it a secret."

"The war's over?"

"No, silly. But our adventure is."

"Spill the beans."

She downshifted, the clutch plates chattered in protest then finally caught. In between fighting with the dying clutch and sticky gear shift, she said, "We, my darling husband... are going... HOME!"

Do every act of your life as if it were your last.
Marcus Aurelius, Roman Emperor

From what I could gather from Ava's breathless recounting, the submarine *USS Tang* was "inbound our station" to pick up General MacArthur, Ava, and me and return us to the United States. The rescue mission was due within days. Possibly as soon as tomorrow evening, depending on how easily the submarine could evade the Japanese picket boats.

The truck crested the rise just as Ava finished spilling the beans. Two guerilla fighters materialized out of the low-lying scrub and waved us on.

"Cat got your tongue?" Ava said to me.

"Sort of."

She looked at me sharply. "Everything okay?"

"After what you just said, no—at least for me."

Another guerilla waved her to park in a spot beneath a scrubby grove of trees to hide the truck from view during the daytime.

She gave me a long look. "So… you're not *just* reporting back to Mac about your recon mission?"

"No."

"You're having a big-time pow-wow?"

"Yes."

"Involving you in an 'active' role?"

"Roger your last."

Instead of answering, she hit the brakes, halted and pounded on the back of the cab. "Last station, folks. Everybody OUT!"

As they poured out of the back she leaned over and kissed me hard. "The happy lieutenant kisses the lieutenant colonel and doesn't give a damn about a court-martial."

I returned her kiss. "But I do."

"Worry wart." She opened her door. "Let's go see the boss."

I held the *USS Tang's* decoded flimsy in my hand. The paper was wrinkled and creased from other hands fussing and fiddling with it long before me, including General MacArthur. Like all coded messages, way short and sweet:

EYES ONLY
FROM: O'KANE, CDR
COMMANDING
TO: MACARTHUR, GNL
COMMANDER U.S. FORCES

RENDEZVOUS YR LOCATION
NLT 24 HRS FR TIME STAMP.

EXTRACTION INCL:
S. CARTER, COL
A. JAMES, LT
1925 ZULU

MSG ENDS

I handed it to Hek, who placed it inside a well-worn leather folder. Amazing how this desolate outpost in the middle of the South Pacific could maintain such solid communications with friendly forces. God only knows where they kept their encryption unit and radio setup. But guaranteed, the Japanese would never find it. These Hawaiians knew more than how to *Hulu*; they knew how to hide.

The smoky kerosene lantern inside the cave cast harsh shadows on Mac's craggy face. He looked like he belonged on Mt. Rushmore—the others; Tony, Ava, Kennedy, Gunny, gathered with me in the largest of the caves carved out by lepers long ago, who, like the guerillas, were outcasts in their own way.

"Good news, sir," I managed to say at last.

"Surprising news indeed," Mac said.

Ava said, "But how could they act so quickly?"

I felt a rush of happiness. "Because Orlando made it out alive and blew the whistle. He's the only one who knew where we were heading."

"I concur," Mac said. "You have stalwart companions, indeed, colonel. Something to be treasured both in war and in peace."

"Especially war. And, sir—"

He held up his hand like Caesar silencing a centurion. "May I have the opportunity of presuming what you're about to say?"

Puzzled, I could only nod for him to continue.

"When I served in France I led a series of raids on German-held trenches. Highly successful, too, I might add."

"Congratulations, sir."

He waved away my compliment. "When duty calls you must heed its cry."

"Yes, sir, and I—"

"You read the decoded message from Commander O'Kane?"

"Yes, sir."

"You saw your name listed, along with Lieutenant James's for extraction?"

"Yes, sir."

"But based on the presence of this United States Navy Lieutenant— Kennedy is it?"

"Sir, yes, sir."

"You're planning on leading your own raid—not on German trenches—but on this Japanese Navy flying boat."

I nodded. "Sergeant Lewis's original idea, while clever, is not enough to disable an aircraft this size. That's why Lieutenant Kennedy has agreed to—"

"Assist you in attempting a modified version of the raid."

I was getting annoyed at his constant interruptions—not to mention his uncanny clairvoyance.

"Could we at least present our proposed mission, sir?"

Mac checked his watch. "Pray, do so, but just the highlights. We need to prepare for our evacuation." He turned to Hek. "You've detailed a protective force, just in case?"

"Absolutely, sir. But the odds are slim. The Japanese mostly treat this place like a…"

"Like a leper colony, which it is."

"Yes, sir."

"Indeed." Mac swiveled his gaze back to me. "Proceed."

We quickly described the highlights: the vulnerability of the fueling station, Gunny's confidence in marshalling the guerilla forces to draw off the Japanese during the attack, and Kennedy's determination to fire his precious torpedoes into the heart of the *Kawanishi*,.

While each of us took our turn, Mac methodically filled his corncob pipe with tobacco. He finally lit it just as Kennedy was describing the course he would take to reach the aircraft.

Mac held up his pipe like a stop sign. "Shoaling rocks on these islands. Could rip your hull to pieces."

"Affirmative, sir, but that flying boat got in there because they blasted a good-sized channel to do so. That's where I'll head."

Puff... puff... nod...

"Proceed."

Kennedy finished his part. Then I wound up the final pitch and delivered it by describing the effect of five hundred pounds of TNT—or a *thousand* pounds if we were lucky with two torpedo strikes—upon the tens of thousands of gallons of high-octane aviation fuel in the *Kawanishi's* fuselage and wing tanks. I especially liked my last line:

"Those damned H-bombs are going *down*, sir, not blowing *up* the Panama Canal."

Mac nodded but didn't break into applause or anything like that. Instead, he said, "What's your opinion, professor? Will these despicable weapons detonate when the flying boat explodes?"

Professor Rasetti, who had been sitting still as a statue while listening to us, came to life. He was Italian. remember.

"*Impossibile.* A fission/fusion reaction requires an application of force in a concentric manner. An explosion of the type Colonel Carter just described would be asymmetrical."

"No thermonuclear explosion?"

"None." He frowned slightly. "Of course..." He spread his hands and fell silent.

"Out with it."

"There is the possibility of damaging the core and causing radiation contamination. But that would be a local event."

"On local inhabitants." Gunny grinned. "Who just *happen* to be the glorious Sons of Nippon."

"Indeed." Mac said, then puffed for a while, saying no more. In the silence, the pre-dawn sounds of waking birds found their way into the cave. The smell of a cooking fires triggered my empty stomach to add a mighty growl to the silence. I acted like it was someone else's stomach.

Kennedy fidgeted uneasily then finally said, "Sir, I need to head back to the base."

"Of course. And choose those torpedoes well, young man. I know they're thorns in your side."

"With all respects to Lieutenant James, sir, they're thorns in our asses."

Ava laughed. "No apologies needed. I work in Hollywood, remember?"

Kennedy said to Mac, "When you get back stateside, sir. Would you *please* tell those idiots at New London that the Mark Eights are useless? There's scuttlebutt about using aerial torpedoes instead. That would be a dream come true. No black powder launches. Just roll them off the deck and away they go, then BOOM."

"I shall indeed convey your message, lieutenant. You're dismissed, and Godspeed with the coming mission. America thanks you for your bravery."

Kennedy and I exchanged a quick look. Neither one of us spoke, but the question floated in the air between us, thick as fog. But with no answer forthcoming, I nodded confidently to the young naval officer, who flashed me a grin and a thumbs-up, then hurried out to hightail PT-109 back to Maui and tuck her into the tunnel before Japanese eyes woke up and started to pry.

I turned to the group. "How about you fellas grab some chow, and then some shut-eye?"

Tony and Gunny got my drift and cleared out. Hek hesitated slightly, then caught on as well.

"C'mon, professor," he said. "Let's rustle up some *poi* and pineapple."

Rasetti shuddered and made a face. "Such food you eat here. I pray every day America will hurry up and win the war, so that I can go back to my beloved country."

Hek said, "Better food in Italy?"

"Better everything."

"Except *il Duce*, right?"

"Benito Mussolini is a pig in search of a spit."

"My kind of guy!"

Hek draped his gorilla-sized arm around Rasetti's narrow shoulders and walked him out like a cop collaring a drunk. "How about we roast some pineapple first?"

MacArthur emptied his pipe and made noises like he was leaving too.

"Sir," I began. "I need to say something."

Tap…tap…tap… went the pipe. "I'm not that dense, colonel. You've been saying it all along in so many ways. This would be in reference to the upcoming mission?"

"Affirmative. I want—correction—I *need* to go on it."

"I know that. But I also *need* to obey orders from my superiors. So do you, colonel. General Patton wants you and Lieutenant James back with him at the Presidio. And despite your obvious desire to strike at the Japanese in a meaningful way, you will do so as that superior officer sees fit—back in California."

I gave him five whole seconds to let his pompous words sink into the earth where they belonged. Then I began.

"Sir, two years ago, the Nazi's killed my wife and baby. I can't bring them back. But I'm damn well going to bring back a world without Hitler and Tojo. And if it means resigning my commission to avoid your lousy orders, then I resign, effective immediately."

Mac stopped tapping his pipe.

Ava said, "Ditto his last, sir."

Mac smiled. "You, too?"

"Going on the mission? Yes, sir. I'm going on it with my guy and screw your lousy lieutenant bars."

To Mac's credit, he put away his pipe before making eye contact. When he finally did so, his gaze felt like he was stripping off a layer of my skin. But when he regarded Ava, his features softened somewhat.

Ava went for the chink in his armor. "Ever read the scriptures, general?"

Puzzled, he drew back. Not easy to stop a four-star in his tracks, but her question did the trick. "I am somewhat familiar with the King James version, but no, not chapter and verse."

"Neither am I," Ava continued. "But my mother always used to read a little each night before supper. Sort of like saying grace, but a bit longer on some nights. Anyhow, the gist of one of my favorites is about Ruth— you remember her, don't you?"

He nodded.

Ava sailed on. "Ruth had this thing about sticking with someone no matter what. She said, 'Whither thou goest, I will go, and where thou lodgest, I will lodge.'" She slipped her arm in mine. "Thy people shall be my people and—"

Mac said, "—and thy God shall be my God."

"I wouldn't exactly call Sam a god." She pecked my cheek. "But he sure as hell is my honey."

Mac stared at his pipe then put it away, as if resisting the temptation to dither. When he looked at us this time, his gaze felt more fatherly than imperial.

"We've been through a lot together, the three of us."

"Yes, sir," I said. "On a life raft in the South China Sea... prisoners on a Japanese sub."

"Then managing a daring escape by plane."

"Bet they're still talking about that in Tokyo."

His smile shifted into a glare. "You're serious about resigning your commissions without proper authority?"

"Absolutely, sir. We quit."

"Are you aware that the United States Army will prosecute you to the fullest extent for desertion in the face of the enemy?"

Ava and I looked at each other. The world with all its confusions and complications disappeared. We really *were* made for each other. I guess what I'm trying to say is, whither *she* goest, I would too.

"Yes, sir."

I'm not a mind reader, so I can't begin to describe what then took place in the mind of General Douglas MacArthur. I can speculate, of course. But I'd rather not because I can never do justice to the complicated, interlaced thought patterns that had enabled this man to become commander-in-chief of all naval and military forces in America. Leaders are born, true, but they're made as well. Mac was both. Patton, too.

He went over to the wall and pulled down the map we'd made for the Kaho'olawe briefing. He began rolling it up. "General Patton will blow his top like one of these infernal volcanoes when he finds out I left you two behind."

I heard him say the words, but they didn't register at first. "You mean I can—we can do this? With your permission?"

"I won't have officers under my command tearing up their commissions in the middle of a war. Makes me look like a tyrannical overlord."

"We wouldn't want that, sir," Ava deadpanned.

He glanced at her sharply, but her sweet, innocent face stopped his suspicion. (Ava was—and still is—a tremendous actor.)

Mac handed me the rolled-up map like Robert E. Lee must have surrendered his sword to Ulysses S. Grant at Appomattox. "Besides, they'd hang you for desertion in the face of the enemy."

"Desertion? We were going to do the exact *opposite*."

"Precisely."

He smiled, as rare as snow in July, then added, "But the difference being, now you'll be doing so as commissioned officers in the United States Army, while under direct orders from your superior officer—your *most* superior officer, I might add."

"General Douglas MacArthur, commanding, thank you SIR!" Ava pecked him on the cheek. Horrified, she stepped back and snapped off a razor-sharp salute. "Forgive my indiscretion, SIR."

Mac couldn't hide his smile. "I can't wait to see the look on George's face when he finds out I've superseded his command structure."

"He'll have a fit," I said.

"And we'll have quite the tale to tell," Ava said.

Mac's pleasant smile faded. A haunted look came into his eyes. "Ever since this war began, my orders have sent brave young men and women to their untimely deaths. While I, on the other hand, have been spared to fight another day. I sometimes wish…"

He stopped and stared into space.

In the awkward pause that followed, I said, "Do you celebrate Christmas, sir?"

My curveball question got his attention. "Excuse me?"

"That star at the top of the tree. When I was a kid growing up in Key West, we always put that on first—then all the other decorations afterward. Ever do that?"

"Yes, yes, I suppose. But what—"

Ava said, "What Sam means, sir, is that you're like that star at the top for the rest of us to follow—whether you like it or not."

He frowned. "I absolutely detest that singular distinction."

"Too late, I'm afraid."

She boldly stepped forward, brushed the dust of his *samue* outfit and re-adjusted his hat like a mother getting ready her child for his first day at school.

"You do your duty, sir, and we'll do ours. Fair enough?"

He stiffened like a pine board and opened his mouth to chastise her for egregious behavior to a superior officer. Then he thought better of it, harrumphed a few times to clear his throat and finally said, "You and the others are going in harm's way. Take the greatest of care not only for yourselves, but for the sake of our nation. We need brave men and women like you to win the peace."

"That's a deal, sir," Ava said. "And we need a brave man like you shining bright on top of the tree."

As it turned out, the *USS Tang* sent its much-awaited signal that very afternoon – they'd just cleared the picket line and would soon arrive on station, two miles off Kalaupapa. Much too risky for a daylight extraction, they would remain submerged on the bottom until nighttime.

When you live on land it's hard to imagine that water covers over seventy-percent of the earth. But if you live in the Hawaiian Islands, you live with that fact almost every day. Not just by gazing at a far-off horizon dotted with clouds drifting over the vast Pacific Ocean and feeling like an ant, but also living with a truth embedded in the primitive part of your brain that says, "I need to eat. I am surrounded by water. How will I survive?"

The Polynesians figured that out by worshipping the gods that "gave" them the ocean. And in return, the "Great Waters" gave them fish, shellfish, cephalopods, mollusks and seaweed. Another gang of gods in charge of the earth gave erupting volcanoes, whose molten lava created land upon which to grow taro, cocoanuts, sugar cane, and a myriad of other farm crops that could sustain life, not to mention calm down the brain long enough to learn how to dance the *Hula*. Coincidentally, that traditional dance was on tap for tonight. Not only for fun, but for tactical reasons, too.

Nighttime sweeps over the islands like a velvet-black cape, silencing all living creatures, save critters who slither and slink in the nocturnal hours. Otherwise, all of Hawaii seems to take a deep breath, roll over, pull up the *tapa* cloth covers, and sleep the sleep of the just. But on this night, the guerillas and lepers would raise hell instead.

At first, MacArthur thought the idea far too risky. Much better to conduct the extraction under cover of darkness. That's the way things were done by the book—Standard Operating Procedure and all that.

But Hek stood his ground as he stood before Mac outside the cave. Sheltered from view by the surrounding scrub and trees, the stocky Hawaiian prince-in-exile (as I liked to think of him) drew the outline of Kalaupapa on the black pumice sand—in particular, the area of the leper colony nearest the pier.

"The sky will be clear tonight and a full moon. Like daylight out on the water. The Japs have observation towers along the ridges here, here, and here. If they spot anything suspicious they'll bring down artillery fire so fast your head will spin—before it separates from your body, that is...sir."

Mac considered this, then brightened. "I see... then what you're describing is not just entertainment, but an effective diversionary action."

"Especially the *hula*, yes sir. We'll stoke the fires so bright that their night vision will go all to hell if they stare at us too long. And I guarantee you they *will* stare."

"Why should they?"

"Because they're garrison troops stuck an occupied island. As far as they're concerned, nothing ever happens on Molokai, except for down in the leper colony, where tonight, the crazies are having another party— drums and music included. Back in the old days, this colony was true madhouse. No morals to speak of, just desperate people condemned to die before their time. One debauch after another—until Father Damien showed up and brought a little law and order and common sense."

"That's history. What about now?"

"Folks still party. But that's because sulfa drugs have put the brakes on the disease and they're celebrating instead of going crazy with fear."

"But how do you propose I get out to the sub?"

"By outrigger canoe."

"Won't they see it?"

"They'll see the canoe for sure. But not you in it. We've got that all planned out."

Mac considered this, then fingered the "scrambled eggs" embroidered on his iconic hat. "I look forward to the day when I can wear this again."

"We do too, sir," I said.

He regarded me for a moment, his face grew somber and then he sighed. "If only it were a year from now, we would already know the outcome of our efforts to outwit the Japanese and destroy that nefarious weapon."

"*Weapons*, sir. They've got two of the damned things."

"Indeed. History will record whether we succeeded or not."

Hek stood up. Up until now I thought his barrel-shaped chest was big. Somehow it got even bigger. "Ten years from now, sir, Hawaiian children will read in their history books of how their fathers and mothers uncles and aunts, and grandfathers and grandmothers took back the islands from the enemy. And how the great General Douglas MacArthur returned to thank them for saving his life so that America could take back democracy for the world."

"I shall do just that."

"We'll have a parade down Main Street in Honolulu to celebrate."

"Excellent."

"There will be one more thing, sir."

"Yes?"

"*Hula*."

You can reduce the complicated, baffling, astonishing art of magic to a single word:

Diversion.

When it works, you can perform wonders, because in the end, magic is nothing more than the *illusion* of the impossible. For instance, if I can get you to follow the motion of my right hand, I'll palm the coin in my left and "pull" it out of your ear or—in our case—return the commanding general of American forces to his rightful place by diverting enemy eyes from its happening beneath their very noses.

By using the *Hula.*

Of the twelve male dancers at the party that night, three were lepers, the rest were Hek's guerillas fighters. But since all of them wore the same palm-leaf woven crowns, tapa cloth shawls, and loincloths, the only difference—and you had to be close to notice—was that the lepers had some "clubbing" going on with their fingers, and one of them was minus most of his left ear. But otherwise, they were dues-paying members of the scariest group of dancers I'd ever seen.

Ava and joined the crowd gathered in an open field near St. Philomena Church in Kalawao, the original site of the leper colony. Located on the desolate, windswept eastern side of the thumb-shaped, tiny peninsula, Father Damien and his sufferers had built a simple, white wooden church where they could pray to a God for the comfort denied them by their fellow man.

In the late 1800s, the Hawaiian government decided to abandon Kalawao in favor of the more weather-sheltered Kalaupapa, two miles away on the western side, where we first landed three days ago. That said, the cruel dumping ground remained, only the location had changed. Same lousy "church," just a different lousy pew.

Ava and I both wore our conical straw hats to hide our features from the Japanese guards manning the observation post high on the sea cliffs, a mile-and-a-half away. Too far away to see our faces, true, but better safe than sorry. Mac was dressed the same but nowhere in sight, as that was part of Hek's grand scheme to get him out to the submarine without being spotted.

The bonfires helped, too.

Being short of wood, diesel fuel lent its muscle to the three roaring blazes that Hek and the lepers had started an hour ago, and by now were going great guns. Nothing like bright light to reduce your night vision to nil—especially that of bored enemy soldiers. All they could see from up there would be human shadows stretching out across the scrub land until they flickered and danced against the sides of Father Damien's church.

Hard to estimate how many folks were gathered here tonight, but counting our guerilla force, well over a hundred. Hours earlier, the colonists had made their way pilgrim-style from their settlement. They traveled by foot along the primitive road that led past our hideout in the Kauhakō crater. As they trudged past, we joined them in their journey and mixed in with the others, including Lieutenant Robinson.

As always, the young navy nurse seemed to march more than walk, so clear was her reason for being on this planet – to put flight to Hansen's disease once and for all—with the help of a *lot* of sulfonamide.

As for the special *Hula* planned for tonight, what little I knew about it I had learned during my stopovers in Honolulu when I flew for *Pan Am*. Back then, it was your standard ukulele-strumming, steel guitar twanging, pretty Hawaiian girls swaying back and forth stuff that Hek informed me was *Hula 'auana*.

"We call it 'missionary dancing,'" he said. "But the tourists love it."

Ava said, "I think it's beautiful."

"Didn't say it wasn't. But that's not what *Hula* means to Hawaiians." He gestured to the male dancers, who by now had lined themselves up in preparation to begin. "Get ready for *Ha'a Koa* style."

From what I'd learned from Hek during our trek over to Kalawao, the Hawaiian warrior class conquered their enemies more from brute strength than sophisticated weapons.

"Feel my arm," he said as we walked along. "Upper bicep."

I felt the heavily tattooed, hard-as-rock muscle. "Glad we're allies."

"Those who weren't, paid the price—back in King Kamehameha's time, and now, too."

"He must have been something. A regular George Washington uniting all these islands."

"With stones and spears instead of muskets. Kamehameha was a warrior long before he was our king."

The dance began.

First of all, forget strumming ukuleles and pretty girls' arms waving up and down like the ocean. These male *Hula* dancers charged out of the starting gate like the ancient *Koa* warriors they represented – half-crouched, arms upraised, eyes flashing, bare feet stamping the earth, while two other warriors pounded on hollow gourds that gave the rhythm to their choreographed movements.

The men ebbed and flowed like a single organism – their line abreast formation shifted to flank, then wedge, then single file, while the lead warrior, a young man almost as big as Hek and nearly as muscled, maintained a steady call and response chant with his fellow warriors.

Lieutenant Robinson joined Ava and me, her eyes bright, big smile, hands clapping in time with the pounding drums.

"See their leader?" she shouted to be heard over the booming drums.

"He knows his stuff," I said.

"So glad he's taking sulfa. His Hansen's will never get worse."

"Looks normal to me."

"Get closer and you'd see thickening of the skin, hypopigmentation here and there, some open lesions, but his days of getting worse are over—as long as we can keep giving him the drugs."

"How are your supplies?"

"Okay for now, thank God. But we'd better win this damn war soon. No telling what Tokyo will do to these poor people."

"He looks like he can take care of himself."

"He can. Thanks to Parke-Davis Pharmaceutical —watch, here comes the best part."

Clenched fists SLAMMED on naked chests, eyes wide, cheeks puffed out, tongues waving, grotesque faces on the dancers to frighten a potential enemy. The disfigured lepers' faces blended in a common rage that infused the warrior dance.

The flickering fire lent a macabre feeling to the moment. If a Japanese soldier had the misfortune of showing up at this moment in time, he'd not last long, considering what the warriors did next.

Their chanting, taunting, aggressive shouting reached a crescendo. Some picked up stone clubs, others long spears, while the rest grabbed bone daggers and wooden swords imbedded with sharks' teeth. The drumming grew louder, as did their chanting, faster and faster, until at a signal from the leader, the warriors dashed forward across the open field and down to the beach where two outrigger canoes waited.

Hiding in one of them was Mac – once more a stowaway, once more at the mercy of others.

Ava said, "Poor man spends more time hiding than commanding."

Hek laughed. "Damn good thing he's not fat, or his stomach would poke out over the gunwale."

The crowd followed to watch what happened next. Another fire was blazing away on the shore to light up the canoes. From tall poles attached to each canoe bow a lantern gently swayed in the night sea breeze that had picked up.

When the *Koa* warriors got to the canoes, they separated into two groups, six to a boat, and began taunting each other. Step... shout... tongue out... face grimace... step... shout... on and on they ranted for at least a full minute, challenging each other to do what was about to happen next.

All the while, dark shadows hid the shape of General Douglas MacArthur beneath a tapa cloth in the outrigger closest to me.

The leader bellowed a command, each group dashed to their respective canoes, grabbed hold of the gunwales and launched them through the surf. The moment they cleared the shore, the warriors took up their tulip-shaped paddles and the race was on.

They dug in with a vengeance, while their respective steersmen used paddles to slew the canoes toward their destination – Okala Island, a tiny, cone-shaped, tree-covered, lava promontory poking out of the water like the tip of a giant finger, a mile offshore to the east of where we stood.

Back when the leper colony was first established on Kalaupapa, the sailing ships carrying the unlucky patients from Oahu would weigh anchor out by that tiny island. The ships captains, terrified of catching the mysterious disease, would often order their crews to toss the poor souls overboard and make them swim for Kalawao.

Most made it, but many drowned. Back then, maybe a better way to die, considering the slow deterioration of life and limb that awaited them when they staggered onto the beaches of this dumping ground for the broken-hearted.

But tonight, that same small island out there with its near-vertical cliffs, was a symbol of hope not despair.

A combination of a full moon glittering on the water and the bow lanterns helped the us follow the outriggers' swift progress. Each of us cheered for the canoe of our choice. A familiar routine, no matter who you are, or where you live in the world – it's us versus them, the good guys versus the bad guys, baseball teams competing—however you want to call it—sides taken, favorites chosen, and each of us hoping "our guys" would win.

This so-called "race," then, was the final step in the diversionary plan we had sorted out a few hours ago—with Mac's final approval, of course. Right about now, based on our coded signals with the *Tang*, a tiny rubber assault raft manned by the submarine's onboard contingent of Marines was racing for the same island—but from the *opposite* side, hidden from view.

The enemy soldiers in the observation tower would be drawn like moths to a flame at the sight of the lanterns bobbing up and down on the boats, and *not* what was simultaneously happening on the other side.

By now, the outriggers were within a couple hundred yards of Okala. Two miles beyond, the *Tang*, having dispatched the raft, would be hovering beneath the waves at periscope depth. I tried to imagine Commander O'Kane down in the control room, peering through the periscope while his crew looked on, powerless to do anything except wait—and pray—for their team's safe return, along with their four-star cargo.

Tony tugged at my sleeve, "Hope to hell this works, skipper."

"You and me both."

Hek whistled once, sharply, to get my attention and pointed to his left. About a mile off shore, the dark shape of a Japanese patrol boat slowly chugged left to right, maybe making five knots. The brilliant white, lancing stab of its searchlight swept over the waters and locked onto the racing canoes.

"Damn it, he's early," Hek said. "Not supposed to be due for another hour."

"Maybe the lookouts called him to check out our party."

"Hope that damn sub is deep."

Ava said, "What about the sailors in the raft?"

Hek frowned, turned and shouted for the group to cheer louder. All of us did, as if this were some great celebration. Somebody started playing the ukulele, while others jigged and jagged in an impromptu *Hulu*. "Party Time in Leper Land," that was us, all right.

Would it have any effect? Who knows? We just kept at it, while the enemy searchlight did its own version of a cop stopping you for speeding, playing over the outriggers, then over the island. When it swept over us, we cheered like movie fans at a premiere. Ava cheered the loudest and waved like one of her one of her overwrought movie fans.

The outrigger canoes disappeared behind Okala Island, and with it went the light from their lanterns.

The Japanese patrol boat was still a half-mile from the island. Whatever was happening behind that piece of volcanic rock was hidden from them—and from us too.

So, we danced and shouted even louder.

Remember, there's no such thing as real magic, only distraction while the ordinary takes place. And in our case, either Mac was tumbling into the *Tang's* raft, safely into the waiting arms of the Marines, or the whole thing was a colossal bust. Blind to what was really happening, I could only clap and shout along with everyone else and cheer for my favorite outrigger.

A light from a lantern peeped out from behind the island.

Then another, as both outriggers emerged heading for shore, the bogus race still on. And as they did, the piercing-bright searchlight swung away from the tiny island like a moth to a flame and played upon the flashing paddles of the Koa warriors as they dug in for all their worth.

The drumming onshore increased as one of the outriggers drew ahead. Would they be the winners?

Then the other outrigger came abreast and edged ahead.

What had been a brightly lit contest suddenly became pitch black as the Japanese searchlight snapped off. The effect silenced the crowd—but only momentarily. As our eyes readjusted to the bonfire-lit scene, we cheered the lead canoe now well ahead of the other.

All I could figure was that the captain of the enemy patrol boat finally decided that the natives were being natives – ho-hum – and swung his boat around in an arcing curve to chug back to its base on the eastern end of Molokai.

And he was right, of course – these natives *were* being natives – cunning, resourceful, creative Hawaiians, who—providing we got good news from the *Tang* in the next hour—had been wildly successful in saving the life of America's military commander-in-chief. And in the process of doing so, extended a mighty middle finger to General Tojo in

Tokyo and another one to Admiral Hidaka in Honolulu. After he let Mac slip through his fingers the first time around, that arrogant idiot somehow managed to stay in command. Not this time, though. *Seppuku* was on his dance card for sure. And the thought of him committing ritual suicide by disembowelment warmed my heart.

Tony, a clairvoyant as most good mechanics are, stuck out his hand and I shook it. "Well, skipper, we snookered that asshole Hidaka but good. That'll teach him to mess with us."

"We're not home free yet."

"Yeah, yeah, I know, but we did it! We got Mac off!"

"Let's hope so."

"I *know* so. Just take a gander at those warrior guys," he said. "Their faces say it all."

He had a point – the *Koa* fighters acted like a football team after winning the Rose Bowl, hooting and hollering and waving their paddles like victory flags. Not just the winning canoe, but both sides jumped for joy.

Ava reached their leader ahead of me and was questioning him. Just as I arrived, she turned and said, "He's on his way!"

"For sure?"

The tall, muscular young man nodded. "He was in our canoe. Got a little tangled in the Tapa getting out, but in the end, he barely got his feet wet."

"What's your name, son?" I said.

"John 'Aukai."

"Put 'er there, John."

He looked at my outstretched hand but didn't move.

I looked him straight in the eye. "That's an order, soldier."

He looked at Ava, then back at me. "I'm not a soldier, sir."

"You are in my books, and you just led these men on one of the most important missions of the war. Plus, you made it back to tell the tale. Now put her there."

Still he hesitated.

Ava said, "He won't bite, honest."

"Yes, ma'am, but…well… we're not supposed to… to mingle."

"John…" I warned him.

He finally surrendered and extended his hand. For a moment, I felt the roughness of his palm and his slightly disfigured fingers caused by the leprosy. But most of all I felt grateful, both for his courage and for the sulfonamide treatment that had halted the progress of his terrible, wasting disease.

Hek joined us and clapped the boy on the back. It sounded like two trees colliding. They exchanged rapid Hawaiian, none of which I could follow. But Hek soon shifted to English.

"I'm putting this guy on my team. Okay by you, sir?"

"Any man who can do what he just did, is on board big time."

John looked slightly uneasy. "I need to check with the settlement chief. We're supposed to—"

"You're on the sulfa drugs, right?" Hek said.

"Yes, sir."

"Then you're on the team. I'll talk to your boss."

Tall to begin with, the kid stood even taller. "I...I... don't know what to say."

Ava smiled. "How about 'thanks?'"

He stammered out his gratitude, his voice breaking—not because it was hard to speak, but when your feelings take charge, sometimes your vocal cords get lost in the shuffle.

Tony and Hek melted into the shadows and made their way back to the crater to await word from the *Tang*, while we waited.

And waited...

They say "no news is good news" but I don't see it that way. Maybe that's because I'm an airline pilot. Not knowing a given outcome—in this case, whether or not General MacArthur made it safely onboard the sub—is like not knowing how much fuel is left in my airplane. It makes for a mighty tense cockpit atmosphere.

But my personal anxiety didn't spill over into the party atmosphere that continued for the next hour. For good reason – we couldn't just close up shop and trudge home. That's not how parties end. The celebration had to fade away under its own power.

To give it some spark, we had more *hula* dancing, but this time two young women from the settlement performed the more modern *Hula 'auana,* with ukuleles strumming, melodious singing, and hands weaving through the night air.

Ava, Lieutenant Robinson and I sat with a group of guerilla fighters and lepers, including a very tired John 'Aukai. The dancers finished. Three more took their place—two female dancers and a singer.

Gone were the strumming ukuleles and "missionary dancing." In their place, the deep bass BOOM of a hide-covered drum. The drummer, one of the guerilla fighters, repeated the same beat over and over again, as if in a trance. An older woman standing beside him started singing, while the two dancers "acted" out a story that Nurse Robinson explained.

"She's singing about *Pele,* the volcano goddess. Passionate, fiery, unconventional."

"My kind of gal," Ava said,

"Me too. Of all the gods and goddesses that Hawaiians celebrate, *Pele* is the one whose lava created the very ground we're sitting upon."

The dancers moved in unison to the right then to the left, symbolizing waves sweeping back and forth over a beach.

I said, "Seems pretty calm and relaxed to me."

John joined in. "That's because this dance is not about the creation of the islands. It's about... well, it's about..."

Robinson smiled. "It's about love. And about how *Pele's* goddess sister—how do you say her name, John?"

"Hi'iaka."

"Yes, and she's the dancer on the left?"

John nodded.

"And *Pele's* on the right. Her spirit has flown over from the "Big Island" to Kauai and taken human form so that she can watch *Hi'iaka* dance the *Hula* with her new lover—but soon she'll do a lot more than just watch."

The goddess *Hi'iaka* broke away from *Pele,* and, arms waving like graceful palm trees in the breeze, she drifted closer to where we were sitting.

"Uh, oh," John said and hunched up his shoulders as if to minimize his size.

Closer.

He shook his head and waved her away. "Too tired."

Robinson said, "*Hi'iaka* now dances with the handsome young chief—what's his name?"

John hesitated, nervous, then said, "*Lo'hiau*. They want me to be *Lo'hiau*."

"You know the dance?"

"Yes, but after what we just did out there I…"

Hi'iaka's fingertips brushed against John's leprosy-roughened cheek. She smiled. Her hips rotated invitingly. He did his best to smile back. Nods and nudges and smiles and chuckles from the others as they watched the seduction of this young, strapping man.

John gave a deep sigh and shrugged in surrender. The drum rhythm shifted as he rose effortlessly to join his partner. With every step he took toward the dancers, he seemed to grow taller and taller. He raised his arms to greet *Hi'iaka*. His bare feet dug into the blood-red soil with absolute confidence as he twisted and turned in unison with the goddess.

"Who *is* this kid?" I said to Robinson.

"His family was big in local politics—until Pearl Harbor, that is. Played football at Punahou. Great athlete. Going places they said, until Hansen's disease got him instead. Now he's an outcast like all the others."

The drums gave way to sticks clattering in a sharper rhythm as the two lovers began moving as one. While they danced, the woman playing the part of *Pele* circled them, her eyes locked onto Prince *Lohi'au*, her arms reaching out to him but not daring to touch—not at first, that is—but the faster they danced, the closer she got.

The drums paused, Prince *Lohi'au* swayed toward the beckoning *Pele* – her hands weaved back and forth, casting a spell. Closer and closer he moved until their fingertips brushed once, twice, then intertwined.

Ava whispered, "Spider's got her fly."

The narrator sang, as *Pele* danced with *Lo'hiau*, his face glowing with passion, while a mournful *Hi'iaka* danced a few steps in pursuit of her sister, her pleading arms outstretched, but to no avail. Back they flew to the "Big Island."

As the dance continued, it became clear that *Pele* wanted the prince all to herself.

But soon, *Hi'iaka* "flew" from Kauai to plead for her lover's return.

At first, *Pele* agrees.

But later, she breaks her word. In a fit of jealousy—remember this is the goddess of volcanoes—she buries her sister's lover *Lo'hiau* beneath a river of molten lava.

The drummers paused in that crowning moment when *Lo'hiau* squirmed beneath the imaginary "lava," then stopped moving.

"He's damn good," I whispered to Robinson.

"He knows what it's like to die."

Ava said, "Poor kid."

The singing began again. The "narrator" chanted a slower song, while *Hi'iaka* rose from the side of her dead lover and circled him, her arms lifted, beseeching the heavens above, while *Pele* weaved back and forth, hands covering her eyes, as if mourning her rash actions, unable to take them back.

Robinson said, "*Hi'iaka's* prayers reach her brother, another god, who takes pity on the prince and breathes life into him once again."

The drums pause for a heart-stopping moment.

Lohi'au's eyes open.

He rises from his lava grave and swirls around *Hi'iaka*.

Pele fades into the shadows as the music reaches a crescendo and the reunited lovers dance as one.

While watching John's smiling face, I couldn't help thinking about the medicine he was taking to stop the spread of his leprosy. That "magic" drug was acting like *Hi'iaka's* brother, magically breathing life back into *Lo'hiau*.

"Will he ever get out of here?" I said to Robinson.

"You mean re-join the world?"

"He barely seems affected."

"Enough to get him here."

"I meant later."

She pondered this for a while. "So far, the sulfonamide is controlling the spread of the bacillus. But it's still too early to tell if it's going to be the silver bullet that kills leprosy once and for all."

Ava said, "I hope for everyone's sake it does. John's such a handsome young man."

"The girl who's *Hi'iaka's* good-looking too," I said.

Robinson said, "Her name is Kala. She's in the early stages as well. Unlike her brother, who's back at the settlement with the other serious cases. None of those could make it over tonight."

Kala, a tiny thing compared to the Hek-sized John, stood there looking up at him. From the way she paid attention to his every word, she was flirting to beat the band.

Ava read my mind. "Ladies and gentlemen let's hear it for love."

"Amen," Robinson said.

Tang's coded message, when it finally arrived back at Kauhakō Crater two hours later, was one sweet word:

SUCCESS

As I read it, I wondered if we could say the same one day? Natural enough thought. When you're standing at the bottom of Mount Everest, you wonder if you'll ever make it to the top. But if you want to find out, you've got to take the first step... then the next....

I handed the flimsy to Hek. "When can your men be ready?"

"Gunny figures a couple days. Need to ammo-up, plus Anakoni's got to gather the canoes over at Maui."

"Any sooner?"

Hek turned and called, "Gunny, the colonel needs you."

The grizzled Marine shuffled over, while munching on some kind of bone with shreds of meat hanging from it.

"What's for dinner?" I said.

"Roast Jap."

I let that slide. Ava taught me when you play second banana, *stay* the second banana. "Hek says a couple days to get everything ready. They're supposed to be gone by then. Any sooner, do you think?"

Gunny pointed the bone at a group of guerilla fighters near the mouth of the cave. Hunkered down on their haunches, they chatted among themselves. "Hek and I briefed them on the basics. They're divvying up who does what."

"So?"

"So... we head out tonight for Maui. Then I figure—"

"You mean tomorrow night, Gunny. It's almost three in the morning."

He chewed some more. "Time flies when you're having fun, sir."

"And?"

"Figure another day to prep there. Then it's off to the races."

"How about twelve hours."

Chew... chew... then.... "Aye, aye, sir."

"How many men?"

Hek turned around and counted. "Twenty, including Gunny and me."

I did the math. "Ava, Tony, and me, makes twenty-three. Hope we can all fit on the PT."

"Twenty-*four*, sir."

"Say again?"

Gunny worked at the bone to get the last bit. Then used it as a pointer. "Our wop professor wants to come along for the ride and watch the fireworks." Gunny raised his voice. "C'mon over here, doc, and tell the colonel what you told me."

Professor Rasetti hustled over like his pants were on fire. Before he even opened his mouth, I knew this was a man on a mission. Unshaven for days, his shirt halfway out of his pants, his slender, expressive hands slashed the air like knives as he spoke, while his grasp of the English language did its best to keep up with his Italian.

"You are going to do this thing, *si? E vero?*"

"If you mean the mission? Yes."

"*Grazie di Dio* for what you will do for the world. I helped Saburo Yamasaki give birth to a monster—*corezzione—DUE mostri*—and now you must send them back to the hell from which they came." He stopped to catch his breath, eyes bright, face red.

"Calm down, professor. You been hitting the torpedo juice?"

"*Mai, mai!* You do not understand. None of you do. I have seen what these monsters can do."

My mouth went dry.

Hek had the same thought. "You've set off one of these things already?"

"*Sì e no.* An underwater test at one-third the tritium levels. But...*mio Dio...*" He trailed off and shook his head. The Italian professor looked to be in his early forties, tops, but a lot of grey hair... I wondered when it started turning.

He prodded my shoulder. "*Colonello Carter, signor,* do not leave me here to stare at the blood on my hands for doing what I have done. *Ti songiuro,* you must let me help in any way I can."

"I understand how you feel, professor, but—"

"No, you do NOT! I was going to—how you say the word… *come se dice sabotaggio?*"

"You're saying it right, 'sabotage.'"

"*Grazie.* When Saburo, he tells me what they were going to do, I decide that very moment to change the core-implosion firing sequence so that the bomb will never work. But that night, when I found out you were coming…"

He pointed to Gunny.

"All I could think of was getting a far away from that terrible place as I could."

Gunny said, "And you made it, professor, safe and sound."

"*Sono codardo,*" he whispered through dry lips, eyes shut. "I am a coward. I should have stayed and sabotaged both bombs. It is you who are the brave ones."

We stood in awkward silence.

I finally said, "How do you say, 'balls' in Italian?"

He looked puzzled, *"Palle."*

I touched my crotch. "I mean these."

He started. "Ah, *si… coglione.*"

"For you to escape that hell hole took real *coglione*, right, Gunny?"

Gunny chewed on his bone and nodded at the same time. Then he muttered, "Big time. Swam out. Could've been shot any moment. Balls you got, doc."

I said, "And if you hadn't escaped, we never would have known what was going on over there."

Hek said, "I agree. Without you, none of this." He pointed to the gathered guerilla fighters.

By now, the men were leaving to get some well-deserved sleep. Not every night did you dance like *Koa* warriors *plus* race canoes to save a general. Smiles and jokes among them, and a beaming John 'Aukai, who towered over the others, making for a giant-sized caboose to the freedom fighters' train.

Without sulfa drugs, that poor guy would still be back at the settlement, cut off from the world and all that it had to offer. But now he was back in it, albeit a world filled with danger and death. Notwithstanding those grim facts, his shy smile and salute to me as he passed, told me it was a world he wanted.

The professor watched them go, his face naked with yearning. What to do with this guy? Then it came to me.

"Professor, I saw where they put the first bomb. Do you know where they'll put the second one?"

"*Si.*"

"I mean *exactly*. CG will be a big deal."

"CG?"

"Center-of-gravity. Those things are monsters. They've got to be placed in the correct spot. Too tail-heavy and that plane will never take off."

"I have seen the mounting posts for the second one."

"Then get your gear together. You're coming with us."

He lit up like Christmas. "I can help?"

"Yes, you can. I don't know the first thing about firing torpedoes, but Lieutenant Kennedy does. You two need to put your heads together and plan the run. They've got to hit just the right spot."

"'Heads together'?"

"Turn of phrase… means thinking like a team."

"*Ho capito.* I will do anything you ask. Just let me be a part of this mission."

"Like Hek said, you already are."

"*Bravissimo.* No more sitting in a cave and despising myself." He thumped his chest. "From now on, I take ACTION against my enemy."

He spun around and marched off. We watched him go.

Gunny cleared his throat. "Do we really need him, sir?"

"No. But he needs us."

While waiting for our night departure onboard PT-109, Gunny and Hek spent the following afternoon re-briefing the guerilla fighters on the

244 ·

upcoming mission. The plan, like most good ones, was simple, not complex, with easily interconnecting parts:

1. PT-109 takes up station five miles off shore of Kanapou Bay, torpedoes armed and ready. There we await the signal to begin our attack run on the flying boat, anchored just offshore of the weaponizing base in Kaukamaka Gulch.

2. Gunny and a small detachment of guerilla fighters in outrigger canoes land to the northeast of the base to take up observation positions.

3. Simultaneously, Hek and his troops land near the base camp of the Japanese garrison troops, ten miles southwest on the shores of Honokanai'a Bay.

4. At a signal from Hek, PT-124 slams the army garrison with mortar fire to simulate an artillery barrage, causing all hell to break loose.

5. Hek and his team the hit the base with all they've got.

6. The attack draws away the guard detachment from over at the weaponizing site.

7. Once Gunny confirms their departure, he signals us.

8. We start our torpedo run.

9. We blow that beautiful beast of an airplane to kingdom come, and by doing so, de-claw the Japanese tiger for good—or at least until we can grow nuclear claws of our own.

PT-109 was minutes away from arriving at the leper colony. Fortunately, the Hawaiian gods were on our side. They sent heavy cloud cover to hide the moonlight from revealing the torpedo boat for all the world to see. The clouds brought a pretty stiff wind too. If it brought rain as well, that could help mask our attack.

But if it developed into a storm, that would be a different story. No access to weather reports, we'd have to rely on traditional methods of forecasting; like asking a Hawaiian elder at the Maui base, who knew these seas and skies like you know the street where you live.

The cloud cover also helped hide the guerilla troops hunkered down along the breakwater from the enemy observation towers on the sea cliffs. They blended into the dark grey, jumbled piles of lava rocks. Two of the larger "piles" must have been Hek and John 'Aukai.

Thanks to Hek's immediate acceptance of the young man into the guerilla group, the other fighters followed suit. Funny how a leader's approval can trickle down to the masses and get them to go along too. That, plus the sulfa drugs doing their magic, made for a new world dawning for that kid. And for the rest of the world too, thanks to people like Nurse Robinson, who joined Ava and me in the small shelter near the concrete pier that jutted out into the tiny harbor.

Even though the night air was relatively warm—almost seventy degrees—I felt the occasional shiver.

Ava spotted it right away. Not much that woman misses. "You okay?"

"I'm fine."

"Opening night jitters?"

"Just a little chilly. Sea breeze I guess."

"Me too." Robinson snugged her nurse's case around her shoulders. "Hard to believe a few hours from now it'll be in the mid-eighties."

We watched in silence as the PT boat drifted closer and closer to the small concrete docking pier, where two men from the colony waited to catch the mooring lines. A muffled revving of the engines in reverse, a low whistle from someone on the boat deck, and the lines snaked out to waiting arms.

Robinson saluted me. "Good luck and good hunting, sir."

"See you tomorrow."

"We'll keep the home fires burning."

"You do that. And keep up your good work with these folks. They're lucky to have you."

"Works both ways, sir."

She turned to Ava. What started as a salute between equals turned into a quick embrace and whispered words. There's a limit to military protocol. Especially when the stakes are mortal.

Sniffing back tears and blowing her nose with a resounding "honk," Ava joined me as I headed for the boat.

Lieutenant Kennedy shook his head in wonder as he witnessed the long line of guerilla troops swiftly scurry on board to take up position, cross-legged, on every available inch of space on deck, and below.

When Ava and I joined him on the bridge, he delivered a sharp salute and grin, "Welcome to the Staten Island Ferry, sir."

Ava said, "Permission to come aboard, sir?"

Kennedy started slightly, then returned the salute. "So granted—that you, Lieutenant James?"

"Face camouflage. The latest rage. What do you think?"

"I didn't even recognize you."

"Good."

While Ava fussed with her utility harness and ammo pouches, I added, "General MacArthur ordered this mission to be a family affair. We happily complied—how are you fixed for torpedoes?"

"They're fine-tuning the ones we're going to be using."

"You don't sound confident."

"Can't lie, sir."

"Appreciate your candor."

"The Kennedy clan is nothing if not honest—excuse me, sir, we need to cast off before Tojo on the cliffs decides we're not just doing our usual social call." He cupped his hands and called out softly, "Let go forward, let go aft."

He advanced the throttles slightly. The engines muttered as their propellers dug in reverse and backed us away from the pier. Within seconds, the moody, cloud-covered darkness swallowed up the boarding dock as though it never existed. In its place, the vast darkness of the open ocean swallowed us up in turn – a small wooden boat bristling with guns and guerilla fighters on their way to change the course of history. Or die trying.

But the clamor and clanging from all the frantic work going on in the PT's secret base in Maui had to happen first. And plenty of it, as we glided up to our mooring inside the lava-tube cavern. Its curved, roughened walls acted like a sounding board and echoed and re-echoed the noise of preparing for war.

Most of the guerilla fighters hopped off the PT boat like monkeys escaping the zoo before it even tied up. Accustomed to the pitching and swooping of war canoes under sail, the hour-long journey to Maui had been like a cruise on an ocean liner by comparison, requiring nothing for them to do but twiddle their thumbs and gossip about who did what to whom.

All that would change tonight, the moment they boarded their double-hulled war canoes for the ten-mile journey across open ocean to Kaho'olawe. With their weapons and munitions safely stored in waterproof center sections of the canoes, their hands would hold paddles instead of guns, and their thoughts would center on one thing only – the next stroke, and the next, as they drove their sleek canoes forward.

To get of Gunny and Hek's additional troops to our final destination without half of them hanging on to the gunwales, *Kahuna* Anakoni had somehow scared up another twin-hulled canoe to handle the influx.

The fighters soon clustered around two war canoes tied up, elephant-style, bow-to-stern in the side channel. They'd be the first to leave. We couldn't begin our attack until after their assault had started. And, considering PT-109 could close the distance separating us from Kaho'olawe in no time flat, Hek would radio the go-ahead, then we'd arrive like a shooting star with our torpedoes hot and ready to shoot.

Risky for us to use the radio, I know, what with Japanese listening stations peppering the islands. But no matter who you are, complacency invariably sets in during occupation and makes a mockery of military discipline. Better to be dodging bullets than swatting flies, which is what the troops mostly were doing in the Hawaiian Islands, while busily dreaming of home.

No fly swatting tonight, though, as our guerilla fighters pointed and chatted in Hawaiian about God only knows what. Similarly, Hek, Anakoni, and Gunny were deep in discussion by the two smaller, outrigger-style canoes tied up behind the big ones These would carry Gunny and his small team of fighters to a point just north of Kaukamaka gulch. From there, they'd keep an evil eye on any troops that stayed behind after the call for reinforcements came and engage them if needed during our attack from the sea.

As for Hek's diversionary attack, we were counting more on human nature than military logic with our plan to peel off the guard force in the gulch. When your neighbor hollers his house is on fire and needs a hose, you come running with yours. You don't think about the sparks spreading to your own roof. You just run.

By now, Hek and Tony and the other fighters had a lot of experience fighting the Japanese. What they had learned so far, is that military textbooks always call for leaving a reserve force to deal with a possible flank attack. But when under fire, the Asian mind instinctively works toward the common good, rather than the selective. Like ants, if you will – the colony takes precedence over the individual.

Plus, we also knew that "plans" go out the window the minute bullets start flying. That was probably tattooed backwards on Patton's chest so that he could read it in the mirror while shaving every morning. At least I think so, considering his remarkable consistency in respecting that axiom to date.

He was also a firm believer in another axiom – war between fighting men—and women—is a zero-sum game. Wins and losses balance out— maybe not right away but eventually.

I asked him once, "If that's true, then why do we go to war?"

"Because we can," he said.

While our guerilla forces prepared for their mission, Tony and I stared at a torpedo resting on a reinforced pedestal, its innards open to the world like an autopsy victim, as two sailors tinkered with its propulsion system at the stern.

At the other end of the twenty-one-foot weapon, Kennedy gently patted the warhead like a baby's bottom. "Five hundred pounds of punch. If only we could land it."

"We will, sir," one of the sailors said. "We've got her ass-end working to perfection."

"Holding pressure okay?"

He checked his watch. "Been like this for a solid hour. Tight as a drum."

The other sailor nodded in conspiratorial agreement.

Kennedy explained the how compressed air, combined with burning alcohol, created steam that drove gears that spun the torpedo's shaft-mounted propeller. Capable of almost forty-miles-an-hour, this deadly weapon could travel almost ten miles, maximum. All we needed was a measly two hundred yards… six hundred lousy feet.

Kennedy peered into an open access panel in the torpedo's mid-section. "Gyros?"

A slight hesitation. Doubt in their eyes. Kennedy grinned. "Don't worry boys, for once in your lives, my firing angle is going to be zero."

He cleared up their puzzled looks by explaining that instead of angling the port and starboard torpedo launch tubes outward like they normally would during an attack, they would fire their two forward torpedoes directly over the bow, zero deflection. The distance-to-target was so short and the *Kawanishi* stationary, it would be like shooting a fish—albeit a BIG fish—in a barrel.

They grinned at that.

Kennedy said, "Button her up, grease her good, and let me know when we're locked and loaded."

Twin salutes and determined "yessirs!"

Such military respect and professional bearing seemed odd coming from two young sailors wearing Hawaiian shirts and ratty-looking hats. One had a fairly decent beard going, while his buddy's was a bit on the straggly side. But that's how you build *esprit de corps* when you're far from home, stranded in the middle of nowhere, and living hand-to-mouth.

I left Tony to kibitz with the torpedo whiz kids, while Kennedy and I returned to the boat – he to his duties, and me to track down Ava.

I found her and Professor Rasetti in the tunnel's makeshift mess hall area, deep in discussion by the stainless-steel coffee urn. Amazing how resourceful you can be in a war zone. Where did all this stuff come from? Not a clue. Nor did I spend an ounce of time thinking beyond the question because the answer—as most answers are during war—would be unbelievable, anyhow.

Ava handed me a cup of the piping hot brew. "Glad you take it black, all they've got is condensed milk."

Rasetti was like a kid in a candy shop. "This is unbelievable. So many things happening all at once."

"We're at war, professor. I'm sure you saw the same thing going on over at the gulch."

"The what?"

"Where that nutcase Jap scientist of yours is holding court."

His face was blank at my slang.

Ava took his arm. "What my husband's saying, is that you friend, Saburo, he—"

"Saburo Yamasaki is *not* my friend." Rasetti spat on the ground. *"Basta così*, not anymore."

Ava was unfazed at the guy's over-the-top style. "Tell the colonel what you told me about what they were going to do."

He reared back. "You mean what they *will* do unless we stop them."

"Relax." She patted his arm. "Let's assume that we blow up those bombs of yours into smithereens, okay? And what you're about to describe never happens—but go ahead, tell Sam about the Oahu flyover they were planning."

His description came out in a flurry of broken English, but basically the gist was this: after takeoff just before dawn, the *Kawanishi* would *not* head east toward the Panama Canal—at least not at first. Instead, they would fly west toward Oahu. The twenty-five-minute hop was nothing compared to the five thousand-plus mile journey that followed directly afterwards.

Oahu would not be sleeping, no, sir—as per orders of whoever was the new commanding officer—assuming Admiral Hidaka already performed his *seppuku* thing—the Japanese inhabitants would be out on the streets, banners at the ready, fireworks at hand, voices ready to cheer the grand moment when the largest airplane in the world made her low approach for a lumbering farewell flyover.

They would be witnesses to the final step in the fulfilment of Tokyo's dream of the "Greater Asian Prosperity Sphere." With the Panama Canal out of action and the Aleutian Island chain occupied, the warlords' design for Japan's new world order would finally come to pass.

What better way to cheer this epoch-making moment than by witnessing the rising sun climbing in the east, while the *Kawanishi* roared overhead and then turned toward the sun. Like a single organism united with one purpose, they'd open their mouths and shout the classic Japanese word.

Caught up in his storytelling, Rasetti gave us a sample, *"BANZAI!"*

The effect was startling. Everything around us ground to a halt. The guerillas and sailors stared at us., while the Italian stood there, breathing hard, like a tenor finishing an aria in *La Bohème*. I quickly shooed everyone back to work.

"You're sure about this flyover thing?" I said when things settled down again.

"Saburo showed me the orders—in Japanese, of course, but he translated them."

"This guy speaks Italian?"

"English. Science needs a common tongue. We have chosen yours."

Ava frowned. "This guy's not much of a scientist—at least anymore. Seems more like a warmonger."

"Come se dice—"

"Warmonger means someone who wants war and will do anything to get it."

"Mi scusi, but you are wrong, *signora."* Rasetti deliberated for a moment. Then said, "Saburo Yamasaki's ancestors were *Samurai* warriors. War did not matter to them as much as how they *acted* in the war, or the battle, or even a sword fight. Saburo is without a doubt the most brilliant scientist I have ever known, but his *Bushido* gets in his way."

"My turn to ask."

"Bushido is a *Samurai's* code of honor. His morals must be absolutely strict, his discipline firm, his devotion to his master absolute."

"Meaning Emperor Hirohito?"

He shook his head. "No. While it's true that the emperor is a god Saburo worships, General Tojo is his master, his *daimyo,* and he is absolutely devoted to serving him, *Samurai* style. He once said—"

He stopped, smiled, and shook his head ruefully.

"Go on..."

"A *Samurai* warrior carries two swords in his belt. Only they can carry two. It is tradition. The long sword is the *katana* and the short one is the *wakizashi.* Each razor-sharp, each hand-forged.

One night, Saburo and I drank too much *sake* and he showed me his swords. Beautiful. Deadly. Not like the bomb we were building, and the one from Tokyo – they were—and still are—a tangled mess of wires and steel plates, but they *will* work, this I know for certain.

"Saburo called the bombs his new 'swords.' The *katana* will strike the west locks, the *wakizashi* the east."

"Meaning Panama?" I said.

"Si."

Always be prepared for death,
whether your own or someone else's.
Yamaoka Tesshu – *Samurai* warrior

The lights flickered once, twice, then went out. Whatever I had been saying to Anakoni and Hek about our war canoes stopped mid-sentence. A sharp whistle. An answering whistle. A banging sound. A curse, then someone laughed.

"You on it, Duvall?" a voice shouted.

"Affirmative, chief!"

More banging. Fairway shouting. Oil lanterns appeared here and there, more for navigation than illumination. You don't want folks tumbling into the water in an underground cave.

Somewhere in the darkness, Ava laughed, and others joined in. I tell you, that woman can work a room like nobody's business. Movie stars. What a world they live in—especially in the dark.

I said, "Where do you get your power?"

Hek laughed. "From the enemy, of course."

Anakoni explained how the Maui-based guerillas had tapped into the central feed line that delivered electricity to the nearby town of Makena. From there, they ran a secondary cable down to the tube cave.

"Where'd they find cable?" I said.

"From the enemy, of course." Hek said.

Anakoni added, "Such idiots, the Japanese."

As if in answer, the lights flickered on… off… then on again. Cheers here and there. Scattered applause. This time they stayed on. Word filtered back from the depths like relay race.

"Junction box… breaker bad… Duvall's a genius… no, he ain't… yes, he is."

The guerillas resumed stowing their weapons in the central cargo sections. Hard to believe that Hek and Tony and I had been in that same place a few days ago, jammed inside a Tahitian racing canoe.

They say that "work expands to the time allotted." I'm here to say that the reverse is true, too—in wartime. In less than a week—seven short days—we had gone from being kidnapped in San Francisco to this secret hideout in Maui, preparing to attack an enemy base.

A *week*.

I said as much to Hek who nodded. "Time is on our side, now. So are the gods."

Anakoni added, "*Ali'i nui* speaks the truth."

"Who's he?" I said.

Anakoni pointed to Hek, who shook his head, and then they went back and forth in Hawaiian, it got a bit heated.

Finally Anakoni shook his head. "I called him 'chief.' Every time I do that he jumps all over me."

"Because I'm *not* a chief, damn it."

"*Yet,*" Anakoni said. "But one day you will be. After we drive the Japs from our islands."

I said, "That's why we're here."

The two men glanced at each other – Anakoni concerned, but Hek stone-faced. But that didn't last long. His face melted into a familiar grin. "Colonel Carter, the great *Kahuna* Anakoni meant *all* of our enemies: Japan....and America included—no offence."

"None taken—I think."

"Don't take this the wrong way, sir, but—"

"—but your country took our islands the wrong way." Anakoni said.

"I don't know my history that well."

Hek said, "That's okay because we do. The Hawaiian people lived it. While it's true your missionaries came to do good for the savages, but thanks to sugar, they did right well, too."

Anakoni grinned. "I love that saying."

Hek poked his friend's chest. "You and your family didn't do so bad, either. Tourist canoes, surfing…"

"Bread crumbs!"

Another verbal tennis match in Hawaiian. I let them go at it, while Hek's guerillas stored the last of the automatic weapons and rounds for their small, 60mm mortar – a pop-gun compared to the two, 80mm mortars mounted just ahead of the charthouse on PT-124. Normally used for harassment fire, those big guys would be used to fix the enemy in place while Hek's attack force disembarked from their war canoes and landed on the beach.

The 124 and 109 also carried pairs of Mark V Spin-stabilized rocket launchers, eight rockets per unit. Not as big a punch as the mortars, but they could do major damage if fired in salvoes.

The faraway cough and rumble of PT-124's engines starting up echoed and re-echoed through the tunnel. The noise died away quickly as they throttled down to a muttering idle. Even so, Hek and Anakoni still had to raise their voices to be heard, but by now their arguing had pretty much run out of gas.

I said, "I remember that beautiful feathered cape in the cave in Oahu."

Anakoni lit up like a movie fan. "Kaneana Cave?" He turned to Hek. "You *wore* it there?" Gone was his sophisticated 'been-there-done-that' attitude displayed when I first met him. Now he was officially gaga over Hek.

"No way." Hek folded his arms across his chest. "*Kahuna* Kalola wanted me wear it to rally the troops like I was Kamehameha, for God's sake."

"Why not? You've got his blood somewhere in you."

"Don't forget the crown," I said.

He winced at that.

Anakoni whistled in appreciation. "That too? Man, I wish I could have been there. I'd have had you wear it for sure." He punched Hek lightly on the shoulder. "You're royal blood, braddah. One of these days you're going to rule these islands like you ruled the football field—this guy, we called him the bulldozer—we'd give him the football and he'd cross the goal line every time like nobody was home but the goal posts."

"Not every time," Hek said with a frown. But you could tell he liked the attention.

Anakoni poked him in his chest. "You'll bring back our constitution, too, brah, right?"

Hek slowly nodded in a kingly way. "Make it even better this time."

That was a new one on me. "You had a Constitution?"

"Colonel Carter, we had us a whole damned *kingdom* before America stole it."

"Hey, don't look at *me* like that."

Hek's frown melted into a smile. "Don't worry, sir. I'll make you head of my Royal Hawaiian Air Force."

"Good benefits? Retirement package? Nice place overlooking Pearl?"

"A *lanai* to die for, guaranteed."

That got us smiling like kids at recess. Nothing like dreams to make reality bearable.

The flickering lights brought us back to the real world and the task ahead. No coronation feasts, no *Hula* dancing, no celebratory parade in Oahu to celebrate "King Hekila's" coronation. For us instead, a ten-mile journey across open ocean to a desolate island to destroy weapons of unimaginable power.

I confess for a moment, the task seemed utterly impossible. How could we ever pull it off? No chance to practice. Not enough time. Nothing more than a few hastily-convened planning sessions earlier that day, with nervous-looking troops staring at Gunny's crudely-drawn maps of the two assault areas on Kaho'olawe.

Simple was the word of the day: Hek would lead the main assault in the south to draw troops back from the gulch, while Gunny's smaller force of ten men would polish off any soldiers that stayed behind. On Gunny's signal from shore, PT-109 would commence its run up the dredged channel and fire its two tuned-up torpedoes into the *Kawanishi's* guts.

From what other information we could glean from Professor Rasetti, things were coming to a head faster than we thought. The flight was imminent. The discouraging thought of arriving there to behold an empty bay with the flying boat and its deadly payload long gone was enough to give me a case of the hives. And enough to rattle Gunny, too.

The chalk kept breaking during the briefing, as he sketched out attack directions with swooping arrows. He cursed the breakage on the high humidity. But nerves had something to do with it, too, I'm sure. Make no mistake, Gunny was the perfect embodiment of what the United States Marine Corps considers the backbone of its fighting men; a veteran, battle-tested, non-commissioned officer not afraid to take chances, give orders, take orders, and get the damn job done.

But everyone, even veteran NCOs have their limits. And just when I thought Gunny had reached his, he surprised me—as he always did.

"We can *do* this, gentleman," he shouted to the group. "And we'll do it the way we've done everything so far – with our eyes on the prize...." He pointed to his glittering, dark-brown eyes. "Do it, troops."

As if attached by a single string, the guerillas imitated Gunny's gesture by pointing to their eyes, too, repeating "Eyes on PRIZE."

"Hearts beating as one." He THUMPED his chest.

No need to prompt them. They did the same, with resounding BOOM.

He grabbed his crotch. "Balls tucked up tight."

"Up TIGHT!"

Grim determination shifted to raucous laughter, including mine.

0200 hours

Go time.

No beating drums, no marching bands, no fiery speeches.

Just men dipping paddles into the salt water, war canoes gliding silently away from the narrow stone pier, and heading for the cave opening, with Hek in the lead canoe, arms folded, staring straight ahead, bound for the garrison site on Kaho'olawe.

Minutes later, three smaller outrigger canoes followed. Gunny an arms-folded mirror image of Hek. Change the guerilla fighters' modern-day war gear to bare chests, loincloths, and stone weapons, and they could have been ancient *Koa* warriors on their way to conquer a rival prince on a neighboring island.

Funny to think of a beach bum like Hek being a prince, but he was proving himself to be one worthy of wearing a kingly crown. I don't believe that blood has anything to do with one's heritage. But I do believe that the spirit world works in strange ways. And while King Kamehameha lived long before my time, it seemed that tonight his spirit was alive and well inside that hefty-sized Hawaiian.

Ava, Tony, and I stood on the pier watching them depart. The only sound echoing and re-echoing inside the cave was the faraway rushing hiss of the ocean waiting to carry them across to Kaho'olawe.

Behind us, work continued on both PT-109 and PT-124. The latter would depart in an hour to support Hek's landing. Kennedy's a half-hour later with us on board to meet our destiny.

Did all of this look good on paper and blackboards? You bet. Sounded great, too, when we strategized how to coordinate the attacks. But like

General Patton said, everything goes out the window when you-know-what hits the fan and the bullets fly.

Ava said softly, "God speed and good hunting to those brave young men."

Tony said, "Amen to that, ma'am."

"Do you mind not calling me that?" Ava said. "Makes me sound like I'm old enough to be your mother."

"With all due respect, ma'am. You ain't my mother by a long shot."

"That's a compliment?"

"A fact."

"From now on, it's 'Ava,' okay?"

"You got it."

She turned to me. "Permission to peck you on the cheek, sir."

"Granted."

She did so, twice, in fact, then stepped back and saluted. "Permission to touch up my makeup? My green's wearing thin."

"You're beautiful nonetheless, but so granted."

Tony and I watched her make her exit. And not just any exit. Hollywood struck it rich when Paramount Studios discovered Ava James. People say stars are made not born. And maybe that's true for other actresses. But after two years of living with this woman, first as her head-over-heels boyfriend, then as her husband, I can say that this particular 'star' was born like the real ones outside the cave.

And while it's true, the heavy overcast hid their celestial presence at the moment, they were still up there just the same, burning bright. In like manner, streaks of camouflage grease paint hid Ava's face, and her shapeless fatigues masked graceful curves. But beneath it all, that movie star was burning bright as Polaris. So damn bright that even now, she gave off that certain "something" that the rest of us don't have—but can damn well appreciate.

Tony said, "With all due respect, Skipper...."

He let out a soft wolf whistle. Ava's sharp ears picked it up. She tossed off the smallest of waves in regal acknowledgement. Professor Rasetti standing on the deck of PT-109 witnessed the same thing we did.

A friendly wave from Ava to him, and one in return from a man who I'd never seen smile. And not only Rasetti, but the two sailors kneeling by the torpedo launch tube who were following her progress the way flowers turn toward the sun – in this case a star. They shook their heads in mute admiration.

Tony said, "Looks like Professor Egghead over there appreciates the finer things in life."

"As should we all." Then I tried to shift the topic. Not easy when Ava's around, that's for sure. "Ready for a little C.G. computing with the good professor?"

"Aye, aye, skipper. Besides, it'll get Rasetti's mind where it belongs."

"Hope he's right about where they'll mount the other bomb. We've only got one chance."

"Two."

"What do you mean?"

"Two torpedoes, skipper. Only need one to break her back. The burning fuel plus the weight of *fourteen* frigging engines on her big-ass wings will do the rest."

"Thanks for the reminder that gravity is on our side."

"Thank God not me. He's the one who invented it."

After years of being rated as a "Master of Flying Boats" for *Pan Am*, I knew from long experience that there's no such thing as being completely ready for a complex journey.

Whether taking off west from San Francisco across the Pacific to land in Hong Kong eight days later, or doing the reverse, there would always come a time when I would make a final check of the instruments; fuel, cylinder head temperatures, oil pressure, hydraulic fluid pressure, and on and on, then move the flight controls through their full range for the last time.

Then I'd make a big deal of clearing my throat so as not to croak as I casually turned to my copilot and said, "Cast off all lines."

Lieutenant Kennedy didn't clear his throat (I made a note to advise him later on this trick), so he sounded a bit like a frog, when an hour later he shouted, "Cast of all lines!"

The first to slither free was the one through the bullnose on the bow. As it came free, he twisted a small lever beside his throttle quadrant that had three words etched on it: "Ahead, Astern, and Stop." "

I said, "I thought only ships had annunciators."

Kennedy patted the wooden wheel. "We may be small, sir, but we're just as old-fashioned as the big guys."

His annunciator was connected by cables to an identical one in the engine room with three arrows pointing to three matching words: "Ahead, Astern, Stop."

When Pappy saw the arrows move on his smaller version (one per engine), he manhandled the shift levers on the engines just like you'd shift a car—but in this case, thanks to an aircraft-style carburetor and a supercharger, you'd be shifting over five *thousand* horses that gobbled five *hundred* gallons of AVGAS an hour, when going full speed.

With her bow swinging clear, Kennedy nudged the throttles slightly as the deck crew let go the lines from the stern cleats. Only a handful of sailors remained behind – on sick call or guard duty. They stood at attention and held their salutes as we passed them and headed for the cave opening.

I checked my watch.

0245.

Yawned twice. The first time because I was sleepy, and the second because I was nervous as a cat. And like a cat, I yawned to reduce the tension I felt—mostly because from now on I had absolutely nothing to do but witness either the success or failure of a mission that by any stretch of the imagination was decidedly desperate.

That whale-sized Japanese Navy flying boat carried the seeds of devastation, not only to the docks in Panama but also to the free world. We only had two measly "harpoons" with which to stop it.

If Japan somehow managed to succeeded in cutting off the United States from the west by plugging up the Aleutians and doing the same to Panama, we'd have no choice but to negotiate a peace of some sort. Sure, democracy would survive—long enough, I hoped, for General MacArthur to drive Hitler back into his cave and roll a boulder in front of it.

But America would be lessened in stature both globally and economically. The balance of power currently teetering back and forth would come down with a crash—on the wrong side of America and the wrong side of history.

I pondered these depressing possibilities while Kennedy's crew repeated what PT-124's crew had done thirty minutes before – but in our case, equipped with a radically different array of armament than our sister boat– most notably, 30mm mortars and a whopping big 40mm Bofor bow gun. Beefed-up with such heavy armament, she was like a gunboat.

By my watch, the 124 must be on station by now, awaiting orders to support Hek's landing—which should be happening soon. So far, we'd received one brief Morse code message to confirm this, but didn't respond beyond a brief "dit-dah-dit" (the letter 'R' for "received.").

Our radios could also receive voice transmissions, but the Japanese had great RDF-triangulation gear. Fortunately for us, they were notoriously slack in pursuing their contacts—unless they detected prolonged communications. So far in this unconventional guerilla warfare that Lieutenant Kennedy and his boats were waging, they'd managed to escape detection. Best not to tempt the gods, though. Not ever.

I was left to imagine what was going on with Hek and his team. I did my best not to think for an instant that it would be a textbook operation. Patton's warning about SNAFUs rang in my ear, even though he was thousands of miles away, doing God knows what.

All I could do was hope that the confusion of a multi-pronged attack upon lazy, bored, garrison troops would create a shock wave – first to stun them into immobility, then a barrage of 40mm cannon fire from PT-124 to cut off any retreat to the hills.

That's when the call would go out for reinforcements. And *that's* when the troops over in Kaukamaka gulch would come running, scrambling, still half-asleep, barely dressed, their officers and noncoms screaming at them as only Japanese soldiers can. The cavalry was coming!

And *that's* when we would attack.

Ten minutes from now.

I checked my watch. Hard to imagine such a thing. But I tried, and at the same time tried to be realistic. I checked my watch *again*, as if I could stop its ever-moving second hand.

Where was Gunny? Had he and his team landed safely? No way of knowing. Managing my racing thoughts was like chasing black cats inside a coal mine – nothing to go on but instinct, common sense, and a lot of hope.

Earlier, when Gunny prepared to depart with his smaller attack force in the outriggers, we spoke briefly. To be honest, more me talking and Gunny nodding and grunting now and then as he adjusted his combat pack webbing and patted his ammo pouches to make sure all was in order.

Everything about him had subtly changed. He seemed slightly shorter, as if his rangy, rawboned frame had contracted slightly to conserve his energy for the mission ahead. He'd served in the Marines long enough to have seen combat in other wars before this one. And now, with his front-line, guerilla-style experience gained during the past two years of Hawaii occupation, he'd become a specialist at poking sticks in the Japanese wheel of war. Tonight the biggest stick yet.

"You're dressed to kill," I joked.

His lean face tightened. "Aye, aye, sir."

"So much for my speech to rally the troops, huh?"

That got a grin.

"Listen, sergeant, I just wanted to——"

"Sir…" He held up his hand and I fell silent. When a Marine gunnery sergeant lifts his hand like that, I defy you not to fall silent too.

He dug into one of his ammo pouches. But instead of pulling out a submachine gun clip, he handed me a folded envelope.

"Do me a favor, sir?"

"Name it."

"If you make it back and I don't, would you mind——"

"C'mon, this isn't a war movie, sergeant."

"No sir, it's not. It's a goddamned *war*, and this is a letter to my daughter Sarah who lives back in Idaho. In case I don't make it, I want her to know some… some things."

I quickly took it. "Sorry, sergeant. Of course, I will."

Then I laughed. It happened unexpectedly. Gunny gave me "the look," as I quickly tried to explain my nervous reaction to a thought I'd just had about my own mortality. As I went on and on, Gunny put up his hand again and I slammed on the brakes.

"You'll make it back, sir. No worries in that department."

"What makes you so sure?"

He leaned closer and whispered, "Because you're a goddamned *officer... sir.*"

He reared back and smiled—the way a tiger might smile in anticipation before it pounces. I didn't dare do anything but smile back.

Thanks to the continuing overcast skies, pitch-black darkness waited for us as PT-109 cleared the camouflaged opening to the cave. Gunny was already long gone with his team. Hek, too, along with PT-124. "Nobody here but us chickens," as the saying goes. But in our case very brave chickens armed with torpedoes.

I stood beside Lieutenant Kennedy in the flying bridge, while Ava and Tony and Professor Rasetti took up residence in the small day room, with the torpedo men. Based on Rasetti's insistence on the bomb placement, Kennedy had calculated the depth settings and the angle-of-fire that would deliver the TNT warheads to their target.

If the *Kawanishi* had been an average-sized flying boat, a few well-place rounds of 20mm cannon fire would have sent it heavenward to that Rising Sun in the sky, and that would have been that. But with a plane this immense, cannon fire would be like poking an ice pick in a car door. We needed the punch only torpedoes could deliver.

Providing they blew up.

I shoved that fear inside my head to a place where all my scary thoughts live. Remember, I was the guy who got Kennedy to agree to this mission in the first place, with my "Let's-count-on-the-forty-percent-times-the torpedoes-*do*-work" speech that he bought hook, line, and sinker. Time for me to bite that same hook.

As my father used to say, "Thoughts make things, not the other way around." No way was I *not* going to think otherwise than those tin fish working the way they designers *thought* they would.

But... the fact remained that the failure rate of the Mark 8 was huge. They dove for the bottom, with their depth mechanisms nutty, or ran round-and-round in circles because of a busted gyro, or worst of all – bounced off the targets, their exploders bent or broken.

Bounced.

To increase our odds, the torpedomen had done their best to fine-tune two of our four. Then had even put small protective "caps" over the exploders to keep them from shearing off, if the torpedoes struck sideways. They also "locked" the depth mechanisms to zero. The harbor waters were too shallow to risk anything deeper. Ditto for the gyros set for zero degrees – we would be firing straight down the pickle barrel.

They had done what they could. Now we needed to do what needed to be done.

Kennedy flicked on a small ultraviolet light that caused the phosphorous numerals on his engine instruments and compass to glow brightly in the darkness.

I was impressed at the visual effect. "We should have those in airplanes."

He tapped the compass. "I'll put it in the suggestion box, sir."

We maintained a cautious ten knots until we cleared the small inlet.

"Keeping our wake down," Kennedy explained. "That's what they spot first."

"Don't need that tonight."

"Don't need it *ever.*"

My knees felt the first swell of the open ocean before my brain did. Behind us, nothing but the shadowy darkness of Maui's low-lying hills with its inhabitants sleeping the sleep of the occupied.

Impossible to see further north to *Haleakelā*, the shield volcano that makes up most of the island. Over ten-thousand-feet high, the dormant volcano is but one of the many "tips" of Hawaii's volcanic "icebergs," whose impressive mass extends thousands of feet into the depths until it finally reaches the ocean floor.

The Hawaiian Islands began with fire. Tonight, we were adding our torpedoes to the blaze—not to give birth but bring death to a flying boat carrying men determined to drop hydrogen bombs with the destructive force of twin volcanoes.

We absolutely *had* to succeed.

Kennedy interrupted my nervous reverie. "Sir, you flew flying boats before the war, right?"

"Affirmative."

"Thought I recognized you."

"How so?"

"Back in thirty-nine, I flew on a clipper—the *Dixie Clipper* as I recall. From Ireland back to New York My first flight across the ocean. Pretty sure you sat at my table for dinner."

I looked at him again, this time more closely, trying to place his face. A hard thing to do, because I had sat through many a meal on many a clipper, doing my best to be a shining example of the kind of *Pan American Airways* in-flight attention we gave to our prestigious, well-heeled customers.

"I had more meat on my frame back then," he added.

"Sorry, but I…"

"Doesn't matter, sir. But I do remember how calm and collected you were when one of our engines started sputtering and backfiring. I almost panicked, but you just kept on eating your dinner and making small talk. That calmed down everybody—especially me."

"All an act, believe me. While the guys on the flight deck were jumping out of their skins, my job was to make sure I didn't drop the peas off my fork. How'd I do?"

Kennedy laughed.

We motored on, lost in our thoughts, while our engines gulped their high-octane AVGAS like a thirsty man finding an oasis in the dessert. The lookouts tucked into their respective gun tubs swept the port and starboard quadrants ceaselessly with their binoculars. If there was something to see in that inky darkness, they'd spot it. All I could see was a wall of nothingness rising from the dimly-lit sea.

A thought came to me. "What were you doing flying from Ireland? Those tickets cost a fortune."

"Remember a ship called the *Athenia?*"

"Rings a bell, but…."

"British passenger liner. A Nazi U-boat sunk her off the coast of Ireland back in thirty-nine. Hitler denied it, but…"

"Nazis are Nazis—*now* I remember…wasn't that—"

"—the straw that broke the camel's back. Yes, sir. The Brits declared war after that."

It all came back in a rush. I even remembered the headlines:

LINER ATHENIS TORPEDOED AND SUNK.
EMPIRE AT WAR!

The Canada-bound liner was filled with over a thousand passengers, including Canadian, American, and British citizens. Plus over five hundred Jewish refugees fleeing the madness of Germany's ruthless anti-Semitism.

Struck by two Nazi torpedoes, the *Athenia* stayed afloat long enough for other vessels to rescue a large number of passengers and crew. But over a hundred people died, either from drowning, or killed outright during the initial explosions.

Kennedy said, "I was in London representing my father, to help make arrangements for the American survivors to get home safely. Once that was done, I flew home. Still in college. My senior year."

"Wait a second. You're *that* Kennedy? Your dad, Joseph Kennedy, was the Ambassador?"

" '*Was*' the ambassador is right. Nowadays he's twiddling his thumbs back in Boston."

"While his son fights a war."

Kennedy patted the wheel. "Suits me fine, sir. My brother Joe's in it too. He's a bomber pilot. Four-engine stuff."

"B-17s?"

"Last I heard, yes."

I took the measure of this skinny kid – his water-stained service hat clamped down over a shock of unruly hair, jaw clamped tight, cheekbones gaunt, and a smile that wouldn't go away.

"That a new shirt?" I said.

"No, sir." He fingered the brightly-colored Hawaiian short-sleeve shirt plastered against his thin chest from the force of the wind. "Only wear it on special occasions."

The wave action picked up, now that we were well into the channel that separates Maui from Kaho'olawe. The PT boat's bow BOOMED into the crests and sent showers of spray over the forward third of the boat, including the bridge—and us.

"Sorry about that," Kennedy shouted to be heard over the deep-throated roar of the engines, now revved up to full speed. Even though

most of the exhaust sound was routed underwater via mufflers, the
wooden deck vibrated like a tuning fork.

"You okay, sir?" Kennedy said.

"Been through worse."

"Flying, you mean?"

"Be surprised how hard thunderstorm clouds can be."

That got a laugh.

The radio operator poked his head out from the deckhouse. The wind
nearly tore the flimsy scrap of paper out of his hand.

"Message from the one twenty-four, sir. Shall I read it?"

"Proceed."

"Not much. Just the word 'Green.'"

Kennedy laughed. "My favorite color."

"Yes, sir."

"Signal strength?"

"Not great, but I got it."

"Keep your ears peeled."

He disappeared like a Jack-in-the-Box in reverse.

Kennedy patted the wheel. "So far so good."

That single word carried a long story behind it. But because Japanese
RDF hounds were on the prowl for our radio transmissions, my
imagination supplied what the word "green" meant:

By now, PT-124 had lobbed mortar rounds onto the hapless garrison
troop's camp to soften them up before Hek took over with his team.
And not only mortars but also the massive CLANG and BANG of the
124's deck-mounted Bofor cannon slamming 40mm shells into the
supply stores and fuel depot.

Then—even as I imagined it—into that wreckage and confusion Hek
and his guerillas were racing full speed, screaming at the top of their
lungs, firing their weapons, for sure, but thirsting for the closer, hand-to-
hand combat their *Koa* warrior ancestors had practiced in the distant
past, as Hawaiian princes battled each other to conquer the islands.

What little I'd seen of the guerilla fighters sparring with each other
back on Molokai made me glad to be on a speeding PT boat instead of
running for my life to escape the rage of a Hawaiian warrior who sought
to break my bones—and my spirit.

I come from a world where Colt .45s and Winchester repeating rifles conquered the West. The Native American Indian's tomahawk and bow and arrow didn't stand a chance against the white man's black powder and lead bullets. But the Polynesian culture was thriving centuries before men started using modern-day lethal weapons that allowed death from afar.

No, the *Koa* killed you close up.

Forearms CRASHING against your face, fists SLAMMING your mid-section. A shark-teeth-studded dagger RIPPING across your face, while a massive thigh upended your balance, sending you to the ground, where a stone-lashed club SMASHED your brains out.

Close-up.

Like that.

And if my imagination matched even in small measure what I'd seen Hek and his Hawaiians practicing, then what they were doing right now for real was turning those Japanese soldiers' sweet dreams into brutal nightmares.

Kennedy hollered to be heard over the engine nose, "Lenny! Time to target?"

The XO poked his head out of the chart room. "Little under ten minutes, sir."

Kennedy stabbed a small button on the control panel and a bell rang shrilly. He shouted into the speaking tube, "Now hear this: battle stations torpedo. Battle stations, torpedo."

Just as he finished speaking, the starboard lookout's high-pitched voice cracked as he shouted, "Bandit bearing zero-one-zero degrees!"

"Range!" Kennedy shouted.

"Estimating two miles and closing fast."

"Good eye, Marvin."

Indeed.

I saw absolutely nothing in the darkness. The XO scrambled out from below in an instant, binoculars in hand.

Kennedy growled. "Radar's useless, right?"

"Working fine, bu nothing on the scope, sir."

Plenty up here though, as men scrambled around everywhere, and one determined woman, who made her way forward and wedged herself behind me in the crowded cockpit.

"Got your six, sweetheart," she whispered in my ear. Nothing like Ava James's voice in your ear, especially in the middle of all hell breaking loose.

"Stand by to lay smoke," Kennedy said. "Guns up!"

A strange-sounding, whistling shriek rose above the deep engine roar.

Night turned into day as an aerial flare exploded a thousand feet overhead. Its blueish-white phosphorous light lit us up like convicts on a prison break.

Our twin-fifties banged out their response. Their tracers lobbed high in the air toward the approaching silhouette of a single engine floatplane unlike any I'd ever seen before: cigar-shaped, single-float, low-wing, with a circular air intake in the front and a rear-mounted pusher propeller. As it flashed overhead, it managed a short burst of cannon fire that passed harmlessly to starboard.

Kennedy shouted, "Spotted our wake. Damned phosphorescence is a 'Kick me' sign."

While I couldn't see the effect because of the aerial flare, I'd seen how ships' propellers churning up the night sea could trigger phytoplankton to light up the water like a theater marquee. That's what this night fighter pilot must have spotted and now he had us in his sights.

We had him in ours, too, but not for long. His turn-rate was dizzying. How many G-forces was he pulling? And what's more, why didn't those strange-looking wings with tip-floats break off from the stress?

While my body was in a high state of alarm and concerned with self-preservation in the midst of mortal danger, my mind followed the plane into its tight turn. I couldn't help but admire both the designer and the pilot for a perfect marriage of man and machine—albeit a killing machine that, as my body reminded me with a pounding heartbeat, with a pilot who wanted to kill *me*.

"Lay smoke," Kennedy ordered, the spun the wheel like roulette in Vegas and we slewed to starboard.

Seconds later, billows of white smoke gushed from the smoke generator mounted on the stern. What the chemicals were I haven't a clue. What I do know is that when they combined under pressure they produced a dense curtain of ever-expanding, dense, fog-like smoke.

To me, this was a dumb maneuver because while the smoke was great, we weren't *inside* it. Even easier to spot us, in fact, and that's exactly what the night fighter did. His second pass was lower than his first. I'm guessing a couple hundred feet off the water. Clearly, he wanted to strafe us with his tracers and watch our fuel and munitions go up, taking us with it to meet our maker.

Our engine sound diminished, as did our speed.

Odd.

A quick look at the throttle quadrant—Kennedy had closed the left throttle only and twisted its annunciator arrow from AHEAD at ASTERN.

He shouted into the talk pipe. "Do it Pappy, DO it!"

Down in the engine room, Pappy was already slamming the baseball-bat-sized gearshift lever on the port Packard from neutral to "reverse."

Kennedy rammed the throttle forward and PT-109 did the damnedest maneuver I've ever experienced – we slid *sideways* as the reversing engine pulled us one way while the center and starboard engines pulled us the other, spinning us on our own axis. Then, with power chopped again on the reverse engine, we shot straight into the billowy fogbank of smoke.

And as we entered the clouds of nothingness, Kennedy cut all the throttles. The silence was a blessing at first, but then the strange-sounding, snarling roar of the plane overhead as it searched for its prey. If it had any kind of down-looking radar we'd be sunk for sure.

Tony shouted from somewhere in the mist. "Got to be some kind a turboprop, don't you think, skipper?"

Kennedy started to answer, but I touched his arm. "He means me, lieutenant. We used to work together at *Pan Am*—Tony! Yes, I figure that's what he's got. Hell of a noise, though."

"Hell of a plane."

Ava said, "Is this stuff okay to breathe?""

Kennedy said, "It's okay. Just feels strange."

The smoke generator continued spewing its cloaking screen of safety. But only a matter of time before that pilot sorted out where we were hiding. A very short time.

Kennedy cupped his hands and shouted, "Ready port and starboard depth charges. Set depth for minimum."

Ghostly shapes scurrying around in the fog, answering, "Aye, aye, sir."

What the hell was he up to?

The plane engine noise increasing, louder and louder.... then the metallic BANG-BANG-BANG of his wing-mounted cannons sending 20mm rounds into a cloud bank floating on the ocean, with us hiding inside.

Blessedly, not a sign of tracers, save for one glowing streak high overhead. I didn't envy the pilot his task. What should have been a turkey shoot had turned into a cat and mouse game, thanks to our smoke screen. Granted, the cat had teeth, but so did this particular mouse.

"Standby to drop," Kennedy said.

Lenny raised his arm high. "See me, okay, guys?"

"Aye, aye!"

"Hear me?"

He clamped a signaling whistle in his teeth and blew a test whistle. They gave him a thumbs-up.

"Make more smoke!" Kennedy said as the plane made another pass.

Just as it zoomed past our port side, missing us by at least a hundred yards, Kennedy hit full throttle and we shot out into the clear, trailing a rooster tail of billowing smoke tendrils.

By now, the enemy's aerial flare had hit the water and gone out. But even before I had a chance to feel relieved, another one lit up the night sky.

Instead of weaving back and forth, we continued straight ahead like a dart. I'm no seaman, but it rubbed me the wrong way not to take evasive action of some sort.

Ava shouted, "There he is!"

As she cried out, the bright beam of a searchlight blossomed on the strange-looking airplane's starboard wing. Its merciless, ice-cold blue light painted our boat bright.

Our twin-fifties opened up and sent tracers looping in an arc that fell behind the plane as they tried to get its range. Hard as hell, though, when an airplane's closing perpendicular to your course.

"Here we go!" Kennedy spun the wheel until it became a blur. The powerful Packards thrust the wooden boat hard to starboard and the bow crested like a surfboard across a series of waves.

Nobody could aim worth a damn during that maneuver, including the enemy plane coming straight at us. The 37mm and 20mm cannons on our bow got their range, and vice-versa.

"NOW!" Kennedy shouted.

Lenny blew his whistle and chopped his hand downward.

On the stern, sailors on both sides released can-shaped depth charges and they disappeared into the boiling smoke.

"Depth charges away, skip—"

The XO's chest exploded in a burst of reddish haze. The impact of the enemy's cannon shell threw him forward against the starboard machine gun turret. He collapsed like a rag doll onto the deck.

Ava dropped on her knees to his side. Kennedy glanced down, shouted a curse, but kept at the wheel, now jinking to port and starboard to throw off the floatplane's aim.

By now the plane was about a quarter mile from us. Our combined closing speed had to be at least two-hundred miles-an-hour. A miracle if any of our rounds had hit home, and a tragedy that one of them had struck down the XO.

The human brain is a marvelous survival instrument. When it senses imminent, mortal, danger, it can slow down time.

Slipping on ice, falling in slow motion, having time to brace yourself... A car swerves into your lane... enough time to judge its trajectory and escape collision?

Happening here too:

The Japanese float plane is less than a hundred yards away...

My brain makes it seem to be closing in slow-motion. Close enough now to see its cigar-shaped fuselage with its enormous air intake in the nose, its odd, downward canted wingtips that serve as stabilizing floats to the center one, and the winking flash of its wing cannons seeking to kill us all.

A muffled, faraway BOOM of a depth charge exploding beneath the water... followed almost instantly by another.

The plane flashes overhead, just skimming the top of our smoke cloud, when two billowy columns of whitish-grey water burst forth into the air above the smoke screen to create a vertical "wall" of ocean that nothing can penetrate—let alone a fragile airplane made of aluminum and filled with the flesh and blood of a fighter pilot intent on doing his duty as he crashes straight into it.

The yellow-red flash of exploding aviation fuel lights up the interior of the water column as it slowly collapses back into the depths from which it came, taking with it what's left of the enemy plane.

Volcanoes built the Hawaiian Islands with fiery violence. We have done the opposite.

Time speeds up again.

The cheering sailors whoop and dance at the sight.

Ava's missed it all – she's still crouched over the body of the dead man.

I confirm in words to Kennedy what his eyes already know.

He shakes his head in disbelief. "Lenny's gone. Jesus."

Ava stands. The XO's bloody dog tags in her hands. "Where can I stow these, sir?"

Kennedy takes them and stuffs them into his pocket. "Can you...?"

"Will do," Ava says.

While we resumed our course for Kaho'olawe, she and Sparks the radioman carried the body below

One by one, sailors from various sections of the boat made their way forward to deliver damage control reports. Bottom line, we had taken some cannon fire that busted up the deck and chewed up the transom a bit. But miraculously, nothing more than that.

Which is no surprise.

Only in war movies does machine gun and cannon fire hit the targets like a carnival shooting gallery. In real combat, when real bullets are flying you're lucky if anything hits anywhere near where you're aiming. Both sides are so intent on hitting and trying *not* to be hit that it makes for an unpredictable madhouse where luck plays as strong a part as does gunnery training.

Yes, you need to know which end of the .50 caliber machine gun to point, how to load magazines, how to lead targets, how to calculate deflections, but in the end? You either get a few holes punched in your boat deck and your ass-end spanked—like we did—or you go up in a mushroom-cloud of exploding AVGAS, because a single tracer round puncturing your hull tanks is all it takes to change your world from here to hereafter.

Kennedy turned to me. "We're getting close. See if Sparks has any word from Gunny, yet. "

"Aye, aye, sir."

"Uh, you got that backwards, colonel. I'm just a Lieutenant JG."

"On a boat there's only one boss. You're him."

I ducked down into the charthouse. By now, Ava had gone forward into the crew quarters to stow Lenny's torn-up body. Sparks was back at his station, tweaking the radio, his hands bloody from carrying the XO, and they shook slightly.

I said, "Time we heard something from Sergeant Lewis and his team."

"Yes, sir. Been monitoring the frequency. Nothing yet."

Kennedy's internal clock was spot-on about wondering about Gunny. By my watch, he should be in position with his guerilla team just north of the bay.

His beat-up, over-used SCR-300 transceiver was less than reliable, but it's all we could scrounge up in the time we had. Its tubes were on their last legs, the handset kept cutting out, and the forty-pound pack was all a man could manage. But our one and only only connection to the him on the shore—short of semaphore flags and smoke signals.

"You doing okay?" I said.

"Nossir." A deep breath. "The lieutenant's chest…. just a big hole."

"I know."

I fished out my handkerchief, uncapped my canteen and soaked it. "Here, clean your hands. They'll get all sticky as the blood dries."

He managed to wipe his right hand clean, then bolted upright as if shot and clapped his headsets hard against his ears.

"Roger, Jarhead," he said. "Receiving you four by three. Say again your last."

He leaned closer to the small radio unit, as if closing the distance would help him hear better.

"In position… troops withdrawing… activity onboard aircraft…"

My heart skipped a beat. Were we too late? Then I remembered Professor Rasetti's comment about the plane flying over Oahu in a grand *Aloha* gesture just as the sun was rising, and then flying east to the Panama Canal and sending to kingdom come, and with it, America's war effort.

I calmed down. Another hour before sunrise. They must be doing some kind of preflight onboard the *Kawanishi*. Probably scientists doing last minute fussing and fretting. And well they should. Two hydrogen bombs were a hell of a payload. If they went off by accident, they'd take out half the Hawaiian Islands—maybe more.

Sparks scribbled down more of what he was hearing, and then signed off.

Kennedy listened to my report, delivered verbally moments later, because he had his hands full, not only with the wheel, but with the fate and fortune of his boat and crew.

The basic gist—based on Gunny's radio message—was that Hek and his fighters seemed to have accomplished what they set out to do. We had no way of knowing any specifics, however, because Sparks had been unable to raise them on their frequency—at least so far. (They had an even crappier radio than Gunny's.)

Bottom line: whatever the guerillas and PT-124 had done to the garrison base must have worked, because they had got the Japs panicking and calling for reinforcements from the gulch, which is all we needed.

Kennedy glanced at his compass, frowned and spun the wheel until he was back on course. "Doing too many damn things."

"How can I help?"

"When the time comes, you'll stand beside me... where Lenny was standing. Got it?"

"Got it."

"Raise your arm straight up so that my guys can see you. When I say 'fire,' chop your arm down. I'll start with the starboard torpedo, then port. One right after another. Got it?"

"Aye, aye."

"Now, head below to the dayroom and tell the torpedomen I want to see them on the double."

"On my way."

The boat crested a wave just as I turned to go, and I slipped on the wet deck. Arms flailing, I grabbed the radar mast just in time and managed to stay upright.

A bark of laughter from the port machine-gunner, then a quick, "Sorry, sir."

"For my next trick, ladies and gentlemen," I said.

Both gunners laughed.

A small table had been set up in the middle of the dayroom. Six men crowded around it, staring at a scroll of paper with all sorts of angles and notes on it. Torpedoman Mate First Class Andrew Jackson Kirksey was holding court, while the others stared intently at what his thick forefinger was slowly tracing on the paper.

"Skipper's going to be firing almost in salvo, so be on your toes, gents. Two men to a tube. One down, one up. If the lead gets hit, I want you to shove him aside and take over. Got that?"

A chorus of 'aye-ayes.'"

"Johnston and Harris, you're starboard. Starkey and I will handle port. The rest of you bums will…"

"Pray," someone said, and that went over big time.

I let the nervous laughter dissipate, before repeating Kennedy's topside order.

When I finished, the torpedomen double-timed out of the dayroom, leaving Tony, Professor Rasetti, and me. I told them the latest from Gunny, including the fact that they were already pre-flighting the flying boat for the mission

Rasetti nodded. "The fusing is a complicated process. You can only do it to a certain point, then the final part must happen in the air."

"Who does that, the bombardier?" I said.

He looked puzzled. I explained what that term meant. He shook his head. "It will be Saburo, I am certain. It must be his hands that do so. He would trust no one else."

"Complicated?"

"Somewhat. Altimeter settings, fuse delays, arming sequences."

Tony said, "Perfect. We blow up the bombs *and* the bad guy all at once. Two for the price of one."

Rasetti said, "If only we could blow up the knowledge too."

"No luck there, professor. Pandora's box is wide open, right, skipper?"

"Right."

"And I am the man…" Rasetti slid his finger across the paper until it rested on the crudely-drawn representation of the *Kawanishi*. "…who helped them do it."

If the skies had been clear, the zodiacal light, or "false dawn," would have given away our northeast approach to Kaho'olawe. Many times during my career I had witnessed that eerie, pale blue harbinger of the sunrise-to-come. It never failed to lift my spirits, as if the sun were saying, "Hang on for another hour or so, then I'll be shining bright."

But today, as we neared the desolate island, the heavy overcast skies hid that promise. Fortunately, it also hid us from prying Japanese eyes. Had that enemy seaplane pilot radioed our position before we downed him?

Possibly.

But even if he had, very little time had elapsed since his aircraft shattered into a thousand pieces that the enemy could barely react other than record his message. Besides, at the moment, they had their hands full beating back Hek's guerilla assault.

This thought—and others—raced through my mind as I hurried topside to re-join Kennedy at the helm. Even though I'd seen Lenny the XO do his signaling and was glad to help out, I felt like the new kid on the block.

When I arrived, Sparks popped out from the chartroom long enough to holler, "The 124 reports fuel dump gone. Suppression fire continues." Then he dove back below.

Kennedy slapped the wheel. "YES! I knew Izzy could do it with his Bofors. Packs a hell of a punch."

I'm no munitions expert, but I'd seen how big those 40mm shells were on Lieutenant "Izzy" Kovar's boat. And the thought of just one of the incendiary versions punching through the steel shell of the enemy's fuel storage "tank farm" was enough for me to picture the chaos that could result.

A faint, reddish-yellow trace of what must have just happened to the fuel dump lit up the undersides of the clouds over the southwest corner of Kaho'olawe. The low-lying shape of the island seemed to rise from the depths as a result. Where before only the endless expanse of open ocean, now an island loomed. Had we been shipwrecked; the sight of land would have been a joy to behold. But in our case, the adrenaline rush of impending danger instead.

"Anything yet?" Kennedy shouted.

Both seamen in their gun turrets had their binoculars glued to their eyes, piped up.

"Negative, skipper."

"Ditto, sir."

When Tony, Hek, and I had reconnoitered earlier, the flying boat was moored offshore. That wouldn't be the case now. Based on what Rasetti had told us about their plans to load the second weapon, combined with the Gunny's earlier recon and the Kagusaki brothers' sketches, the flying boat would now be tied up tail first to a dock to facilitate weapon loading. That second nuclear weapon was big and crude and not worth risking loading onto a barge and floating out to the plane. The mountain would come to Mohammed, that's for damned sure.

A series of flashes on the other side of the southern promontory. Tall sea cliffs masked the source of the explosions. But regardless of where the explosions were happening, for sure, Hek's guerillas were pounding hell out of that base and making our work on the northern side much easier.

Maybe "easier" is not the right word, but you know what I mean. When you're getting ready to take dead aim on a four hundred-foot long jumbo flying boat and need to pickle your torpedoes in the exact right spot on the fuselage where the fuel tanks are, you need all the help you can get—including me standing beside Lieutenant Kennedy, waiting to do my part.

Ava crouched on the hatch ladder leading below to the charthouse. She reached out and grabbed my leg and shouted something. But Kennedy advanced the throttles just as she did so, so I shouted for her to repeat it.

She cupped her hands, "I SAID... you sure know how to show a girl a good time!"

Flashing sparkles of gunfire in the distance cut short my reply. Small arms fire. Our gunners swung around like predators seeking prey.

Kennedy shouted, "Hold your fire!"

As we approached from the southeast for our attack run, what little pre-dawn light that managed to make it through the thick cloud cover lit up the lifeless-looking, reddish-black, mass of pockmarked volcanic rock known as Kaho'olawe. The Japanese had sure picked the right spot to do their dirty work. The over-grazed, under-watered, desolate scrap of land showed its sullen face to us as if to say, "I dare you to come closer."

We did.

So far, the dark green-painted flying ocean liner was lost in the murky shadows. About a mile from our target, I *still* couldn't pick it out to save my life. Rasetti insisted that they would have moved it to the loading pier by now. Had it taken off already?

"Any joy?" I shouted to the lookouts.

"No sir."

Kennedy made a small course correction. "Don't worry, it's there, colonel... I can smell it—standby torpedoes one and two!"

His command took me by surprise and I stood there like an idiot, watching the port and starboard torpedomen crouch down beside their firing stations. Our plunging motion through the waves and the rushing wind whipped back their hair like rodeo riders. Their steady hands gripped the launch levers.

Ava tapped my leg. "Wake up, flyboy!"

UP shot my arms. I felt like an idiot.

Kennedy said, "Sir, you don't need to do that until I say, 'ready to fire.'"

"Ready to fire, got it."

DOWN went my arms.

The boat SLAMMED into another cross wave, bounced, then settled down again. It's eighty-foot length and fifty-six tons helped minimize the motion, but if I didn't remember to keep my knees flexed, I'd regret it.

"Target bearing zero-three-zero!"

Kennedy spun the wheel to line up with the target, then shouted through the speaking tube. "Pappy... ready engines two and three... keep an eye on my signal!"

After the torpedo launch, we'd do the same skidding, pivoting, 180-degree reverse maneuver we did to hide from that enemy float plane. This time, though, an even more abrupt maneuver because we'd be reversing *two* engines to YANK us around the narrow passage that the enemy had blasted through the coral reef for the *Kawanishi*.

If I hadn't seen Kennedy already pull off that amazing maneuver once before, I'd have said it was impossible. But Pappy was down in the engine room getting ready to slam the gearshift levers into reverse as we got ready to do the impossible *again*.

In the distance, a fiery exchange of tracers looped back and forth in the gulch, where the research labs and administration buildings were located. Then a small explosion. Must have been one of the Gunny's guerilla mortars finding a target. More gunfire. Clearly, not all the enemy troops had gone running help repel Hek's attack.

I pointed that out to Kennedy, who grinned. "Too late, this American fox is already in the Japs' hen house."

The endlessly long shape of the *Kawanishi* flying boat emerged from the shadows to become the whale-sized target of our dreams.

That smile of his. Like a flashbulb going off. "And here comes our big, fat, dinner."

Lights were on in the cockpit and the myriad of portholes dotting her slab-sided fuselage. Lights on the loading dock, too. Shadows of people darting up inside the plane's massive rear loading hatch. Half of it folded up into the fuselage, the other half angled down as a ramp.

Plane, dock, beach, hills finally appearing, too, where seconds before just the murky black mass of Kaho'olawe and brooding clouds overhead.

Ava shouted, "Thar she BLOWS! Moby Dick!"

The lookouts laughed, which helped relieve the rising tension.

"Ready to fire!" Kennedy shouted.

I spun around and faced the torpedomen. UP went my arms. Their faces turned to me, waiting for my signal. Time started slowing down again, I could feel it happening: the relentless, pounding roar of the engines diminished to a distant, eerie buzz in my ears, the HISS of the water as we sliced through it faded to a whisper....

Everything moved in real time, but I began seeing each element in crisp detail:

Kennedy's hat tipped back on his head, his tousled brown hair blowing back over his forehead like a thoroughbred's mane.

Ava's mouth is set in a straight line. Her tongue flicks out like a snake's to moisten her lips.

The starboard torpedoman—his name I forget—looks at me like my daughter Abby at her birthday party about to tear open my present as soon as I say, "Go ahead, honey."

The American flag—or what's left of it after countless miles of open ocean travel—shimmering and shaking in the fifty-mile-an-hour wind.

My arms ache but I don't care.

The *Kawanishi* looks as big as a skyscraper on its side. How in hell can that damn thing fly?

Doesn't matter. After we're finished she'll never fly again.

Goodbye, big bad girl.

Kennedy angles his head this way, and that way, I can feel it coming. Which torpedo will go first?

"Fire ONE!"

My left arm DOWN and the port torpedoman YANKS the launch lever backwards.

A muffled BANG as the black powder charge explodes against the launch plug. The twenty-one-foot-long, Bliss-Levitt Mark 8 torpedo leaps out of its tube, soars over the bow, and arcs into the water. The ocean swallows it up in an instant.

"Fire TWO!"

My right arm DOWN, and a repeat performance, this time the starboard side. My time sense slows the torpedo's rush out of the greased launch tube, its arcing path over the bow, and its splashing entry into the water. Feels like the slow-motion movie of an Olympic high diver. Only difference being, this one weighs over two thousand pounds.

Impossible to see the torpedo wakes. Still too dark out. But wait a second... over there to starboard... a whitish streak, then nothing.

Our engine noise rises—like they would if you depressed the clutch in your car while going full speed. Pappy must be SHOVING those gearshift levers like mad.

"Hang on!" Kennedy shouted, then SLAMMED the throttles forward.

But before the propellers could bite into the water to slew us around in the opposite direction, a shudder rippled through the ninety-foot length of the boat from stem to stern.

Then a harder lurch as the hull struck something underwater for a second time. So hard that we slewed around like a drunk on black ice. Kennedy applied full throttle, but only got half a response.

A muffled voice through the speaker tube.

"Say again!" Kennedy hollered.

But before he could get an answer, the engine room hatch aft of the dayroom flipped open, Pappy climbed halfway out and bellowed. "Lost two shafts!"

The Packards were roaring, but we continued slowing. The good news was that the engine going forward still had its shaft and screw attached and turning. The rest of the news was bad.

The radioman popped out of his chartroom. "Taking water forward, sir."

"How bad?"

"Two feet...rising fast."

A massive explosion off the port bow. A water column shot upward, carrying tons of volcanic rock, black sand, unlucky fish, but nothing else. True to the Mark 8's lousy reputation, the gyros had tumbled after all, and it dove like porpoise. Since its fuse was set for ten feet, once past that depth it became armed and didn't know where the hell it was heading until it exploded against the shallow bottom.

Just like us.

Except we were still moving—not away from the action, but straight for it. I understood Kennedy's quick thinking. To stop moving was to sink. Forget abandoning ship. To keep moving would at least get us to shore. What waited for us when we got there was awful to contemplate. But floating around in the water, waiting for a vengeful Japanese patrol boat to machine-gun us was worse.

Sixty seconds earlier we had been a fighting machine doing a fine job.

Now, just so much slow-moving junk.

And what the hell happened to the other torpedo?

Not a clue.

Time stood still.

Then...

In the midst of the murky morning light, I swear I "saw" an airplane instrument panel clear as crystal. Instead of reaching out and grabbing the control yoke, I grabbed Kennedy by the shoulder instead. "Head for the plane."

"I'm not a *kamikaze*. No way."

"I'm a *pilot*, goddamn it! Don't you understand?"

Didn't take him long to do the math.

Then that wonderful grin of his. "Aye, aye, skipper!"

*Arouse a bee and it will come at you
with the force of a dragon.*
Takeda Nobushige, Samurai

Kennedy spun the wheel, hit full throttle, and the bow slowly swung toward the *Kawanishi* flying boat. With only one still-functioning engine, our forward speed was nothing to write home about. Still, that single, supercharged, screaming-loud Packard 4M-2500 was tearing its heart out to bring us up to speed faster than I thought possible.

Then I thought about something else... cupped my hands and shouted, "Hold your FIRE!" I turned to Kennedy, "Sorry, skipper, but I don't want anybody shooting up our ticket out of here."

"You're serious about *flying* that thing?"

"Affirmative."

"You're nuts...sir," he said.

"You want to ram it instead? Make your parents cry when they get the telegram from the war department?"

"No, sir, but you're... you're crazy."

"That makes two of us—aim just aft of her loading ramp. See if you can come alongside."

"I can try, but..." He spun the wheel twice as much as usual to keep on course. "Losing rudder fast."

Tracer fire looped out at us from shore. Our twin-fifties poured back a lead-filled answer to whatever Japanese soldier was stupid enough to tempt his fate. Our bow-mounted 37mm opened up too. More tracer fire, but this time coming from the beach to the right of the plane. Directed—not at us—but at the Japanese gunner. *Had* to be Gunny and his team. What must he be thinking?

I said to Ava, "Flash message to Gunny, voice channel, in the clear: 'Mission aborted. Meet at plane.'"

"Wilco."

She dove below to get Sparks going on the radio.

By now, PT-109 was about five hundred yards from shore, heading straight toward it, which brought our spin-stabilized rocket launchers to bear. Mounted on either side of the chartroom slightly aft of the bow gun, each launcher had eight Mark 50 rockets. Crewmen were already traversing them outward so that the back-blast would hit the water, not the deck.

Kennedy was miles ahead of me in the rocket launching department, and said, "See that firing panel to your right? Push the upper right button and it should light up. The others will come on when the circuits close."

I stabbed at it. "No luck."

"Try again."

I did.

"No dice."

"It's *got* to be working—here, take the wheel. Let me see what's going on."

The wooden spokes felt warm in my hand but the wheel spinning so loose that I wondered if the cables were attached at all. The bow kept wanting to swing away from my aiming spot on the dock. It was all I could do to keep her on our heading.

Meanwhile, Kennedy's hands flew over the rocket launch control panel like he was playing a Steinway baby grand. The lights flickered once, twice, then came on full, lighting up his face and his jubilant smile.

"Stand clear of the launchers!" Kennedy hollered. He could have individually fired each of the five-inch rockets, but chose the "SALVO" button, instead. This would trigger a sequential circuit that fired all sixteen, each a fraction of a second after the previous one.

"Rockets AWAY!"

A bright yellow-white bloom of light as the first missiles WHOOSHED from rifled-steel tubes that imparted a spin to stabilize their trajectory. The solid rocket fuel burned fiercely, unstoppable in its thrust. One after another they darted out, WHOOSH... WHOOSH... WHOOSH.

What the target was remained a mystery. Enough to know that wherever those rockets would land, each carried a twelve-pound punch of TNT. The resulting explosion would destroy something – flesh and blood, research papers, fuel supplies, didn't matter. What mattered was striking back—hard.

The rocket propellant burned out quickly, having done the job of lifting the projectiles into a high-curving arc toward the shore. Impossible to track them in the darkness. But seconds later, easy to see the rippling flashes of reddish-yellow light as they detonated on the research facility and bomb assembly buildings. Then, a tremendous explosion, whitish-blue, without sound at first, but when the shock wave reached us I felt it SLAM into my chest. Liquid hydrogen was my best guess from the violence of the blast.

"Hoooeee!" Kennedy crowed. "Navy one, Tokyo nothing!"

The crewmen cheered raggedly but kept firing. Bloodlust was up and running free.

Kennedy took over the wheel, "Got it, sir. Thanks."

He spun the wheel and almost immediately, the boat swung obediently back onto a precise course, as if sensing a sea captain was in charge, not a flyboy.

No question now as to the extraordinary size of the *Kawanishi*. Enough daylight now to separate the dark-green giant from the rising sea cliffs of Kaho'olawe.

The soft glow of lights from inside the cockpit and observation windows that dotted the four hundred-foot-long fuselage gave it a strange sort of life. The most light came from the "step up" section at the rear of the fuselage, by the loading ramp. Directly above, the plane's tail assembly continued its astonishing climb to a twin rudder configuration, each gargantuan slab of aluminum at least eighty-feet tall.

I'd only seen the aircraft once before, when Gunny and I and Tony made our hasty reconnaissance. Then, it had just been a winged whale that I needed to harpoon. I could have cared less about anything more than that. But now it had become our salvation.

Maybe.

Closer now. Figures on the dock running inside the plane.

I shouted to Kennedy over the roar of our solitary engine and the incessant BANGING and CRACKING of our deck guns.

"Ever watch *Sea Hawk*, skipper? Errol Flynn taking on the Spanish Armada? We're going to board that flying boat the same way, like pirates, and get the hell out of here."

Kennedy was a fast learner. He didn't hesitate an instant. He cupped his hands and bellowed, "All hands, break out small arms and prepare to board enemy vessel!"

Less than a hundred yards from our ticket to ride.

Ava stuck her head out from the chartroom. "Gunny got our message. On his way."

"Better hurry," I said. "We can't do this alone."

"The hell we can't," Kennedy said. "My guys will—hey, easy, old girl, don't DO to this to me."

He spun the wheel hard, while shouting in the voice tube. "Pappy, losing rudder. Can you do anything?"

A muffled response and Kennedy cursed as we began a slow drift to port. Nothing he did to the wheel seemed to stop our change of direction. At this rate we'd end up foundering on the beach, short of our destination and ripe for the picking.

I estimated our forward speed to be about ten knots. Not anything to write home about, but considering our battered and broken hull was taking on water at an alarming rate, the old girl was doing her best.

By now, most of 109's crew had assembled outside the dayroom, Tony and the professor among them. The men fussed and fiddled with a collection of rifles, sub-machine guns and hand grenades gathered up from God knows where. These were sailors, mind you, not seasoned foot soldiers. Whatever effect we were going to have would be more shock than skill.

After conferring with Kennedy on our plan of attack, I hurried back to the men.

"Once inside the plane, fellas, no hand grenades. And watch where you fire. That big-ass bird is going to save our lives, providing we don't kill her first. Read me loud and clear?"

A chorus of "yes sirs" and nods. Most of them looked scared to death. Nothing I could do about that. Felt same way. Probably more so.

"Hiya, boys!" Ava's voice had that "Hollywood ring" to it.

Their faces swung to her like flowers to the sun.

"May I?" She grabbed a Tommy gun from one of the seamen and brandished it in the air. "Which end of this darn thing do I point at the bad guys?"

Laughter.

She shot me a sideways glance and rolled her beautiful eyes. In that moment I felt the full value of Ava James, not only as my wife, but as a woman put on this earth to show the rest of us how to face the world—

no matter what comes your way—with your chin up, eyes open, and your heart filled with love.

The engine changed from scream to dull roar.

Kennedy voice rose above the clatter. "Brace for collision!"

A quick glance over the bow and still on course! Whatever he did to pull that off was a mystery. But then, my praise died in my throat – a grinding lurch and we slewed to port. We barely had time to grab something to keep from sliding off the deck as PT-109 swung even further to port.

"Brace, BRACE!" Kennedy shouted.

Seconds later, fifty-six tons of PT boat collided with the loading dock.

A massive CRUNCHING sound as the bow splintered the planks and pilings into toothpicks....we rose up, then settled down like a giant walrus coming ashore.

Then silence—or what passed for silence.

Only the distant crackling of sporadic gunfire as engagements continued. My guess was that Gunny was executing a withdrawal and protecting his rear as he did so.

Lieutenant Kennedy led the charge, while shouting at the top of his lungs. His crew took up the cry and we thundered across the planked deck like a herd of angry buffalo—and one gazelle—Ava, whose banshee-shriek was even more scary. Two sailors stayed behind to man the .50-caliber gun tubs and provide covering fire. We'd call them in when the time was right.

Our boarding plan—if that's what you could call the last-minute scheme Kennedy and I worked out—was to secure the plane with the minimum of force—meaning not to shoot the thing to pieces. I needed a flyable aircraft. That said, I'm a reasonable man, especially when the plane I wanted to fly didn't belong to me in the first place. Bound to be damage from resisting forces. I just hoped it wouldn't bad enough to ground my desperate dream.

The last time I was inside this monster-sized airplane, darkness hid most of her details. Sort of like standing inside a cathedral with the lights out – you *know* it's a vast space even though you can't see it.

Different this time. Lights blazing everywhere.

In the distance, the spherical, wire-covered mass of one of the H-bombs partially blocked the view of the other one mounted behind it. Wire-strand cables secured them to cradles, with their wheels chocked on twin-rails running the length of the cargo deck.

I don't know how Jonah felt when the whale swallowed him up. But I felt like I was in the same situation—only with a flying machine instead of a leviathan-sized mammal. If I could get inside the "brain" of this beast, I just might get her to do my bidding.

Figures darted away from the 109's cavalry-like charge. But one of them stood stock-still with his hands up.

"Don't shoot, fellas!" he cried in perfect English. "It's me, Kagusaki the baker!"

Kennedy, Pappy and his enginemen managed a few waves as they raced past him in pursuit of the fleeing others. Ava and I came to a halt when I recognized the short, plump Japanese man who had met us on the plane the night we reconnoitered it.

"Brah, what you people DOING here?" he gasped.

"Torpedoes missed," I said.

"Not that one. Look."

We followed him about a hundred feet forward to a spot on the starboard side of the fuselage. He stopped and pointed down. "Look familiar?"

Scratched with green paint and dripping water, the nose of the Mark 8 torpedo protruded about halfway into the fuselage. Despite all the hard work our guys had put into making sure this thing would explode, its contact trigger (once again!!!) must have bent on impact.

From what I could imagine, it had made like a porpoise at the end of its run and penetrated the *Kawanishi* just above the waterline. We'd take on water during takeoff, but only a small amount, providing they got rid of it and plugged the hole right.

Ava said, "Duds-ville."

Kagusaki let out a WHOOSH of relief. "Lucky me."

"You aren't kidding," I said. "Wait a second, how'd you end up here?"

"My turn for guard duty. I started to jump ship when the attack alarm sounded, but the other guard tried to stop me."

"Where is he?"

Kagusaki patted his short sword. "With his ancestors—but wait a second, what are YOU doing here?"

"Scared of heights?"

He shook his head.

"Lucky you."

Gunfire from outside echoed off the fuselage interior. Each and every one of the bundled wires snaking through the bulkhead stringer holes, every rod, every tightly-stretched cable angled this way and that way—everything I saw inside this incredible plane had a specific purpose.

So did I.

The cockpit was almost a football field away from where I stood. I wanted to take off running but had to wait until Kennedy and his men got back with whoever they'd managed to capture. The Japanese were notorious for not wanting the shame that came with surrender. Too many stories about soldiers pulling the pin on hand grenades and dying for the Emperor. Hell of a way to run an army.

Kagusaki shouted, "There they are!"

Kennedy in the lead again. But limping big time, his left pant leg bloody.

"Where'd you get hit?"

"The little son-of-a-bitch knifed me."

He held up the short Japanese *tantō* dagger, blade still bloody.

Behind him, hands raised high, three bedraggled Japanese – two civilians, one military. Behind them, a gaggle of gun-toting sailors. Then Tony, followed by Rasetti, smiling like the Cheshire Cat.

"Where are the rest of your guys?" I said.

"Pappy's still searching, I sent the others to the gun turrets—they look like the same twenty-millimeter Oerlikons we've got. This bird's a regular flying battleship."

"We may need them all before this is over—who's this one in the flying gear?"

"Found him hiding near the flight deck. That place is like a greenhouse up there, by the way. For your sake I sure hope he's got something to do with driving this beast."

"We'll soon find out—and these guys?"

By now, Professor Rasetti had made his way up to face the shorter of the two Japanese civilians. They both wore khaki pants and neatly laundered white shirts, like twins except for the size and age difference. One in his early thirties, the other—my guess—in his mid-fifties.

And even though the Italian scientist towered threateningly over the older of the two, his broad-face with narrow features was the picture of serenity as he calmly regarded Rasetti then said in perfect English, "I see you have returned from the dead."

Rasetti spun around, staring at me but pointing accusingly at the man. "*This* is Saburo Yamasaki! The man who would destroy the world to gain the stars."

Yamasaki rolled his eyes. "Italians… Every word an opera."

"But it is true, you viper. Deny me. I *dare* you!"

Yamasaki ignored him and turned to me, his gaze as cold as a shark's. "And you are?"

"Your worst nightmare."

"Ah, another Italian."

Ava laughed. "Hardly. But that's not a bad idea because we really *are* your nightmare—so, tell me, Professor Atomic, where's the 'off switch' for these super-bombs of yours?"

Yamasaki ignored Ava as if she were a monkey that somehow managed to speak and continued staring at me. "America is only delaying the inevitable, you know."

Kagusaki the Baker stepped up to the scientist. I thought he was going to clobber him, and so did the professor. But minus his dagger he was sunk. Instead, Kagusaki rattled off some Japanese. I have no idea what he said, but it sounded threatening. The professor's chest slowly rose and fell, and his eyes squeezed shut behind his glasses as he blithely weathered the tirade but did not respond.

When done, the ex-baker now soldier turned to me. "No dice, sir. He's got his *samurai* blood up, for sure. But I watched these two guys working on that bomb over there. They were doing something to that thing on top that looks like a washtub. See it?"

Rasetti said, "That is the fusing mechanism."

I said, "Know how it works?"

His uneasy look was answer enough.

I took a deep breath. One step at a time. Action leads to discovery. Discovery leads to decisions. I turned to Kennedy.

"Lieutenant, we got us a live torpedo over there stuck like a harpoon in the side of a whale. We can't take off until your guys disarm it and shove it out."

"So we hit the target after all!" He opened his mouth to give the order, but before he said a word, a couple torpedomen took off running. "We got this, sir!"

That said, the torpedo weighed over two thousand pounds. Fortunately, only the nose had made it through, so the majority of the weight would act as leverage to aid the combined muscle of desperate men.

A flurry of shouting from outside.

Machine gun fire. Small stuff, but insistent. Flames licked PT-109's shattered bow wedged in the busted-up dock. A crowd of guerillas scrambled over her mid-section, with Gunny in the lead.

The tall, lanky, old-timer leaped over the torpedo launch tube like he was running hurdles in the Olympics. The shorter, more compact Hawaiians swarmed across the deck and followed their leader as he jumped down onto what was left of the dock. Two of them stayed back to help our sailors provide covering fire.

Then a surprise.

From below decks of PT-109, a figure staggered out with a body draped over his shoulders. He looked up, his face desperate. Sparks! That kid wasn't going to let the XO's body fall into Japanese hands.

Gunny spotted him and waved his hands like a demented traffic cop. "Kepano, give that guy a hand. The rest of you, move, move MOVE!"

The guerillas pounded past him, up the boarding ramp, then inside the plane. Gunny caught sight of me, grinned and saluted. "Fancy meeting you here, Colonel Carter, sir!"

"A small world, Gunnery Sergeant Lewis. Prepare for takeoff."

"You kidding me, sir? In this thing?"

"It's an airplane. I fly them, you know."

"Then you'd better do it damned fast. We kicked over a hornet's nest back there. Hear them?"

I turned to Kagusaki. "Know how to close this ramp?"

"Yes, sir."

"Then show this guy, quick, because I need you to come with me."

I cupped my hands and shouted for Tony. He came running, rifle in hand – a far cry from the tools he used to wield to magically transform coughing, backfiring, engines into purring kittens.

Within seconds, Kagusaki showed him how to raise the ramp then close the two upper parts that were folded inward against the bottom of the upper deck like an *origami* sculpture.

I said, "After I get the engines up and running, Gunny calls in the rest of his troops. Tony, you raise the ramp, then haul ass up to the flight deck and lend a hand."

"You got it, skipper." Tony whistled in appreciation. "Twelve turboprop engines. Still can't believe it."

"Four jet engines, too."

His eyes sparkled. "She's a beast."

I turned to leave but he caught my arm. "We can do this, skipper. I *know* we can."

Gunfire in the distance. Closer.

A sailor kneeling by the ramp entrance, hollered, "Bad guys incoming!"

Kagusaki cried, "STOP! That's my brother!"

A Japanese soldier wearing tall leather boots and officer rank chevrons on his collar leapfrogged over PT-109's deck then onto the dock. Both hands in the air waving a sheathed officer's sword with a white handkerchief tied to it he thundered closer and closer.

Gunny bellowed, "Hold your FIRE!"

The officer scrambled up the ramp and embraced his brother – two battling bakers who did a hell of a lot more than make cookies.

"Nice sword, Riku," Kagusaki said. "Where'd you get it?"

He brandished it. "Where do you think?"

Its menacing shape gave me a chill. Something about that gentle curve of that razor-sharp steel made me wonder how many heads had been severed from their bodies by order of Japanese Imperial Army generals.

Saburo Yamasaki spat at Riku and shouted, *"Uragimono!"*

Riku laughed and shouted back in English. "I may be a traitor to Japan, but I am a hero to America, right, Hinata?"

Both brothers found this remark extremely funny.

Gunny's voice carried a nervous edge to it. "Need to haul ass, sir!"

I traced some wires to what looked like an intercom and headset. "Once you hear the engines going, put this on and listen for my orders."

"How the hell does it work?"

"We both need to figure that out—stand by on the loading ramp, Tony."

"Aye, aye."

I grabbed Kagusaki and towed him over to the Japanese prisoner wearing flight gear – quilted life vest, goggles and cap.

Chevrons on his sleeve.

Officer rank.

Lieutenant maybe?

Couldn't be older than his mid-twenties. Navigator? Assistant flight engineer? Somewhere low on the totem pole for sure. An "Indian" not a "Chief." But someone who knew far more about this plane than me. We would go exactly nowhere without him.

I said to Kagusaki, still smiling at his brother's earlier remark. "When I talk, you translate. I won't look at you, I'll look straight at him. Got it?"

"Yes, sir."

I said to the officer, "What's your job?"

"*Anata no shigoto?*" Kagusaki rattled off.

The kid stood tall and looked me straight in the eye. " *Kōkū pairotto three-shu.* "

"Says he's an aviation officer third class."

"Jackpot. Let's head for the flight deck—on the double."

"Colonel…what's 'on the double' mean?"

"Step on it."

"Got it."

Lots of shouting, but then the flight officer, with a prod from Kagusaki, took off running, while I shouted over my shoulder, "Ava, time for work—Tony, see you soon!"

"Aye, aye, skipper."

On the way forward I passed a group of sailors clustered around the protruding nose of the dud torpedo. They had already found some wooden poles to use as crowbars. How they got the torpedo out would have to remain a mystery because I had my own share of them to solve—and solve fast in the next ten minutes or all our hard work was going down the drain.

Impossible to do such a thing, of course. Get this monster in the air in ten minutes. Pre-flight, engine run-up, taxi, and takeoff for one of our Boeing Clippers customarily took nearly an hour of relentless switch-throwing, dial-twisting, and throttle-shoving.

And doing all of that according to a detailed checklist, item by item, so that we could bring a complicated creation of aviation machinery not only to life, but then to soar above the clouds and cross the ocean.

And not just the pilot and co-pilot.

Add to their preflight duties, the flight engineer's sacred ritual of monitoring his myriad engine instruments, dials, and meters – oil pressure, hydraulic pressure, rate-of-fuel indicators, cylinder head temperatures, manifold pressure, batteries, generators, fuses—all ticked off, one-by-one, against an equally complex checklist that he would follow with the calm, detached deliberation of a heart surgeon.

The radio operator, too, equally lost in his many duties of tweaking receivers and transmitters, RDF loops, antenna spools, wireless keys, and microphones—to name just a few.

And last but not least, the navigator, whose real work lay ahead, but still needed to be certain of his tools that would faithfully lead us from Point A to Point B across the ocean, like charts, dividers, bubble sextant, chronometers, drift flares, pencils, parallel ruler, protractor, and his sacred *Weems* close at hand to help him master the art of celestial navigation.

As for us?

Just Ava and me, running like crazy to catch up with Kagusaki, who clambered up a ladder leading to the center deck of the *Kawanishi*.

Ava said in between breaths , "This thing's ... like a ship…"

"No kidding."

Are we there, yet, daddy?"

"Very funny."

"Straight out of a movie… don't you think?"

"Needs… a happy… ending…"

Climbing the ladder myself, I shouted to Kagusaki and the prisoner, "Slow down!"

Arriving on the next deck and hustling fast. Fleeting glimpses of long racks of folded-up seats. Like being in a movie theater.

Must be for troops.

Kagusaki said it could carry nine hundred. How come we never even knew they were building something this big? Easy. Impossible for westerners to spy on Japan. Proof of that here, for sure.

Ava pounded my back. "Errol Flynn this time…. He'll play you…."

"Not Bogey?"

"Smokes too much… couldn't run… like us."

A voice calling from high above. "Hi, sir!"

A sailor manning one of the dorsal turrets leans down from his rotating cupola and waves. His is one of four such gun turrets dotting the length of the fuselage, with two more identical turrets mounted on the tail – stacked on top of each other like flapjacks. What a plane!

"Fire at will, sailor. We're all on board except the guys on the 109 giving covering fire."

"Aye, aye, sir! These things pack a real wallop."

Ava tugged me. "C'mon, we're losing them."

We ran another hundred feet—would this plane never end? Ladders leading upward into the darkness, open hatches leading downward. How many tons of aluminum in this thing? Miles of wiring? Thousands of man-hours to create such an airplane?

Finally, something familiar-looking – a set of broad steps on a curving staircase leading up to the flight deck I'd once seen on a lark a few days ago but now could save our lives, if we could just get all our ducks in a row—and fly.

"Ladies first," I said.

"Not a chance, skipper." Ava shoved me forward, "Curtain going up!"

Up until this moment, the flight deck of Pan Am's Boeing 314 *Yankee Clipper* had been a vast improvement over the workspace on our Martin 130s or Sikorskys, or for that matter, any other plane I'd ever flown. Like going from a cramped roadster to a Cadillac limousine.

But *this* was like the entire club car on the *Twentieth Century Limited*.

Easily thirty feet long by twenty feet wide, the *Kawanishi's* flight deck began with three rows of nicely cushioned seats for the privileged rear-ends of VIP generals and admirals who wouldn't deign to descend below decks and mingle with the troops in "steerage."

Ava patted one of the seats. "Nice digs."

To be honest, it felt more like the bridge of an ocean liner than an airplane. Kagusaki and the pilot blocked what I was most interested in – the flight controls. But first things first. I stopped Ava by the flight engineer's station, the length of an upright piano and just as tall, with three towering columns of instruments of all shapes and sizes.

"Any of this ring a bell?"

Her eyes flitted over the setup. "Most of it, yes, but it's all in Japanese lettering—what do they call it?"

"Kanji."

"Kanji —anyhow, it's pretty familiar stuff. Numbers are numbers, thank God."

Her eyes never stopped moving as she rattled off the obvious – RPM, manifold pressure, oil temperature, Rate-of-fuel gauges, and *fourteen* engine throttles—twelve red, and four yellow. She ran her hand across them like sweeping the keys of a piano. "I'll need the arms of an octopus."

"No you won't. They've got gang-levers, see?"

"Got it—yellow for turbojets, yes?"

"Affirmative."

"Look over here…" She pointed to a panel of dials and switches that had red-painted lines leading from fuel tank selection switches, then over to fuel-flow indicators, then up to tank fill indicators. "I like this road map they did for fuel management—we're going to need it."

"We should be doing that with our planes."

She fell silent, absorbed in a process known only to people who fly can understand – I call it "shaking hands." If you're a pilot, you may call it something else. But regardless of what term you use, until you've made the mental decision to implicitly trust your airplane's instruments the same way you trust your body and mind, then you're not ready to fly—and the plane will punish you for it.

Call it a marriage, a union, a bond—whatever—that altimeter, that RDF needle, that ILS glide slope indicator are equal partners with you in the sometimes perilous but always pleasurable process of leaving the face of the earth and being at one with the sky.

I said, "Time to earn your flight pay, lieutenant."

"May I pray first?"

I kissed her quickly. "Say one for me."

"Only if you say one for the jets. I haven't a clue how to get them going."

"See that row of switches just above the yellow dials? The ones with the covers?"

She flipped open one of the safety covers to reveal a toggle switch. "Just like the ones we use. Damned copycats."

"Those are the igniters. Those dials beneath should be your bus switches from battery to generator. You'll need them to get the compressors spinning to a certain RPM before you kick in the igniters."

"How do you know this stuff?"

"America's no stranger to turbine engines. We've got our own in development."

"You never told me that."

"You never asked—and besides, I wouldn't have told you because it's top secret."

"Not anymore."

"Look, just focus on turning the props. Hold off on the jets until Tony gets here. He's been on board these things back at Oahu. I quizzed him about it, and he can lend a hand."

"But he's a mechanic."

"Mechanics know everything. Pilots don't."

But we have instincts. And right now, all I wanted to do was satisfy my craving for what I knew was waiting for me at the pilots' station.

No matter how many instruments airplane design engineers manage to cram into a control panel, they build that mountain of information upon a foundation of six critical instruments:

1. Horizon indicator
2. Airspeed
3. Altimeter
4. Vertical speed indicator
5. Turn-and-bank indicator
6. Compass

Nowadays known as a "six-pack," back in 1943, beer only came in bottles and flight instruments came—not with digital numbers that click up and down—but with clocklike "hands" that spin round and round.

As I got closer and closer to that sacred place where flight begins, I ignored the plethora of switches, dials, levers, and buttons on a column to my right and a zillion more switches on a panel to my left and focused on how the Japanese designers had laid out their version of the "six-pack."

First glance was comforting.

What I needed to get this bird into the air was staring me in the face. Fortunately, the Japanese used color coding on the airspeed indicator like we do to indicate DNE (Do Not Exceed) speeds, Stall with flaps speed, operating range, and the same color coding for the cylinder head temps. Red is red, no matter what language you speak.

I sat in the left seat, buckled my chest-straps, rubbed my hands together, then turned to the junior pilot and twirled my forefinger around in a tight circle and grinned like we were drinking buddies.

"Hai?" I said.

He frowned, of course.

I nodded to Kagusaki, who pulled out his *Nambu* pistol and dug it into the kid's chin and whispered in his ear.

The pilot's eyes—narrow with anger—got wide with fright. Another nudge with the pistol and a stream of Japanese poured out.

"He's saying something about a list."

"No kidding. A checklist for sure."

Then another thought came to me. "Put the gun down. Ask him if he's married. Has kids."

"Huh?"

"Ask him!"

He posed the question. A look of surprise softened his face—if only for an instant—but long enough for me to see a husband and father hiding behind the scared-shitless face of a young man who thought he was low man on a totem pole, but was now at the top—albeit with a different tribe than the one he was used to saluting.

He raised his finger. One.

I fiddled with the multitude of throttles to my right – twelve props and four jets. How in the hell could I ever manage to—the kid's name. "What's his child's name?"

A brief hesitation. A gentle nudge with the pistol.

"Niko."

"Boy or girl."

"Musoko"

"His son."

"Got a photo?"

He nodded.

"Let me see it."

No matter your culture or country, if someone asks to see your kid's picture, you show it. He fished it out of a well-worn wallet the size of a deck of cards with half of them missing.

Jackpot.

Not only a cute kid. All kids are. But being held in the arms of his beautiful, young, kimono-wearing wife. I caught my breath at a memory of Estelle and Baby Eddy, that stabbed my heart like an arrow. But before the memory of my wife and child returned full-blown, I sent it back down into my heart.

"Mother and son?" I said.

Kagusaki did the honors, *"Haha to musoko?"*

The pilot's prideful smile quickly surrendered to a dutiful scowl. The fish was nibbling, but hadn't bit.

From inside my beat-up wallet, I slid out the water-stained, well-thumbed photograph of Estelle holding Baby Eddie in her arms – his christening day, wearing the same white, lacey outfit my mother wore at *her* christening. Estelle smiling, Eddie about to howl—but not yet. I couldn't help but grin.

I handed it over to the pilot. "My wife and son."

Kagusaki translated.

"The Nazis killed them both. Atomic bomb. Washington, D.C. *Tell* him."

The pilot listened.

"Killed them the same way that asshole professor back there wants to kill innocent people in Panama."

"I don't know the word for 'asshole.'"

"You'll think of something—tell him!"

"Darling…" Ava's warning voice didn't complete the sentence, but I knew what she meant. The clock was ticking and four hundred feet behind me the world was coming apart at the hinges on an enemy dock in the middle of an unfriendly sea. But so what? If I didn't get this Japanese pilot on my side, we were sunk at anchor.

I took both photos and propped them up in front a bank of hydraulic pressure gauges mounted on the throttle pedestal. Why the hell they had put the gauges there was a mystery. Maybe ran out of room on the panel. But perfect for my purpose.

"Hai?" I said as I patted the control wheel, then twirled my finger again in the universal sign for "let's get this plane in the air."

We stared at each other – man-to-man, and I prayed husband-to-husband and father-to-father, not as sworn enemies fighting a war declared by old men who wanted blood instead of peace. Just two fellow aviators in a tight spot that we needed flying away from—fast.

I smiled slightly and raised my eyebrows in anticipation. C'mon, kid…

The pilot slowly raised his hand and nudged Kagusaki's pistol barrel away from his chin. Then he picked up a ringed binder, opened it to the first page, looked at me one more time… then said something in Japanese.

Kagusaki translated, "Battery switches on."

Bingo.

"Where are they?"

The kid pointed to a bank of them above the oil temperature gauges.

"We're in business!!" I said and flicked them on—all six.

Seconds earlier, we'd been trapped inside a dimly-lit, dead-like world of buttons and switches. But with a JOLT of twenty-four volts DC, our world blossomed into a universe of dinging chimes, rapid clicks, and trembling needles on countless dials. Every instrument had its own back light, every switch lit from beneath, and everything bathed in reddish, overhead light that helped our night vision.

No doubt about it, the Japanese had built a plane to end all planes, bigger than anything on earth. And they had done so completely under the radar of our so-called intelligence service. Germany's, too. I'm betting. Did the Nazis know about this? My guess is, hell no.

The Japanese understood—and still understand—racism better than you think they do. And not only do they understand its evil ways, they have learned to make it work *for* them, not against them.

Admittedly, not at this moment in time, when military idiots were running their nation and busy raping and pillaging the Pacific southeast.

But in the years that followed their defeat, they moved from darkness into light as easily as you or I move from one room to another.

How?

Don't ask me. Ask them.

So...how would this damn girl fly? I pulled the massive control wheel toward me. But instead of the heavy "clunkiness" of cable-driven flight controls that I was accustomed to, the control column glided back and forth with hydraulic-boosted efficiency.

I darted a glance at my co-pilot (I was thinking of him in those terms now, not the enemy.)

He saw my amazement and nodded with pride.

"What's your first name?" I said.

Kagusaki found out, and then laughed.

"What's so funny?"

"His name is Kaito. It means helpful."

I patted the throttle quadrant. "Kaito, my friend, let's get this big-assed girl going!"

While we plowed through the checklist—correction—while Kaito did and I followed like a trained monkey, Ava continued her hectic labors at figuring out where to push this, and where to pull that. Because of thousand-plus hours spent ferrying bombers as a WASP (Women's Airforce Service Pilot) she knew her way around multi-engine aircraft.

Yes, this beast had *twelve* props and *four* jets, but think of it this way—because trust me, Ava was thinking this way too, and so was I—a piano has eighty-eight keys, right? Fifty-two white, thirty-two black. Lots of moving parts—like this damned whale with wings. But... pianos have octaves, right? Seven to be precise. Figure out one of them and, brother, you've figured them all.

Thready-logic, I know, but it holds true in music and in flying. Our first "octave" is airspeed, angle-of-attack, power, thrust, and attitude. Sort that out, honor it religiously, and the rest is commentary.

A *lot* of commentary, I'll admit, as we pounded through the checklist and got the turboprops turning one by one.

I'd never seen one in action before, other than in hush-hush secrecy on a General Electric prototype running on a test bed. Back then, I had done my best to understand terms like "compressors," and "annular burners," and how the the exhaust thrust *also* spun the propeller that, in turn, spun the compressors that fired the burners in an endless cycle… but I left most of details to the experts, like Orlando.

By now, along with a few choice curse words from Ava, engine temperatures were slowly climbing on eight of the twelve turboprops. Hard to see them in action in the dim, dawn light. We only had some outside observation lights that Kaito had turned on for us. At the moment they showed the fast-spinning discs of eight, four-bladed propellers humming away at idle while their operating temps climbed to stabilized levels.

Kaito called out in something in Japanese.

Kagusaki said, "Number nine."

While I cracked the throttle open, Kaito flicked on the boost pump and fuel ignition switches located on the center overhead control panel. Then he held down the spring-loaded start switch. Somewhere buried in the miles of bundled cable, the signal went out to start spinning compressors inside engine number nine.

At a predetermined RPM, the igniter "cans" lit up the vaporized fuel spraying into the combustion chamber, and the incredible circle of cause-and-effect was born that makes the whole of a turboprop engine greater than the sum of its brilliantly-engineered, meticulously manufactured parts.

Footsteps pounding up the circular staircase. If it was the bad guys, we were dead. If not, then any further delay in getting this plane in the air was out of the question. So I kept at the task at hand.

"All buttoned up, skipper!!" Tony's voice rang out. "Everybody's inside, so you can haul ass—excuse me, ma'am."

The chattering, faraway BOOM-BOOM-BOOM of twin twenty-millimeter cannon fire from our dorsal turrets rose above the turboprop SCREECH and put a period at the end of his sentence.

"Mooring lines?"

"We're free as a bird—how we doing, lieutenant?"

Ava said, "Props okay, but I'm getting nowhere fast with the jets. They're lit, but that's about it."

Tony grabbed a seat affixed to rails and slid it beside her "What we got going here?"

. I left them to their work and slowly advanced the throttles with *both* hands—how the hell else do you manage twelve engines?

Kaito shook his head, reached over and slid a locking bar at the base of the throttle quadrant that ganged them up in a variety of combinations.

"How do I say, thanks?" I said.

"Arigato."

"Arigato, Kaito!"

He bobbed his head slightly. *"Doutiashimashite."*

I tapped the RPM gauges and then pointed to him. "OK?"

"OK."

I needed him to sing out when I reached my limit on what these weird-sounding engines could do. A lifetime of listening to the happy hammering of piston engines was a hard habit to break.

No matter the maker – be it Pratt & Whitney, Allison, Packard, or Wright, my ears could detect the slightest of hiccups coming from ignition issues or bad fuel. But turboprops? Just an endless, screeching howl from the turbine blades as they shoved out hot exhaust and spun the variable-pitch propellers.

I slid back the window and stuck my head out to get a fix on how were situated in relation to the shoreline. I had an unobstructed view because the slab-like wing was over one hundred fifty feet *behind* me. That was the good news. The bad news was not being able to see the pylon-mounted engines without literally standing up and turning around. They, along with the wing, were in the next county, on *top* of the wing instead of faired into the leading edge like most planes.

For sure, dawn was coming like it had since time began. Thank God for the gloomy cloud cover keeping us from being silhouetted against what would otherwise be an ever-brightening horizon.

A few flashes of gunfire in the distance. Then a towering SPLASH of water about two hundred yards off to my left.

Mortar fire?

Probably.

Time to get the hell out of town.

I ducked inside and goosed more power to the engines. Needles rising on the gauges. A quick look to Kaito, who surprised me with a "thumbs-up" sign. Where the hell did he learn that?

I found the intercom button on the control wheel.

How the hell did it work?

It took Kagusaki only a few back-and-forths with Kaito for me to figure out how to operate the press-to-talk switch. Within seconds, Gunny's croaking voice came on the line.

"Sir, they're breathing down our neck!"

"We're on our way. Once we're our far enough for our tail turrets to bear, have your guys shoot up the PT boat. Aim for the depth charges and the remaining torpedoes. See if Lieutenant Kennedy has any other suggestions. It's his boat."

"*Was*, you mean sir."

"Also, find the radioman and send him up here—the guy carrying the body from the boat."

A brief pause. Sounds of gunfire in my headset.

"Got it."

"Lieutenant Kennedy too. We need a navigator."

"Where we headed, sir?"

"Home."

I turned to shout something at Ava, but Kaito hollered at me while pointing at the temperature gauges.

Flashing red lights above four of the twelve gauges. My blank stare was all he needed to jump out of his seat.

Kagusaki thought he was escaping.

Me too.

But only as far as the engineer's station about ten feet behind us, where he muscled his way in between Ava and Tony. His hands flew over a series of small levers that I could only assume had something to do with those rising temperatures. The turboprops didn't have cowl flaps like radials, so what could it be?

But wait a second... they had to have some kind of cooling vents, because after Kaito did what he did, the indicator needles on those hot engines trembled slightly, then surrendered to green-ville on the dials.

By the time my co-pilot resumed his seat, all but one of the warning lights had gone out. He pointed his finger at it, the way you'd point a gun, then pretended to fire a "shot." He owned moment, because the red over-heat light flickered out just as he did so.

He blew on his finger to cool off the "barrel"—and even more dramatic, didn't even make eye contact with me—just another day at the office for this clever kid who knew a thing or two about American movie westerns.

Kagusaki and he went back and forth while I advanced the port throttles to swing us north to make room for the towering twin tail to clear the dock, but not too much. I needed those double tail gunners to chew up that PT-boat.

With the target swinging into view, the dorsal turret directly behind the flight deck opened fire. Its tracers overshot the boat at first, but then walked backwards until the rounds started raising white splashes all around the dock. Then all hell broke loose when the double-stacked tail guns joined in. Imagine four 20mm cannons pounding shells into the wooden hull of a PT-boat. Add to that, gunfire from five other dorsal turrets who now got into the act.

The 109 didn't stand a chance.

The hailstorm of cannon fire found the depth charges first. The "cans" went up in a brilliant white flash that temporarily blinded me. But I kept looking anyhow. How could I not? The combined efforts of Gunny and Kennedy's gunners were making mincemeat out of any enemy soldiers stupid enough to be anywhere near what was left of the loading dock.

Her fuel tanks went up milliseconds later, probably from sympathetic ignition not gunfire. We hadn't been carrying full load, but I bet at least a thousand gallons of hundred-octane went up in a reddish-yellow fireball that rose two hundred feet in the air.

Exploding somewhere in the midst all those hellacious fireworks was the crowning touch – two TNT-packed torpedoes. Pieces of this and scraps of that went flying everywhere.

A hell of a show.

Tony stood beneath the long, teardrop-shaped canopy that arched over the flight deck and regarded the chaos taking place on shore. "Fourth of July in February, skipper."

"Roger that."

Now to get this winged whale into the air.

My headset crackled and buzzed. Then Gunny's voice. "Sparks and the loo-tenant on the way, sir."

"They know how to find us?"

"One of my guys is showing them—wait one."

A pause. A muffled shout. Gunny cursed. Then "Sir, unidentified craft just laid a spotlight on us."

"Open fire, for God's sake."

"Negative. The lieutenant belayed the order. Says it's one of ours, but how the hell does he know?"

Seconds later, the "unidentified" craft answered the question for us, when a very-recognizable PT-124 overtook our lumbering flying boat like the hare breezing past the tortoise. It reduced speed and crossed in front of us to take position directly below and to our left. Its Aldis lamp began flashing Morse Code, that I repeated aloud, and made sure my intercom was still on. I wanted Gunny to pass it along.

"Message from PT-124 follows – 'Good luck… good… hunting… give them… hell.'"

They must have witnessed our takeover of the flying boat, while on their way back from their diversionary mission on the southwest side of the island. Had it worked perfectly? I doubt it. Nothing's ever perfect in war. Men had been killed and wounded on both sides.

But if PT-124 was here, pacing us like a happy Irish Setter after a hunt, then somewhere out on the open ocean, two war canoes filled with Hek and his guerillas were racing back to their secret base. That made me feel good.

Mission accomplished—sort of.

Ava shouted, "Jets lighting up!"

"For real?"

Tony added, "Two burning and two on the way, skipper."

"Great. We'll need them."

Kaito pointed his stubby finger at the already-rising temperature gauges on the middle instrument panel. Then he made an "OK" sign. I made one back. Yes, we were both commissioned officers. Yes, we both had sworn solemn oaths to defend our respective nations from aggressors. And yes, we were mutual enemies. But we were pilots, too.

And when the complex, interconnected, myriad parts that make up an airplane work the way they're supposed to, you can't help but feel the kind of feeling we both had when we saw instrument-based proof that eight thousand pounds of additional thrust were slowly but surely building inside the four cylindrical shapes mounted on top of our wing outbound of the turboprops.

"Twelve turning and four burning," Tony said.

"Thank you, sir—and madam."

Hard to predict wind direction because the wave action was subdued. I had to guess from the west. Not the first time I've had that problem during water takeoffs. If you don't have it sorted out right, Mother Nature will do it for you by "weathervaning" you in no time flat. Not a problem in most cases, because you've got plenty of room to maneuver. But in our case, being in the lee of Kaho'olawe, we couldn't take off to the west without running smack into the volcanic landmark.

I had no idea of the takeoff run of this beast. True, she barely had a payload – less than fifty men and two multi-ton bombs. But the weight of her fuel alone must be staggering, and her sheer size would mean miles of "runway" before she finally took to the sky.

Kagusaki shouted, "Look!"

I followed his pointing finger to a bright stab of light coming from a searchlight at our two o'clock position and closing fast. My guess was a couple of miles, but it's hard to predict distances with no outside references. My heart wanted it to be another PT boat, but my head said, "hell no."

"We've got company, folks," I said, then mashed the intercom button on my yoke. "Eyes right, everybody. Two o'clock... enemy vessel of some sort... closing fast."

Gunny took up the warning, and I left him to marshal the sailors and guerilla fighters manning our gun turrets. The vessel was out of range of our weapons, but not vice versa. I incendiary rounds striking our fuel tanks could spell the end the same way we ended PT-109's life. Yes, this was an enormous plane, and yes, it presumably had enough power to fly. But the only way she could take to the air was if her wings could lift her off the ground—or the water in our case.

Despite her size she had the same fragility of a paper kite – two sticks joined together in a cross, covered with tissue paper pulled taut. When tethered by a string, its papery surface resists the thrust of the wind, and in doing so, it leaps into the air. But break that precious wood joint and BOOM, it collapses on itself.

"Incoming!" Ava shouted.

She must have seen the flash of cannon fire, but impossible to chart the path of the shell against the pale grey, dawn sky. We had to wait for it to land—which it did, with a violent, vertical tower of white water about a mile to our left, almost hitting the shore.

A ranging shot for sure, and a bad one, thank God.

"They can't have radar," I said.

"If they did, we'd be up in smoke by now," Ava said,

Tony said, "I agree with the lieutenant. They're old school."

"Any guesses what it is?" I said.

"Probably the *Shimushu*," Tony said. "Jap escort destroyer. Saw her at Pearl a couple times. She's like the local beat cop in these islands. Somebody must have blown the whistle during the attack and she came running."

Another round. Closer.

"What kind of guns?"

"She's got five-inchers that pack a punch. But can only fire the forward one at the moment."

Bad news. Our 20mm rounds would bounce off her. The only way out of this was to keep accelerating.

Easy to say, but…

The airspeed indicator showed us barely hitting thirty knots. Faster than the *Shimushu*, true, but the faster we went, our takeoff angle would widen to a broadside, and she could bring her full complement of guns to bear. Even though she was "old school" without radar, her gunners understood the art of deflection shooting and could lay down a hailstorm of shells as we accelerated.

So, instead of running like a frightened deer, I retarded the starboard throttles and advanced the port ones to full power.

Kaito made a questioning grunt. I ignored him, as our bulbous nose slowly swung to starboard in response. The rounds fell further away. Once lined up head-on to the *Shimushu*, I advanced the starboard throttles to stop the swing. I had to aim straight down the pickle barrel to minimize shell hits and take my chances that the deck crews couldn't react in time.

"Wait a second," Tony shouted. "I think—no, I know for *sure*… Tojo's not firing at *us*, he's going after the PT boat!"

"Tony's right!" Ava laughed. "He thinks we're the *good* guys!"

Here, all along, I figured *we* were the target. Guilty conscience, I suppose, because, in truth, the *Shimusu* wanted the blood of the mosquito boat blasting through a triple water column of four-inch rounds that straddled her perfectly. Had she been stationary, the next shell would have done the trick. But she was hitting close to fifty miles-an-hour, her bow tearing through the waves like they were tissue paper.

"Go Woody!" Kennedy shouted from somewhere behind me.

He and Sparks had made their way forward during our takeoff run. Now they had a front-row seat to a battle royal between the heavier-armed but slower escort destroyer and the over-powered, over-sexed, Elco Patrol Torpedo boat.

Let them duke it out.

Time for more speed.

I tapped the four yellow throttles and said, "*Hai?*"

Kaito's eyes darted across the dials – RPM, fuel flow, temperature, then he shouted, "*Hai!*"

I slowly advanced the jet engines to full thrust. Each packing two thousand horsepower would give us eight thousand more horses to pull us through the water.

The airspeed indicator was just crossing the fifty-knot mark. Liftoff speed for a forty-ton, Boeing 314 Clipper was about seventy-knots fully-loaded. Tony and I estimated this monster to be at least three hundred *tons* of aluminum, steel, and plexiglass. We'd be lucky to get airborne at one hundred-twenty, unless we could play with the flaps.

But "playing" is not something you do with an unfamiliar aircraft. And if ever there was an unknown bird, it was this winged behemoth.

And yet… the control yoke was the same. Rudder pedals, too. Throttles, airspeed indicator, compass…. I was in the same church-of-flight, just sitting in a WAY different pew.

I tapped the airspeed indicator and moved the control yoke slightly, as if rotating for takeoff.

Kaito finger stabbed a point just below one hundred ten knots and I felt a touch smug. Good guess on my part, but I needed to consult with my attending physician—Ava.

I shouted over my shoulder to her, "He calling liftoff at one-ten—make sense?"

A slight pause as she ran the numbers through her pilot's head. We were two surgeons staring down at a strange patient.

"With decent wind, maybe. She's a beast—uh, oh, RPM on six and seven."

Tony said, "On it, no sweat."

A quick over-the-shoulder glance – the two of them were working their engineering station like twin pianists – hands flying, switch-flipping. In response, my throttles mimicked their throttles via electro-pneumatic servos.

"A hell of a plane," I said as I watched our airspeed climb faster and faster.

90... 100....

By now, Lieutenant Kennedy stood directly behind me, peering out the canopy at "Woody" Ferguson's impudent attack on the destroyer escort. Ever since I realized the Japanese thought we were friendly, I'd been nursing the *Kawanishi* further and further away from the warring parties, now well off to port.

Streaks of red-orange tracer fire from the escort's secondary batteries laced the air to compete with PT-124's neon-red, fifty-caliber answering fire. I'm sure their forward deck cannon was pumping 40mm rounds at the escort, but not enough daylight to see any strike results.

"He's only got two fish," Kennedy said. "C'mon, Woody, you can do it."

"So can we," I whispered to myself as the airspeed indicator needle trembled against the 105-knot mark.

I tapped the photos I'd put up on the instrument panel—my Estelle and Kaito's wife.

"Hai?" I said.

He nodded.

Time to fly.

Twelve turboprops, four turbojets – 32,000 pounds of thrust shoving a winged whale through the water. Did she feel any lighter on the controls?

A little.

Hard to judge.

Seaplanes can take forever to break loose from the surface tension of water. To help do that, they have a "step" built into the hull that creates the right amount of turbulence. Instead of a continuously smooth line along the hull, the fuselage "steps" upward about two-thirds along the way to create a notch in the hull. In our case, "up" meant about twenty feet.

Right about now, ocean waters were foaming in confusion from the turbulence caused by that step. I felt it in my rear end—the "seat of my pants" as it were—that she wanted to fly. Seconds earlier, I wouldn't have dared try. But now, I knew because *she* knew. No longer a "whale" or a "beast" or a "monster." The *Kawanishi's* wings were taking on her three hundred-plus tons of weight and turning a wallowing denizen of the deep into a beautiful, gigantic *geisha*.

And she was all mine.

I wiggled the control wheel then gestured upward with my thumb. Kaito nodded and reached over to "guard" my throttles from accidentally shifting from their full takeoff position. Extra protection because Ava and Tony were doing the same with their matching throttles. When you're doing business with a skyscraper with wings, it never hurts to have friends along to lend a hand.

A little back pressure now. Not too much. Just a touch. A flying boat likes to lift off by herself—"fly off" as it were—without human interference. Once airborne our marriage would begin, but for now, I did my best to let my "date" do her thing without me.

A slow rise upward, then an equally slow fall to kiss the South Pacific goodbye one more time...then finally she rose like an express elevator. Did she ever! So fast that her nose pitched up and we almost stalled.

"What the hell?"

Stick forward to level out and she responded quickly. Our airspeed recovered, then kept climbing... 140...150... I knew Kaito was smiling at my "slipping on a banana peel" moment, but pride refused to let me look. He knew how she flew, but I didn't risk him on the controls—not yet, at least.

We had ballooned up to almost five hundred feet and were still climbing. I began a shallow turn to port—not to take up a heading, but to see what the hell was happening on the ocean below.

Kennedy held a pair of binoculars to his eyes. Who knows where he found them.

"A hit!" he shouted.

"Us or them?" I said.

"Them. A gun hit—c'mon Woody, don't get so damn close."

I continued our slow climbing turn to port until I brought both combatants into full view. Like Zeus and his fellow gods on Olympus, we had a ringside seat to the battle between the *Shimushu* and PT-124 on the waters below.

The Elco ninety-footer was three-quarters of the way through a three hundred-sixty-degree turn. Her phosphorescent wake sketched an almost perfect circle. Less than a thousand yards separated the hunter from the hunted.

Kennedy whistled in admiration. "I know what you're up to Woody... DO it!"

From our ever-increasing height—now almost a thousand feet AGL, a bright orange-white flash on the deck of the PT boat as the black powder charge shoved a Mark 8 out of its launch tube. It splashed into the water with a phosphorescent bloom.

"Number four, number FOUR!" Kennedy shouted.

FLASH, the second torpedo shot out to join its twin.

The foaming blue-white wake from the first torpedo's tiny steam-turbine-driven engine aimed it straight at the escort. That meant its gyro was actually working. And miracle of miracles, the second one too! Two fingers of death screeched across the water.

"Perfect angle, Woody!" Kennedy said. "Praise the Lord for torpedoes that work."

"Amen!" Tony said.

Thanks to the torpedoes phosphorescent wakes, the *Shimushu's* lookouts saw what was coming, and the nimble-footed ship was already turning toward them to "thread the needle" and escape damage.

Meanwhile, PT-124, her job done, skidded hard to starboard to keep her profile to a minimum, while putting as much distance as possible between herself and the escort's' five-inchers and 20mm.

Without warning, the first torpedo leapt from the water like a hooked sailfish, then dove for the bottom – a victim of a tumbled gyroscope.

"Business as usual," Kennedy growled.

Free from one threat, *Shimushu's* quick-witted captain ordered the helm hard-a-starboard to veer further away from the remaining torpedo and improve his chances.

Kennedy shouted, "Check it out! Number four's rudder's gone haywire."

I risked a quick look, but not for long, because we were nearing the bottom of the cloud ceiling and I'd have to transition over to instruments soon.

Then he whooped with laughter. "I can't believe it!"

Instead of hissing past the escaping destroyer escort and into the open ocean, the opposite appeared to be taking place. As if connected by an invisible string, the Mark 8 was curving to port *toward* the target. True, a defective torpedo like all the others, but its frozen rudder control was steering it on a converging course with the enemy, who had made the mistake of turning too—and now couldn't turn back in time.

Less than three hundred yards separated them. The ship's twenty-knot top speed was no match for the torpedo's relentless thirty-six. Would it hit the ship? Not if she could help it. Every weapon on board was firing furiously at the approaching messenger of death.

Splashes everywhere, but no hit yet. Good news for Woody and his crew as they continued their high-speed escape. What a story they would have to tell when they got back to Maui – what began an attack on a Japanese super-bomber had morphed into an airborne hijack that rivalled escaping from Alcatraz in its odds for success.

Kennedy pounded on the plexiglass canopy. "C'mon… *c'mon!*"

The first wisps of cloud cover streaked past the canopy. Any second now, we'd disappear into the dark-grey mist and be flying blind until we found the top of the cloud ceiling.

"BINGO!" Kennedy shouted.

A towering white column of water and smoke rose from the *Shimushu's* fantail. While not a direct hit to break her back and send her to the bottom, the torpedo's warhead had wiped out the rudder and single screw, rendering her dead in the water. As proof, she was already losing way and slewing to starboard.

What happened next, I'll never know, because my eyes locked onto the artificial horizon indicator to keep our wings level as we finally entered the misty soup.

I adjusted our rate-of-climb to a stately two hundred FPM. An airplane this big moved through space and time in a completely different manner than, say, a twin-engine bomber or single-engine fighter. Gnats compared to a condor.

I risked a quick look at Kaito, who was attending his tasks as co-pilot – monitoring our engine performance and various other duties, but at the same time angrily bending Kagusaki's ear in a big way. I let them go at it for a while without interfering. My hands were full—literally—with the control yoke.

How in God's name did they manage to boost the controls on this this aircraft? The ailerons and flaps were located on the trailing edge of the massive wing, two hundred feet behind me. The rudder and elevators were four *hundred* feet away.

Yet, when I moved the control yoke, it had less tension than Patton's loathsome C-87, and even less than *Pan Am's* Boeing 314 *Yankee Clipper*, whose control inputs frequently took the muscle of both pilots. Both of those hefty, four-engine birds were cable-controlled. But the Japanese engineers must have figured out some kind of hydraulic boost system that did most of the work. The only thing it *didn't* do was take the worry out of trying to kidnap the *Kawanishi*.

Kaito and Kagusaki tailed off their exchange. The interpreter patted the co-pilot on the shoulder like they were brothers. Kaito shrugged off the gesture like poison.

"What's going on with you two?" I said.

"Discussing the fortunes of war."

"Meaning?"

"He's up here safe and sound watching us blow up his fellow warriors down there."

"Baloney. Tell him we blew up a rudder and propeller and part of the engine room. Most of his brothers-in-arms will live to see another day."

"Most but not all. You know what I mean, sir."

I did a quick instrument scan. "Keep an eye on him. I don't want any *banzai* bullshit going on."

Kaito shot me an accusatory look at my mention of the B-word.

"Tell him no offense."

They went back and forth some more. Kaito finally nodded briskly, then returned to his monitoring duties, a frown still plastered on his face. Not much progress in the "take-it-easy,-we're-all-just-friends" department.

"Like I said…"

"Yes, sir, I'll keep an eye on him."

We broke out of the overcast at six thousand feet. Below us, a slowly-rolling, muddled mixture of dark grey and lighter cumulus. Above us, the rising sun turned the pale-blue sky rosy-pink.

Not the Japanese "Rising Sun" Whose rays I'd seen on too many damned flags lately. But the real one, shining bright and blissfully unaware of the war raging on this pretty little planet we call "earth."

But not pretty forever.

While the sun had its own thermonuclear explosions taking place on its fiery surface, we carried the seeds of an identical force deep inside the cavernous belly of our flying boat.

I caught Kaito's eye, pointed at the sun, smiled, and gave him a thumb's up. He shrugged slightly and turned away. This was not a happy man. But a necessary one. Without him in the right seat, I was flying blind, even in VFR conditions.

Our destination?

I had one in mind.

Step by step walk the thousand mile road.
Miyamoto Mushashi - Samurai

W/hat did the man say who jumped out of the airplane without a parachute?

"So far so good."

Which is how I felt when Lieutenant Kennedy "walked" the navigation dividers across the map spread out on the chart table of the navigator's station located aft of the pilots' station. The stand-up table was similar to the ones we used in the Boeing *Clippers*—with one exception – sized for the lesser-statured Japanese, Kennedy had to hunch over to do his calculating.

I hunched over next to him, more from nervous tension than need. I was a trained navigator. So was Kennedy. And while his expertise was water-based and mine aerial, "stars are stars and the sun is the sun," and the last thing he needed was someone breathing down his neck with a second opinion on where the hell we were, and where the hell we were going.

So, while Kennedy marched the divider's needle-sharp points across the vast Pacific and counted out loud to himself, I called out to Ava who was spelling me in the left-hand seat, "How's the autopilot holding?"

She gave me a thumbs-up. "Pegged on zero-six-one degrees, captain."

A plane this big was built to fly on incredibly long missions, but impossible without a dependable autopilot. While hand-flying is at the heart of aviation, maintaining straight-and-level flight for hours on end is best left to a machine.

"Keep an eye on it," I said. "And get ready for a course change soon."

"Roger."

Fortunately, our co-pilot Kaito had thawed out enough to demonstrate how to use the autopilot. While somewhat similar to the Sperry A5 we used in our Army Air Corps bombers, it had its own quirks. But with some sharp questions and Kagusaki's quick translating, I sorted out how to set the inputs that would control the *Kawanishi's* three axes of flight – pitch, roll, and yaw by sending inputs to her ailerons, elevator, and rudder, respectively.

From what Tony had gleaned, our flying boat had a combat radius of almost ten thousand miles—that meant the Japanese could fly nonstop to New York City, bomb it, and fly all the way back and land in Oahu and *still* have fuel to spare. Not a lot, mind you, since the distance was nearly ten thousand miles, but enough.

Not that we were going to do that. But for sure, the Japanese war planners had taken full advantage of the plane's combat radius when planning their mission to bomb the Panama Canal locks and return, which was nearly the same mileage.

"Close, but no cigar, Tojo," I thought to myself, and allowed myself a brief feeling of smug determination. I mean, look at us... 10,000 feet above the ocean, engines humming perfectly, heading due east with their precious Panama Canal bomber in American hands.

I said to Kennedy, "Wouldn't it be nice if we had an auto-navigator, too?"

He sniffed dismissively. Way too busy trying to calculate the correct course that would lead us to our destination in the New Mexico desert.

Yes, I said *desert*.

Question of the hour – could we land this behemoth of a flying boat on Alamogordo Army Airfield's two thousand-foot runway, where Ava and I first flew General Patton? No choice in the matter now. PT-109's dud torpedo had punched a hole in the fuselage, so we had to opt for concrete instead of water. Thank the gods she was an amphibian like our PBYs, with retractable landing gear.

But then, I wondered if Kaito had any hands-on experience in setting her down on land and my nervousness ratcheted upwards along with my blood pressure. Too many questions, not enough answers.

Ava turned in her seat and hollered, "Tony, howzit going back there? Miss me yet?"

"Big time, lieutenant, but I'm managing."

My chief mechanic had propped his feet up on Ava's now-empty chair, leading the life of Riley. Based on his relaxed posture, everything was working perfectly.

I couldn't resist. "How's our fuel flow?"

"Stand by."

He CLUMPED his feet onto the deck, then leaned forward to ponder the twin row of fuel-flow dials to his left. He tapped one of the dials, then another. Satisfied, he gave me the OK sign.

"She's got a hell of an appetite, skipper."

"Good thing we've got plenty of food."

"Long as we don't run up against headwinds—you're serious about New Mexico, right?"

"Affirmative. We're carrying the Holy Grail—not to mention a couple Knights of the Round Table as well."

"You mean the wop and the Jap scientists?"

"Professors Rasetti and Yamasaki, yes."

"That Italian will talk their ears off. The Jap? Good luck with that guy."

"Doesn't matter. We've got two of their bombs. Actions speak louder than words."

He whistled appreciatively. "What a haul. Hope we can pull it off."

The thought of failure turned me back to Kennedy, who by now was jotting down a series of numbers to aid him in determining our LOP (line of position) on the chart.

Soon he would shoot the sun and calculate where we were in time and space—providing we could still see the sun. At the moment, it bathed us in brilliant light. But not knowing what kind of weather lay ahead, we needed to make hay while it still was shining.

Years ago, as a young aviator in *Pan Am's* navigation class I'd memorized this sentence – "Celestial navigation is the use of angular measurements between celestial bodies and the visible horizon to locate one's position in the world on land as well as at sea."

Easy to say, not easy to do.

Not if the sun is too low on the horizon, or the stars hidden behind heavy cloud cover. Not if the parachute flare you dropped to calculate your drift doesn't light up. Or the drift meter can't register how much the wind is shoving you off course.

Radio beacons are man's best friend, but they only work over land. Back stateside, Ava and I could easily fly General Patton from point A to point B anywhere in the country by following a series of Morse code dots and dashes transmitted from ground stations.

But out here in the open ocean, all we had were the navigational instruments Lieutenant Kennedy was using to calculate our position. One of the most important ones was the *Nautical Almanac.* The Japanese version was in Japanese, of course, and its entry for "Increments and Corrections for the Sun" was gibberish. But the multiple columns of numerical tables representing minutes and seconds were in Arabic. That's all that mattered. True, we were in a different "church" but all the "pews" were the same – declination, Greenwich Hour Angle, Sight Reduction Tables—the works.

Even the Japanese bubble sextant was familiar—to me, at least. And after a brief explanation of the differences between this type of instrument and the one Kennedy used on water, he caught on fast, especially how the "bubble"—similar to the one in a carpenter's level— served as a "horizon" when you can't see it because of low cloud cover.

He headed off to shoot the sun through the plane's astrodome, a small plexiglass observation dome protruding through the top of the *Kawanishi's* fuselage just aft of the greenhouse-sized cockpit.

I left him to his calculations and crossed over to the radio operator's station, directly behind the engineering station.

I felt like a doctor "doing rounds" but when you're the captain of an airplane, no matter the size, the only way to make sure everybody's doing the right thing at the right time is to see for yourself. I'd learned that the hard way on a trans-pacific flight for *Pan Am* when I *assumed* the navigator's compass settings were identical to ours on the flight deck. I lived to tell the tale, but barely.

Sparks, the PT-109's radioman, sat hunched over, peering at the triple stack of transmitters and receivers, whistling a tuneless sort of tune. Now and then, he'd reach out, twist this dial and flip that switch.

"Any progress?" I said.

He made a final adjustment to a frequency dial the size of a small dinner plate before answering. Then he turned to me, his face serenely confident. "Getting there, sir."

"By the way, what's your name? Other than Sparks, I mean."

He brushed back a tousled shock of red hair. "Radioman Second Class John Maguire, sir."

"How long you been in?"

"Two years, four months."

"Days?"

He thought for a split second. "Nineteen—counting today."

"Girl back home?"

"Yes, SIR."

"She call you 'Jack?'"

"When things are okay, yes sir. But when they ain't, it's 'John.'"

"Those radios. Think they'll be 'okay' too?"

He hefted a pair of earphones. "Radios are like women, sir. They all look different, but deep down they're all the same—just like guys. Frequencies are like that, too. The same all over the world—take this VHF job the Japs got here—it powers up differently, but at heart, it tunes right in."

He put on his headset, flipped a switch, gave a listen, grinned, then handed me the headsets.

A hiss of static, then a burst of Japanese. More static, then more Japanese. Terse. Formal.

"What is it?" I said.

He shrugged, "Kagusaki'll know. But based on this frequency range I'm guessing it's CAP pilots reporting in."

"Don't know what that means."

He tweaked the RDF before responding. "Can't determine direction yet—but anyhow, CAP means 'Combat Air Patrol.' Most likely coming from planes off those carriers that sailed from Pearl a while back."

Seemed like another lifetime when I witnessed the Japanese Navy strike group departing Pearl Harbor the same day Ava, Mac, and I arrived – two enormous Japanese fleet carriers, their flight decks packed with aircraft, four heavy cruisers, a destroyer squadron, a flurry of destroyer escorts, and at least two fleet submarines.

"Let's hope we don't run into them," I said.

Sparks grinned. "It ain't like we're flying a Navy PBY, sir. The Japs will think we're the good guys, like that dumb destroyer did."

"That's what Kagusaki thinks, too. Hope you're both right."

Lieutenant Kennedy passed behind me, saying, "Got us a fix, skipper."

I joined him at the chart table and waited as he thumbed through the almanac, ran his finger up one column of figures then across to another, did some final calculations, then finally jotted down:

20° 58'44"N+150° 40'35.7"W

"That a seven?" I said, pointing to the final number.

"Yes, sir."

"Thought it was a one. Hmmm... Borrow your pencil?"

I drew a tiny line, or serif, through the downstroke of the numeral seven. "Europeans do this to make sure they don't mistake it for a one."

Kennedy sketched an identical hash-marked seven on a scrap of paper. "Good idea. How'd you learn that trick?"

"The hard way."

Neither the time to tell him about being lost in the middle of the Pacific Ocean on my first flight for *Pan Am* as navigator for the *Hawaiian Clipper*. Nor the place to tell him how I had spent years patiently climbing the promotion ladder rung by rung, from junior flying officer, to radio operator, to flight engineer, to navigator, with my hungry eyes fixated on the right-hand seat in the cockpit, first as a co-pilot... and then finally—hopefully—reaching the left-hand seat as captain. Then, the absolute pinnacle of Mount Everest by becoming a "Master of Flying Boats."

But my nightmare of being lost on that awful night wiped out my dreams of glory. Crouched over the chart table, I had *finally* got a drift calculation that made sense and convinced myself we were no longer wandering in the watery wilderness.

By taking advantage of the harsh light from the parachute flare on the ocean surface, I used the etched reticules in the viewfinder to determine my drift angle.

All I had to do was observe in which direction the waves moved. Then, using a series of dials and a small pencil I could determine the compass heading necessary to remain on course.

I would also calculate ground speed by using a separate calculator and a stopwatch. While our drift meter was a godsend for a navigator, using it at night required the accursed parachute flares. Those damned things came from the devil himself.

The third flare—thankfully—had worked and I confirmed our compass heading, current position and airspeed.

Finally!

By my triple-checked numbers, we were now on proper course. Three hours and nineteen minutes from now we would be landing in Oahu.

I reported the same to the mighty Master of Flying Boats, Captain James T. Fatt, who occupied the left-hand seat like Caesar did his throne. His wish was our command. And that command was our doom if we hesitated.

A giant of a man, both by reputation and bulk. He'd flown biplanes in the First World War, barnstormed across America in peacetime, flown the mail through rain and snow and gloom of night, until he finally achieved a pilot's version of nirvana by becoming *Pan American Airway's* senior pilot.

I was terrified of the man. And I loved the man. Both at once.

Fatt snatched away my slip of paper showing our position, speed, and ETA. He shoved his reading glasses onto the tip of his whiskey-reddened nose and looked at me before he looked at the paper with my hastily-scribbled notations.

"You sure of this, son?"

"I am, sir... now, I mean."

He peered over his glasses like an overweight Ebenezer Scrooge. "Clarify *'now'* Mister Carter, if you please."

"Two of the drift flares burnt out before I could get a reading."

"God DAMN it, I told them about those GOD damned things going out on us."

"Yes, sir."

"This number right here, a seven or a one?"

I took back the paper and my mouth went dry. It could be either.

"Let me check, sir."

Like a yo-yo, I spun back to double-check—thank God I'd written it in more legible handwriting on the chart when I first calculated it! Then I spun back to Fatt.

"A seven, captain."

"Gimme' your pencil, *Mister* Carter."

He proceeded to do what I had just done for Lieutenant Kennedy.

He handed back the slip of paper. "See the difference?"

"Yes, sir."

"Lesson learned?"

"Yes, sir."

He tucked his reading glasses into his shirt pocket and patted them like an old friend. "If that had been a one, we'd be sleeping with the fishes tonight. Instead we'll be dancing with the girls—ever dance the *Hula*, Mister Carter?"

"No, sir."

He swayed back and forth slightly and smiled but said nothing.

I thought about Fatt's long-ago "*Hula* girls" as I slid my finger across the empty space on the map to the spot where Kennedy had just penciled a tiny "X" to mark the spot.

According to his calculations, we were now two hundred forty-two miles northeast from Kaho'olawe. We'd been cruising at one hundred-eighty knots for a little over an hour, apparently minus any serious head winds, and also minus the turbojets.

I had Tony shut them down soon after takeoff. They'd helped us get this fat girl off the ground, but their fuel appetite was voracious. I did some quick math—depending on winds aloft, we could conceivably arrive in New Mexico in a little over sixteen hours.

When I announced this to Kennedy he shook his head. "Hard to believe that sixteen hours ago I was sound asleep in Maui."

"You'll be sleeping stateside by tomorrow night."

He didn't look happy about it.

"Why the long face?"

"Sir, I signed up to fight the enemy."

"And you've done a hell of a job so far. Plenty of chances to keep on doing that. But nothing wrong with a few nights between clean sheets and a shave stateside. It'll make the world look –and feel a lot better."

He rubbed his beard. "Hate losing this."

"Join the Royal Navy."

That got a grin.

"Sam!"

From the tone of Ava's voice I was at her side in seconds.

She peeled off her earphones and handed them over. "Gunny's off the rails—listen!"

We swapped seats and I keyed the transmit button.

"Carter here."

"Sir, that dago Rasetti's gone plumb loco, not talking English, won't let us get near the bomb. He's got a damned gun."

"Where's Yamasaki? That nut-case scientist."

"Out like a light. Rasetti socked him one, then went native. Better get your ass down here, sir. NOW!"

"On my way."

As I got near the tail of the plane, I ducked behind the massive shadow of one of the H-bombs squatting on its delivery pallet like a malevolent Easter egg. I could see my breath from the ice-cold chill coming from its surface. Thirty yards ahead of me, the other bomb sat on its delivery pallet as well—*with* Professor Rasetti crouched on top, pistol in one hand trained on Gunny, the guerillas, and the sailors. In the other, a length of rope held taut.

"Good morning, professor!" I shouted.

He turned.

Gunny and the others made a rush for the bomb, but I shouted, "STOP!"

They froze.

I did my best to stroll forward instead of bolt. Rasetti kept his pistol trained on me as I drew closer. Guns pointed at me give me the shakes. I took a deep breath to relieve the tension. Something about the overly-dramatic quality of Rasetti perched on top of a hydrogen bomb in a Japanese super-sized flying boat, reminded me of *The Maltese Falcon*, a great detective novel written by Dashiell Hammett. A great book, and an even greater movie with Humphrey Bogart playing the detective, Sam Spade.

Bogie was much better playing that gumshoe than portraying me in *Mission to Manila*. Probably because Sam Spade's such a great character in a novelist's mind, while I'm just a schmuck who got tangled up in the web of war and was fighting his way out.

Including now.

I thought to myself, "What would Sam Spade do?"

Then I had it. "Nice pistol you got there, professor. *Nambu* is it?"

"*Arresto!*" he shouted.

I was within fifteen feet of the bomb. But towering ten feet above me, the Italian was miles away from being grabbed. A hell of a tableau – *Man with H-Bomb Holding Gun in Hand.*

"How many rounds that thing got?" I said.

He shrugged.

"Think you have enough to kill us all? Let's see… How many are there?" I counted to myself, mumbling away. "I count twenty-six—including your fellow scientist, Professor Yamasaki. By the way, how's the jaw, doc?"

Yamasaki refused to acknowledge my existence.

Rasetti said, "It is not my gun that will kill us. It is this rope in my hand that will release the energy of the sun!"

I smiled—Spade would have done that—then I slowly applauded—he would have done that too. "Nicely played, professor. Ever been an actor? You must have because you sure took us for a great ride with all your bullshit patriotism."

"I am not acting. I am telling you the truth."

"C'mon, you don't want to blow us up. Why don't you come down here and let's talk it over."

His face shifted from anger to astonishment to an almost maniacal smile. "*Aspett!* Wait! *Madonna mia,* you think *I* am the one?"

"Well…what'd you expect? There you are with a gun in one hand and what I assume is some kind of lanyard in the other. One yank and we're one with the sun."

I turned to Yamasaki, "Right, professor?"

He rubbed his bloody jaw but said nothing.

Rasetti shook his head. "You are wrong. It will not explode when you *pull* the rope. It is only when you *release* it that it starts the timer." He shouted at Yamasaki, "Am I right, *bastardo?*"

Silence.

I took the leap—not physically—but just as precipitous as I went full Sam Spade. "Then turn loose of the damn lanyard and be done with it. I want to meet my maker, see what he looks like. Don't you?"

"*Assolutamente no!*" Rasetti pointed his pistol down the side of the bomb. "Look just beneath that square panel. See the lid that is half-open? Look inside. Tell me what you see."

I did so. First a tangle of wiring, then beneath it…

"Some kind of red light."

"It is on because this hydrogen bomb is *armed.* Something that should *not* have happened until the plane was an hour from the Panama Canal."

"But you wanted to blow us to kingdom come right away, so you did the deed."

"I never *touched* it! It was Yamasaki who did this. When I saw him run for the bomb, I knew that he... he..."

Gunny spoke up. "Things went nuts when these two jokers went at it. We broke them up, but the wop and him fought over the lanyard until this one hightailed it to the top and started in with his gibberish. Glad he's finally speaking English."

Rasetti said, "You *must* believe me, colonel. I am saving us from instant death."

I looked back and forth from him to the sullen Yamasaki. "I will, providing you keep a good hold of that rope while we figure a way to rig it safe—Pappy, you're Navy. Solve this and step on it."

"Yes, SIR!

PT-109's engineman grabbed another sailor and they hustled over to the bomb. Hard to call it a bomb. More like a gigantic tangle of cables and wiring wrapped around a steel sphere, sitting on a wheeled pallet. Like one of those balls of string you see made up from all sorts of lengths of colored twine, wrapped round and round until it's the size of a huge weather balloon.

There had to be some way that Pappy could turn this damned thing off.

I crossed over to Yamasaki, who stood between two beefy guerilla fighters, rifles at the ready. His eyes explored something of interest on the deck beneath his silk slippered feet.

"Nice embroidery on your footwear," I said. "Going somewhere special?"

That got me a quick glance. I've got to say that you don't *ever* want a guy to look at you the way this guy looked at me. Ever seen a shark's eyes? It's not that they're evil or anything like that. They're just empty.

Blank.

Like looking into an abyss.

I mean, there's got to be a brain inside making things go round and round for the shark, but by the time intelligence reaches its eyes, it's a bottomless pit that I dare you to stare at for more than a few seconds without getting a chill.

Yamasaki's eyes were like two coal-black marbles staring full force at me, as if measuring my soul for a trip to hell. A bit over the top with that description, maybe, but remember, I was still in my Sam Spade mode, taking what I thought were heroic actions, but only because I was pretending to be a heroic person. Or in my case, a solid, dependable, been-there, seen-that, private dick like Humphrey Bogart, who had to get the "Maltese Falcon," or die trying.

"What's with the lanyard, professor?" I said.

Silence.

"Moving on to a new topic, then. Is the other bomb armed?"

Nada from Mr. Sphinx.

I kept staring at him while I raised my voice, "Gunny, check the other bomb. That panel thing. Make sure we don't have *two* lights lit up to blow us to kingdom come."

"Aye, aye, sir."

Muffled footsteps as the men raced off to check.

Rasetti called out to them, "It's on the other side—no, not there, *there*. Look down. *Madre di Dio*, I pray it is only this one."

A long silence, while we waited.

Something in the set of Yamasaki's shoulders told me we had nothing to worry about—relatively speaking, of course. There was only the one bomb, true—but Jesus wept—a *hydrogen* one.

"Why arm just this one?" I said to him. "And why now?"

His hooded shark eyes widened ever-so slightly. Had I not been watching closely, I wouldn't have seen it, but I was.

I poked him in the chest, hard. "Why only one?"

He clenched his hands but kept them at his side.

"Negative on the light," Gunny called out.

Then a sailor shouted, "Line secured."

Rasetti clambered off that bomb like it was on fire. He crouched down and traced where the lanyard led to the arming box.

"Careful, professor," I said. "You don't want—"

Rasetti waved me into silence. He stiffened. "I need a flashlight! Quickly!"

A sharp command from Gunny and his guerillas swarmed over the vast interior in search of same. Their voices echoed off the high-arching side walls and bulkheads as they jabbered back and forth in Hawaiian.

"What are you looking for?" I said.

Rasetti's face was grave. "What I do not want to find."

Yamasaki smiled and finally spoke. "You *will* find it, Antonio."

The Italian gasped but stayed where he was.

"*Ua'loa!*" A guerilla came running with a yellow, box-shaped "battle lantern" already turned on. As he ran, its bright-white beam danced over the longerons and stringers that held the fuselage together. Down here, buried in the depths of the aircraft, hard to imagine we were flying through the air at over two hundred-miles-an-hour. More like scurrying around like mice in a cathedral.

Rasetti grabbed the lantern and played its light inside the arming box.

By now, the bomb had gained an even coating of frost. Rasetti's fingerprints dotted the surface. He gasped and darted back. At first, I thought he got an electrical shock. But when he turned to face us, it wasn't electricity that caused it, it was terror.

"*Madre di Dio,* why did you *do* this?"

Yamasaki said, "Because they never listened."

Rasetti turned to me. "How high are we?"

"Ten thousand feet, why?"

Yamasaki turned to me. "When we passed five thousand feet, the bomb armed itself."

It took a second for that to sink in. "Then *un*-arm it."

A long pause.

Rasetti said, "We cannot. The deuterium has entered the fusion chamber. "

"What the hell does that mean?"

Yamasaki said, "It means that all the kings horses and all the kings men cannot put Humpty-Dumpty back together again."

Rasetti said, "If we descend below five thousand feet, the weapon will explode automatically."

"And us along with it," Yamasaki added.

"But the rope!" Rasetti shouted. "Why did you want to—"

For the first time, Yamasaki became animated. "They would not listen to me, so I decided to serve my Emperor instead his warlords. He is my *shōgun*, not those lackey admirals and generals who want to rule the entire world. They do not understand that Japan only wants to take her proper place upon it and receive the respect she rightfully deserves."

I said, "You're out of your mind, you know that?"

He folded his arms across his narrow chest, spread his feet slightly, and bent his knees.

Rasetti pointed to the lanyard now secured to a metal, frost-covered pipe. "How did you bypass the timer? And why? This way the bomb would have exploded *inside* the airplane!"

Yamasaki stuck out his chest. "What do you do to keep out robbers? You either build a wall so high or you dig a hole so deep they cannot pass."

"What are you talking about?"

A long pause. A Mexican standoff but with Japanese players. Gunny edged his way closer to us, while the others stood there, as stupefied as I was at the thought of this insignificant little man holding our fate in his twitching hands.

Yamasaki licked his lips and smiled. "Oahu."

Rasetti's eyes about popped out of his head. "Do you mean——"

Yamasaki looked past all of us and into a world of his own devising. He gazed at something we couldn't see. He spoke as if we no longer existed.

"The Aleutians!" He spat out the word. "Miserable rocks in the middle of nowhere. And Panama? Blow up canal and you do not gain victory. You open the gates of hell, instead."

Rasetti stepped closer like a man watching a rattlesnake but determined to touch it. "You were going to explode the bomb over *Oahu*? That was your so-called 'hole' in the ocean?"

Yamasaki smiled but didn't look at his fellow scientist. "One... single... bomb and Japan would have had what she has wanted for a hundred years... a *thousand* years."

"What is that?" I said.

He slowly turned to face me. Those eyes of his... at least when a shark looks at you, you know it's alive. Yamasaki's eyes had that flattened look that only dead people have. Yet, he was still breathing and talking.

"Colonel!" Rasetti grew even more agitated, as if to offset Yamasaki's eerie calm. "Remember... this plane was supposed to fly over Oahu before heading for Panama. People waving flags. Bands playing. A great celebration."

Gunny did the math. "Then ka-BOOM?"

Yamasaki's right hand jerked slightly as he nodded. "With Oahu gone, and Kauai and Molokai, too, the hole would be so deep that Japan would finally be secure from invaders. She would become the epicenter of the

Great East-Asian Co-prosperity Sphere. Safe to grow, safe to rule, safe to serve her people forever."

I said, "Not anymore, mister."

It was like I'd slapped him as hard as I could.

His dead eyes sharpened into life. So did his right hand. He ripped open his flimsy-looking short-sleeve shirt—buttons flew everywhere— and he pulled out a small dagger from his waistband.

With two swipes of his razor-sharp *tanto*, he slashed the arms of his guerilla guards, who spun away, shouting in pain. I've seen *Kendo* swordsmen fight in matches, and the speed of their strikes is so blindingly fast that you don't realize they've struck until they've scored. Same thing with this scientist-turned-*samurai*.

It's a scientifically-proven fact that high stress affects your time-perception in such a way that you can perform certain feats of strength and movement that you could never have done under ordinary circumstances. This dagger-wielding, unhinged nuclear scientist making a beeline for the bomb was far from ordinary. By doing so, he triggered enough stress to fill an ocean.

Even with sensory slow-down working to our advantage, Yamasaki's speed and skill was stunning. As I took off after him, three guerilla fighters and a sailor went spinning, also wounded from his whirlwind slashing left and right.

Gunny calmly watched him fly past him like a race car at the Indianapolis 500, while I, on the other hand, was determined to tackle this little demon, even if it meant I suffered God knows what from that knife of his.

Yamasaki reached the frost-encrusted bomb and slipped on its climbing rungs as he scrambled up to cut the detonation cord. One slash with his knife and we'd meet our Maker.

"Hey, Professor!" Gunny shouted.

Yamasaki turned toward the voice.

He waved his KA-BAR in the air. "Want to trade?"

Then he flung his knife like first pitch on opening day. The blade barely had time to rotate back to front before burying itself in Yamasaki's right shoulder.

The force of the strike flattened him against the bomb. The icy slipperiness caused by the liquid hydrogen inside made him lose his balance. He slithered down the side of the giant sphere, bumping and banging along the way until he collapsed in a heap at the bottom.

A gang of Gunny's guerillas dove on him, while a sailor tore the *tanto* from his grip.

"Secure that *samurai* shithead." Gunny shouted.

Not for nothing do sailors know how to tie knots. In less than thirty seconds, Yamasaki lay on the deck, trussed up like a turkey minus the stuffing.

Gunny stood beside me, alternating his attention between observing the proceedings and wiping his knife blade clean of the professor's blood.

I said, "Where'd you learn to throw like that?"

"My daddy taught me."

"Where'd he learn?"

"Marines. Got gassed at Belleau Wood."

"They called that one the 'War to End All Wars.'"

"Yes, sir, until this one came along—by the way, that son-of-a-bitch bomb is still ticking, you know."

"The five-thousand-foot thing, you mean?"

"Aye, aye, sir. We go below that, and we go up in smoke."

I let that inescapable fact float in the air. Even though we'd landed our scientist "shark" on the dock, Yamasaki had left behind a far more dangerous one still swimming in the water—in our case the air. Oahu and its inhabitants, and the surrounding islands with their unsuspecting souls had been spared being vaporized for the sake of this madman's twisted notion of geopolitics.

But the moment our altimeter went below five thousand feet, the barometric triggers inside the bomb would do what they'd been designed to do all along. We would be "promoted to glory," as the preacher says, sending what was left of our vaporized souls to the Pearly Gates.

"I'm not quite ready to die, Gunny. You?"

"Still loving the good life, sir. Especially above five thousand feet."

"Let me get on the intercom and update the flight deck. Then let's reconvene by the bomb to discuss our options."

Gunny slipped the knife into its scarred and nicked scabbard and turned to go.

I said, "Permission to shake your hand, Gunnery Sergeant Lewis?"

He examined his callused paw. "Wait one. It's a little bloody."

He doused his hand with canteen water, wiped it on his pants, then grabbed my hand.

"*Semper fi,* sergeant."

"*Semper, fi,* colonel."

Ava's voice on the intercom was a combination of astonishment and calm reserve—if you can imagine such a thing. But that's what happens if you can handle two opposing concepts while keeping a level head—which she most certainly can.

Yes, we had saved the plane—and the mission—by disarming our straightjacket-worthy mad scientist bent on rearranging the world to fit his *samurai* sensibilities. But a mixed blessing because now we had a fully-armed bomb that would explode no matter what. You may have heard of "Fail Safe." This was "Fail Deadly."

"But why?" Ava said.

"Tokyo's way of making sure the bomb exploded no matter what. Like a dead-man's switch."

Memories of inter-city streetcar operators back in Key West. While his hands moved the myriad controls necessary to guide the trolleys to and fro, his left foot was always firmly planted on a pedal—the "dead man's switch." If he took it off for whatever reason—most likely if he died or was incapacitated—the trolley's emergency brakes would kick in and it would screech to a stop.

In our case, the opposite outcome. If the plane encountered enemy action during its attack on Panama and fell from the sky, the barometric triggers—providing they were set—would automatically set off the bombs. Yamasaki had preset one of the triggers. Then rigged the lanyard. A double-play that had *almost* worked. But as Captain Fatt used to say, "'Almost' only counts in horseshoes."

A long pause while Ava ran our dilemma through her mental gearbox. What to do next? By now, the guerillas had dragged Yamasaki off to one side and lashed him to a fuselage stringer. He sat there cross-legged, as impassive as the Buddha minus his beatific smile, while Gunny and

Rasetti knelt by the bomb, peering at something beneath the sturdy pallet upon which it rested.

I took a deep breath and let it out slowly.

Had life taken a different turn... had Gunny's KA-BAR missed... none of us would be standing here staring at a gigantic, frost-covered, malevolent beachball smothered with wires and tubing, packed with an atomic bomb to pull the trigger, and liquified heavy hydrogen as the "gun" that would cause the thermonuclear chaos.

Ava said, "You're positive the other one's safe?"

"If you can imagine any bomb to be 'safe,' it is. Rasetti checked it."

"And you want to take the safe one..."

"To Los Alamos, after we get rid of this hot one."

She laughed. "You're crazy, you know that?"

"So, what else is new?"

"It's starting to rub off on me, because I'm nuts enough to think we can do it—once we're at ten-thousand feet, that is"

"Let's punch a hole in the ocean."

"Poor fishies."

If you've never dropped an H-bomb out of a transport aircraft—and I'm pretty sure you haven't—the methodology for doing so is not that complicated: a pallet, a set of rails on the deck, and parachutes that delay the drop time long enough for the plane to escape the blast.

Simple as pie.

The bomb was another story, of course.

And while Rasetti did his best to explain how the damn thing worked, I got down on my hands and knees to figure out how it rested in the cradle. All that mattered to me was that it *did* work. He went on and on about how the atomic primary fission "trigger" would compress the hydrogen stored in concentric "thermos" bottles of liquid hydrogen. Surrounded by a uranium "pusher" the blast would compress the liquid deuterium, which in turn..."

You see where this is going.

I repeat, not only *could* it work it *would* work, and we had to get rid of it before that happened.

"How many chutes?" I said. "I count six, three to a side."

Gunny said, "Agreed. But how do they release?"

"There's got to be a common static cord somewhere—this it?"

Gunny traced the static line from chute to chute and nodded as if checking off a clipboard. "Pretty damn simple."

"Why be complex?" I said.

The bomb's massive steel pallet sat on eight flanged wheels, four to a side, that rested, in turn, on steel rails spiked onto wooden ties to displace the weight of the load on the plane's main deck. These delivery rails ran back twenty yards to the second (unarmed) bomb. The *Kawanishi's* aircraft engineers were no idiots. To maintain the plane's center-of-gravity, they needed to keep the bombs a specific distance from each other for the wings to maintain their proper angle-of-attack.

After dropping the first bomb on Panama's Gatun locks, and losing tons of payload, they would have to do some rapid trimming of the flight controls or she'd go into a nose-down attitude faster than you could blink. My guess is that to deliver the bomb, they would go to max power, then nose up, do a gravity release and be dialing in nose up-trim all the while. That way they could counter the drastic CG shift before it got out of hand.

At least, that's how I figured it.

Anybody can fly a plane straight and level. That's why God invented autopilots. But to divest yourself of a forty-ton payload and *not* turn into a dart that hits the bullseye called "earth" as a consequence, takes some pre-planning—and praying.

Gunny said, "Wait a second… lookee here."

We bumped heads examining a junction box of some kind beneath the sphere. A throttle cable snaked out from it and we traced it to another junction box—smaller—halfway up the side of the bomb.

Gunny used his KA-BAR to pry open the box. Inside was a simple altimeter and what looked like an aneroid relay—a switch that responds to changes in barometric pressure.

"*Scusa mi.*" Rasetti's dirty fingernail entered my field of view and tapped the face of the altimeter.

"See this yellow hand? It is set for one thousand feet. When the bomb reaches that altitude it will explode."

"What about the five-thousand-foot thing?" I said. "Won't it blow up on its way down?"

"*Nessun problema.* What do Americans call a street where you can drive in one direction?"

"One-way."

"*Essatto.*"

He went on to explain that the moment the bomb fell, an accelerometer would identify the sudden negative-G force as an official "drop" and activate the ignition relay. The "dead-man" switch would shut off, and the sensors would wait for the bomb to reach its pre-arranged altitude. When that happened, they'd send a signal to the second box, and...ka-BOOM.

"It arms as it drops, you mean."

"*Sì.*"

"Makes sense. The bombs would have to explode low enough to take out those locks. Otherwise they could get back in business."

Rasetti smiled. "Not only the locks, colonel, but the combined blast radius is twenty miles. The Isthmus of Panama is only thirty-five miles wide."

Gunny blurted, "Nothing left but ocean."

"The Atlantic meets the Pacific?" I said.

Rasetti shook his head. "Not that dramatic, but with the lakes drained and the locks gone... *Che sa?*"

I tried to picture the chaos. Whatever was left of Panama would take years to set right again.

Rasetti was ahead of my thinking. "Of course, the radiation from such a blast would contaminate the land for a very long time."

I tapped the side of the ice-cold sphere—but not too hard, mind you. "This son-of-a-bitch is going in the drink."

"And the other one?" Rasetti said.

"Home to poppa."

While not exactly "ticking," we still had one hell of a dangerous bomb onboard. Once I got back to the flight deck and briefed the folks, their faces looked how I felt—tense as hell. All of them, that is, except our co-pilot Kaito. Gone was the sullen resentment I'd seen on his kisser for the past hour. In its place was outrage—not at me, for a change, thanks to Kagusaki.

What did the trick? His translation of our screw-loose *samurai* Yamasaki's crazy-ass plan to blow up half the Hawaiian Islands and end the war.

Kaito spat the word out. *"Kamikaze baka!"*

"He says idiot," Kagusaki explained.

I pointed to his and my family photos on the instrument panel. "War is not healthy for living things."

Kaito pondered Kagusaki's translation. While he didn't exactly reach out and shake hands, I at least felt that we were on higher ground than when first we met.

Ava said, "When do we get rid of it?"

"As soon as Gunny gets his guys to clear the rails for a drop."

She put on her "all-business" face. "I'll monitor it for you."

She took off her headphones and wriggled out of the left seat.

Helen of Troy's face may have launched a thousand ships. But Ava's had done more. On the silver screen first, then as a multi-engine ferry pilot in the Women's Auxiliary Air Force, and now, as a commissioned officer in the Army Air Corps, she represented the female fighting spirit unlike anything anyone had ever seen before.

"At ease, lieutenant," I said.

She gave me the "look."

You don't *ever* want Ava James to do that to you. Trust me.

"Yes, colonel?"

Forget launching ships. Ava's face could freeze a thousand icebergs.

"I still need you on the flight deck."

"With all due respect, sir, whatever the hell for?"

"In case…"

She raised her eyebrows and I promptly ran out of gas.

"You need a commissioned officer down there. Lieutenant Kennedy can't leave, you can't leave, Tony can't leave, but I damn well can."

She patted the left-hand seat. "Your table's waiting, sir. Meet you on intercom."

She was right, of course. The peaceful co-existence of officers, non-commissioned officers, and enlisted personnel was essential. Each complements the other. You screw up that balance at your peril.

I risked a quick glance at Kennedy; his face a mask of neutrality. Then the slightest of nods—not to me specifically, but to the logic of Ava's doing what needed to be done.

"Before you head out, here's what we're going to do," I said. "Everyone listen up, okay?"

I turned to Kaito, and with Kagusaki's help, described my plan to jettison the live bomb. I figured it would closely parallel how Kaito and his crew would have done the same during their Panama Canal attack, but I wanted to make sure.

Kaito's nods and *"Hai's"* (meaning "yes") encouraged me.

Then I explained how we would open the rear boarding doors, and partially extend the ramp.

Kaito frowned, wagged his finger, rattled off a long phrase and ended with, *"Ōku no ton."*

Kagusaki said, "He says the bomb weighs many tons. Do not extend the ramp any more than five meters, or the bomb will break it off."

"Hai," I said.

Kaito seemed startled at my clumsy Japanese.

"How do I say, 'You know best.?'"

"Anata ga chumon suruto."

I had him repeat it a few times, while Kaito looked on. Was he smiling? Hard to say. But his mouth looked like it was losing the battle of staying serious.

I finally looked him straight in the eye and said, *"Anata ga chumon suruto."*

That got a sharp nod that I took for a bow.

I continued with the rest of my plan, including kicking in the turbojets and then nosing-up into a sharp climb, kicking free the wheel chocks and making the drop.

Kaito and I went back and forth about the ideal climb angle. Mine was more radical than his. My guess is that the young pilot wanted to go "by the book"—for their previously agreed-upon Panama Canal plan—but I wanted to jettison the monster bomb as quickly as possible, then get the hell out of Dodge and keep riding—in our case East, not West.

In the end, I compromised and lessened my climb angle by five degrees, which pleased Kaito. Seems he was concerned about the post-

drop pitch-angle shoving us into a deep stall. And he had a point: losing
a multi-ton ordnance load all at once plays havoc on your slipstream.

Had they ever done this before? I asked.

Only with smaller test loads. Much smaller.

All theory, then.

I lessened my planned angle-of-attack even more, then explained to
Ava that after they kicked out the restraining wheel chocks, to make sure
that Gunny and his guerillas and Kennedy's sailors shoved like hell on
that dolly to speed things up.

"Got it?"

"Yes, sir."

As Ava headed for the crew stairwell, Sparks called out, "Lots of
traffic all of a sudden, sir." He clamped his headphones tighter.

I had Kagusaki listen in on another pair. He sat beside Sparks, head
tilted, lips moving slightly, while jotting on a piece of paper. When he
finished, he read it through and shook his head.

"Not much sense to this, sir. Different call signs from different
aircraft. Something about flight levels, and fuel reports, and then it
faded."

"Any RDF?" I said to Sparks.

"Got it as far as rough heading. Two-four-zero degrees."

"No land in that direction."

"No, sir."

Kennedy piped up, "Fleet aircraft? C.A.P.?"

"Possible." I said, "What are the odds they know we stole the plane?"

Ava promptly said, "Twenty to one they still don't."

"How so?"

She shrugged and ticked off her points on her fingers. "One, Gunny
and his team took out Kaho'olawe's radio towers first thing. Two, Hek
and his team did the same on the base. Three, PT-124 sank the escort
that *thought* we were the good guys. Four, twenty to one we got away
with it."

I pondered this. "How about you, lieutenant?"

Kennedy said, "I'm not as sold on it, sir. I'll give you fifty-fifty chance
they think the Panama mission is still on."

"Even minus the Oahu flyover that never happened?"

He shrugged. "I side with Lieutenant James on that one. But here's an important fact: if there's one thing that rarely works out here, it's electronics. Radio signals bounce all over the place, salt air screws up the insides, rust moves in when you least expect it. If Oahu never heard from us, they'd be worried for sure. But they wouldn't panic—at least not yet. I think we've got a fifty-percent chance of that not happening for a few more hours."

"Brief your gunners to keep a sharp eye, just in case. If we get jumped, I don't want to go down without a fight."

He looked around the spacious flight deck. "A plane this big would take a lot of punishment before that happened, sir. She's a flying battleship."

"With mighty thin skin. "

"Aye, aye."

He lifted up a sheet of paper. "Before I go, here's my ETA—winds aloft permitting, of course."

I examined his figures: twelve hours, ten minutes to Alamogordo Army Airfield, New Mexico. Home sweet home!

Then I put on the brakes.

I refused to let my mind get ahead of the storyline. Plenty of time later to figure out how to penetrate American-controlled airspace along the California coastline without being brought down like Captain Ahab harpooned Moby Dick.

Time enough later to sort out the challenge of landing a multi-ton seaplane on a concrete runway that may—or may not—absorb her massive weight. Time enough later to think about a thousand more details that may or may not need attention if the Japs caught us trying to escape.

By now, Ava and Kennedy had reached the access stairway. He went up to brief the gunners, she went down below to drop the bomb..

I wanted to shout, "Be careful!" to them both, but kept my big mouth shut and my mind in the present.

The next half-hour was a blur of action below, as Gunny and his team cleared the way for the bomb cradle to roll backwards when the time came. The six-wheel device had locking pins on the aft-facing wheels. Once pulled, our H-bomb train would leave the station.

The lashings for the parachutes had to be double-checked. So did the primary static line used to yank them open. Affixed to the top of the cargo bay, the line needed proper anchoring. The secondary backup lines too. Once in place, they draped down like maypole ribbons, each attached to one of the chutes.

I had learned from Rasetti that the chutes were designed to delay the drop long enough for the *Kawanishi* to escape the shock wave from the bomb blast. Upon the initial drop from 10,000 feet, a much smaller pilot chute would pop open and yank out the larger parachutes. Reefed at first to survive the shock from the opening, all six would quickly blossom into full size.

Ava was right to insist on being down there with the launch team. It's one thing to get a job done, but without strong layers of management it can go haywire fast. I pictured Gunny and her as two Prairie Dogs popping up from their respective holes to make sure the coast is clear, then popping back down again to make sure the digging is proceeding as planned.

The chronometer on my instrument panel registered 0630 hours. We'd been airborne since just before dawn. Over the past hour, the solid cloud cover that had saved our bacon back at Kaho'olawe had steadily broken up into large sections of open sky above and empty ocean below.

From our height, the water looked glassy-smooth. Had I seen whitecaps at this altitude, we would have been in for some serious winds. But considering the high pressure front passing to our northwest, its prevailing winds were accordingly brisk and would slow our speed over the ground—ocean in our case.

I raised Ava on the intercom.

"Time to drop?" I said.

"Gunny says fifteen minutes. But that's optimistic. This damn thing is gigantic. Don't want to start it rolling until were absolutely ready."

"Cloud cover's breaking. Don't know for how long—do I have time to grab a drift check?"

"Go for it."

They *must* have that gear stowed somewhere. I double checked the autopilot settings then said, "Kagusaki, I'm heading back to the navigation station. Keep an eye on the store."

In seconds he was at my side. "Won't touch a thing."

I lowered my voice. "Make sure our co-pilot doesn't either."

The baker smiled. "No worries, sir. He's still steamed up about Yamasaki wanting to take us down *kamikaze* lane by blowing up Oahu."

He turned to Kaito and rattled off some Japanese. The copilot frowned at first, then laughed and said something back.

"What'd he say?"

"When the war is over he'll be the only Japanese officer that gets medals from both sides."

It took Kennedy and me digging through a rack of steel cabinets above the navigator's table to find a wooden box about the size of a shoebox. Inside, the Japanese-made drift meter nestled on a green velvet-covered, cushioned frame like the Crown Jewels.

But this was only the top half of the unit that contained the prism sight, graticule circle, and ground speed calculator. All familiar stuff to me despite its foreign manufacture. Planes don't recognize national borders. Neither do pilots if given a choice.

"That's it?" Kennedy said.

"Only half. The viewing tube's probably mounted near the chart table."

It took only seconds to find what we thought at first was just a metal plate, but it turned out to be a rotating cover that slid open to reveal mounting lugs. How in God's name they figured out how to route the viewing tubes down through the decks to the bottom of the plane was beyond me. Somehow, along the way, they would have had to amplify the light to deliver a readable image.

But all I cared about was inserting the top into the base. A twist and two solid clicks, and the drift meter start vibrating ever so slightly. It could only mean one thing.

"We're in luck, this thing's gyro-stabilized."

I squinted through the cushioned eyepiece – a blur of greyish-white at first. But a twist of the focus knob and the ocean surface directly below us came sharply into view. But not the bouncing, jumping, trembling image I'd seen so many times when navigating for *Pan Am.* The gyroscope in this Japanese-made drift meter damped all vibration. Accordingly, the ocean glided past, rock-steady.

"Take a looksee."

While Kennedy did so, I positioned the tiny pencil stub the drift meter used to record wind direction. Similar to the B-5 unit installed in Army Air Corps planes, this one also used a small pantograph to transfer the pencil tracings from the pointer inside the viewfinder onto a frosted glass graticule next to the eyepiece.

"Great view," Kennedy said, then surrendered the unit to me.

I explained what I was doing as I went along. How I used the small pointer to trace the direction of waves, and how the small pencil on the pantograph duplicated my tracings. Once I'd done three sets, I rotated the frosted glass with the penciled lines until they matched the etched horizontal lines.

According to the calculator, we had a twelve-degree nose-left drift. We needed to change our compass heading accordingly. I hollered out to Kagusaki. "Have him dial the autopilot to zero-five-seven degrees. And confirm."

"Yes, sir."

"Time to sort out our groundspeed—grab that stopwatch."

Kennedy picked it up.

"On my count start, and stop when I say 'stop.'"

"Yes, sir."

I pressed my eye to the cushioned eyepiece. Whatever was on my mind up to that point—and it was a lot, including being at war, stealing an enemy airplane, and getting rid of a hydrogen bomb—all of it disappeared when the wave sequence I wanted came into view. I picked a spot with my pointer.

"Start…"

I followed the flickering, dancing spot on the ocean as best I could. And when it finally left my view I had Kennedy stop the watch. Then I showed him how to use the metal-dialed computer to align with the time, which in turn showed true airspeed versus indicated.

"Two hundred seven knots," I said. "Not bad, considering."

"Can I take a look?" Kennedy said.

"Be my guest."

He looked through the eyepiece and grinned like it was a telescope showing him the night sky. I left him to his fun and turned to leave for the pilot's seat.

"Uh, oh." Kennedy said.

His stiffened posture didn't bode well as he crouched over the viewfinder like a man peeking through a keyhole.

"Wakes, sir. Lots of them."

"Ships?"

"My God."

He turned to me. "Aircraft carriers, too!" He looked back into the finder. "Damn, it's got to be that fleet from Pearl…"

"Direction?"

"North by northeast."

We were heading more easterly. "Let's pray they don't spot us."

I wasn't back in the left-hand seat more than thirty seconds when Ava's voice said in my headsets, "Ready to drop this ugly thing."

"Stand by to do just that."

"You sound happy, sir."

"I'm more than happy, lieutenant, I'm ecstatic."

"Because…?"

"We're going to do more than punch a hole in the ocean with that thing."

I quickly explained what both Kennedy and I figured must be part of a Japanese carrier strike force heading north. Ava beat me to the punch line.

"They're heading for the Aleutians!" she crowed.

"Supporting the invasion."

"Supporting Davy Jones instead. Let's DO this thing, skipper! Opening the ramp now."

Kagusaki let loose a volley of Japanese, while pointing out the window at my nine-o'clock. Then in English. "Airplanes!"

I followed his pointing finger, but all I saw at first were puffy white cumulus clouds slightly below our flight level of ten thousand feet. Then a formation of planes briefly shot out from behind a cloud then disappeared again.

"They're after us!" Kagusaki said.

Fighters, not float planes. Flying this far from land, they *had* to be carrier CAP. I keyed my intercom.

"Lieutenant James, belay opening the loading ramp! All gunners hold your fire. Repeat, hold your fire on approaching enemy aircraft. Do NOT fire unless fired upon!"

The chorus of "Wilco's" and "yes sirs" faded as I stripped off my headphones and raced back to the navigator's station. I reached around a baffled Kennedy and grabbed the leather aviator's helmet and white silk scarf I'd seen hanging there earlier, along with a flight jacket and a couple of woven straw baskets.

I left the leather jacket on the hook. And the helmet was so small I couldn't get it over my head.

"Your knife. Quick!"

Kennedy pulled out his KA-BAR.

I slashed the back, so I could squeeze the small cap over my head. The leather almost split completely, but held. I pulled the goggles down onto my forehead.

"What are you...?"

"You'll see."

The white silk scarf was soiled from use. I shook it out full length, then wound it around my face so that only my eyes could be seen.

My voice was muffled as I said, "How do I look?"

"Like hell, sir."

"Perfect."

By the time I got back to the left seat and buckled in, three Japanese Navy fighter planes flying echelon left had taken position off our left wing. Kaito pointed to the right. Three more, echelon right.

I felt both relieved and terrified. Relief because if they had known what *really* happened back at Kaho'olawe, they'd have gunned us down long ago. Kennedy was right about lousy radio communications out here.

But I was also terrified that they might find out at any second and come after us like angry wasps. The Japanese didn't believe in self-sealing gas tanks in any of their aircraft. Ours were filled with tens of thousands of gallons of high-octane avgas. True, she was bigger than Moby Dick, but incendiary cannon shells would be harpoons heading straight for her heart. Talk about a fireball.

"Sparks, you got anything?"

"Lots of chatter, sir."

"Kagusaki?"

Our translator sat beside the radio operator, his headphones pressed to his ears. A grin split his face like a sunrise. "They're shouting *Banzai!*"

A whoosh of relief.

I looked out the window and thanked God for the *Kawanishi's* almost five hundred-foot wingspan. The carrier fighters were keeping their dutiful distance off our wingtips, which meant they would have to have eagle eyes to see past my cobbled-together disguise as the chief pilot.

I lifted my hand and waved furiously.

The faraway flight leader nodded, then waved back. A fluttering of hands from the other pilots, too. Waggling wings. Then a series of sharp salutes, which I returned.

Kaito sat there staring straight ahead during this love feast from the Japanese Navy. Hard to sort out how he felt about all this. Had the tables turned and I was a captive in my own airplane, I'd be scheming like mad to do something. As much as he loved his family, he'd become a naval aviator. Did he want to fight for the Emperor or for Japan? Was there a difference?

One by one, the planes peeled off and dove away. Within seconds, the sky was empty again, save for the cumulus clouds and the bright sun.

"*Sayonaras*" given and received over the radio.

Kaito's hands rested in his lap. Where he was in his mind I don't know.

I keyed my microphone. "Open cargo doors and ramp out. Standby to drop."

Gunny's voice. "Aye, aye, sir."

"Where's Lieutenant Carter?"

"With the launch team. I'm at the door with the static lines."

I stripped off my cheesy Japanese pilot's disguise, checked the autopilot to be sure it was functioning correctly, then hurried back to Kennedy and drew him aside.

"I'm going to drop this thing. Keep an eye on the co-pilot, okay? First sign of trouble—"

"Aye, aye, sir. I know what to do."

Over to Tony.

I put my hands on his shoulders and leaned down to whisper. "Going full power in a few seconds. Jap pilot may try to retard throttles. No clue on how he'll react. Kennedy's got his eye on him. You too. Got that?"

"Loud and clear, skipper."

"How you doing?"

He patted the bank of engine throttles controlling our twelve turboprops and four jets. "Beats hell out of changing Jap oil and eating lousy rice."

Back I went back to my seat like a shuttlecock, strapped in, took a deep breath, disconnected the autopilot and took over the controls. I risked a look at Kaito, who continued staring forward.

"*Hai?*" I said to him.

He nodded.

I risked everything and wiggled the control wheel – the universal signal that you're transferring command to your fellow pilot. Kaito darted me a sharp look. Time stood still.

"*Hai,*" I said, and wiggled it again.

He slowly reached out and wrapped both hands around the oversized control wheel. Did this kid have that much stick time in this beast? If Japanese navy aviation was anything like *Pan Am*, the answer was "hell no." Our junior pilots got very little PIC, Pilot in Command, but a LOT of time pre-flighting and doing every menial task the senior pilots didn't want to do.

Had to be the case here. But whatever had been going on in that brain of his up until this moment flew out the window, because his hands and feet were fully occupied flying the largest plane in the world. I hoped his heart was too.

Kagusaki stood between us, leaning forward, eyes bright, waiting to translate.

"Prepare to drop," I said.

He translated. I gripped the engine throttles and began a slow advance to full power. Kaito took a deep breath, but more from excitement than anger. He didn't know about the ships Kennedy had spotted through the drift meter. For all he knew, we were punching a hole in the ocean and he was the prizefighter chosen to do so.

As for what else was down there? Hard to say, considering it had been a while since we'd seen the carrier strike force. We were not on converging courses by any means. So… maybe we'd just poke a hole in the waves, after all. Well, it'd be one hell of a hole, that's for sure.

"Light me up!" I shouted to Tony.

I watched as the jet engines' RPM rose quickly. Had we been on the ground it would have taken much longer. But since we were already clipping along at over two hundred knots, the turbines spun up quickly to four thousand RPM indicated.

"Lighting off," Tony said.

One by one, the spinning turbines came to life inside the pylon-mounted jet engines. Our airspeed needle climbed inexorably toward three hundred knots. Amazing thrust coming from those four little engines! Here, along we thought the Nazis had a lock on modern-day warfare. If Adolf could see us now!

"Standby," I said into my intercom. Kagusaki echoed me in Japanese. How do I say, 'together'?"

"*Issho ni.*"

I made eye contact with Kaito and repeated it as I took hold of the wheel with him to share the load. He nodded confidently, which made me want to laugh. If I had a dime for every time I tried to act calm and collected when I was terrified, I'd be a wealthy man.

That said, I'd like to say that the high temperature on the flight deck caused by the canopy's greenhouse effect made my hands sweaty. But that would be a lie. It was flop sweat. Pure and simple. I had no idea how rapidly the *Kawanishi* could climb or descend. No idea how any of this plan would actually work.

When my father wasn't engineering steam locomotives for the *Florida East Coast*, he loved building furniture. Nothing major, mind you, just humble things like stools, end tables—stuff like that. He'd spend hours reading the plans, lining up his tools, sharpening his chisels and saws. Then he'd start.

And never look back.

He used to say, "I talk to the plans before I get going. But once I pick up my tools, the plans talk to me."

Our plans were on the table. Time to pick up the tools.

"Chocks secure?" I said on the intercom, more from nervousness than concern. If Gunny and Ava didn't have their act together by now, they never would.

"Secure!"

"Everything else nailed down?"

"Aye, aye."

"Here we go... stand by for my call."

I nodded to Kaito, and together we pushed forward into a shallow dive. The horizon began climbing as we started falling. In less than thirty seconds, the altimeter unwound to nine thousand feet, while the airspeed needle touched the yellow quadrant, indicating three hundred fifty knots. The red quadrant beyond, our DNE—Do Not Exceed—speed was four hundred, but I didn't dare risk it.

"Now!"

We slowly, firmly, pulled back on the control yokes together. The response time was glacial, but steady. The positive G's squeezed a bit, but no more than you'd expect in a carnival ride as the *Kawanishi* changed flight attitudes with the ponderous grace of a drunk who didn't want to look drunk.

The altimeter began climbing. We brushed through a small pocket of cumulus clouds, a slight darkening of our world, then bright sunshine again as we climbed to where Icarus met his maker, the sun.

But this time we would be sending the sun to the earth instead of the other way around. True, not the real sun, but the *idea* of the sun, with the thermonuclear rage of hydrogen atoms fusing under tremendous pressure, and then releasing a type of energy unknown on earth until people like Saburo Yamasaki and his kind walked down the long, lonely, deadly road with no turning back.

No turning back for us either.

Fifteen degrees up-angle... twenty... airspeed falling faster than I expected. Reaching the top of the roller coaster... click... click... click...

"Pull chocks! Go, go, GO!"

Four hundred feet behind me I prayed that Gunny, Ava, and the rest were doing the right thing with eighty tons of rolling death on wheels, leaving the world of sanity, on its way to insanity.

No time left, had to nose down or stall.

"Bomb's AWAY!" Ava shouted.

We shoved the nose down just as the airspeed needle trembled at ninety knots, our stall speed. The *Kawanishi* tried to fall off on a wing, but our preemptive nose-down maneuver helped her fulfil her singular desire to fly, no matter what her idiot pilots did otherwise. Planes are like that – trim them for level flight, leave them alone, and they'll fly all day without your help. You might say they're *built* to fly and *want* to fly.

Me too.

Considering we were ninety tons lighter, meant less mass to shove through the air, and accordingly, the flight controls were now slightly more free-moving than before the drop.

"Ramp closed?" I said over the intercom.

"On its way," Gunny said.

"Do not—repeat—do not look back. Remember."

"Aye, aye, sir. That thing rolled out of here like the *Twentieth Century Limited.* A perfect drop. I can still see the chutes. All six deployed on the button. Our stuff should work like that."

"Eyes inside. Button up those doors, tie yourselves down, and get ready for a rocky ride."

With the combined square footage of six parachutes slowing the fall, the bomb's velocity was twenty feet-per-second. Because we'd reached eleven thousand feet during our "zoom-climb," I estimated we'd have about seven minutes to get the hell away from ground zero before the bomb blew up. But folks who live their lives based on estimates soon learn they're merely place markers for reality. That monster could blow at any second.

Did I mention the shock wave?

Meant to.

Earlier, Rasetti had described how their proof-of-concept H-bomb went off in the South Pacific, and how the shock wave capsized one of the observation frigates, ten miles from ground zero, I figured we'd run away as fast and far as we could. But after the initial flash of light from the explosion, we'd have to turn the plane around and face the shock wave or risk getting wiped out ourselves.

Total silence on the intercom.

The deed was done.

Nothing to do now but watch the second hand on the instrument panel tick-tick-tick away until time ended and eternity began for whoever and whatever was on that ocean.

Was I thinking about the men inside those ships down there? You bet. Did I feel sorry they'd soon be dying for their beloved emperor? Oddly, yes. Over the years I had made many Japanese friends from my *Pan Am* days. They were pawns in a deadly damned game called "war."

So were we.

While ethics and morality have a place in this world, they didn't on the flight deck of a hijacked enemy plane in the middle of the Pacific Ocean in the middle of a shooting war set off by politicians, generals, and greedy businessmen.

Beyond a blur of thoughts which revolved around preserving the lives of the people in my airplane, I had room for one more thought that I sent out to whoever or whatever might be waiting for me in the Great Beyond.

"Forgive us our trespasses," I whispered.

At first, just light.

Whiter than white. Brilliant, all-consuming, it flooded the flight deck and turned a peaceful February morning into sharp-edged, flash-bulb-like world.

I shielded my eyes as best I could by squinting. Fortunately, the brilliance quickly faded to pinkish-white, then blood-red.

Time to face the music. Had to move fast. The *Kawanishi's* turning rate was that of an ocean liner.

"Full power!"

"On it, skipper!" Tony said.

The engine throttles trembled, then edged forward as I swung the yoke to port and nodded for Kaito to assist. Rudder input on this whale was a feat of strength. The controls must be hydraulically assisted some way. No way could cables do the job alone.

I lowered the left wing to steepen our turn. Not *too* steep, though. While other bomb was lashed down tight, I didn't want to take any chances. Harmless as a weapon, but as a twenty-two-ton chunk of steel it could rip the belly out of this plane if it tore loose.

The nose kept swinging…swinging… past clusters of cumulus clouds blood red from the distant, mammoth-sized fireball that stretched across the horizon. Inside its ever-swelling size, raging cyclones of white-hot fire swirled. Beautiful and deadly—all at once.

The shockwave from the controlled chaos was rocketing toward us at over one thousand feet-per-second. Could we make the turn in time? The compass kept swinging...

"Everybody brace!" I shouted.

Ever been punched in the face?

If you have, you can skip over this paragraph, because that's exactly the effect the shockwave had on the *Kawanishi's* airframe. It stopped us cold. For a millisecond the air vanished over the wings and disappeared from the turboprop and jet intakes.

Disappeared.

Gone.

Shoved us backwards so fast that we dropped from the sky like a KO'd boxer with a glass jaw smacking the mat. But fortunately, the shockwave thundered past as quickly as it arrived, leaving an aftermath more chaotic than the initial impact.

The plane wanted to nose down and be done with flight. Kaito and I couldn't pull back yet because we had little or no control authority. The slipstream passing over the elevator was still mushy.

"Let her go!" I shouted.

Kaito didn't understand English, but he knew from my tone of voice what I meant as I kept the control yoke forward, wings leveled, and watched the airspeed indicator start to climb again.

The pitot tubes on the fuselage created the vacuum needed to tell me when we could get this bird out of her death dive. Eight thousand feet... seven... six...five....four...

By my nerve-wracking count, it took fifteen impossibly long seconds for the chronometer on the instrument panel to measure our descent into hell. Fifteen seconds of staring at the approaching ocean is an eternity. I don't recommend it. But the minute we achieved sufficient airspeed, Kaito and I began the slow but steady pull on the controls that first halted the dive and then leveled us out at approximately five hundred feet above the turbulent ocean. Then we began a slow but steady climb east, away from the still-burgeoning mushroom cloud.

The two of us I exchanged the kind of look only pilots can understand. When you've gone through the wringer and discover that you made it safely to the other side in one piece, you get that "look" in your eyes that your fellow pilot recognizes as his own as well. If you've ever seen an older pilot and wondered why he has those tiny wrinkles at the corner of his eyes, let me tell you, it's not age alone that does it, it's experiences like the one Kaito and I just went through.

I pointed to our family photos on the instrument panel and gave him a "thumbs-up" sign. For the first time I saw the hint of a smile. Then it went away. But I saw it.

"Jesus, Mary, and Joseph," Kennedy said. "Would you take a look at that."

He was standing on the narrow platform beneath the navigational bubble, looking backwards.

"I *told* you not to..."

"No worries, skipper. I'm just looking for the first time."

None of us needed to poke our heads inside that plexiglass dome. The mushroom cloud was big enough to see from where we sat on the flight deck. The cloud I'd seen in Hanford, Washington when we blew up the plutonium storage facility a couple years ago was a puffball compared to the towering column of boiling, roiling smoke and watery debris that continued to rise.

I guessed it at 50,000 feet by now, and still furiously climbing and swelling out at the top into a "cap" that might have been twenty miles in diameter. Hard to guess from our distance. Not just because we were far away, but because we'd never seen such a gigantic cloud like this before. The Grimmest of Reapers had swung his scythe. What was brand-new to us on that fateful day would one day become commonplace.

A joyful whoop caused everyone's head to turn – Ava and Gunny stood at the top of the crew ladder, both panting to catch their breath.

Ava shouted as she hurried forward. "Mission accomplished! Let's see what happened."

I said, "You haven't seen it yet?"

Gunny said, "Hell, no sir, guys crowding every viewing port and gun position, so we decided to get a balcony seat instead."

"Welcome to hell." I pointed up at the broad expanse of plexiglass panels that made up the *Kawanishi's* flight deck canopy. Beyond it, the mushroom cloud, now brilliant white from the sun with even brighter flashes flickering inside. God only knows what was still going on in there, and what had been caught up in the maelstrom.

Ava stared in silence, then said, "That's what the sun's doing all the time?"

"All day, every day," I said.

Gunny turned to me. "I think we just won the war."

"Providing we get that other bomb home safe and sound—it's lashed down okay?"

"Sleeping like a baby, sir. Never budged during the roller coaster ride we got from the shock wave."

Another voice called out, *"Ecco qua, signori e signora."*

Professor Rasetti stood by the ladder and pointed to the mushroom cloud. "Astonishing, is it not?"

He strolled toward us with casual grace, like he was ambling along the *Via Condotti* in Rome on a summer evening instead of being inside a flying ocean liner, thousands of feet in the air.

I turned to Gunny, "Where the hell is—"

"Ah, yes, sir, about that Jap scientist. Funny you should ask."

"Where *is* Yamasaki?"

A long beat of silence. Then Ava looked heavenward. "With his *samurai* ancestors—what's left of him, that is."

I opened my mouth to ask the question, but Gunny answered it. "Seems he slipped—wouldn't you say so, Lieutenant James?"

"Looked like that to me, Sergeant Lewis."

"Slipped and fell right out of the open hatch."

"Definitely an accident," Ava said.

I stared at them and they stared at me.

The drone of the airplane engines.

Lieutenant Kennedy watching the proceedings with the trace of a grin on his face.

Tony leaning forward from the engineering station, his eyes narrow with suspicion.

Rasetti finally said, "They are lying, of course, my colonel."

"And why would that be?"

He shrugged. "Because they want to hide the truth."

"Which is?"

He drew himself up like a witness in court. "War is not the killing of innocent women and children. If that bomb had exploded over Oahu..." He paused. "But it did not, thanks to you and your brave soldiers and sailors. Now it is gone forever—*grazie di Dio*—and Saburo Yamasaki along with it."

He tapped his chest. "*Sono io.* It is I who sent my colleague to the hell he deserves. I who shoved him out of the plane. I who murdered him."

I pondered his words—his confession, if you will.

"Not murder, Professor Rasetti," I said. "Your colleague's plan to use that weapon on innocent civilians made him an enemy combatant of the highest order. And as such, he was subject to the rules of combat that permit the very action you took. It's not murder, my friend, it's war."

I put out my hand. "Thank you."

He stared at it, then at me, then finally shook my hand and smiled. "*Piacere e mio.*"

"What's that mean?"

His smile vanished. "The pleasure was mine."

Control the enemy before he controls you.
Miyamoto Mushashi - Samurai

"What are you smiling about, darling?"

Ava's voice called me forward through time. Seconds before, I had been shaking Professor Rasetti's hand onboard the *Kawanishi*. Now I was back in the present—1968—and my wife was smiling at me, head tilted slightly to one side, calculating the meaning of my thousand-yard stare into 1944.

"He had a hell of a grip," I said.

"Who did?"

"That Italian professor. The one on the plane."

She smiled her trademark "Ava James" smile. Twenty-five years had passed since we had dropped the Japanese H-bomb. But where Father Time had taken his toll on my face, he'd made Ava's even more beautiful. True, no longer the Hollywood pinup girl that every soldier and sailor wanted to kiss; nowadays, she played more serious roles on the silver screen, and had been nominated for an Academy Award—twice.

She leaned over the red velvet rope that separated visitors from the famous surrender table on the forward flight deck of the *U.S.S. Arizona*.

"I can still see Uncle Georgie sitting there, holding out the pen for them to sign," she said.

"While packing his pearl-handled six-guns."

"Well?" She frowned. "They still carried their swords, remember?"

"How could I forget?"

It's a good thing we don't remember every damn thing that happens to us over a lifetime. We'd go crazy. Only certain moments when time stands still are the ones that sit on the shelf, happily waiting to spring to life the moment they're triggered.

This was one of them. And seeing the bronze surrender plaque set into the *Arizona's* wooden flight deck released a flood of memories that almost drowned me.

For an instant, I was transported ten thousand-feet above the Pacific Ocean once again, escaping the fury of the world's first hydrogen bomb exploded in anger. But over two decades had passed since that terrifying moment. Today, I stood on the deck of the *U.S.S. Arizona* Memorial in Pearl Harbor, home at last.

On December 7, 1941, the battleship *Arizona* had narrowly escaped death from the Japanese attack. Half-shattered, she managed to limp back to Puget Sound Naval Shipyard in Seattle, where they converted her into an oddball-looking aircraft carrier that got the job done, starting with Doolittle's raid on Tokyo. The first of many new aircraft carriers to come, she continued serving the fleet throughout the four-year war that followed.

Towed to Oahu to honor the twentieth anniversary of the Pearl Harbor attack, the Navy had converted her into a fitting memorial to commemorate the sacrifice of the thousands of soldiers, sailors, marines, and innocent civilians who died in Oahu on the day that Acting President Frances Perkins told the world, "would live in infamy."

The inch-high, raised bronze letters on the plaque said simply:

OVER THIS SPOT
ON 2 SEPTEMBER 1945
THE INSTRUMENT
OF FORMAL SURRENDER
OF JAPAN TO THE ALLIED POWERS
WAS SIGNED
TO BRING TO A CLOSE
THE SECOND WORLD WAR
THIS SHIP AT THAT TIME
WAS AT ANCHOR
IN TOKYO BAY

Inscribed around the plaque's circumference was the latitude and longitude of that historic spot in the placid waters of Tokyo Bay where the "grand fleet" of American and Allied warships had gathered.

35°21'17 North 139° 45' 36" East

"It was hot for September," Ava said.

"Humid, too."

"Good thing I wore my hair short back then."

We'd been invited to attend the surrender ceremony and witnessed the proceedings from the cramped quarters of the ship's island. A tight fit but a great view of the thousand-plus soldiers and sailors taking up every inch of available space on the flight deck to watch the Japanese generals lay their swords on the table, and the silk-hatted Emperor's representative sign his John Hancock on the dotted line.

Ava had made captain by then and was heading for major. We were back to our old job again – flying the good general from here to hell and gone. By then, she was spending more time in the left seat as Pilot-in-Command than me.

Gone was our lousy C-87A four-engine cow. In its place, the sinuous, sexy, Lockheed *Constellation* – an airplane that fit Ava's curvy figure. A figure, I might add, that had gotten suspiciously bigger and bigger in the region of her belly, which required her to take time out in late 1944 to give birth to our son, a healthy baby boy named Peter George Carter.

The blessed event took place nine months to the day after my co-pilot Kaito and I managed to land our *Kawanishi* KX-1 flying boat at Alamogordo Army Airfield, after an eighteen-hour journey across the Pacific.

As usual, Ava was reading my mind. "Smiling about that landing you made?"

"Hardly call it that."

"Any landing you can walk away from..." she said.

Funny how memory softens the edges where necessary. You couldn't even call it a controlled crash the way we encountered Runway 34 at Alamogordo. By my estimate, we had five thousand feet of smooth concrete waiting with open arms for our multi-engine whale that had grown multi-tire landing gear "legs."

But at the last moment, even with full flaps and nose-down trim, she decided she wanted to keep on flying. Planes are like that. Piper Cubs are fine when that happens. You can let them dawdle a bit before surrendering to gravity. But when you've got a four hundred foot-long aircraft staggering along near stall speed, you can't waste a moment being too high above the runway.

Silence on the flight deck – that interminable time during a landing sequence when you wait upon lift coefficients and angles-of-attack to surrender to gravity.

Nothing doing.

I risked a quick look at Kaito, who shrugged his shoulders and rattled off something.

Kagusaki translated. "He says, don't blame him!"

"I'm not, damn it!"

The concrete continued racing past beneath us while her massive wings kept loving the airflow. The marshmallow-like ground effect caused by the wings was tremendous.

"She won't stall!" I shouted.

Tony shouted, "Go around!"

"Can't."

No way could we horse this girl around for another try. Flaps would take forever to nurse back up. We'd cartwheel into the desert. Forget it.

Halfway down the runway now.... images of the airfield flashing past – neatly-parked rows of B-24s and B-17s being used for training bomber crews. A couple squadrons of P-47s, too. While their brothers would soon be raising hell in North Africa to support General MacArthur's invasion, we mushed along in New Mexico.

Two P-47s flew just off our wingtips and slightly above, finishing their job of escorting us for the past two hundred miles when we first entered New Mexico airspace. Once we had done so, the P-38 *Lightning* pilots who had escorted us up to that point, peeled off and scooted back home to tell the tale of escorting a Japanese Navy seaplane the size of a skyscraper across the Arizona dessert.

Hotshot fighter pilots love to talk, and these two guys off our wingtips would have a great time in the Officers' Club telling their buddies how the great Colonel Carter pranged his landing big time.

Two-thirds of the way down the runway now, and the damn girl *still* floated along like the star attraction in Macy's Thanksgiving parade.

If you can't beat em, join 'em.

I yanked the gear handle UP.

Kaito gasped and tried to reverse my action but I shouted, "No!"

A deep groan and shudder as six pairs of twelve-wheeled bogie trucks began tucking themselves back up inside the hull. Our amphibian was turning back into a whale.

I added power to slow down our sink rate and pulled back slightly on the controls. Needed time for the gear to fully retract.

"Landing straight ahead," I shouted. "On the damn desert!"

Kagusaki did his best to translate.

The concrete runway ended... the macadam run-off extension ended... the desert began...

Captain Fatt would have been proud of me. At least I imagined him congratulating my decision to keep flying instead of trying to force a stall. I pretended the sand and gravel below were the calm waters of the lagoon at Wake Island.... Barely any wind... slowly descending until the hull kissed the waves....

Gravity eventually won out because it always does.

The *Kawanishi's* wings finally gave up the ground-effect ghost and her green-painted aluminum hull brushed against the scrub and tumbleweed once...twice.... three times and then...

We didn't "land" so much as slowly grind to a stop, wings level, wing floats stranded twenty feet above the desert sand. The pool -table-like level terrain and minimum of rocks had acted like a file that smoothly "sliced" off fifteen feet of our double-bottomed hull. Tons of aluminum scraps left a grooved trail that made it easy for the crash trucks and ambulances to find us.

Bottom line, everybody safe and sound, including "The Bomb." As for the *Kawanishi*, after the intelligence guys got their fill of taking photos (and stealing souvenirs), they salvaged the engines (fabulous design, by the way. Who says the Japanese are the only ones who copy? We sure as hell copied their Ne301 turbojet technology.) The rest they eventually cut up and melted down for the war effort. But Ava and I were long gone before they destroyed that fabulous flying boat that had saved our lives.

"Thought I'd find you here."

My son's voice called me back to the present again, just like Ava had, moments before.

Parents are trained to hear the voices of those they love. That's why you can hear your kid's voice across a crowded room. I turned to greet my "Petey," who now preferred "Pete," standing before me – a tall, handsome young man of twenty-four, looking sharp as a tack in the moss-green uniform of a United States Marine officer.

Oahu's late afternoon sun across the harbor glinted off the first lieutenant bars on his broad shoulders and his Navy "Wings of Gold" on his proud chest. Even though Gunny was long gone to that parade ground in the sky, my "war stories" about him had captivated Pete ever since he was a kid. Becoming a Marine was never a question for this boy. Always a fact. Ditto, when it came to being a pilot, too.

"What do you think, Pop? They do a good job on the display?"

"I'm speechless."

He laughed. "That's a first."

Ava pecked his cheek and straightened his tie, while I excused myself and strolled down the *Arizona's* flight deck to where six B-25 twin-engine bombers stood parked on an angle, nose-to-nose on the stern, with an additional one aimed straight ahead, as if waiting for the FO to lower his green flag and send her on her way to Tokyo.

Half the bombers wore American markings and half the Soviet "Red Star" – the same way they had in 1943 when Colonel Doolittle rumbled off the deck to lead America's joint strike mission against Japan. A mission that Orlando Diaz and I unexpectedly found ourselves going on at the very last minute.

I saw Orlando's sturdy legs before I saw him. He stood by the last B-25, painted to resemble the exact same one we had flown in on that fateful day in '43, when the *Arizona* took a torpedo hit, all hell broke loose on the flight deck, and we exchanged "hats" from being observers to participants in the historic raid.

"What do you think, partner?" I called out.

He turned around and smiled like Christmas morning. A sprinkling of grey hair where black had always been, a little more stooped than when we were younger, but his milk-chocolate-smooth face was blissfully free from the wrinkles that had invaded mine.

He patted the fuselage. "Still can't believe we pulled it off."

"Twenty-eight years ago we did a lot more daring things than we do now. As for me, I'll stick with my good old reliable 707's."

"You do love your jets."

"Roger that."

His face grew somber. "How much longer before the FAA steals your wings?"

"Two years, four days, and…" I checked my wristwatch, then gave up. "Keep forgetting Hawaii's six hours later than New York."

He shook his head. "You're going to miss flying the 747. I saw the prototype in Seattle. She's a giant. They're calling her a 'Jumbo Jet.'"

"Hells bells, we could have stuck two of her inside that *Kawanishi*."

Orlando laughed at that. Understandable. He'd never been inside that beautiful beast. But I had.

"Maybe Ava and I will fly on a Jumbo one of these days... after I retire, that is."

We looked at each other. Two old eagles, flirting with sixty but pretending it hadn't been a long time since we first rolled off this very flight deck and joined Doolittle's squadron.

But Orlando was right... in two years I'd be sixty—mandatory retirement age for airline pilots. Sure, I could still fly as a private pilot, but not in "the deep blue ocean where the big ones play." That's how Captain Fatt described what it was like to fly *Pan Am's* clippers. I'd done it, too, and still was—just not landing on the water anymore.

Those days were long gone. I'd been flying our South American route lately—Buenos Aires, Rio—a different world down there for sure, happy people who knew how to make time stand still.

Whenever Ava got time off from Hollywood, she'd fly standby on one of my trips. During layovers in Rio, we'd sit on the beach and marvel at "Sugarloaf" mountain rising from the sea. Good memories. Peaceful times. Not talking. Just being.

Orlando didn't have to worry about age restrictions. As *Pan Am's* District manager for Transpacific Flight Operations, he could keep working at our center at Honolulu International as long as he liked.

He'd come a long way from being a grease monkey in Key West, hungry for airplane work. So had I, from being an eager kid desperate to fly anything with wings to commanding a four-engine, jet-powered commercial jet airliner with two hundred souls onboard who trusted the aircraft and crew to get them where they wanted to go.

Orlando said, "When's your boy shipping out?"

"His squadron joins the fleet tomorrow."

Orlando kicked one of the main gear tires. "I swear we haven't learned a damn thing."

"Vietnam, you mean?"

"The wars just keep on coming, Sam. Ours...then Korea... now this."

Pearl harbor was filled to capacity with ships painted Navy grey. The destroyers and cruisers I could sort out. But the auxiliary ships like tankers, amphibious ships, and cargo were a confusing blur of grey steel and mysterious superstructures.

All but one of them, of course.

From where we stood, I could just make out the masts and flight deck of the Amphibious Assault Ship *USS Jeremiah James Lewis*, LHA-3. On her flight deck, the CH-47 "Chinook" assault helicopters' rotor blades were folded and tucked in tight like sleeping birds.

Below decks, scores of young Marines rested in their bunks. But soon the *Lewis* would be carrying these young men to meet their fate, hopefully not like Gunny's on that sad day in 1945, less than a year before the war ended.

I never learned the dirty details, only read the commendation that posthumously awarded that grizzled old fighter the Congressional Medal of Honor for saving the lives of his besieged fellow soldiers during the invasion of Hawaii. Gravely wounded, he led a counterattack on an enemy position and so overwhelmed it that it turned the tide of battle—at the expense of his valiant life.

It only seemed fitting that a navy ship designed to land Marines into harm's way should be named after one of America's greatest heroes who did just that.

And into that same harm's way, an aircraft carrier waited somewhere out there on the "deep blue waters" to take on board my son's squadron of Douglas A-1 "Skyraiders."

These massive, propeller-driven, single-engine aircraft were an anomaly in the jet engine era. But they got the job done. That's what mattered. And what mattered even more to me as the father of a wonderful son was that the VFA-25 squadron "Spads" were built like Mack Trucks. Despite taking ground-fire that would doom a more fragile craft, they had a well-earned habit of always finding that arresting wire and arriving safely home.

"Ever think about going back in?" Orlando said. "You're a big shot general. How many stars again?"

I punched him lightly. "Cut it out."

He grinned. "Two? Four? Lost count."

For the record, I'm a retired brigadier general. One star. One story."

"Patton was good as his word, wasn't he?"

"Meaning?"

"I got out a bird colonel and you got your star."

The mention of General Patton's name brought me back to where I was standing. I looked down the length of the flight deck.

"You remember the day Tokyo called it quits?" I said.

Orlando knew what I meant. He could read my mind like I could read his. We'd known each other ever since we were hell-raising nine-year-olds, outrunning the cops in in the shadowy side streets of Key West.

Orlando said, "Old 'Blood and Guts' could act as good as he fought."

"You mean making them surrender on the *Arizona*?"

"Exactly. That stunt of his made Mac's surrender ceremony in front of the Reichstag look like a tea party by comparison."

General George H. Patton had stood by the microphone that day and gave a command performance—if you've seen the newsreels, you know what I'm talking about. But let me tell you something, I saw and heard the real thing that day. Especially, those twin, pearl-handled Colt .45s of his, just waiting for trouble to start, while "Uncle Georgie" read them the riot act in a voice edged with menace.

But no trouble from the Empire of Japan on that bright and sunny, hot and humid September day in Tokyo Bay, when the Emperor and his military quasi-government, faced with the threat of losing their nation, decided to stop fishing and cut bait.

I never found out whether or not Patton was pleased that he'd beaten Mac to the punch by getting the Japanese to fold their tents first. The Nazis managed to hold out until the following February, 1946, when Russian forces captured Adolf Hitler in his famous bunker. The Third Reich's "fall" after that was more like the *Hindenburg* dirigible bursting into flames and crashing to the ground at Lakehurst, New Jersey.

So much for the thousand-year Reich.

Japan's surrender had been more stately. After we foiled their master plan of building an isolating "wall" running from the Aleutian Islands down to Panama, Patton invaded the Hawaiian Islands. A year later, armed with thermonuclear weapons, he marched ever westward across the Pacific to the Philippines, then on to Japan's doorstep.

Once we got within spitting distance, a light switch went off in Tokyo – one day, all-out war, then, "Uh, oh, *that* didn't work out, folks." Next day, they were at peace: "Hey, let's do what the Americans say."

A wise and most efficient choice. "Forget *banzai* charges, folks. Let's embrace the free market, and among other things, make automobiles a thousand times better than the rust buckets being turned out in Detroit, not to mention wildly innovative electronics that RCA and GE will stare at like kids in candy store without a penny in their pockets."

The longer I live, the more I admire the Asian mind. It sees the whole. Westerners see just the part, but arrogantly, declare it's the whole. They see the long game. We see ping-pong but think it's chess. I don't expect either culture to ever change. But I do hope that occasionally we can help each other out when and where we need it the most.

But war is what happens instead. Most of the time.

Like now.

"Jack knew better," I said, referring to President Kennedy's escalation of American involvement in Vietnam, from "advisors-only" to draft call-ups, to my son Pete about to drop bombs and fire rockets on the Viet Cong.

"You ever tell the man that?" Orlando said.

"Once. And it didn't matter. Kennedy was smart enough to become president but dumb enough to get suckered into war."

"Politics."

We left it at that. I refused to spend another second getting hot under the collar with Jack Kennedy's failure to resist the magnetic pull of "The Red Menace Taking Over the World" as preached by his foreign policy advisors and saber-rattling generals.

The drumbeat had begun with Truman in the early 50s, then Eisenhower took over, and now Kennedy was on board, doing his best to halt the spread of communism. Ideology versus ideology, true. But also, young men versus young men. Bullets versus bullets, bombs versus bombs.

Nothing had changed. Nothing ever would. Just different names for the same damn thing. The future? Jack's two terms in office were done in November. LBJ looked to be a shoo-in over Nixon. Both were consummate politicians, but my money was on the guy from Texas, not that shifty-eyed weasel from San Clemente.

I turned to Orlando. "Joining us for dinner, or do you have to work?"

He smiled. "The Royal Hawaiian, right?"

"I figured why not, for old times' sake."

"He shook his head. "Sorry I missed your great adventure. It all started there, right?"

"Yes, it did. But if you hadn't escaped from the Nazis that night in San Francisco and blown the whistle, Ava's and Mac's and my chopped-off heads would have been stuck on pikes in Tokyo—so don't let me hear you complain, let me thank you instead."

"You're welcome."

"Dinner's at eight. That okay?"

"Got a ton of paperwork, but it can wait—when you going out on your trip? I haven't checked the boards lately."

"Day after tomorrow. Idlewild."

He frowned that special frown operations folks have perfected. "Cutting it a bit tight, aren't you?"

"How are the loads running?"

He shrugged but said nothing. I hoped that was a sign that he'd find some space-available seats to get Ava and me back to California. From there, I could catch a red-eye to New York and pick up my South American trip.

Orlando motioned to where Ava and Pete stood in the distance. "You'd better tend to business."

Ava was holding both Pete's hands. She stood on her tiptoes to kiss him on the cheek.

I said, "That kid's a tall drink of water. Wonder how he fits in that Spad of his."

"Same way you did in that seaplane on the submarine—what was its name?"

"The *Seiran*. Aichi made them. Hot little buggers."

"They're making twin-engine commuters nowadays. Too small for us, but nice."

"Let's hear it for peaceful aviation."

He nodded, then stuck out his hand. "Thanks for inviting me, Sam. Been meaning to check this out for quite a while. They did a good job—the memorial, I mean."

"So did we."

We shook hands, his paw just as big and just as meaty.

"See you later, *General* Carter," Orlando said, then pulled a salute.

I returned it. "Take charge of the company, *Colonel* Diaz."

I about-faced and headed toward Ava and Pete.

By now, late in the day, the tourist crowd had thinned out. Just a few stragglers here and there, wandering here and there on the vast expanse of the historic flight deck. Nobody paid any attention to this middle-aged man wearing tan slacks and a flowery Hawaiian shirt that his wife picked out for him because she said it matched his eyes.

I took her word for it.

Only a short distance separated me from Ava and Pete—maybe thirty yards, at most. But with each step, my journey back in time spanned fifty-eight years of living on God's good green earth and flying above it in beautiful airplanes.

Raising hell with Orlando in Key West as kids… learning to fly from a barnstormer-turned-mail-pilot when I was seventeen… fast-talking my way into a radio operator's job with Juan Trippe's fledgling *Pan American Airways System*… then climbing and clawing my way up the seniority list to become Master of Ocean Flying Boats.

I thought about the people who had loved me into being – my mother Rosie and my father John, now far beyond the clouds, singing with the choir of angels. Along with them, Estelle and Baby Eddie, gone in a nuclear burst of light that had lit the fires of World War Two.

Gone too was my mentor, Captain Fatt, felled by a Nazi bullet. Generals Patton and MacArthur, too – men that history had chosen to save America from Hitler and Tojo—long-gone heroes but never forgotten.

I thought about where we all would be by this time tomorrow: Pete's *Skyraider* squadron would be with Task Force 77 sailing for the South China Seas to fly sorties over Vietnam.

Me? I'd be checking weather reports and passenger loads at *Pan Am's* flight ops center to see if Ava and I could wrangle a "non-rev" hop back to the mainland.

My New York-Buenos Aires four-day-tripper was scheduled to depart the day after tomorrow—and Orlando was right – a tight fit if I didn't make all my connections. But after a lifetime of flying from point A to point B, and then back again, I knew things would work out somehow. They always did and always would. Maybe not the way I wanted or hoped for, but worked out for sure.

Did I know this truism when I was an eight-year-old boy, staring skyward at that barnstormer buzzing rooftops in Key West? Not a chance. But fifty years later, seeing my son laughing at something Ava just said, and then turning to face me, his eyes still innocent but learning fast, I knew that he would make the sky his home the same way I had. Borne by wings to dance with the clouds, challenge the tempest, salute the rising sun, and bid farewell to the waning moon, my son would learn that things always work out in the end.

And if they don't, keep flying until they do.

Sam Carter
Key West, Florida
January 7, 1976

Paul Lally is a novelist and Emmy award-winning
television and film writer/producer/director.
He lives in New Hampshire.
His previous novels are:
AMERIKA
AMERIKA: Call to Arms
RISE AGAIN
RISE AGAIN: To the Colors
RIDE THE TITANIC
SILK

Find out what's coming next at:
www.paul-lally.com
or
E-mail him at:
paul@paul-lally.com